THE LEADER OF LORS

BOOK II IN THE ATRIIAN TRILOGY

BY

FAWN BONNING

Printed in the United States of America
ISBN-13:978-1496169686
ISBN-10:1496169689

This book is a work of fiction. Any references to real people, events, establishments, organizations, or locales are intended solely to provide a sense of authenticity and are used fictitiously. All other characters, incidents, and dialogue are drawn from the author's imagination and are not to be construed as real.

Cover design by Donediditmyself Graphics

THE LEADER OF LORS

DEDICATION

For my mother, my hero.

PART I

CHAPTER 1

Chrisssstaaa...

Snapping awake, Christine grappled with the phantom of tangled sheets, flinging them aside, keening and kicking till they tumbled from the bed. Frantic eyes skimmed a room cloaked in darkness, and a strangled cry escaped at the movement along one wall—mere shifting silhouettes of swaying branches from beyond the window.

Pressing a hand to her mouth, she drew in a shuddering breath, one that exited as an anguished moan. Tears welled as shame flooded—yet she could not keep trembling fingers from tracing tainted lips, sinfully caressing the lingering remains of the forbidden kiss.

Rolling to her side, she grabbed a pillow, hugging it tight as the ragged breaths leveled off. She swiped at a lone tear, fighting to keep others from following. Too many had been shed since her return. Her vow to forget Atriia and forge forward was proving drastically difficult. There were moments when all of the carefully suppressed memories shot out and slapped her in the face, the blow rocking her to the very core.

She put a hand to a cheek still warm with the stinging aftermath. It was unthinkable to desire this man, and indeed she would not permit these thoughts during the waking hours. It was only at night, during the deepest of dreaming, they did surface, forbidden thoughts of one fraigen dropper. Like a slinking shadow, he would creep upon her, dark and dangerous, hands of silk gliding along her skin, cruelly caressing—the weight of him, pressing, possessing—his warm breath at her ear, whispering…

Squeezing her pillow, she turned her attention to the window where Luna's soothing smile was filtering through the filmy sheerness of curtains, her hazy beams casting shadows upon the wall. Branches, dressed in fluttering leaves, were dancing in a warm summer's breeze—a dark, mystical ballet.

A crib was seated against the same wall serving as the ballet backdrop. Within, the baby stirred, her lips smacking in slumber, dreaming of suckling at her mother's breast.

Christine looked to the clock on the night-stand, the large, luminous numbers informing her that it was ten minutes past two. Soon, hunger would be pulling Rebecca from sleep.

With a deep sigh, Christine ran a hand underneath her nightgown to trace a finger lightly along the newest scar. They had been right after all, those of Atriia who said she owned no hips for birthing babes. At almost nine pounds, Rebecca had proven too large to pass naturally through the birthing canal. And so she had been pulled perfunctorily from her mother's womb, perfect in every way—plump and pink, ten fingers, ten toes, a healthy set of vocal chords, and a mat of deep auburn curls plastered to her skull.

Sam's child. It was a fact she didn't care to dwell on. But it was becoming increasingly evident with every passing day as Rebecca's face began to take on Sam's features. Around the eyes especially, eyes which had gradually darkened to a deep cobalt.

Christine rolled to one side, her gaze settling on the small form within the crib, feeling her heart swell at the sight. It was hard to believe she could love anything so much, a love so deep it made her ache. But even as consuming as this love was, it could not be called pure, for it was tainted by guilt. Though the child was only six months old, there were moments when a certain expression, a certain mannerism made it painful to look at her. For this, above all else, Christine resented Sam the most.

Once again, a stirring sounded from within the crib. Slipping from the bed, Christine padded across the room to peer down upon an angel on Earth. The child's cherubic face was framed by rampant russet curls and held lambent eyes round as saucers in the darkness. At the sight of her mother, the babe kicked her legs and reached out with a celestial coo. As usual, she had awakened jovial.

Christine reached for her angel, pulling her to her chest, clutching at a creature so excruciatingly exquisite. A plethora of fervent kisses placed about one plump cheek brought forth a hearty giggle.

Slipping an arm from her gown, Christine bared her breast and the babe latched on, the tiny hands burying into the folds of her nightgown to knead contentedly. Love suffused Christine as she peered into shimmering eyes of innocence.

She felt a lump form instantly in her throat, felt the sob attempt to wrench its way past. How could looking into a face of such unparalleled beauty bring about such unprecedented pain? She loathed herself for such maliciousness—loathed Sam for his selfishness.

Moving to the window, she slid the curtain aside to peer out over the grounds, her gaze gliding over the swaying amber grasses of the fields and on to where they abutted the forest in the distance. Slowly, her eyes shifted to where moonlight shimmered on dark waters—her beloved pond.

Icy fingers caressed her neck and a fine sheen of moisture seemed to materialize instantly along her brow. A knot, like a lead weight, anchored firmly in the pit of her belly.

Her beloved pond was calling her.

There was no denying it any longer. At first the sensation had been subtle, a mere wisp of a whisper, one which could easily be construed as an overactive imagination. But the sensation had been steadily intensifying over the weeks.

With a shiver, she pulled her eyes away and shuffled weakly to the rocker, needing the soothing motion more to ease her own angst than to comfort the suckling babe. Rebecca's eyes were half-mast as she nursed, obviously oblivious to any malevolent beckoning.

Christine brushed a downy curl from the child's forehead. She would ignore this calling, this beckoning, as best she could. And if it became overbearing, then she would pack up her things and move away. Though financially, it was impractical, she knew it was inevitable, for even as she struggled to bury the memory of her brother, her mother was doing everything in her power to keep it alive—his room where nothing had been disturbed—his Bronco where it remained parked in the drive—his toothbrush still hanging in the bathroom—his shaving gear sitting in the cabinet.

She would move in with Kyle as he'd been begging her to do for months.

Christine closed her eyes as she rocked, the heaviness in her chest having nothing to do with the child nestled there. It was Kyle—the way he looked at her with such longing, the way his lips lingered lovingly on her cheek when her own lips were turned so hastily away. The way his gentle arms held her when she needed comforting. He hadn't faltered once when she told him of her pregnancy. He'd stood by her side every step of the way. He was the most patient man she had ever known—and the most handsome. The mere thought of his dimpled smile made her knees weak. Yet she couldn't bring herself to open her heart to him, a heart she feared may have been mangled to beyond mending. It was the voice, that deep within, warning that betrayal was imminent. She blamed Sam for that as well.

She gazed down upon a cherub drifting into slumber. Though her mouth continued to suckle, she drew no milk. Christine drank in the beauty—the moist puckered lips, the dark lashes fluttering against fair skin, the tiny hands entangled in her nightgown. So delicate and vulnerable, so completely dependent upon her. She would not subject her to danger, would do whatever it took to ensure her well-being.

She rocked the sleeping babe, comforted by the feel of her, the warmth of her, the powdery fragrance. Shadows on the far wall continued with their fluttering moonlit ballet. Beyond the window, a breeze gently gusted—and she heard it—ever so softly, just beyond the panes. Like a forlorn lover, dark waters were wooing her, a wily whispering, gently insistent—

Chrissstaaa…

Chrisssstaaaaa…

CHAPTER 2

"Christine."

Christine pursed her lips thinly. "Yes, Clifford."

"Ignore them."

Squirting window cleaner on the glass of the freezer door, Christine began to wipe it down vigorously with a wad of paper towels. "Ignore who?" She glanced over the counter to where the three patrons sat at the booth snickering behind their ice cream cones.

Clifford sidled a bit closer. "I can see you want to kick some ass," he whispered. "Remember that you have more class."

"Cliff…you're killing me. Besides, I never claimed to have any class."

Pulling a box from under the counter, Cliff slid out a fresh sleeve of cones. "You have more class in your little toe than they combined will ever know."

Christine continued with her sturdy scrubbing. "Who eats that much ice cream? They're here almost every night."

Clifford slid the glasses back up the bridge of his nose with a finger on the frame between his eyes. "Yeah. If I were to guess a thing or two, I'd say they want a word with you."

The buxom blond woman leaned in to whisper something in her boyfriend's ear, and he glanced in Christine's direction with a smug grin—then mumbled something to the man seated across from him, spurring him to glance over with an ice-cream coated smirk.

"Why don't you go in back," Clifford suggested. "Fold that pile of rags—the whole stack."

"I'm fine, Cliff, really," Christine insisted as she continued with her manic scrubbing. “I was just thinking about Saturday. Kim and her boyfriend are flying in for Becca’s birthday. She’s turning one already. Can you believe that?”

“Christine—I believe that spot is clean.”

Realizing the door she was scrubbing was quite literally squeaky clean, Christine moved to the adjoining door, giving a few furtive squirts of glass cleaner. “Josh Radworth and Calvin Barnes.”

Cliff glanced over at the only occupied booth. “Yes ma’am. They played ball with Sam.”

“And that’s Carol Dillon, Sam’s ex. She thinks I killed him like I did Sanchez. Everybody does.”

Cliff carefully loaded the cone dispenser. “Let them think what they may. Perhaps they’ll know the truth someday.”

“I don’t blame them for wanting answers. They loved him. Everybody did.” She watched as Cliff pulled a jar of candied cherries from under the counter and began to wipe it down with a damp rag. “Including you,” she added.

Placing the jar on the counter, Cliff ripped off the protective plastic cover. “He was a good guy, I cannot lie.” Wrenching open the lid, he spun it off, then leaned heavily on the counter to peer inside. “He was the only one who talked to me in school—even though I wasn’t cool.” There was a quiver in his voice. He cleared his throat to flush it out. “Remember the cherries?” he asked. “How he got mad at me for putting so many on your sundae?”

Pausing in her polishing, Christine peered through the glass at the bins of ice cream lining the bottom of the freezer, twelve different delicious flavors in all. She nodded as a lump formed in her own throat. “He really pissed me off that day.”

“You had steam coming from your ears—and bolted before shedding tears. The next day—you both disappeared.”

She looked to where he was staring into the wide-mouthed cherry jar as if into a deep, dark well.

“Clifford. Do you think I hurt Sam?”

He hesitated, then shook his head, his attention still held by the bobbing cherries.

Her vision blurred as the tears welled. “I loved him, too, you know. I would never have hurt him."

"Stop saying loved." His eyes were troubled when finally he turned them to her. "The way you use past tense does show—there may be much more that you know."

The group at the table across the room broke into snickers over something that may or may not have had anything to do with her. Still, she whipped her head around. "Do you mind!" she snapped. "What the hell is so funny, anyway?"

"Well," Carol Dillon drawled. "Excuuuuse us. We're just trying to have a good time—in spite of the company," she added.

"Yeah? If you have something to say to me, just say it."

Cliff took hold of her elbow. "Christine, let's go in back for a—"

"Where is he?" Carol blurted. "Sam? I know you know."

"Yeah," Josh said, leaning back on the seat and folding his arms across his chest. "You know."

"I don't."

Josh gave a disgusted huff as he shook his head. "Liar."

"Okay," Cliff said, pulling his apron off over his head. "I think it's time for you to leave. Don't force me to roll up my sleeves."

Carol snorted, throwing a hand to her stomach. "What a freak," she brayed. "Don't force me to roll up my sleeves? Are you kidding me?"

"Cliff the stiff," Josh said, standing to lean his impressive line-backer frame back on the table. His biceps bulged as he crossed his arms across his chest. "You gonna kick my ass, big guy?"

Calvin Barnes—one of Sam's best buddies and the star quarterback for Collin Ridge High for four years straight—slid out of the booth and sauntered to the door, throwing his unfinished cone in the trash bin. He put a hand on the door as the trashcan lid swung back and forth with an irksome squeak. "Let's leave," he suggested, "before Cliff the stiff rolls up his sleeves." He shivered and produced an exaggerated frightened face, prompting his friends to laughter.

Retrieving her purse from the seat beside her, Carol slid out with a smirk. “Leave it to a freak to hire a freak,” she sneered, then stopped at the door with a hand on her hip. “Sam always defended you, you know,” she directed to Christine. “Nobody dared say anything bad about his creepy little sister if he was around. And how did you repay him? Stab him a hundred times? Cut him up into a thousand tiny pieces? Bury him somewhere in a shallow grave?”

“Get out,” Christine whispered as a tear spilled over.

“You’ve got dark circles under your eyes. What’s wrong, little sister? Can’t sleep at night? Somebody haunting your dreams?”

“Out!” she screamed, trying to push past Cliff, though he put an arm about her shoulder to restrain her. “Out, yon blasted bligart!”

“Let’s go,” the Barnes boy said, pushing open the door, sending the cowbell to a clunky clanging. “This shit is getting too weird.”

Carol rolled her eyes as she turned to exit. “Fucking freaks,” she mumbled.

CHAPTER 3

Christine glanced to where Vince stood on the grassy bank. He was gazing out over the pond with his hands in his pockets, watching the family of mallards skim across the sparkling surface toward the pier. He was dressed in khaki shorts, a blue polo shirt, and brown loafers, his typical casualwear. He was fine as far as step-fathers went—polite enough, kind of quiet, though a bit of a neat freak. He was a private sort, and though he never said anything to Christine, she knew he didn't appreciate the attention she brought to the Clavin residence. It wasn't nearly as bad as it had been in the beginning, only an occasional reporter ringing the phone or the doorbell. Vince always managed to turn them away gently. And he was gentle with her mother. That was the important thing. She was so much more fragile these days—and with good reason.

Christine's eyes drifted to where Kim and Ryan stood on the pier, tossing out bread. Ryan seemed like a great guy. He had remarkable green eyes and he made Kimmy laugh a lot. What more could a girl ask for?

With a sigh, Christine searched the water's deceptively calm surface. There could be no more putting it off. The summoning voices—be they in her head or no—had worn her down over the last six months. They called her name derisively now, not the subtle whispering as in the beginning. Caterwauling wrenched her from sleep at night with sleep-clothes clinging to a sweat-soaked body and a heart sounding like a herd of buffaloes stampeding through her brain. They were no longer trying to coax her to black waters, but demanding insistently. It was time to make a move before they consumed her.

She looked across the picnic table to where Kyle sat sipping on a soda and was embarrassed to find his eyes upon her. His beautiful deep-blue eyes were filled with concern.

"What is it, Chris?"

Christine fidgeted on the bench as she used her fork to push the food around on her plate; potato salad, coleslaw, baked beans. "I've been thinking."

"I can see that. Something bothering you?"

She smiled shyly, her resolve wavering at the thought of living under the same roof with one who read her so effortlessly. She looked over to where Rebecca sat in her highchair, a fistful of potato salad en route to her mouth. She managed to get a small portion to its intended destination, though most ended on her left check. "I've been thinking about your offer—about your spare room."

For a few moments, it appeared as if Kyle didn't fully comprehend. She watched as slowly realization dawned. He cocked his head as a crooked grin formed.

"I insist on paying rent, though. Now, don't say no, Kyle," she added quickly at the expression on his face. "This isn't negotiable."

"What about your classes? You'll never be able to afford rent *and* tuition."

"I'm going to ask for more hours at work. I don't think Cliff will mind—if he doesn't fire me first," she added with a frown. "I wouldn't blame him."

"That won't happen," Kyle said with a dimpled grin.

Christine fidgeted. "If I had any sense of decency, I'd quit. He's losing customers because of me."

"So quit. I'm Mr. Moneybags now that I'm head mechanic at Riley's. I really don't need for you to pay rent. I don't want you to. And I'll take care of your tuition. It's not a big deal. That way you can concentrate on school and raising Becca."

She faced him squarely, determined not to back down. "It's not negotiable," she reiterated. "Either I pay rent, or I don't move in."

Kyle studied her intently, the wheels spinning furiously behind his deep blue eyes.

"Just say okay, Kyle," she sighed wearily. "You know better than try to make sense of me."

"Okay," he chuckled. "It really doesn't make an ounce of sense, but—say you want to paint pink elephants on my walls, I'm shopping for pink paint."

She grinned sheepishly as she dropped her eyes to her plate. He wasn't telling her anything she didn't already know. "Pink elephants, huh? I'll have to think about that one."

"Are we ready, boys and girls?" a voice filtered in—her mother coming down the stone walk. She was carefully balancing the birthday cake—a pink googly-eyed dinosaur with purple spots. She was flawless as always, tall and slender, wearing a pale-yellow sundress and white sandals. Her dark hair was pulled back into a ponytail beneath a wide-brimmed straw hat.

"At the sight of the approaching cake, Rebecca sat up at attention, then squealed and clapped her potato-salad hands, a wide grin popping into place on her potato-salad face. While Kyle was preoccupied with Becca's reaction, Christine studied his profile—the line of his chin, the dark curly hair, the dimpled cheeks. He was horribly handsome. Almost too handsome.

Her fingertip went to the scar on her cheek, one very fine, barely detectable, and then to the other which crossed her throat, this one thicker and more defined. She pulled her hand away when Kyle looked to her, and their eyes locked for a few long moments, before she lowered hers.

Once she was under his roof, he would begin to press her for the answers she'd been so carefully avoiding. He would start pressing on other more—intimate matters as well, no doubt.

She glanced over to where the tall reeds swayed ever so gently. The water shimmering in the sun didn't appear ominous. The sky—crystal blue with only a smattering of thin white clouds—didn't seem portentous of doom.

Rebecca began to babble as the cake drew nearer, clapping her hands and kicking her legs, and Kyle chuckled, then stood with a handful of paper towels to clean her hands and face.

He was going to make a wonderful father. It was time to move forward, to begin the life she'd dreamed of for so many years while imprisoned on Atriia. She'd been imprisoned since her return as well—by her own crippling fears. It was time to tear down those walls. She was free now, free to pursue her dreams, her happiness, and that's exactly what she intended to do.

When Kyle sat back down, she smiled warmly, and when he reached across the table, she took the hand offered, squeezing it tightly. He had good hands, strong but gentle.

"It's going to be fine, Chris," he promised.

She looked into eyes like shimmering sapphires, multi-faceted eyes the deepest of blues, eyes pleading for her trust. She nodded, trying to stave off the welling tears, trying to push out the consuming fears. "Okay," she whispered, "pink elephants it is then."

CHAPTER 4

Christine rolled to her stomach yet again. She eyed the boxes lined against the wall—all of her belongings packed neatly and ready to go. The night outside was still and dark, the sliver of a moon offering little light. Occasionally, the hoot of an owl broke the stillness. The calm outside, however, did not reflect the turmoil which raged within her.

Rolling to her back, she kicked the covers off, feeling flushed despite the cool night. In the crib, the newly-turned one-year-old slept soundly, unaware of the acute anxiety ravaging her mother mere feet away. Rebecca had thoroughly enjoyed her first birthday, shoveling handfuls of cake into her mouth and licking the icing from her fingers with great relish. The balloons had fascinated her, as had the wrapped gifts, especially the giant ball gifted by Kyle. Half the day she'd spent hobbling about on her newfound legs, kicking and chasing it about while giggling so hard it induced hiccups. The sun and exercise had taken its toll on the child. She'd teetered on the edge of sleep in her highchair, coming dangerously close to falling face first into her spaghetti dinner.

Shivering, Christine fumbled for the covers she'd just kicked away, pulling them to her chin, wondering vaguely if she was coming down with something. "Yeah," she whispered. "It's called cold feet syndrome."

Kyle had seemed different as he'd said his goodbyes. Nothing overtly obvious. Subtle body language; the way he held his mouth as if suppressing a grin, the way his sapphire eyes held a certain glint, the way his fingers had brushed along her back as he leaned in for his good-bye kiss, his lips lingering on her cheek much longer than usual. And the kiss had been dangerously close to her lips.

Rolling to her stomach yet again, she fluffed the pillow and plopped into it, half burying her face as she hugged it close.

~~~~~~~~~~

The creak of the bedroom door pulled her from the drifting state—her mother's nightly check-in. She heard her move to the crib—heard the rustle of covers as she adjusted Rebecca's blanket—then the groan of the floorboards as she moved to the bed. Christine waited to feel her own bed covers adjusted and the kiss on her forehead, thus to complete the nightly ritual.

Bringing a fist to one eye, Christine tried to rub away the blurriness. Perhaps her mother was having anxiety about the move as well. Perhaps she needed to talk. Perhaps she wanted to talk her out of leaving.

As her senses cleared, it occurred to Christine that a peculiar smell had entered along with her mother, one unusual, one familiar—earthy—musky—wet…

Christine's eyes flew open as an alarm went off, a blaring in her brain.

Scrambling to a sitting position, she threw the covers to the floor.

The scream caught in her throat at the sight of the large hulking figure at the foot of the bed, one with a frame which certainly did not belong to her mother. There was barely enough light coming in through the window to make out the features. Only the eyes were discernible, these glistening like shiny black diamonds. "No," she breathed, the word barely pushed out past a throat constricted in fear.

He was soaked through, the breeches clinging to his thighs, the dark hair hanging in long wet strands to broad bare shoulders. She could smell it emanating from him—the musky pond scent. He was cradling something in his arms—a bundle of stolen treasure, booty wrapped in a blanket, a blanket she instantly recognized.
~~~~~~~~~~

Pivoting suddenly, he vanished through the bedroom door.

"Sam!" she screamed, and was instantly up and running. She didn't see the puddle, one which took her feet out from under her like an oil slick. She went down hard, her head cracking on the hardwood floor with a thick thud.

Clambering back to her feet, she stumbled to the stairs where she teetered at the top, her head spinning, her vision clouding as blackness threatened to overtake her. Grabbing the banister, she stumbled down the steps and through the living room toward the kitchen. She screamed at the sight of the back door standing wide, then barreled through it into the still night, speeding toward shimmering waters in the distance, frantically pursuing the dark figure intent on eluding her.

He was too far ahead. She knew she wouldn't catch him. And so she screamed his name again and again, pleading with him as he made his way to the end of the pier.

He stopped for a brief moment to fumble with his trove of treasure, repositioning it—before leaping in feet first.

She was screaming as she hurtled down the pier, her eyes searching desperately at the dark waters below it. There was evidence of his entry, the surface churning, the rippling sending small waves to the shoreline, but neither Sam, nor his stolen stash, were anywhere to be seen.

With a frantic shriek, she leaped in after them.

The shock of cold water forced the air from her lungs. Struggling back to the surface, she sputtered and flailed as she tried to regain her senses. She considered for a brief moment that she'd been dreaming, sleep walking, and the water had awakened her from a nightmare. Sam was dead. She had seen him dropped, had witnessed the last breath leave his body, the spark of life leave his eyes, had witnessed this time and again, replaying the moment of his death in her mind over and over, torturing herself, lamenting the loss of a beloved brother, cursing him, cursing herself for wanting, needing, yearning for the part of him that was Hannen.

She considered wading back to the shore and returning to the house. Certainly Rebecca would be sleeping soundly in her crib.

A cry escaped her as she felt a tug from below, the caress of silky waters at her legs drawing her down. A whirlpool began to form, swirling lazily around her. She struggled against it, futilely kicking to stay afloat. In that instant she knew, dream or no, the decision to turn back was no longer her own.

Panic seized her at the realization of where she would resurface if she went under—black waters swarming with fraigens, their razor teeth anxious to rip her limb from limb—and as she began to thrash, desperately fighting against the grips of an invisible foe, she failed to take the vital breath needed before she was pulled under, a breath without which she would never survive the torturous journey to Atriia. She was screaming as she was dragged downward, and when eventually she did decide to take the vital breath needed, cold liquid was all that filled her lungs.

CHAPTER 5

The pressure in her lungs was excruciating. Her stomach knotted and she sputtered, retching as water and mucous poured from her mouth and nose. As air entered her lungs, she cried out at the pain of re-inflating organs. She was spinning in the darkness, struggling for consciousness, for breath, this being squeezed from her by the woodslink wrapped so tightly—a death grip. She tried to scream out, but only a thin moan escaped.

She heard it then, the hiss of the hideous creature, it's breath hot against her neck as it nuzzled—the soft flick of its tongue as it tasted her—the others which followed, up over her chin toward her mouth. It hissed her name, deep and raspy, the moisture of its breath entering her parted lips. Not wishing to bear witness to her own painful demise, she let darkness take her, drifting away on a tide of merciful oblivion as the beast began to devour her…

CHAPTER 6

Droning sounds penetrated through the haze—voices, she realized as the murkiness cleared, voices muffled by the wall separating them. Slowly, her eyes adjusted to the darkness. It was a small room with no ceiling, the wooden beams and rafters of the roof exposed overhead. Dim moonlight filtered through a single window, casting a luminescent glow upon her where she lie upon the bed. A cold rag lay draped across her forehead. She reached for it, then drew in a sharp breath at the pain, one released as a weak moan.

From the corner of her eye, she caught movement, a dark figure standing from where he sat on a cot beside the door. Though his features were in shadow, she knew instantly who kept vigil.

She sat up quickly, and instantly the room went dark as pain enveloped her. Dropping her chin to her chest, she fought against faint. "Becca," she moaned.

"Safe," he replied, the raspy voice sending shivers through her. As if on cue, Rebecca's sweet giggle sounded from beyond the room, this answered by a woman's laughter.

"No," Christine groaned as the looming figure stepped closer. "You—I saw you—saw you…" The room was spinning, her mind reeling.

"Aya, Christa."

She felt the hair at the back of her neck stand on end as he took another step, bringing his face into the filtered lighting. She quickly turned her face away from the sight of his unmasked.

"Christa—"

"No!" she gasped, pressing her palms to throbbing temples.

"Lie back," he said as he moved in. "Yon did have one difficult passing through the lairs."

"Stay away!"

"Christa—"

"Stay away, Sam!"

The name stopped him in his tracks. "Hannen," he corrected.

"Fine! Stay the fuck away—*Hannen*!"

Nausea engulfed her. She had just antagonized Sam like old times. Conflicting emotions tore through her at the realization that he was alive, elation and revulsion butting heads in her gut. She looked down to where she gripped the covers and discovered why this act created such pain. Her fingers were scraped and swollen, the torn nails crusted with dried blood. Even in the darkness, she could see bruises running the length of her arms. By the feel of it, her entire body had suffered the same afflictions.

There came a light knock, and then the creaking of hinges as the door was pushed open and a woman's head poked through. "Aiyee! This lita did hear speakings. Is she well, then?"

"Aya," Sam replied sourly. "She is that."

"Apologies, Reesla," the woman directed to her. "Trollers have been sent for, but the closest are in Rostivane. The foul blogarts who did this to yon will doubtent be many longs distanced fore such can arrive."

Christine eyed the woman briefly, a matronly woman with graying brown hair wound neatly at her nape. She wore a plain gray dress and a crisp white apron. "I would like to see my daughter," she intoned stonily.

"One babe." Sam motioned to the woman.

"Aya," the woman replied, disappearing from sight. She returned promptly carrying a lantern in one hand and supporting Rebecca with the other where she sat astride one broad hip. At the sight of Christine, the child threw her arms wide with a shrill squeal.

Christine felt her heart soar at the sight of her angel, and despite the pain of a bruised body, she took the proffered child, crushing her to her chest, breathing in of her scent and placing kisses on her cheeks till she squirmed. The babe was wearing a cloth diaper, a chamois-soft shirt, and a wide grin, seeming physically and emotionally unscathed by her travels through the caverns.

There was obviously something of great interest in the next room. Rebecca seemed intent upon maneuvering off the bed—and so Christine helped her down, and then watched as she tottered out the door with her newly assigned care-giver close behind.

Christine gave Sam a quick glowering glance. "How could you—" Instantly, tears formed, thwarting any further accusations. Swiping them angrily away, she leaned back against the headboard and pulled her knees to her chest, wincing at the pain of a body badly battered. She'd been stripped of her own pajamas. She was wearing a white sleeping-gown and nothing else. She couldn't help but think Sam responsible for this as well. There was the vague memory of raspy whisperings as wet clothes were being peeled away. Another vague memory surfaced as well. She felt the heat rise to her cheeks at the recalling of a ravenous mouth on hers, an indecent devouring.

More tears escaped and she swiped them angrily away as a chill coursed through her. Hugging her knees close, she pulled her eyes reluctantly from the door which had lured Rebecca through, moving them to the very bane of her existence, viewing him in the fresh orb of light emitted from the lantern left behind.

Although she knew it was Sam, the man so intently focused on her bore little resemblance to her brother. Dark, shaggy hair hung to his shoulders, and his clothing—a long-sleeved shirt tucked into form-fitting breeches—acutely accentuated a powerful build. Sam had always been athletic, but there was something dangerously different about this man—the way he carried himself, his stance at the very instant. The fraigen dropper was in her presence—feral, intimidating, sensual. The dark eyes especially, devouring with a dastardly shamelessness. The disfiguring scar shone pale against his tanned skin, deeply indenting his left cheek where much of the flesh had been ripped free, before traveling down his jaw and across his throat like the thick noose of a rope.

He did not turn away from her scrutiny. He held his place as the defiant fraigen dropper he was, his posture challenging. She wanted to confront him, to ask the many questions reeling through her brain. But too many emotions were roiling through her—fear for Rebecca and for herself, frustration at the inability to express these fears, embarrassment at the inability to contain the tears. Pain suffused her very being. It seemed not one inch of her body had escaped unscathed. She was scraped and bruised, ripped and swollen. And to make matters worse, her body was retaliating its abuse. A shiver assailed her, the tremors rattling her teeth. Clutching the blanket with tender fingers, she pulled them to her chin.

But Sam had no intentions of putting off the forthcoming confrontation. Moving to the side of the bed, he towered over her, the hovering hulk of a man bent on defending himself.

She moved her eyes back to the doorway. "Haven't you put me through enough for one day?" she asked, disheartened by the weakness of her own voice.

"One babe," he spoke softly. "She's mine."

It was more statement than question, one which forced the air from her lungs like a fist to the gut. Though the words tried to form on her tongue, the breath to deny his statement was not to be found.

She was saved a reply by a rapping at the door followed by a ganis entering, one tall and slender, the light from behind spilling around flowing white hair.

"Reesla, this is Meshganis Tieslen," Sam introduced.

"It is good to note yon wakened," the man spoke as he approached her bedside. He leaned close to gently prod at her forehead, and she winced as he found a tender spot. "Small one there, and one here," he said, indicating another knot beneath her hair just above her right temple. "The biggest is here," he said, locating a large knot at the back of her head. "We will keep close eye on such. Yon did battle fiercely, Reesla. Yon has bruising head to foot."

"Mine babe, she is fine, then?"

He nodded, his expression turning odd. Sliding a chair to sit by her side, he stroked his beard with spindly fingers. "As one meshganis, I must ask. One scarring on yon belly, I have nayat ever noted such."

She shot an accusing glare at Sam before returning her attention back to the meshganis. "Mine babe was pulled through such."

His eyes shot wide. "Of all Atriia! I was thinking the very thing!" He stood abruptly, putting one hand to his forehead as if testing for fever. "I did know—did know it was such! What is the callen of one meshganis who did such? From where does he hail?"

"Shriver from Greenville."

"Greenville?"

"Far distanced," Sam interjected. "Sleeper region."

The meshganis stroked a long black beard, one which seemed abnormally dark considering his white hair. His eyes were glowing in the lamplight. "What leexer was used to keep yon still? Was it slegg root?"

"Epidural." She glanced toward a glowering Sam.

"I have nayat heard of such." He was speaking only to himself as he began to pace. "I did use slegg root on one hound. But too much was given. The tippets do always waken. Why did one hound nayat? Was yon sent to sleeping?" he directed to her. "Did yon have flustings waking?"

Christine clamped her jaw down to prevent her teeth from chattering as a violent shudder shook her. Noting this, the meshganis stepped close to put a hand to her forehead. "I will fetch added blankets. Katissa," he yelled as he made a hasty exit.

Sam moved in quickly at his exiting, his eyes hard. "That ganis would nayat step on one dung beetle!"

"I only told the truth." Even so, she felt tears of guilt surface. Another bout of shivers shook her, and she brushed angrily at a tear rattled loose.

Sam softened at this. Reaching to his waist, he stripped his shirt over his head in one deft movement, freeing the fraigen to leer at her with one evil black eye.

"What—no—wait!"

Ignoring her, he crawled onto the bed and, lifting the covers, motioned for her to lie down beside him.

“Please leave me alone,” she pleaded, knowing even as she spoke them, the words were pointless. It would have been equally as pointless to resist the hands that forced her to comply.

~~~~~~~~~~

With him pressed so close, she knew he could feel her weeping, but it was no use. The tears would not be denied. She pressed her face into the pillow to muffle her misery, and his response was to pull her closer still.

Wrapped snugly in his embrace, his body was a furnace behind her, spreading warmth through her chilled soul, and though she was loathe to admit it, there was comfort in his familiar embrace. With his face no longer visible, it was almost possible to imagine such an embrace belonged to one Hannen Fallier and no other. It was an embrace she thought she would never know again, and one she had missed terribly.
~~~~~~~~~~

CHAPTER 7

She was shivering. Nausea knotted her stomach as fear consumed her. She was not afraid for herself, but for the fraigen dropper, the man who was Samuel and Hannen, both—the man she loved and loathed at once. This gray and dismal morning would be his last day of life. She felt this as surely as she felt the talon-like grip of PacMattin's hand upon her arm. He would have her witness the horror unfolding, the savage dismembering of the man she loved. PacMattin took great pleasure in her pain.

Drums were beating as the fraigens converged upon Sam. She felt a twisting within, a crushing vise locked on her heart, on her very soul. A wave of nausea swept over her as one fraigen locked onto his leg, one other his arm, and the macabre tug of war began…

She awoke with a start to the sound of rain drumming on the rooftop, drops surely the size of baseballs by the beating the roof was taking. She lay still as her breaths returned to normal. Warmth had once again taken up residence within her limbs, the heat radiating from the body pressed against her from behind.

Lifting a hand to the back of her head, she examined the painful knot, and with this slight shifting, the arm draped across her waist tightened—a reflex in sleep. His warm breaths in her hair were deep and steady, his chest rising and falling against her back in slow, peaceful measures. How many times had she awakened to this very embrace feeling so safe and secure, so very fulfilled? Such was not the case this dismal, rainy morn. The feeling which encompassed her was one of profound emptiness.

As her eyes adjusted to the dim lighting, she made out a small form on the cot by the door—Rebecca sprawled on her back, sleeping soundly. An ember of anger lit at the sight of her, this directed at the man who would so recklessly risk her life.

She pulled her eyes from the child to scan the room—a small bedroom, one used as storage. The wall she was facing held a window with two cluttered bookcases on either side. Though they did contain several books, most of the shelves were littered with vials and beakers and glass jars of various shapes and sizes, the paraphernalia of the mad doctor. In one corner, sacks were piled high, their sides bulging with contents unknown. What appeared to be bundles of herbs were dangling from the rafters overhead, these tied in bunches and hung out to dry.

Her eyes came to rest on the only window. The curtains had been drawn, these thick and dark, revealing nothing beyond. *Atriia.* That's what loomed beyond them. And Black Pond.

Summoning her courage, she carefully rolled to her back and attempted to inch her way from beneath Sam's arm, but he instantly stirred, then pushed to one elbow to peer down upon her with sleepy eyes.

Snared beneath his arm, she was forced to face him squarely as his eyes poured languidly over her features, seeming to drink in every minute detail. Her breath caught in her chest as they slid back up to meet her own.

As if on cue, the pelting rain eased, so all that could be heard was her own racing heart pounding in her ears. She attempted to protest, went so far as to open her mouth to do this very thing, but it seemed words escaped her yet again. She was peering into the eyes of the fraigen dropper—savage, wanton eyes divulging his desires with implicit clarity.

"Sam." With some effort, she forced the word out, and he stiffened at the name, the hunger in his eyes defusing.

Pushing past his arm, she slid to sit on the edge of the bed, awakening the bumps and bruises with a vengeance. With her back safely to him, she hung her head between her shoulders, trying to focus on the floorboards at her feet as the dizziness passed. "How can you be alive?" she spoke weakly. "I saw you…" She squeezed her eyes tight at the memory, trying to keep the tears at bay.

"Dropped," he finished for her.

She nodded numbly. Shutting her eyes could not keep the memory at bay, an image burned into her brain forever, haunting her waking thoughts, her dreaded dreams—the blood, the twisted limbs, the pale swollen face, the glimmer of life slowly fading from his eyes.

"I think *I was* dropped," Sam spoke softly from behind her. "I did note them—mine brathern, mine malla and fallar—Bocksard…" His voice faltered at the mention of this last, and Christine felt her own tears well at the thought of all who had perished at the Rez of Fallier.

"And then I did waken," he continued, "to this very boarding, this very bunker."

"Where are we?"

"Skirtings of Huyetti," he informed her. "One small cassing nayat five longs from Black Pond. We are in the rez of Sy Tieslen—one meshganis yon did meet. Same did mesh mine rippings, did save mine life."

Christine looked to where Rebecca slept so soundly. The child's face was turned toward them, the pale countenance framed by dark ringlets. A lump formed in her throat at the sight, as did tears in her eyes. "You would risk drowning the baby—to bring her to this godforsaken place?"

He gave a deep sigh. "I did nayat know there was one babe. I do swear on Sola. It was only yonself I did mean to bring back."

Burying her face in her hands, she shook her head as the tears began to overflow. "Why? There's nothing here for me. *Nothing!*"

In an instant, he left the bed, moving around it to kneel before her. Forcing the hands from her face, he brought them to his lips, holding them tight. "I love you, Christa. Do you hear me?"

Closing her eyes, she shook her head vehemently, hating the torrent of tears, hating the quivering lip and the painful palpitating of her heart.

"I can nayat stop mine heart from feeling as it does," he spoke in hushed tones as Becca stirred upon the cot. "I did try—as Sola shines, I did. It belongs to you and no other."

She shook her head emphatically, hating her slumped shoulders, hating the chin dropped down upon a hitching chest.

Suddenly, he shot up off his heels, inducing her chin to pop up and her eyes to pop open.

"You belong here with me," he insisted, leaning close, his eyes challenging. "Rez Fallier is being rebuilt as we speak. Come back with me. Share mine rez—and mine callen."

Shaking her head, she made a feeble attempt to pull her hands away from his.

Undaunted, he held tight. "Christa Fallier," he spoke, trying the name on his lips, and liking the sound by the grin that formed. "Yon can nayat stop yon heart from feeling as it does either. It belongs to me."

"Naya," she hissed. "It belongs to Kyle. He has my heart! And I took his name!"

She witnessed the shadow of doubt darken his features, and then he was probing, drilling with eyes intent on unearthing untruths in the words she'd spoken. They dropped down to her hands—where no ring rested.

There came a prickling of panic. "I can't give you what you want! I can't. You're my…" Her voice faltered on the word, for even as she thought it, she knew it wasn't entirely true. The eyes peering at her so unscrupulously did not belong to her brother. They were far too intense, devouring her in a way Sam's never would. How many times had she lost herself within these very eyes? How many times had she found herself in them?

She dropped her eyes to the vicious scar on his cheek, then down to the new scar that ravaged his shoulder, then over to the chain hanging about his neck, a thin strip of black braided leather. A charm dangled from it, resting in the cleft of his chest in the vicinity of the fraigen's toothy grin. It was a fraigen scale.

"The very used to drop PacMattin," he whispered, having seen the path her eyes had taken. "It did still rest upon one rafting, in one spot of foul dried devon's blood. Yon did well, Christa, as I knew yon would."

Swallowing hard, she looked over his shoulder to the shelves, studying the jars. “I can’t, Sam,” she stated flatly with her eyes safely averted.

He brought her ring-less hands to his mouth, placing a gentle kiss upon each in turn. “Sam is gone, Christa,” he rasped throatily. “Look at me. Lay eyes upon this ganis, Lita Fallier,” he insisted, moving into her line of vision so she was forced to comply.

She cursed the endless well of tears and the quivering lower lip, biting down on this last to prevent such. The breath had left her body and she was having difficulties drawing it back in again.

“Who do you see?” he whispered.

She felt her resolve waiver. It was Fallier the fraigen dropper who knelt before her, his face horridly ravaged by one fierce fraigen, the very creature inked upon his chest, the very creature he had so selflessly sacrificed himself to so that she might live. He was badly scarred, yes. He was magnificent, dark and wild and beautiful. His eyes were black and smoldering. They took her breath away with their shameless intensity.

He was leaning into her—and she to him. It seemed she had found her air, the breaths coming in quick succession. And then her breaths were mingling with his as he took her bottom lip between his own. The pounding in her ears was deafening, drowning out the siren trying to ring out reason. She could not remember placing her hands behind his neck, but they were there, clinging, for she was floating backward, being guided to the bed ever so slowly.

As his weight settled solid on top, she moaned against his mouth, and not for the pain of bumps and bruises, for this had quickly been overridden by a painful desire. How she had missed the body of the fraigen dropper on top of her, the scent of him, the taste.

He was savoring her lips as he ran his fingers into her hair, and she followed suit, her fingers trembling.

A thought pushed into her muddled mind. Her hands had not encountered the ties of a face mask. She had thought him ashamed of his disfigurement. But it was something entirely else which had shamed him.

Her eyes flew open. Her senses reeled, a strange vacillating between passion and revulsion—and she began to struggle against him.

Pushing to forearms, he propped himself above her, his face close, his warm, shallow breaths mingling with her own, holding his place doggedly despite the firm hands pressing against his shoulders.

The smoldering eyes of the fraigen dropper were speaking to her, demanding that the hands pressing against his shoulders travel behind his neck, so to pull him down once again to her own trembling lips. Tantalized and terrified at once, she struggled against their lurid lure.

With defiant deliberateness, he reached between the two of them to loosen the tie at his waist.

The breath caught in her throat at a move so bold, and a hot tear slipped from the corner of her eye as her hands gave in to his bidding, sliding to his neck.

Any remaining resistance was spirited away on a kiss so sensuous, it sullied the senses. She clutched at his neck with her hands, his hips with her thighs as he crushed her beneath him. She was lost—lost…

Salvation came in the form of a mewling cry, Rebecca awakening from a bad dream. Like a slap in the face, it cleared her senses, pulling her from eminent disaster.

CHAPTER 8

Food was being prepared. Seated at one end of the table, Christine observed Rebecca where she sat perched merrily upon Sam's lap. The child was hopelessly taken with him, giggling obligingly every time he feigned attempts to gobble her chubby fingers with a feral snarl. Her tiny hands repeatedly wandered dangerously close to his mouth for the sole purpose of eliciting such an attack.

Across the table from Sam sat the Mas of the rez. He was an odd one, this Meshganis Tieslen, his garb different than any she had seen on Atriia—a flowing layered robe in the purest of whites. His ears were multi-pierced, the dangling earrings running from lobe to upper ear. His hair was not white as she had thought, but very blond, and worn long in back, to below his waist, but short about the face—an Atriian mullet. The shorter hair above his ears had been twisted into tufts and tied off with bejeweled leather laces, the dangling baubles bobbling with his every movement. His beard, one unnaturally dark, had been similarly adorned. He was rolling one such dangling beard-bauble gingerly between thumb and forefinger as he conversed with Sam.

His lita, Katissa, was stirring coarse at the stove. Beside the coarse pot, a large skillet sat steaming. It was filled with scrambled eggs to which she had added thinly sliced strips of meat. Christine's nose told her it was shike strips. It also told her that bread was baking, the sweet aroma permeating the iron oven walls. It was a cozy kitchen, the walls constructed of logs, and with open beam and trusses overhead. Baskets with various fruits and vegetables lined the walls and more dangled from above. Bundles of coarse stalks were neatly stacked in one corner.

Christine shifted in the chair, readjusting the blanket draped about her shoulders, and Sam glanced in her direction, something he seemed to be doing with disturbing frequency. He was obviously of an anxious mind to continue on from where they had left off. She avoided his gaze, not wanting to think on what had transpired. After nearly an hour, she could feel her face flushed still, her lips tender.

The door next to the oven was yanked open and a young boy entered, one owning eleven or twelve years, and lugging two pails at his sides. Straining under the weight, he hobbled across the kitchen, plopping them upon the counter near the stove. "Water is muddied by the raining," he informed them breathlessly.

"As is yonself, Daxter," Katissa countered, motioning to his muddy boots.

With a sheepish grin, the boy trudged back outside where he stomped his feet vigorously before re-entering.

"Did yon note Sura, then," his mother asked as she stirred the steaming eggs. "It does nayat take one entire turning to collect shike's milk, surent. She best nayat be arcing arrows. This malla will snap every last one in two, that be truths."

"The raining did cave one goser boarding," the boy explained. He shook his head to rid it of the drops collected in the tousled blonde curls. He was a striking child, his skin deeply tanned, his hair quite fair. "She does tend to same. I did hand offerings to lend aid, but she is of one foul mood this sol." Moving to the stove, he peered over his mother's shoulder at the food sizzling in the skillet, then reached under her arm, plucking out a morsel of meat and popping it into his mouth.

Mas Tieslen gave a curt snort. "Same's mood has been foul since the arriving of yon lita," he spoke to Sam, giving a nod in Christine's direction.

Daxter chuckled at this. "Aya, Sura does claim same is railed and stunted and that same—"

"Of all Atriia!" Katissa railed, flashing an embarrassed grin at Christine.

"Was nayat mine tongue did speak such," Daxter defended.

"Was Sura."

"Tell Sura firstsup is readied," Katissa interjected, sending the boy trudging back out wearing a sulking frown.

"I do wish to hand many thankings for all has been done for this ganis," Sam said, before launching a fresh attack on the taunting fingers.

Meshganis Tieslen nodded. "Is yon certain, then, yon must take leave right off?"

"Aya. Reesla seems well enough for travel," he said, glancing in Christine's direction. "I will bid ponies and supplies at the next market, then we must be off."

"Daxter will nayat take well to this word, surent," Katissa said as she placed a plate piled with steaming food before him. "And I gest yon does check neath yon carry cover, lest Sura does lie hid neath."

"Spellered," Tieslen said, grinning at Sam. "She does alreadied beg to visit yon rez. I told her she may come when I travel there to birth the nipper."

She strode in the back door then, the Sura of whom they spoke, with Daxter just behind. Christine had expected a young girl and so was surprised at the beautiful young woman who entered, one at least eighteen years of age. She was surprised also at the pants she wore, such attire unacceptable for the litas of Atriia. She also wore ganis footings, knee-high boots of leather complete with holstered blade. She was tall and slender, the blonde hair pulled into a tie at her neck. She crossed the kitchen with an odd limping stride to deposit the milk pail upon the counter.

"Sura," her mother chided.

With a huff, Sura pulled the gilt from where it had been tucked into the waist of her breeches, letting it fall to the floor. "I did nayat wish to muddy mine gilt," she explained before plopping down at the table next to her father.

CHAPTER 9

Christine pushed the eggs around on her plate. There was a tightness in the pit of her belly which left no room for food. He meant to spirit them away, away from Black Pond, away from the tunnels leading home. The packing list was being discussed as they ate; five gosers, two reams of coarse stalks, a bushel of suva, cooking pans, one barrel of spirits, two water barrels, dried swill and shike strips, crouting hooks, crout blades.

"Reesla is in need of footings and gilts," Katissa pointed out. "Mayhap Sura could part with one or two."

Daxter snorted through a mouthful of food. "Such will nayat fit. Sura does own feet big as any ganis."

"And yon does own the biggest mouth in all of Atriia," Sura retorted in a tone which implied he best keep it shut. "Dung beetle brain."

"Silence," Sy demanded. "Reesla did nayat travel these many longs to listen to such blow, surent."

Sura took a healthy swallow of milk before wiping her mouth on the back of her sleeve. "It is mine wondering how same did travel such longs with nayat one gilt to boast."

Sam shifted in his chair. Sitting upon his lap, Becca plucked another bite of egg from his plate and stuffed it in her mouth.

"As yon does well know, Reesla did fall on ill-fating," Katissa offered from her spot at the table.

"Aya," Sura scoffed. "Blacktongues did drop down two ganis escorts, so to stelcher lita garb." There was ill-concealed skepticism in her eyes as she tore off a bite of bread and popped it into her mouth.

"Foul blacktongues will stelcher the footings off their very sasturns if same could gain half one slice for such," Katissa stated firmly.

"Was the ponies they did seek," Sam offered.

"Well, thankings should be handed to Sola for Reesla did escape with her life," Katissa pointed out.

"Did yon pass near Black Pond, then?" Daxter inquired through a mouthful of food.

It was the first question directed to Christine. Caught off guard, she glanced to Sam for guidance.

"Same did pass near to such," Sam affirmed as he set Rebecca to the floor.

"Did yon note her, then, one Loper of Zeria?"

Christine blanched, the mug of milk in her hand nearly toppling as she struggled to right it.

"Daxter, do nayat speak of such blow," his malla chided. "All do know same did fall to fraigens."

"Many do claim she does still walk the shores of Black Pond," Daxter insisted.

"Aya," Sura smirked. "Riding the backs of fraigens, blazened locks flowing in Luna's smile. Only one tot would believe such blow."

"Our Leader of Lors does nayat think such is blow," Sy broke in, "else same would nayat insist on viewing every last blazened-locked lita who does walk one face of Atriia. Reesla should wear one hooded gilt while in traveling, lest she be forced to go before one Zerian council."

As five sets of eyes turned to her, Christine safely averted her eyes away. Gripping the edge of the table, she held herself in place, her eyes glued to the child wandering about the room nibbling on a piece of bread.

"Yon does seem pallored," Katissa spoke at last. "Does yon fall ill?"

The sliding of Sam's chair sounded, grating along the floor as it did along her nerves. "Same is doubtent in need of resting," he spoke softly, and Christie felt a shudder run through her as he skirted around the table to offer a hand. He meant to lead her back to the boarding, back to unfinished business.

"Naya," she spoke weakly, though her conviction was strong. "Such speakings of blacktongues does make mine body ache. I do think I need more sols of resting fore I am well enough for travel."

The ridge of Sam's jaw tightened, sending the vein in his neck to bulging.

"Mayhap it would be best to put off yon travelings," Katissa directed to Sam.

"Aya," Sura chimed in, her eyes lighting at the prospect.

"Aya," Daxton agreed.

"Come," Sam said, riveting Christine with a hard glare. "Yon should lie down."

"Aya, yon should," Katissa agreed. "I will keep watch of Becca."

"Fine then," Christine said, standing without the aid of the offered hand. "We do need to speak on any account."

As soon as he shut the door behind them, she whirled on him, yanking her arm from his grasp. "I'm not going with you, Sam!" she spat. "The only place you're taking me is back home!" She turned away from his stony face, one which appeared unmoved by her convictions. "I don't need your help. I'll figure it out by myself."

"I will take yon back home, Christa. Back to one Rez of Fallier."

"Naya!" she shot back, spinning to face him, angry at his calm demeanor, angrier that she had reverted back to the Atriian language. "That is *not* my home!"

"Yon pale nipper, she did grow to one fine pony," he informed her. "Same is with babe, mayhap two."

"What? How could you let that happen!"

"It was out of mine hands. Hindler did—he did nayat think to keep her separate. Meshganis Tieslen has promised to aide in one birthing, but she will need her malla."

Squaring her shoulders, Christine faced him boldly. "We will go back, with or without your help. I will marry Kyle, and I'll live happily ever after—in my world, Sam. Not here—not with you—not ever!"

His expression didn't waver. He was defiant, stubborn as ever.

"I don't love you, Sam. Not like that."

"Mine callen is Hannen," he rasped. "Same Hannen yon lips did lock with nayat one turning past."

"A mistake," she blurted. "I was still in shock—not thinking clearly—I—"

"Yon can nayat go back, Christa," he stated matter-of-factly. "The way is closed."

She chortled at his vain attempt at deception.

His eyes narrowed. "Does yon think I would have waited two segs to return to you?" he pressed. "I did try every sol, Christa, from the time mine rippings did mesh. The tunnels—they would nayat allow mine passing."

"Right. And I'm supposed to believe that one day they just opened? What, did a neon sign light up, or something? Come on in. Now open for business."

"Naya," he answered, ignoring her facetiousness. "The waters did call to me."

She felt the blood drain from her face.

"Christa—"

Turning abruptly, she moved to the bookcase, scanning the vials and jars, and registering nothing. She swallowed down the painful lump in her throat. "Then we will wait," she whispered, "till they call again."

"And how long will yon wait, then, Christa? Two segs? Five? Ten?"

"Yes, you bastard!" Suddenly the tears surfaced along with the terror at the prospect of a lifetime on Atriia. "And I will have my own boarding till then," she added, forcing the words past a choking sob.

"You can't stay here Christa, not so close to one cassing of Zeria. Lor Zeria, he—somehow he knows yon does still live.

He's—in searching."

Christine felt an uncomfortable crawling along her scalp. Crossing her arms across her chest, she rubbed at the goose-bumps trailing down her arms.

"He holds great power, Christa, the first ever Leader of Lors. Every Lor of this region is sworn to serve him now. Every man, woman, child—"

"I don't care," she stated flatly. "I'm going nowhere with you, Sam. So—fuck off."

A chilly silence ensued. She could feel his eyes on her back, drilling into her. She felt compelled to scream at him, to hurl obscenities along with canisters and vials and anything else she could get her hands on.

She was spared the trouble by his exiting. Only after he'd pulled the door shut safely behind him, did she release the jagged sigh of relief.

CHAPTER 10

Desperation consumed her. The cherubic child at her breast, even, could not loosen the knot that cramped her insides. Though Becca continued to suckle in intervals, it was clear she had drifted into slumber, the suckling mere reflex and not forceful enough to draw milk. Prying her gently away, Christine placed her carefully on the bed, pulling the blankets over her small form.

With clenched fists, she paced the floor before the bed. A day earlier, she had been celebrating Becca's first birthday, a bright sunny day which seemed a thousand years removed from the dreary, drizzly one just beyond the window. To be back in Atriia was incomprehensible. But Becca in Atriia was obscene.

There was a roiling in her belly, anger and hunger combined. She'd declined midsup, then lastsup, opting instead to stew in her room. She didn't want to look at him, didn't want to hear his voice. A shudder ran through her at the mere thought of his eyes touching upon her. That it was not a shudder of revulsion—was beyond appalling. It was the eyes. Hannen's eyes. How easily she had fallen under their spell. How readily her body had responded to his touch. A tingling ensued at the memory, this infused with embarrassment. There was only one thought which stood clear amidst the cloud of confusion. She must escape this man who was not Hannen and yet not entirely Sam, this man who meant to possess her at any cost.

Wringing white-knuckled hands, she peered through the panes at a day darkened by disheartening rain-soaked clouds. Despite the strong desire to crawl out the window, to distance herself immediately from Sam, she knew she could not act hastily, could not endanger the child now so deep in slumber.

Moving to the bedside, she brushed a deep russet curl from the child's forehead and caressed an ivory cheek. The babe sighed heavily in her sleep, stirring at the touch.

A rapping sounded on the door, and a head poked in. "May I have one word, Mine Lita?"

Christine invited the meshganis in.

~~~~~~~~~~

"I am releasing yon from mine care," he stated after a quick examination. "Yon swellings are going down nicely. I do think yon well enough for traveling, Mine Lita."

Christine sighed heavily. "Did Hannen send yon in here?"

He grinned as he located a bauble in his beard in need of fingering. "The ganis is completely spellered. Yon must know this, Mine Lita."

She shook her head as she searched for an explanation which might seem plausible.

"Why did yon travel here if yon does nayat feel the same?" he asked.

Seating herself on the bed, she ran a hand wearily over her face.

"When they brought him to me, I did place him in this very bunker," the meshganis informed her. "One arm and leg both near ripped off. I did fear him one ganis dropped. His face was one coloring of parchment, as Sola shines. His life's blood was gone, yet he refused to go when Sola called. I have nayat ever noted one ganis battle for his life as did he. And the whole while, during fevering, during fits of sleeping, was yon callen he did speak, Christa."

She felt the blood drain to her toes where they dangled numbly off the side of the bed.

He grinned as he fingered his beard bauble. "Such is yon callen, is it nayat? Christa Clavin, one Loper of Zeria? I do nayat know why yon does live—but I *do* know why Hannen does."

She swallowed hard as tears welled. "He lives for yon is one skilled meshganis."

He nodded. "I *am* skilled, Mine Lita. The most skilled
~~~~~~~~~~

meshganis in all of Atriia, save mayhap Shriver from Greenville." He waved away any words she thought to speak. "I have birthed babes, have seamed rippings, set bones, battled illnesses other meshganist would nayat dare, and prevailed. But I am nayat above Sola," he said, moving for the door. "I could nayat mesh mine own litar when she was birthed with one crooked leg. And I did nayat pull Hannen from the hands of Sola," he added as he pulled open the door. "Was yon did such."

As the door was pulled to, a sudden fatigue settled over Christine, weighing heavily. Crawling beneath the covers, she wrapped herself around Rebecca, closing eyes weary with worry. There was a chill in the room, a combination of weather and fear. She snuggled under the blankets until gradually warmth crept in.

~~~~~~~~~~

She started awake at the sound, the creak of a door, or perhaps a floorboard. It seemed she had just closed her eyes, yet the room was darker than it should have been. Obviously she'd been down for some time. She blinked repeatedly, trying to clear the fog of sleep. Reaching out with one hand, she felt for Rebecca.

"Christa."

She gasped at the sound of his voice at her ear, startled that he'd managed to climb onto the bed without rousing her.

Flailing at the covers, she attempted to escape their entangling embrace. He helped with this obstacle, flinging them aside—then was upon her in an instant, one hand cupped firmly over her mouth. He leaned in close. "Do nayat struggle," he breathed into her ear.

She was protesting against his hand, the dampened words nothing but muffled garble. Finally, she ceased these struggles, realizing that attempts to dislodge the granite slab crushing her to the mattress were futile.

With his hand still cupped firmly over her mouth, he pulled back to face her, his lambent eyes demanding compliance. Still, she faced him defiantly, trying to convey her agitation with a glare she hoped was scathing. She expected he would try to reason with her, to try to
~~~~~~~~~~

convince her to go with him without causing a scene. She did not expect the words whispered.

"Let me inside of you."

The sentence chilled her, but the way he said it was just as troubling—the raspy whisper ringing more of require than request. She dared to assume he was speaking along more innocent lines, merely requesting she open her heart to him. But she was to find his words were quite literal. It was not her heart he wished for her to open. Reaching down with his free hand, he forced her legs apart so he might settle firmly between them.

Naked, she realized. He had climbed atop of her stripped of clothing, his intentions dishonorable from the start. She struggled against him, pleading now with what she knew must be wide and frightened eyes.

"Let me inside of you," he repeated, a husky rumbling pulled from somewhere deep within, "and yon will know—you are home."

He removed his hand from her mouth to grip the sides of her face, drilling her with desperate, demented eyes.

She meant to scream, but it was not a blood-curdling cry for help that issued forth when she opened her mouth, but a plea of a different sort, one beyond comprehension.

"Take me, then! Take me home!"

She was dumbfounded at the breathless words her own lips had uttered.

Readily reaching to her knees, he drew them up, preparing to comply.

"Christa."

She came awake with a gasp, gripping the covers in tightly clenched fists. Her knees were drawn up, but only blankets lay draped heavily between them, not the body of a man poised, one primed and ready to ravage her.

Instead, he stood in the doorway, the figure tall, the shoulders broad. "Yon did call out in sleeping," he said, the raspy voice sending shivers through her.

To her left, curled up on the bed, Rebecca stirred.

"Fine. I'm fine," she insisted, her trembling voice betraying her completely, for she was not fine. Not fine at all.

CHAPTER 11

She could not bear to face him across the table, could not even bear the knowledge that his eyes were upon her. She was grateful when the conversation shifted his attention. The traveling vendors were to be in market three sols hence and the list of supplies was being discussed. Daxter wanted a new knife, the smaller blade used to skin crouts. The seedberry seed supply had been raided by tippets, and so new seeds would be needed for next seg's planting. A new wagon wheel was in need of purchase, the old spare having been damaged beyond repair, and Meshganis Tieslen was in need of a variety of roots and medicinal plants. He was especially eager to purchase a new bind which had come out, one scribed by a well-known meshganis from the upper region.

Sam was looking over his list as well, doggedly determined to move forward with his traveling plans.

"Be sure to add footings for Becca on yon listing," Katissa spoke from where she stood scrubbing a pot.

At the sound of her name, Rebecca squealed loudly from the corner where she sat playing with her makeshift toys—wooden bowls she was attempting to stack. Loud sloppy raspberries sounded as she began a new construction, her tiny hands diligently trying to balance the cumbersome bowls.

"I will take measurings for yon footings and travel gilts, Reesla," Katissa continued. "And trust Sy to pick fine ponies," she directed to Sam. It is good yon does choose to stay behind with Reesla. It will give yon one chancing to—plan yon travelings," she said with a wink.

"No—naya!" Christine barked out, suddenly realizing Sam had been scheming. "I mean—I was wishing to travel to market."

"Reesla," Sam urged, his warning clear in the undertone. "Yon is still meshing."

"It is mine wishings to go," she stressed while keeping her gaze carefully averted from his.

"Yon should heed the words of Hannen," Katissa spoke. "Yon blazened locks will draw many eyes and yon has naya papers to state yon has gone before one Zerian council."

"Aya, yon blazened locks will draw many eyes," Sam warned.

"I will color mine locks," she informed, motioning to where Sy sat at the table combing black dye through his beard.

The meshganis paused to peer into the jar of black paste. "I will need to dig more socket rootings, then."

CHAPTER 12

Situated in the back of the carry, Christine held Becca on her lap, the two swaying in unison to the rhythm of the trundling wagon wheels. The babe was enthralled by the sights, her neck craning back to marvel at the gargantuan trees passing overhead, her tiny fingers pointing to the birds and bugs flitting by.

To their left, Sura busied herself mending a pair of slips, the needle and thread being pushed in and out deftly by well-practiced fingers. On the bench opposite them, Sam was teaching Daxter to tie knots using a stick and twine. Daxter, seeming to relish the attention, focused intently as Sam skillfully maneuvered the twine to demonstrate the different techniques.

Sam glanced up yet again from his tutoring to take in Christine's newly acquired dark locks, and she averted her eyes from the brooding gaze. She intended to deal with him one small step at a time. He had relented when she insisted on having her own boarding, moving the cot into Daxter's room, but he remained in a dark mood, his dangerous eyes drilling her whenever they were able. She could feel them upon her at the very moment, burning into her flesh.

She set her jaw, and her resolve. He would be angrier, still, when she formally informed the Tieslen family that she and Becca would not be leaving any time soon.

~~~~~~~~~~

A small home came into view amongst the trees, the first since their departure. Like the Tieslen residence, it was quaintly fashioned
~~~~~~~~~~

of logs and stone. A slim harvest of coarse stalks swayed in a gentle breeze. A carry sat lame, one wheel propped upon a standing stone.

"The Vandergans," Katissa informed them over her shoulder where she sat beside Sy in the driver's seat.

It was but the first of many such homes they would pass, and as they closed nearer to Huyetti, the homes became more abundant, as did the carries, these converging from the many side roads. Several such passed them, moving at a faster clip. And they, in turn, passed several moving slower. Two more were passed pulled over to the side making repairs, one changing a wheel, the other inspecting the hoof of a pony.

Nearly two turnings into their travels, the trees opened upon sprawling amber fields, and the cassing appeared in the distance. Huyetti was small in sizing, no walls of stone to boast her boundaries—only an outcropping of thatched roofs on the horizon. Still, the excitement mounted as she came into view.

"Thankings to Sola," Katissa sighed. "I can nayat feel mine backside any longer. And I need relieve mineself. I did nayat feel like lifting mine gilt behind one tree."

Sy chuckled. "If yon does wish, I will lift yon gilt."

She swatted his shoulder with an embarrassed titter.

CHAPTER 13

It seemed everyone within riding distance had come to market. The cobbled streets were bustling with men, women, and children, all crowding the booths which lined the streets to eye the wares; clothing, footings, kitchenware, jewelwear, weaponry, food, binds.

Balancing Becca on her hip, Christine tried to ignore Sam's smothering hovering proximity as she trailed behind the Tieslen family.

"Aiyee!" Katissa exclaimed at a table piled high with bolts of fabric. "Such colorings are meant for pleasurers, surent." Nevertheless, she and Sura made their way to the front to examine the bold colors, running hands gingerly along the silky fabrics.

Daxter tugged at his father's elbow. "Fallar, can I go speak with Colden? I did note him near the crouting hooks."

His father grunted, and pulling a shiny black slice from a leather pouch, placed it in the boy's palm. "In one turning, meet at the supping tentings."

With a nod, Daxter pocketed the slice and dashed off into the crowd.

A considerable amount of time was spent at a kitchenware stand where Katissa carefully examined the different fry pans before choosing one which seemed to satisfy her in both size and weight.

Mas Tieslen carefully plucked out several different hair baubles at the bead vendor, before moving on to the herb and root vender, this booth holding his interest as there were uncommon medicinal roots which could not be dug locally. While he sorted through these, Katissa and Sura moved on to the footing vendor, sorting through the different sizes.

For Becca, they chose a tiny pair of soft suede boots which slipped on easily. This even seemed to lift Sam's dour mood, he grinning as the babe stomped about, teetering comically in the unfamiliar footings. Seeming to deem them worthy of wearing, Becca squatted down to finger the beadwork.

"My big girl," Christine crooned—before a shout drew her attention away, a ruckus in the crowd. As she watched, several people were shoved aside as a burly brute plowed through the crowd at a full run.

"Stelcherer!" a voice bellowed.

So engrossed was the ganis with peering over his shoulder, that he misjudged his flight route and barreled into a table heaped with candles and perfumes. Delicate glass bottles shattered and wax candles flew in all directions, and the large man somersaulted through the air, colliding with the herb table and with Sy, taking his legs neatly out from under him.

With the lightning speed of the fraigen dropper, Sam closed the short distance and pounced upon the man, and Katissa was not far behind, frying pan in hand. She meant to bludgeon the blogart, but was denied this just revenge as his pursuers converged.

As thc thief was being detained, Sura and Katissa assisted Sam in assessing Sy's injuries. It appeared they were examining his left arm at the elbow—before a crowd formed, obscuring him from Christine's view.

"Becca!" Christine gasped, realizing she had forgotten her in the turmoil. Whirling around, she frantically searched the crowd of onlookers—and spotted her in the distance, a glimpse of red hair tottering away.

Throwing caution to the wind, Christine barreled her way through the crowd, frantic to keep sight of the russet curls weaving in and out. She collided with what felt like a brick wall, a mountain of a man who offered apologies while inadvertently hampering her view.

Shouldering past him, she scoured the crowd, then hurtled toward the blazened locks in the distance. As she drew closer, Christine realized how the child was making such progress. She was being led by a woman, one tall and stout.

"Lita!" she shouted, and the woman turned her head around.

Swooping in on them, Christine scooped the child into her arms, clutching her close.

The woman looked about nervously. "One babe did seem lost," she offered.

"Lost!" Christine gasped. "Lost! So you lead her away, you idiot!" She was attracting attention, curious onlookers pausing to gape, and so composed herself accordingly. "Thanks for nothing," she sneered.

Giving a curt nod, the woman went about her way.

Setting Rebecca on her hip, Christine poured over the angelic face. The grinning child didn't appear any worse for the wear. She was enthralled by her mother's dark hair, fingering it with great interest, even pulling it to her mouth for a tentative taste test.

Christine smiled in spite of her palpitating heart. And as the panic slowly ebbed, it dawned on her that she had unintentionally escaped Sam's clutches. Even as this realization struck her, she spotted him shouldering through the throngs as he scoured the faces.

Without a second thought, she hurried away from him, slipping between two vendors to stand hidden behind the parked wagons. A surge of relief swept through her as he passed by unawares

~~~~~~~~~~

Christine chose her candidates carefully, a couple who appeared to have finished purchasing their wares. The man, one tall and thin, was weighted down with various packages, while the lita, one equally tall but not near as thin, trudged along behind him, huffing and puffing with the exertion of hauling her own weight. It hadn't been difficult to convince the pair that she was one lone lita with babe in need of temporary boarding. And so, her escape had been rather uneventful. With Sola still sitting high in the sky, she sat with Rebecca on her lap while the small wagon strolled leisurely out of Huyetti.
~~~~~~~~~~

~~~~~~~~~~

Rez Axermme was not what she expected. It was a huge sprawling mansion, a rustic blend of logs and stone surrounded by fields of coarse stalks. Her rescuers were the servants of the rez, their quarters separate from the main house, one of more modest means but with several boardings to spare. She was shown to one of these—a small room kept clean and tidy—and then was offered food and drink which she accepted thankfully.

The woman who had so graciously taken Christine under her wing was Antiva. Though her ankles were swollen from the day's market venture, she insisted on showing Christine about the rez, proudly pointing out every tiny detail; polished wooden floors lined with exquisite woven runners, forest-green curtains striped in burgundy, a fireplace large enough for a full-sized man to stand within upright, a supping table of polished wood built large enough to hold not only the Axermme family, but the servers who were considered family.

Two of them were indeed.

"Mas Axermme," Antiva informed, pointing to the ganis in the mural, a healthy man with high widow's peaks, bushy brown brows, and kind brown eyes. "His lita, Antova. Same is mine twin sasturn," she boasted proudly. "And their twin gans, Trenden and Triden. All do travel to Woroff to bid ponies as birthingsol giftings. They did turn five and ten segs this cycle."

"They are eyegrand ganies," Christine said, and Antiva beamed.

~~~~~~~~~~

Christine spent most of the day listening for the approach of thundering pony hooves and for the sound of Sam's fists pummeling the front door. As night crept in, so did a sense of relief, and gradually her breaths became less shallow, her muscles less tense. She helped Antiva prepare lastsup—roasted goser with glazed carrots and onions, those they called coneroots and ringroots. At

Antiva's urging, she commandeered the kitchen to make scullies for dessert, rolling out the dough and smothering it with seedberry jam before rolling it into a fat log and slicing it thin.

Antiva's eyes rolled back into her head when she bit into one of the lightly browned delicacies. "I have been in searching of one scullery aide," she spoke around a mouthful of cookie. "If Mas Axermme does approve, and I am surent he will when he does sample these," she said, pushing the remainder of cookie into her mouth and moaning loudly behind the fingers pressed to her lips to keep the contents in place as she chewed, "yon is more than welcomed to stay."

~~~~~~~~~~

Though her hospitable hosts had heaped her bed with blankets and pillows aplenty, sleep that lun was elusive, fouled by dreams of a hulking figure in frantic search. Unhindered even by the raging storm which ravaged the night, he stood upon a planted stone, his feet set wide, anchored upon a boulder which seemed a part of him. With dark eyes reflecting the jagged flashes ripping across the skies, and hair whipping in the violent, swirling squalls, he raised angry fists high to shake them at the heaving heavens. Like a bellowing beast, he howled her name, his raspy wails riding the gales like a ship on a roiling sea.
~~~~~~~~~~

CHAPTER 14

Christine settled easily into life at Rez Axermme, falling comfortably into the role of scullery lita, working by Antiva's side while Becca tottered about the kitchen nibbling on scullies. It was a rez well run, each servant aware of their duties and performing them efficiently. The fact that the Mas of the rez was away did not entice them to shirk in their duties. In fact, they seemed compelled to perform their duties more efficiently on the chance he might return unannounced. It was clear that fear did not compel them, but love for the Axermme family and pride for the Axermme rez.

No one appeared to be overly concerned about searching into Christine's background. However, her background quickly came in search of her. Only three sols had passed when it came to call.

~~~~~~~~~~

"Yon does have one caller," Antiva informed her, sticking her head inside the door to rouse Christine from where she rested beside a napping Becca. "One Tieslen."

Christine felt the blood drain from her face as she stood.

"One Sura Tieslen," Antiva clarified. "I do know the callen. I do bid leexer for mine swelled legs from one Meshganis Tieslen." She leaned in the door. "It was mine thinking at first one lita was one ganis," she whispered. "Same did ride atop one pony, and wearing ganis garb at that!"

Sura appeared in the doorway behind her. She hadn't bothered to pull her gilt from her britches. Reaching to her riding hood, she threw it back to reveal the neatly wound bun holding her blonde mane in check.
~~~~~~~~~~

“I will bring scullies and seedberry juice, then,” Antiva said as she waddled quickly away.

Sura’s eyes darted briefly about the boarding. The ride had flushed her cheeks.

“How did you find me?”

Sura’s dark eyes were veiled as she faced Christine. “Huyetti is nayat so large one cassing.” She waved her hand to dismiss further elaboration. “There is much on which I do need to speak and few grains to speak such. Mine fallar is on his way to Black Pond to inform Mas Fallier of yon whereabouts.”

“Black Pond?”

“He does bunk on the banks since yon went missing.”

Christine felt her knees weaken. She sat wearily on the bed, and the napping Rebecca tossed in her sleep, rolling to her side.

Sura brushed a flyaway curl from her eyes. “He did spend many luns bunking on such banks once his woundings did mesh,” Sura spoke softly. “He claimed it was to work up the brazenings to once again battle fraigens, but I know this to be untruths. He was waiting for yon then, as he is waiting for yon now—Christa Clavin. Such is yon callen, is it nayat?”

Nausea gripped her at the mention of the name. It was a dangerous name to claim, a name spoken in tot tales throughout Atriia.

Dropping to one knee, Sura bowed her head. “Mine Lita. It is mine grandest honoring to kneel before yon.”

“Sura, please stand. Surent yon can nayat think me to be such.”

Sura did as asked, standing to rub dampened hands upon her thighs. Christine searched the face of the tall, young woman before her. She was wise for her years, but inept at hiding her feelings. She was spellered by Sam, and afraid of the lita who might steal him away.

“I did follow one lun,” Sura admitted. “Did hide in one woodland as Mas Fallier did walk brazened into waters brimmed with fraigens. Five by ten did cower as tippets on the banks while he did dive beneath blackened waters.” Sura’s dark eyes lit at the memory. "Nayat one foul fraigen did dare to challenge him." Her eyes turned somber as she focused back on Christine. "And he was nayat diving for genopé. Why then does he dive to fraig lairs? What does he hope to find at such? Or whom?" She moved to the window to peer out over the grounds. "He was ripped limb from limb when first brought to mine fallar. I have nayat ever noted one ganis so pallored. I did surent think him one ganis dropped. Mine fallar is the grandest meshganis in all of Atriia, for he did bring back one ganis did lose near every drop of his life's blood." She brushed hastily at her eyes, eliminating the tears before they could fall. "Many sols he did lay in fever speaking yon callen again and again." She ran her hands over her hair, pushing stray strands from her face before turning to Christine. "When Mas Fallier lays his eyes upon yon, they do fill with longing. But I have noted nayathing but fear in yon eyes when he moves near."

Christine rose to her feet. "I do only wish to put distance between mineself and Hannen, Sura. As Sola shines."

Sura dropped her eyes to her feet. "Mas Fallier does own one face horridly scarred, but his heart—"

"It's not the scarrings, Sura! Mine heart—it does belong to one other."

"One other?" Sura whispered in a relieved sigh.

Christine placed her hands on a stomach in knots as she looked to the sleeping child on the bed. "We must take leave right off," she whispered. "I wish to return to mine hailing, to the one other of whom I speak. Will you help me?"

Sura bowed her head. "Aya, Mine Lita."

Antiva pushed her way in, huffing with the exertion of pushing the cart. "Scullies and juice for… Yon is overly pallored," she said, looking with concern at Christine.

"Forgivings, Antiva." Christine motioned to the food cart. "Wrap such for travelings," she whispered weakly. "I must take mine leave right off."

CHAPTER 15

Christine held Becca to her chest as the ponies thundered past. She knew there was no possible way for Sam to spot them from the road. Still, she held her breath, the thundering of her heart louder in her ears than that of the pony hooves. Fear gripped her at the thought of Sam passing so near, and also at the thought of where she was headed once he was past.

"Black Pond," she whispered weakly.

~~~~~~~~~~

Sura looked pale as she fidgeted with the reins. She rubbed briskly at her arms as if chilled where they stood hidden in the shadows of the trees. Her dark eyes were riveted on even darker waters. "Will Antiva be true to her word?"

Christine rubbed Becca's back where she sat upon her hip, the babe seeming transfixed by the water as well. "Aya. She will nayat speak that yon did come to call. She will speak that I did leave loner, headed for Huyetti."

Sura nodded numbly. "Yon two did grow overly close in only three sols."

Christine grinned, her eyes misting at the recalling of the tears Antiva had wept at her departure, and at her last departing words—that she was going to miss her scullies overly. "She is a good lita. She will be true to her word."

Sura sighed heavily. "And why Black Pond? Will yon wade into blackened waters, then, with one babe in arms, so to climb upon the backs of fraigens?"
~~~~~~~~~~

“Naya, Sura.”

Sura looked to her then, eyes dark with trouble and brimming with tears. “Why Black Pond? Why does Hannen bunk on same banks in waiting for yon? Why, then, did Lor Zeria do the same?”

Christine recoiled. “Such is untruths, surent.”

Sura shook her head. “It is spoken. Ten sols and luns, Lor Zeria did stand planted on these very banks. His ganist did think him skewed and so did stay close by his side. They did fear he might walk into blackened waters in search of his precious loper.”

A coldness settled over Christine. She clutched Rebecca tighter as a shiver shook her.

“Does Becca belong to him, then, one Lor of Zeria?”

“Naya.”

“Does she belong to Fallier?”

“Naya!” Christine lied with vehemence.

Sura worried her lip as a tear slipped down her cheek. “I should nayat leave yon and Becca here loner.”

“I do insist on such.”

Sura gave a sullen nod of her head, then remounted her pony. She seemed pale as she looked down to Christine for reassurance.

Christine mustered a brave nod. “Go now,” she ordered.

CHAPTER 16

The waters were not calling to her, not even a whisper, and Sola's smile was fading fast. Seated on a tree stump at the edge of the woodland, Christine peered down at the dark waters in the distance. The last of the sunning fraigens had long since slipped into the dark waters, but with Becca in tow, Christine balked at the thought of moving nearer to the water's edge—and as the turnings passed, she came to realize the absurdity of her actions. She had done exactly what she vowed she would not. In her haste to distance herself from Sam, she had put her child in danger.

As Sola dipped, the deep drone of crickets began to chorus. Becca, her belly sated with scullies, busied herself by tottering about in her new boots, examining the different flora which abounded. Coaxing the child upon her lap, Christine did not have to coax her to her breast. With a balled fist, the babe rubbed one eye as she nursed, quickly conveying the tug of sleep.

Christine sighed as her eyes moved back to dark waters. Sam would return to Black Pond when he realized she had eluded him yet again. He would read right through Antiva's fibs. More than likely, he was returning even as the thought occurred to her. Though she loathed the idea, she would return with him to the Tieslen home, there to wait until dark waters beckoned.

A chill struck her as a creature cried out at the water's edge, this followed by a splash as the drink at dusk turned deadly. Off to her right, from high in the trees, a talcar screeched in reply.

Across the pond, at the edge of the wood, she thought she detected movement, dark shadows slinking amidst the foliage, surely a figment of her imagination. All the same, she held the nursing child tighter to her breast.

A shrill whistle sounded, a crout calling out warning of danger, this temporarily silencing the droning insects. Gradually they fell back into sync. It was a comforting chorus, for she knew as long as their night song sounded, no woodslinks were about. There was a prickling at the back of her neck, this more than just a chill creeping in as Sola gave way to slumber. Her eyes drifted back to the woodland beyond Black Pond, this growing more ominous as Luna's blanket thickened. If, by chance, Sam didn't see through Antiva's lies and headed for Huyetti, it was destined to be a long and sleepless night.

CHAPTER 17

The mist drifting up from Black Pond dampened the chilly night air. Christine's shivers would not abate in spite of the warmth emanating from the sleeping child she cradled. Rebecca had grown terribly heavy over the past few turnings and Christine's arms and back ached with the effort of holding her. With some care, she shifted the small body yet again, then slowly swiveled her head around to loosen the crick forming in her neck. As she brought it back around again—she found a blade pressed against her throat.

"On yon feet, lita," a gruff voice ordered.

Startled, Christine struggled to find her voice. She found it instantly as the blade dug deeper. "I do hold one babe," she explained hastily.

"Stand slowly," he ordered, "and turn face to this ganis."

Doing as bid, Christine clutched Rebecca tightly as she faced the stealthy interloper, one who had sneaked up from behind under the cover of the deafening chirring of crickets. He was tall and thin and his clothes were filthy. The front of his shirt was stained dark and Luna's smile gleamed on greasy hair. She caught his stench, one which nearly staggered her—urine and soured food and sweat so old it had turned acrid. His face was gaunt to the point of emaciation, and with an oozing ulcer crowning one cheek and a mouth corrupted by cankers. She knew instantly she was in the presence of a blacktongue.

Holding the knife to her throat, he nervously surveyed the area. "Yon does travel loner, lita," he stated more than inquired.

"No—naya," she lied. "Mine fallar and mine brathern, they should return in mere grains. They do—"

"Silence," he growled, his putrid breath turning her stomach.

"Yon is loner," he reiterated, and with a slight hand signal, brought forth a slew of others from their hiding place within the trees, four in all moving quickly toward a pond glistening like slick oil in Luna's smile. Instantly they went to work, one throwing several crout carcasses at one end, while three divers quickly slipped out of their clothes on the opposite shore.

Icy fingers caressed Christine's scalp as fraigens converged on the bait, the fresh meat creating a greedy feeding frenzy. As the divers waded into glistening waters, she turned her face away, unable to watch. With knees on the verge of buckling, she clutched the sleeping babe to her chest as a harsh realization was forced upon her. She would not be taking Rebecca into fraigen-infested waters—not this night—not ever.

She fought back the stinging tears as the desolation of this revelation struck her. "Pleadings. If yon will take me to Huyetti, mine brathern will hand over many rounds," she begged of the repugnant man who stood before her anxiously surveying the tree line. If he heard her words, he made no sign. "If yon—"

"Silence!" he barked.

A whistle sounded, a warning that fraigens had finished devouring the bait—and the three divers scurried from the water, their night's work completed just that quickly.

Seemingly unperturbed by Christine's presence, the group assembled about them to examine their collection, a meager two to three stones per diver, most smaller than a pea. The putrescent man with the knife carefully deposited the black stones into a small pouch which he secreted away into his pants pocket.

Christine pulled from his grasp as they made to leave. "Mine brathern will hand over more rounds than yon pouch of genopé will ever bring!"

He shoved her roughly. "Move, bligart," he snarled. "Yon will bring naya rounds with one ripped neck." He spit into the dirt, then gave another good shove in the desired direction. "Larid will decide yon worth."

CHAPTER 18

The camp was well hidden deep within the woodland, a grouping of four tents situated about a campfire of glowing embers. The small procession was greeted by a small urchin boy of about six, the ragamuffin curiously eyeing the strange lita with babe in arms. A number of crout skins, each hanging by a fluffy tail, ran the length of a six foot line on the left. And on the right, the skin of a huge woodslink was stretched tight between two trees. Christine eyed the behemoth warily, instinctively clutching Rebecca a bit tighter to her chest.

A thin, mangy hound lifted its head weakly at their approach, then stood at the sight of the small procession, an act which seemed to take tremendous effort. Once on her feet, she shook her head, sending long ears to flopping and slobber to flying and her to staggering sideways. Catching herself, she stood with legs splayed, watching them pass with sad, droopy eyes.

They found this lurid Larid between two of the tents with his pants down around his ankles. A single burning torch shed shadowy light on a scene which sent Christine's heart to thumping painfully.

An emaciated woman was in a most undignified position. Stripped of clothes and bent over a tree stump, Larid had her head wrenched back by a fistful of hair as he took her from behind, every thrust eliciting a tiny yelp of pain.

He didn't bother to break his rhythm as he gave the procession a sideways glance. "Roth," he spat breathlessly. "Yon should have returned two turnings past, blogart!"

He was a repulsive man with long thin legs descending from a bulging belly on the verge of explosion. The torchlight flickered on a face strangely bloated and with several bulging boils. Christine felt the bile rise in her throat as, after a few added thrusts, the repugnant man huffed and shuddered, then threw his head back, howling and beating with fists upon his sunken chest. Shaking nasty snaggles of hair, he whooped and hollered like a madman while the woman beneath him yowled.

Christine clutched the child in her arms, hiding Becca's eyes even though she slept. She closed her own eyes against the sickening scene as terror traveled through her in a series of dizzying waves. Her foolishness had put them in this predicament. In her desperate panic to escape the clutches of Sam, she'd put herself and Rebecca in grave danger, right in the midst of a camp of vile blacktongues. That they were at the mercy of this hideous devon, one who owned not one shred of decency, sent her body to trembling, her mind to reeling.

When she opened her eyes, he was cinching the tie of his pants. The scarecrow of a woman stood beside him, her head bowed, her shoulders slumped, her shriveled breasts sagging. Her dark hair, matted in crusty clumps, was obscuring her gaunt face. To Christine's horror, the urchin boy approached the wretched woman and tentatively took her hand, leading her silently away as the droopy-eyed hound trailed sluggishly behind.

"This lita did sit with one babe at Black Pond," Roth explained quickly. "I did stay hid one full turning to make certain she was loner."

Christine felt her skin crawl as Larid turned his face toward her, one reminding her of a certain janitor who frequented her dreams, one bloated and pale like a full moon. His puffy eyes narrowed to slits.

"I was waiting for mine brathern and fallar," she tried to explain hastily. "Both are most surent in search. They will hand many rounds for mine return."

He hacked loudly and spit a thick wad of mucus into the dirt, one which gleamed in the moonlight, seeming to come alive before her very eyes with a hundred wriggling maggots—certainly a figment of her imagination.

She took a step back as he moved closer, his gait awkward, something wrong with his feet or ankles. His smell preceded him, the reek of puss and maggots permeating his being as if it was rotting from the inside out. He bumped Roth aside, nearly toppling the thin man, then stopped before her, his eyes running the length of her, once, then twice again.

"One tot does own blazened locks," he stated, nodding to Rebecca, and Christine felt the heart hammering in her chest drop to her stomach.

She struggled against the urge to retch. "Mine faller will hand over many rounds for our safe returning. He is one meshganis. Meshganis Tieslen of Huyetti. Has yon heard of him?"

"Auggh," he growled, the maggot-infested phlegm rattling around in his throat. "Huyetti is closely trolled."

"Yon would nayat have to travel into one cassing. We do hail from the outer skirts, three turnings by foot, at most."

He moistened swollen lips with a thick tongue, his slit eyes glistening in the flickering light of the torch. "Does yon hold milk, lita?" he asked, grinning to reveal teeth resembling black mush—and Christine felt the milk within her breast instantly curdle. The food in her belly had soured as well and was forcing its way back up.

Swallowing down the rising gorge, she pressed the back of her hand against her mouth. "No. Naya. One babe does…does drink shike's milk."

Larid's eyes narrowed suspiciously.

Roth cleared his throat nervously as he proffered the pouch.

With a grumble, Larid snatched it from him. Emptying the bag's contents onto his palm, he turned and inspected each shiny black stone in turn. Plucking three of the smallest stones aside, he gave one to each of the divers. Two scurried off with their dark treasure. The third, obviously not concerned about privacy, smashed his between two rocks on the spot and greedily lapped at the residue. The effect was instant, his mouth foaming as he went to the ground.

He rolled to his back, his eyes half-mast and vacant as he stared up at the stars.

“Backtongued blogart,” Larid grumbled, giving the downed ganis a curt kick in the ribs.

Roth cleared his throat, prompting Larid to pluck a fourth black stone from his palm. Pinching it between thumb and forefinger, he rolled it before Roth’s eyes with a taunting grin—then yanked it briskly away as Roth reached for it. “After trapping,” he said. “Aim ears.” Holding up one finger, he motioned to the woods surrounding them. Christine listened as well, her blood turning cold at the stillness. The night creatures had fallen silent.

Danger was in the woodland.

CHAPTER 19

The boy was terrified. He clung to the dark-haired woman who was his malla, his thin chest hitching shuddering sobs. With hollow eyes, she rocked him gently. She was positively skeletal, the woman whom Larid had taken so vulgarly. Though she may have been beautiful at one time, her skin was now stretched thinly over high cheek bones and sagging down into sunken cheeks. Thin lips were set grimly.

Situated on one of the stools surrounding the burning embers, Christine rocked her own child, grateful that she was sleeping soundly. To her right, Roth sat slurping a watery gruel.

As Larid approached with bow in hand, the boy clung tighter to his malla, letting out a thin frightened keening.

"Well, then, brathern," Larid addressed to Roth, his eyes aglow with excitement at the hunt to come. "Let us be off. One woodslink does wait to feel mine arrow pierce its belly. One tippetly tot will draw same surent with all his wailing."

When Larid grasped the boy by the arm, yanking him to his feet, Christine closed her eyes against the terrified face. She shook with the effort not to jump to her feet and claw at the devon's eyes. It was only the babe in her arms who prevented her from doing such. She clung to Rebecca, covering her ears firmly against the boy's pitiful pleading as he was dragged away.

His malla hugged herself, rocking feverishly and humming loudly.

As his last cry faded into the distance, her rocking ceased in an odd instant, and she sat hunched, deflated, her humming halted. The only sound was the crackling of the fire. The woods were eerily silent.

After what seemed an appropriate length of time, Christine shifted Rebecca's weight and stood. "I am taking mine leave, lita," she spoke sternly. "If yon gani does live through this lun, I gest yon does take him and do the same."

The haggard hound lifted its head. Peering into the woods, it whined and shifted nervously.

"He will live."

Christine was startled to hear the woman speak, especially in a tone which seemed so certain.

The dark-haired woman nodded in the direction the hound was peering. "One woodslink does lie hid just beyond there tree line."

Clutching Rebecca tightly, Christine pivoted to peer into the woods.

Picking up a stick, the woman prodded at the fire. "It does search for its mate," she said, motioning toward the skin stretched out to dry. "It will nayat come near one fire. But yon must nayat take to one woodland."

Situating herself back on the stool, Christine worried her lip as she scanned the woods. The thought of woodslink eyes upon her and her sleeping child shot terror into her heart like a poisoned arrow. She would not risk it. She knew all too well the embrace of the foul creatures and did not wish to know such again.

~~~~~~~~~~

There came a rustling from the trees. The hound stood to let out a clipped howl. Christine stood as well, readied to let out a howl of her own. But it was only Larid who slithered from the brush, dragging the boy by the collar. The traumatized child was shoved roughly to his mother's feet where he clung trembling to her ankles.

"One spectless gani did barely cry out," he growled angrily. "Ten rounds! Ten rounds does lie hid in one woodland, and one blasted tippet will nayat cry out!" With this, he kicked the cowering boy in the ribs, forcing out a screech—the cry startling Rebecca awake. "Aya!" Larid snarled. "Now one gani does cry out, then." He
~~~~~~~~~~

drew his foot back once again.

With a cry, the thin woman fell on the boy, covering his body with her own, but was merely assaulted for her valiant effort, taking the blow meant for the boy, and then a few extra added, the blows sending her rolling along the ground. Landing on her back, she writhed as she struggled to get back the air kicked from her lungs.

Larid chuckled at her distress, then raised one booted foot and stomped her stomach.

Rebecca shrilled then, the high squeal breaking through Larid's rage. He turned glowering eyes upon the babe, and as Christine tried frantically to hush her, a hideous grin surfaced upon his hideous face.

"Aya! Aya!" he bellowed. "Such are the wails I seek! Such will draw one woodslink!"

Clutching Rebecca, Christine turned to run, but was quickly detained as his hand shot out, snagging a handful of her hair. Fighting wildly, she snarled as he pried Rebecca from her grasp, only giving her up for fear he might wrench the child's arms from their sockets. The babe's strong lungs protested shrilly at the rough handling and the abrupt separation.

Christine lunged, her claws out, a guttural growling vibrating in her throat. A red haze clouded her vision as she pounced—and so she did not see the fist she ran into.

When the haze cleared, she was on the ground with Larid heavy atop. One of his hands had two of hers pinned. The other slithered inside her gilt to knead one breast roughly. A nasty chuckle sounded, the maggot breath nearly bringing up the meager contents of her stomach. "I do think one lita did speak untruths," he sneered, exposing a mouth of mush. "Here does hide milk plenty."

Christine craned her neck towards Rebecca's frantic cries. Roth was holding her awkwardly as she screamed and squirmed. She held her tiny hands out beseechingly toward Christine, her brimming eyes wide and frightened, her chin quivering.

Pulling his hand from her gilt, Larid pulled the pouch from his pants and tossed it toward the lita who stood cradling her ribs.

"Crush one stone," he ordered gruffly. "With one tongue blackened, one lita will nayat struggle as I fill mine belly with milk." He released her hands to press an arm against her throat, cutting off her air.

Her struggling was in vain, her kicking connecting with nothing, her snarling depleting her air. She concentrated her attentions on the arm-bar choking the life from her, beating and clawing at it.

The pressure on her throat lifted and she drew in breath, the sharp intake pulling spittle down her throat, inducing a coughing fit. And then she was choking again as Larid stuck a finger into her mouth, coating her tongue with a bitter, chalky substance.

"Aya," he sneered, the rot-breath foul in her face. "Ten added rounds will be in mine purse when one babe does bait one woodslink. And warmed milk will be in mine belly. I do have one thing for yon belly as well," he promised, grinding his hips against hers so she might clearly feel the 'thing' he referred to.

A strange tingling filled her head as genopé began to take instant effect, this traveling down her arms and to her legs. She could feel the heat of the fire to her left. She reached toward it, fumbling for a weapon. Curling her fingers around a thick branch, she stove it into the side of his head.

There was a sizzling sound as the smoldering end seared his scalp, then a bellowing as he rolled off of her, clutching at his head. A nauseating acrid odor assailed her, the smell of burning flesh and hair.

Thoughts were scrambled in her brain as she scrambled to her feet to the sound of a raging elephant. But one stood clear. The raging bull would kill her when he recovered, would gore her with his tusks, would stomp her belly into the ground, rip her limb from limb. She knew this implicitly. And so she stumbled to the fire pit and hefted one of the surrounding stones. A surge of adrenaline spewed forth a hearty groan as she lifted it high and brought it down upon his head. There was a sickening thud as his skull caved in with shocking ease—and instantly his trumpeting halted.

Staggering backward on leaden limbs, Christine spread her arms wide for balance. A gray fog was rolling in. She could hear Rebecca screaming, but the cry seemed distanced. Her legs buckled beneath her and she collapsed to hands and knees, her stomach heaving, bringing up a thick, bitter sludge—and then again.

The sharp blow to her head came from behind. Then there was only darkness.

CHAPTER 20

Rebecca's thin cries pulled her from the darkness. It was a weary cry, the cry of a child on the verge of exhaustion, a child who had been crying for some time.

Forcing her heavy lids to open, Christine tried to focus on the small form seated in the clearing. Her tiny face was pale and her russet curls gleamed in Luna's smile. Thin tendrils of mist seeped up from the mossy ground around her. The lun was quiet, far too quiet, not even a lilting breeze to rustle the leaves. The only noise was the keening cry of human bait.

From her spot, lying on her side, Christine watched as small, balled fists rubbed at weepy eyes. The babe's tiny chest hitched pitifully as she drew in breath to voice yet another pathetic whimpering cry.

Christine tried to call out to her, but there was something wrong. She could not speak, could not move—effects of genopé still lingering.

She was not alone. Two dark forms were crouched beside her, hiding behind a tree, watching the lure as well. She could see the dark outline of the bow held ready. One of them gave an excited signal, pointing, and Christine followed his direction to the tall grasses which began to rustle as something stealthy slithered toward the innocent babe. Horror filled her as she watched the serpent's head pop through the grass into the clearing. She tried to scream, but only a thick gurgling sounded. The woodslink paused warily, cautiously surveying the situation, before deeming it safe.

It was enormous, its sinuous body gleaming in Luna's smile as it glided soundlessly toward the keening babe. Only upon reaching her did it raise up on its many appendages, so to put its face at her level, so to reach out to her cheek. The child quieted at the tender caress.

A thin whistle was wheezing through Christine's nose as she looked frantically to the men in shadows. They held their cowardly spot, not seeming to be in any rush to notch an arrow. She tried to call out, but only a thick gurgling sounded. This drew their attention, all the same. Crouching low, they moved toward her. It was Roth's thin face did lean over her first.

"Is yon wakened then, bligart," he asked with a grin. "Just as well, then."

"Aya," Larid agreed, appearing beside him, the word sounding gravelly, as the muscles on one side of his face weren't working correctly. He grinned at her, his bloated face contorting, a most grotesque grin, for half of his face was staved in. A grisly mix of white skull fragments and gray gore glistened in Luna's smile.

"Becca," she forced out past the sludge in her throat.

"Aya, one babe did well," Larid sneered. "One woodslink will be overly slowered, now one tot does weight it down."

Christine's eyes flew to the clearing to discover Larid's words were true. The woodslink was stretched out in the moonlight, lazily digesting the large lump lodged in its belly…

She was gurgling as her eyes opened. She was not lying on a damp bed of leaves, but on the hard-packed dirt beside the fire pit. Her ankles had been bound, as had her wrists behind her back. There was a vile sludge in her throat. She gagged and spit to get the last remnants of vomit dislodged. She had fallen into her own upheavings. It coated the side of her face and clots clung to her hair. Struggling to a sitting position, she searched frantically for Rebecca.

"One babe is well. She does lie in sleeping with Bixten."

It was the boy's malla. She sat perched upon a stool a few feet away from where Larid's body lay, having been dragged a short distance from the fire and turned to its back. The woman's posture was different. Her shoulders were back as she sat almost primly with her hands folded in her lap. The fire had been stoked back to life, the flickering flames casting a sharp edge to the woman's gaunt features. "The ganist have all blackened their tongues," she spoke in a tone devoid of emotion. "When Sola rises, they will draw sticks on which will rip yon throat."

Despite the heat pouring from the fire, Christine shivered.

The woman stood then, and Christine saw what had lain hidden in her lap, the glint of the blade piercing through the darkness. The woman's dark eyes held an odd glint as well, one frigid in the firelight.

Christine struggled to her knees. "Lita," she begged of the approaching woman, "hear me! Hear mine words, lita! I am worth many, many rounds! Ten by ten by ten again!"

If the woman heard, it did not register on her hardened face.

"I am Christa Clavin, lita! Does yon know this callen? One Loper of Zeria! The Lor of Zeria will hand over many rounds!"

The woman halted before her. "And I am Tasta Izaki. I think it only fair that yon know mine callen as well." Christine cringed when the woman reached out to her face—but it was only to caress her cheek with the back of one frail hand—as the woodslink had done.

Christine felt her eyes well at the gentle touch. She tried to beseech the woman with these tear-filled eyes, but the woman's eyes had turned inward. "As Sola shines, lita. I am Christa Clavin! I…"

Christine's voice faltered as the thin woman withdrew her hand. As if in a trance, she slowly strolled around her, halting directly behind.

Christine choked back the sobs so to force out the plea. "Mine babe. Take her to Rez Tieslen, that does sit on the skirts of Huyetti. To her fallar—Hannen Fallier. And yon must take yon gani as well, Tasta," she wept. "He will take care of him and he will never lift a finger to him. Or to you. He's a good man. A good man." Closing her eyes, she braced herself for the fatal slice.

But it was not her throat the woman meant to slice. She instead sliced the bindings at her wrists and then her ankles.

As Christine staggered to her feet, the knife was placed into her hand.

"Make haste," the woman spoke numbly, her shoulders slouching once again. "Sola will waken soon."

CHAPTER 21

Christine stumbled through the thick undergrowth, the thorn-riddled creepers ripping at her gilt and raking her calves and thighs. Try as she might, she could not find the vague trail they had come in on. With the haze of genopé still lingering in her brain, her thoughts were muddled and her limbs shaky. And to make matters worse, she could not appease Rebecca. The frightened child was unremittingly whimpering and squirming, the traumatic events of the night still evidently fresh in her head. And it didn't help that she could not change her wet diaper, or that she had refused Rebecca feeding, not wanting to lose precious minutes and not knowing if genopé might be passed to the child through her milk. The hungry, irritable child fidgeted relentlessly in her arms, struggling to be let down, thus slowing her terribly.

When she stumbled upon a small creek, she stopped briefly to drink and to scrub at the dried vomit coating her face and the front of her gilt, though re-wetting this only worsened the sour smell, thus turning her stomach. Sitting back on her heels, she watched a squatting Rebecca pat at the water with tiny hands, the child cheerful to finally be separated from her malla's hip.

Christine's heart beat painfully in a tight chest as she tried to stave threatening tears and to clear a hazy head. There was an odd quivering in her muscles that she couldn't control, a genopé induced spasming, and gray spots would occasionally roll before her eyes like miniature tumbleweeds. If she could make it to Black Pond, she knew she could find her way back to Huyetti from there. She would contend with Sam, would face him a million times if it meant keeping Rebecca safe.

With a yelp, she shot to her feet and snatched Rebecca up, clutching her close as she scoured the brush, listening—to silence. Her scalp crawled eerily. There were eyes upon her. She could feel them. Shifting Rebecca, she reached for the knife secreted away in her pocket. Fear gripped her as tightly as she gripped the blade. She was far too familiar with the deadly embrace of the woodslink. The memory was anchored solidly in her brain. The sound of her own bones snapping still rang in her ears on many nights while deep in the throes of dreaming. But in all of her nightmares, she had never clutched a babe to her chest, one peering with enthrallment at the blade held out before her.

Christine looked to the skies where the blanket of Luna was slowly slipping away. Sola was wakening. Though pressed for time, she would not leave the clearing by the stream. She would wait, would hold her spot of safety until Sola could shed more light on the vine-entangled brush which most surently secreted a silent serpent.

~~~~~~~~~~

Rebecca was beside herself, confused as to why her mother refused to set her down. With a soggy diaper and an empty belly, she whined and cried and squirmed and pouted and whimpered. No amount of back rubbing or cheek kissing or soft cajoling words could console her. Finally, she buried her face into her mother's gilt to sulk, exhausted by her efforts.

Beams of morning light filtered through the trees about them. Still, Christine could not bring herself to move. Fear gripped her tight as any woodslink, a tenacious embrace. There had been movement just beyond her scope of vision, a rustling of leaves—perhaps caused by a stealthy, slithering interloper. She fought to keep focused past a brain spinning with the aftereffects of genopé. Morning birds should have been trilling as Sola first wakened. Yet they held their song. A gentle breeze swayed the canopy of branches overhead. The trees were thick, Sola's smile only finding its way through on scattered rays. Shadows were deep, too deep to clearly betray any lurking predators that might lie hidden
~~~~~~~~~~

in the brush. Her thoughts were jumbled. The genopé in her blood was scrambling her brain. And so she hesitated, uncertain, as precious seconds sifted through.

As she fought with indecision, the silence was broken by the faint bay of a hound in the distance. The blacktongues were in search.

It was the impetus needed.

With the knife held out before her, she stepped into the shadows—and into a nightmare.

~~~~~~~~~~

She was unprepared for the blow, one which assaulted her the instant she stepped into the trees, was unaware, even, that a woodslink was capable of using its tail in such a way. Like a powerful whip, it lashed out, striking her in the square of the back and catapulting her into the air. A sordid somersault separated her from both Rebecca and the knife as she tumbled head over heels. Landing on her back, she squirmed at the excruciating pain of deflated lungs, wheezing and writhing as she struggled to take in air.

When finally it entered her lungs, it instantly exited again as a gut-wrenching groan. Scrambling to hands and knees, she focused on Rebecca. The babe was protesting loudly at her bumpy landing, even though she sat perched upon a mound of leaves. And she had obviously taken a tumble as well, for a mound of leaves sat perched upon her head. Her cries had attracted the woodslink. It was launching a sneak attack, its sinewy body slithering in from behind.

With a snarl, Christine sprang to her feet and rushed for Rebecca, but the viper's tail shot out yet again, connecting with her left shoulder and sending her flying. She landed on her belly, sliding on damp leaves as if stretching for a home run. Though it was not home plate her hand touched upon, but the hilt of the knife knocked from her grasp on the first assault. Snatching it up, she leapt to her feet, spinning to confront the monster determined to devour her beautiful Becca.

It had changed its approach. Seeming to have deemed the babe
~~~~~~~~~~

easy prey, one incapable of flight, it had abandoned caution, choosing instead to move in directly from the front, its forked tongue flicking in anticipation of the feast to come.

While its attention was on the babe, Christine closed the gap quickly and leapt at the beast, plunging the knife into its body, imbedding it to its haft.

A hideous hissing ensued as the serpent recoiled with uncanny speed, then struck, a blinding blur as fangs like twin hot daggers sank into her forearm. The impact knocked her to the ground, her screams ringing loudly through the silent forest.

The beast released her to writhe and roil, its sinewy serpentine body contorting, its tail whipping dangerously. In its mad frenzy to dislodge the embedded knife, it toppled Rebecca, and Christine bellowed as she scrambled to her feet, certain the desperate serpent would crush the babe in its piteous plight.

With a snarl, she leapt upon the writhing creature, enwrapping it with arms and legs alike. Locking ankles around a body thick as a man's thigh, she clung desperately as strange appendages beat at her, these surprisingly weak—appendages meant for chilly caresses and good for nothing else. Foul obscenities flew from her mouth as she kept her spot, a perfect position it seemed, for try as it might, the flailing creature could not snag her with its fatal fangs. With ankles tightly locked, she grasped the hilt of the embedded dagger and wrenched it loose so to drive it in again, and yet again while the viper whipped its head and hissed its pain.

A haze clouded her vision, one which had nothing to do with genopé. A growling could be heard over the hissing, the sounds of a mad woman in the throes of hysteria. The blade dipped again, sinking deep, a hot knife through soft butter. And then the growling halted abruptly as her ankles unlocked and she was thrown to the ground.

Her vision cleared just in time to see the serpent strike, its head, the size of a basketball, dropping down like a driven ax, its mouth wide, its fangs jutting. She rolled, and the strike meant for her face drove into her shoulder instead, embedding deeply. As she screamed, she realized she still held the weapon, the hilt gripped firmly in her hand—and so drove the deadly dagger into its brain. It convulsed, and Christine cried out as its fangs drove deeper into her shoulder. Its tail whipped out, striking nothing but air, and Christine screamed again as she was dragged several feet, impaled as she was by two searing fangs.

With one final shudder, the serpent went limp at last.

Christine tried to blink away the gray haze intent on claiming her. She could hear Rebecca crying. It was a sweet sound, for she recognized the cry as one of fear, not pain. There was another sound commingled, a dog braying. She turned her head to locate the haggard hound. Slobber flew in sloppy strands as she barked furiously at the lifeless woodslink. Four men flanked the hound—Roth and the other divers—all staring dumbfounded at the fallen lita locked in the jaws of the dropped woodslink. They spun in unison as ponies barreled through the underbrush, the riders atop brandishing blades drawn and readied.

"Drop yon blades, blacktongues!" a gruff voice ordered, and they obeyed instantly, throwing them to the ground as if they'd been seared.

Christine heard the voice only vaguely through the strange buzzing in her ears. Though she fought furiously against it, the gray haze prevailed against her.

~~~~~~~~~~

She came awake screaming as the wookslink fangs were pried from her body. Clutching her shoulder, she writhed on the ground—then struggled to a sitting position, shaking off the tumbleweeds blocking her vision. "Mine babe!"

The man standing over her stepped aside, pointing to where Rebecca was seated on the ground, shaking two crout tails like pom-poms. The hound lie nearby with its head resting on its paws, watching the child's antics with drooping eyes. Roth and his companions sat just beyond, their hands bound behind their backs.

The stranger crouched down beside her, resting back on his
~~~~~~~~~~

heels. “These blacktongued blogarts do claim yon did drop one woodslink loner.”

She looked to where the bound men sat gawking at her.

“Aya,” one of the divers spoke up, “one lita did sit its back—as if one foul pony.”

The crouched man gave a dubious chuckle.

Christine tried to clear her brain of floating debris so as to size up the man hunkered beside her. He was a handsome man with dark curly hair clipped short. He was fair complexioned with dark lashes framing kind eyes the color of olives. She dropped her eyes to the woodslink, her stomach turning at the sight of the knife hilt still protruding from its head. “It did mean to sup on mine babe,” she spoke weakly.

“One lita is devonous,” Roth spoke angrily from his spot. “Same did drop mine brathern—did bash his skull, did spill his brains! It would do yon well to slice one railed throat while she is weakened.”

“He did mean to use mine babe as woodslink bait!” she shot back, leering at him.

The olive-eyed man lifted her bloodied arm, surveying the punctures on her forearm. “It is well woodslinks do hold only weakened poisonings,” he said. Gently peeling the gilt off her shoulder, he inspected the wound there as well.

“Aiyee, Kaltica, do nayat handle one blacktongue,” one of his comrades warned. “Same does crawl with lotice, surent.”

Christine looked to her tattered gilt, one soiled with vomit, dirt, and blood. She thought to deny blacktongue status, but knew her newly blackened tongue would speak otherwise. She lie back as a wave of nausea overtook her, the dark tumbleweeds rolling before her vision.

“Poisoning will bring sleeping.”

She opened her eyes to the man who leaned over her. “Mine babe,” she croaked weakly.

“Yon babe will be safe, lita.” he replied.

She used the last moments of consciousness to search his eyes—warm, olive eyes—and she believed him.

CHAPTER 22

Christine winced with every rut the wagon hit. The troller they called Kaltica was seated high upon a chocolate pony with Rebecca held in front of him. She rode well, clapping her merry hands and fondling the pony's mane as she babbled baby talk. Through half-mast eyes, Christine watched as the troller helped her to sip from his water flask for the hundredth time, watched as slowly the babe succumbed to sleep, resting peacefully against the troller's belly. She was grateful for the kindness of this stranger, for it seemed she could not keep her mind focused. There seemed to be no sense of time or direction. Sweat beaded on her forehead, yet she could not keep from shivering.

But she was not alone in her misery. The trollers had obviously been busy. The wagon was crammed full of blacktongues who all seemed to be having difficulty functioning as genopé worked its way out of their systems. Seated shoulder to shoulder, they moaned a morbid melody as they swayed in unison to the rhythm of the rolling wagon wheels. Shackled as she was to the men on either side, it was difficult to change positions to alleviate the pain which all but encompassed her. It was if someone had taken a sledge hammer to her back and to the back of her head, and there was a constant throbbing pain in her shoulder and forearm that had traveled to her temples. If that wasn't bad enough, the stench of her wagon-mates was intolerable. What little time she spent conscious was spent trying to keep from gagging.

Christine looked back to Becca. What she thought was only a few seconds must have been much longer, for the babe was no longer napping. She was eating what looked like a scullie and seemed to be enjoying it greatly.

CHAPTER 23

The wagon had ceased its movements. This fuzzy realization pulled her up from the depths of a deep and dreamless sleep.

She awoke to find herself leaning heavily upon the dozing blacktongue seated beside her. Sitting up groggily, she grimaced at the pain that shot through her shoulder. She was alarmed by the darkness, this embellished by the canvas sides which had been rolled down. She called for Rebecca—then again, louder as panic set in.

"Yon babe is safe."

There was just enough light to make out the thin woman who sat across from her with one arm draped about her sleeping boy. Larid's lita. Even in the darkness, it was hard to miss the dark circles etched beneath her sunken eyes. She was shivering violently despite the blanket thrown across her shoulders.

"She is with one troller," the lita forced past chattering teeth. "Same did tend to yon woundings."

Christine reached to her shoulder, wincing at the tenderness. The wound had been bandaged and smelled strongly of medicine. Only vaguely did she remember it being tended to, though she thought it had been a dream. "Kaltica? One troller with hair clipped short?"

The woman nodded weakly. Resting her head back against the wagon, she closed her weary eyes as a shiver shook her.

Christine realized her own shivers had subsided, but found a profound weariness had replaced them, one which would not be denied. Beyond the canvas covering, the night was clear and cool, the stars peeking through the seams. Drawing the thin blanket about her shoulders, she drifted into oblivion.

CHAPTER 24

A hand was groping at her breast. Larid was leering down at her with one eye. The other was dangling by a tenuous thread of flesh. Half of his face had been destroyed, half of his skull concave and alive with a mass of wriggling maggots. Many had squirmed their way out of the crater and were dangling in his snaggled hair. "I do think one lita did speak untruths," he sneered, his rot-breath foul in her face. "I do feel milk plenty," he said, his hand kneading. "It will warm mine belly nicely." He grinned to reveal a mouth of black mush, and the eyeball swayed. "I do have one warm thing for yon belly as well."

Throwing his head back, he beat on his chest like an ape, hooting and howling, shaking his head till the eyeball snapped free and maggots rained down…

She came awake with a start as hands closed around her throat, throttling for all they were worth. She clawed at the hands, then beat at the pale face hovering close—Roth, his face contorted in rage. He had dragged his two shackle-mates along for the ride, and did drag hers along as well as he pulled her to the floor. Holding her by the throat, he slammed her head against the wagon bed, straddling her as she thrashed. Her kicks connected with several dozing blacktongues and they bellowed angrily. There was shouting coming from all about, and a woman was yelling, a child screaming, a hound barking—a calamitous cacophony. Forefront in the mixture was spitting and sputtering as she struggled for breath—then a sharp and desperate intake of precious air as Roth was abruptly ripped away. A blow sent him, and those connected, sprawling. Scrambling to his seat, he sat glaring at her as he rubbed his injured jaw. "One lita must be dropped," he growled. "Same did drop mine brathern!"

"The Saker of Toskeena will decide her fating, blogart!" the long-haired troller barked. "Nayat one blasted blacktongue! I should drop yon down where yon does sit!"

"But she is devonous!" Roth insisted.

"Devon—devon," the diver shackled to him mumbled in a genopé delirium. "Same did sit—did sit one woodslink."

"Aya," the diver on his opposite side concurred. "As one devonous pony."

"Silence!" the troller ordered. "Blasted lot of skewed blacktongues!" He looked to where Christine sat on the floor of the wagon-bed, holding her throat. Snatching her by the wrist, he yanked her roughly to her feet, and she cried out as pain shot through her body like a jolt of electricity. She felt herself sway at such excruciating agony, only being held in place by the grip at her wrist. "I did note this railed blacktongue in the jaws of one dropped woodslink," he admitted. "Same did land one luckied blow, surent. Now same did drop one full-sized ganis as well?"

"He did only wish to sample her milk," Roth whined, rubbing miserably at his jaw.

The troller gave her a second look, this one much more thorough than the first, his eyes running languidly down her length and back up again, pausing for an uncomfortable length of time at her heaving chest. He was a tall ganis with dark hair hanging to well below his shoulders. In Luna's smile, she could just make out a scar which traveled from one corner of his mouth to the lobe of one ear where an earring was dangling. His eyes were black and they held a hint of something which did not sit well with Christine, a troubling glint just within their dark depths.

"Mayhap he did nayat ask kindly enough," the troller said with a sly smile, confirming her suspicions.

"What flustings lay here, Harvin?"

The scarred troller jumped at the deep voice, releasing her wrist. "Kaltica. One blacktongue did try to throttle this lita," he explained, motioning to Christine. "He does claim she did drop his brathern."

Kaltica eyed Roth. "Bind the blogart," he ordered. "If any does try to harm this lita, same will be dropped with naya questioning. Is such clear in yon genopé-thickened brains, then?"

Cradling her shoulder, Christine gave Kaltica a nod of thanks. He'd been roused from sleep, only taking enough time to slip on his pants and to grab the blade now held down by his side. He was not as thin as she had thought. He was lean, but strong.

"Is yon injured, lita?"

Christine's hand lifted to her tender throat. "No. Naya. Mine babe. Can I note her, then?"

"She is sleeping. And she is nayat one babe. She is one nipper loping as one babe." He grinned handsomely. "Same did sup one full bowl of coarse, five seedberries and ten scullies, and does drink more water than any pony I have ever rid."

"Has yon ever rid one woodslink?" Roth sneered as his last shackle was removed. "This devon has," he spat, pointing an accusing finger at Christine. "Mine brathern was one decent ganis!" he screamed as Harvin shoved him from the wagon and dragged him away.

Kaltica ran his eyes down her length as he ran a hand through his hair. "Sleep now," he advised. "We do take early leave on the morn."

"Troller Kaltica," she called, halting him as he turned to leave. "Yon has been kind to mine nipper. Thankings."

He gave a grin and nod, and then he was gone.

CHAPTER 25

Bathing in the river had cleared her senses considerably. It was a shallow spot, one littered with large boulders to hide behind. She held the blanket to shield Tasta, and Tasta had done likewise for her, though this thin attempt at modesty had probably been for naught. Most of the blacktongues, still suffering from withdrawal and finding even the simplest of tasks taxing, had shown little interest as they themselves attempted to wash as ordered.

Leaning back against the tree, Christine clung to the thin blanket, her only shield of decency. Keeping her eyes averted from the naked ganist sprawled along the creek's grassy banks, she stared longingly at the clothes flapping in the brisk breeze. Hanging to dry on a rope stretched between two trees was a long line of shirts and trousers. Hanging in the midst of these were the gilts and undergarments belonging to Tasta and herself. Though there was a smattering of thin, grayish clouds sailing across the sky, Sola's smile was bright, and Christine was hopeful it would not be too much longer before it pulled the remaining dampness from the freshly laundered garments—and her hair.

She lifted a damp lock from her shoulder, rolling it between her fingers. It was still a glossy black, despite the gray-tinged suds she'd seen while soaping her hair.

Breathing deeply of fresh air laced with warm sunshine, Christine tried to soothe the uneasiness churning within. Nausea still plagued her, the aftereffects of genopé and woodslink venom combined. On top of that, a debilitating throbbing continuously pulsed in her shoulder, this seeming to gravitate to her temples with annoying frequency. Her stomach did not want to hold food, her limbs were weak and wobbly, and her breasts painfully swollen. She had not wanted to risk passing genopé to Rebecca through her milk, and it seemed the babe was weaning herself in any case, asking continuously for water from Kaltica's flask.

Shifting her weight, she adjusted her position against the tree. The cool waters had helped to alleviate some of the fuzziness from her brain, enough so that she might dwell upon her dire situation. She was unsure of how many days the small convoy had been in travel, unsure of where she was, of where she was headed. What she did know was that she was now considered a lowly blacktongue. She worried about the repercussions of this new development, especially in regards to Rebecca.

She looked to where the small child with the sagging cloth diaper tottered diligently behind Bixten. The thin boy with the swollen belly—wearing nothing at all and seeming not to mind at all—was collecting a handful of wildflowers growing in abundance in the tall grass near the water's edge. His mother was not too far off, huddled inside her own blanket and leaning against her own tree. The haggard hound, Neema, was scavenging about the river's edge, nosing around for morsels of the morning's meal left behind by the dish washers. Two trollers stood watch over the lazing prisoners. Two more were rinsing out a couple of water barrels by the river, those which had been used to wash the clothes in slige to rid them of lotice. The others were busy around camp tearing down tents and tending to ponies.

Resting her head back against the tree, Christine reveled in the feel of Sola's smile on her face as she listened to the tranquil trickling of flowing water.

"Greetings, lita."

She started awake at the voice so close to her ear—then hastily checked the blanket, clutching it to her chest as she peered into the dark probing eyes of the troller hunkered down beside her. At such close proximity, she could see the pale scar was jagged, forming a tight z on his cheek before angling back toward his ear. He held a flower pinched between thumb and forefinger, twirling it before her.

"I did just come from noting one slinkskin," he said, his eyes taking in her freshly washed appearance. "There are many rippings. Yon did battle with brazenry, lita." He offered the flower out to her with a charming grin.

She glanced to the river's edge where Rebecca was chasing her thin comrade in a circle, her merry giggles being carried in on the brisk breeze. The two trollers standing watch had moved down a ways, their backs conveniently turned. Those who had been cleaning barrels by the river were gone. A few yards away, several naked men lie sleeping in the sun, their arms thrown over their faces.

"Do nayat fear this ganis, lita. I do only wish to check yon woundings."

Christine shrank back against the tree as he reached to slide the blanket from her shoulder.

"Aya. They are meshing nicely, then."

Vulnerability suffused her as he leaned in close to her ear, his breath hot as he whispered chilly words.

"I am asking nicely, lita."

Christine felt her stomach turn as nausea stole over her. The pathetic trembling in her extremities could not be quelled. "I am nayat well," she said in a trembling voice which seemed terribly tiny.

He drew back to grin at her as he trailed the flower down her cheek. There was no denying he was a handsome man in a roguish gypsy kind of way, and a man completely aware of such. His skin was deeply tanned, his teeth uncommonly white, his eyes dark and flashing. "I do have one thing may be of aid in mine pocket. One genopé stone, mayhap two."

"I have naya needings of such."

The troller's grin faded. "How many stones does yon wish, then?"

Her stomach roiled, a stirring which had nothing to do with nausea. "I do nayat wish for any stones, troller. I do only wish to be left alone. I am ill. If yon does lay one finger on me, I will scream till mine lungs do burst. As Sola shines, I will."

She witnessed the troller stiffen, his eyes narrow. "Yon would be so spectless, lita, when I did ask so nicely?" And with this, a knife was snatched from his boot, the tip put to her throat. "How loudly will yon scream, then, with one throat ripped wide?"

Of a sudden, the blood racing through her pounding heart had traveled to her head, pulsing painfully. "If it will mean keeping yon foul hands off me, then rip it," she challenged calmly.

The troller's eyes narrowed further, before a small grin surfaced. Dark, flashing eyes poured over her freshly cleansed face. Using the flat of the blade, he lifted her chin. "Yon is likened to naya blacktongue I have ever noted. Yon skin is sweet, likened to one babe's. Yon eyes are clear, nayat clouded. Yon is railed, but does own curves, curves nayat very well hid neath one thin cover." And with this, he yanked the blanket down to reveal the curves of which he spoke.

With a growl, she slapped at his face, then cried out as he wrestled her to the ground. With little effort, he pinned her hands, so to prevent the readied claws from ripping at his face. Pain suffused her, casting black shadows across her vision. But this did not keep her from witnessing the dark eyes light at the sight of her exposed breasts.

The tip of his tongue darted out to wet his lips. "I will ask nicely one last time, lita."

"And so will I ask nicely," a husky voice stated, startling the troller atop her. "Release one lita this grain."

Christine tried to blink the pain-laden tears from her eyes as the sun-dappled figure came into focus—Gaile, the bald-headed troller who worked closely by Kaltica's side. Tasta stood not far behind, holding Becca on her hip.

"Gaile," the scarred troller stammered. "I did only mean to check one lita's woundings, and she did try to rip mine face."

"Yon concerning is kindly, Harvin. But Roltin has been keeping close eyes on such woundings. I did come in search of one lita for this very reasoning. Bandagings and saxter do wait in his tenting this very grain."

CHAPTER 26

It was a spacious tent, easily large enough to sleep six men or even eight, and plenty tall enough for one to stand unhindered, even at the sides. Even so, Christine was uncomfortable enclosed with him, unnerved by the way he continued to watch her so brazenly as she fed Rebecca. Of all times, the child insisted on being nursed. Christine had relented, assured by Kaltica that most of the genopé had already passed through her system. But Rebecca was being difficult. She refused to be covered with the blanket, yanking it away several times, leaving Christine all the more exposed to his bold eyes.

Kaltica didn't seem uncomfortable in the least as he gathered together bandaging supplies. "I will speak with Trost. He will nayat bother yon again," he promised as he pulled up a chair to sit before her. Leaning close, he examined the injured shoulder. "Does it pain yon overly?'

"Naya," she lied, keeping her eyes averted. She felt her heart quicken as he moved closer yet to apply the thick, strong-smelling ointment they called saxter.

"And yon neck?"

"Fine."

"There is bruising."

As he wound the bandaging under her arm and around her shoulder, she tried to concentrate her attention on the nursing babe who did not seem to be thirsty at all, but simply going through familiar comforting motions. Deep blue eyes lined in long black lashes were watching every move the troller made. They blinked sleepily, and a small fist came up to rub at one.

Christine struggled against the growing nausea. Her

confrontation with Trost had left her weak and shaky. She was light-headed, her brain hazy—though not so much she couldn't tell that Troller Kaltica was behaving oddly, his gaze continuously leaving his work to glance upon her face up close.

Finally, his tending to her shoulder complete, he settled back in the chair, boldly eyeing the babe at her breast.

Christine attempted to adjust the blanket—and then drew in breath, holding it in as Kaltica leaned it to gently lift the sleepy child away. With some haste, she pulled her gilt back over her shoulder, watching as he moved the cradled bundle to the bedding.

Pulling the covers over the tiny form, he brushed a curl from her forehead as she smacked pouty lips as if still at her malla's breast.

He was oddly silent as he returned to administer to her forearm, inspecting the puncture wounds briefly before generously applying the salve. "Yon will go before one Saker of Toskeena on the morrow," he said at last.

"The morrow?" she asked, suddenly understanding his strange behavior. "Oh—I—I must hand thankings, then, on yon tendings to me and to mine nipper."

His eyes were unusually cold as he glanced up at her. "And who will tend to yon nipper while yon does stay in one keeper."

Christine blanched at this. "Keeper! But I was nayat one diver!"

"Yon tongue is blackened."

"Such was forced upon me!"

"Saker ValCussin is known to be overly harsh on blacktongues," he said as he wound the bandaging around.

"I can nayat be sent to one keeper! Mine babe!"

Securing the fresh bandaging with a knot, he sat back in his chair, his eyes moving to the babe in slumber. "Yon lia, she is of sound health. Nayat likened to babes of blacktongues. Blacktongued litas can nayat hear the crying of their babes above the foul calling of genopé. One gani in yon band," he said, referring to Bixten. "Same is overly railed, as one gani of one blacktongue will surent be. Blacktongues do nayat hold milk," he stated, scouring her face most brazenly. "And they do nayat ride upon the backs of woodslinks," he added.

"Yon does believe I speak truths, then? That I am nayat one blacktongue?"

"What I believe is nayat of portance. Yon will stand before ValCussin on the morrow. It is he yon must convince of such."

Christine glanced to where Rebecca slept soundly. "Yon could speak for me. The word of one trusted troller will surent sway one saker." She watched his eyes drop to Rebecca. The slumbering babe stirred, kicking off the covers, then rolled to her side to curl into a ball.

Slowly, his eyes made their way back to hers. "The others of yon band do claim yon did drop one ganis."

It was Christine's turn to drop her eyes to the sleeping child. "He did mean to use mine babe as woodslink baiting."

"One lita who does drop one ganis must be dropped in turn."

Christine felt the blood drain from her face as she watched the sleeping babe. A wave of nausea engulfed her and she felt herself sway.

"Christa."

She looked to the troller, hoping against hope he could offer some sort of salvation. She realized too late he had called her by name.

"The other lita does claim yon is Christa Clavin, the very Loper of Zeria."

The air in her lungs left in an audible whoosh. She gave a half-hearted smile as she tried to pull it back in. "Naya," she said, shaking her head. "Mine callen is Christa Clayton. Tasta's brain is skewed by genopé, surent."

"Aya, surent," he agreed.

CHAPTER 27

Christine found it difficult to stand for such a long period in her weakened state. Luckily, Rebecca was in a quiet mood. Sitting on the floor beside Bixten, the babe watched the milling crowd with great interest. The halls were packed, and the line leading to the saker's boarding was moving excruciatingly slow.

When finally the band of blacktongues moved into the crowded courtroom, she heard disputes settled; neighbors squabbling over boundary lines, a coarse farmer looking for compensation for the damage the neighbor's shikes had reaped upon his crop, a merchant trying to acquire payment for wares sent out on a note of promise.

She watched Saker ValCussin as he handed down sentencing with proficient professionalism. His skin was deeply tanned, yet his hair was snow white. He was heavyset, round about the middle, and with a pair of spectacles resting at the tip of his nose.

When finally Kaltica approached him to lay papers out upon the table, Sola was sitting high in the sky. ValCussin skimmed the papers, shuffling through them efficiently. "Troller Kaltica, yon is asking this saker be lenient on the two litas of this band."

Kaltica nodded. "Aya. As yon does note, one does own one young gani, the other one babe."

"Both litas do also own blackened tongues, do they nayat," the saker stated tritely.

Kaltica's fingers tapped the hilt at his side. He took a step closer to the table, leaning in. "Saker ValCussin, one lita is in the late stages of genopé rot. The other has woundings. To stay in one keeper would mean their droppings, surent."

The revered saker peered sternly over the rim of his glasses. "Troller Kaltica, yon has done yon duties, bringing these blacktongues before mine court, as yon has done over and again. Let me do mine duties as well, then. Blacktongues must be keepered, lest every lita with one babe think she might be pardoned for such."

"This lita must be dropped!" Roth shouted out angrily as he motioned toward Christine. "Same did drop mine brathern!"

There was a murmuring throughout the crowd, and ValCussin looked down with confusion to his papers. "Is this truths, troller?"

Kaltica spoke up quickly. "Surely one lita so railed could nayat drop one full-sized ganis."

"Same did bash his brains with one rock! Same is skewed. Is she nayat?" Roth asked of the divers flanking him, and they nodded adamantly.

ValCussin addressed the divers directly. "And all did witness such, then, with yon very eyes?"

They looked to each other, as if unsure, before shaking their heads.

Roth growled angrily. "Yon did all note one skewed lita sit the back of one woodslink, did yon nayat!"

To this the men all nodded vigorously.

Kaltica threw his hands up. "Mine honored Saker, the blacktongued blogarts are skewed, surent."

"Tasta!" Roth blurted. "Tasta did note one lita bash Larid's brain! Was her ganis, fallar to her gan!"

They all looked to the cadaverous woman who had been more than content to watch silently. She seemed to shrink as all eyes turned to her.

"Well, lita? Speak then," the saker ordered. "Did one lita drop yon ganis?"

Tasta looked nervously to Roth, then to Christine.

"Lita," the saker warned, showing dangerous signs of agitation. "It is one simple question. Aya or naya?"

"Loosen yon tongue, yon brainless bligart!" Roth spat, causing a few onlookers to titter.

Tasta squared her shoulders defiantly. "Naya," she spoke firmly. "Was Roth did drop his own brathern," she stated, drawing a collective gasp from the crowd.

With a howl, Roth lunged at her, but was quickly checked by Gaile who elbowed him in the chest, the blow nearly sending him to the floor. Around them, the crowd murmured excitedly.

"And Christa is nayat blacktongued," Tasta continued, seemingly emboldened by Roth's rebuffing. "Genopé was forced upon her tongue. Yon must nayat send her to one keeper. She does own one callen Christa Clavin, one very Loper of Zeria."

A hush fell over the crowd. Christine felt as if the air had been squeezed from her lungs, the words to deny Tasta's statement unable to find their way to her lips with no air behind them. A chuckle sounded in the audience, this followed by several snickers, this escalating to a full-blown uproar. Christine looked to the faces, some with hands clapped over their mouths, ganist and litas clasping their stomachs, some practically doubled over. She looked to ValCussin and was astonished to find him laughing robustly as well.

Removing his spectacles, he dabbed at his eyes with his sleeve as the laughter began to die. "Aiyee, many thankings, lita. I was in need of one good laughing," he admitted as he resituated his glasses. "Both litas will go to bidding. The divers—six cycles in one keeper. Six segs for one ganis did drop his own brathern, sorry blogart."

Roth growled at this, beating his palms against his forehead.

"Yon should thank Sola I do nayat add six again," ValCussin scoffed. "This for blaming the dropping of yon brathern on one Loper of Zeria, her very self." It was a statement he could barely get out before breaking into a bray which sent his rotund belly to bouncing.

The crowd joined in raucously.

CHAPTER 28

Christine peered out over the milling crowd. The poorly constructed platform was raised several feet off the ground, giving her a fine vantage point to observe the perspective bidders. Ganist of all ages and sizes milled about talking amongst themselves while looking over the small group of litas lined up side by side across the stage.

Christine looked to Tasta who stood to her left. Gone was the woman who had so brazenly defied Roth three days earlier. She was now a deflated lita, her shoulders slumped, her head hanging. She seemed unaware of the thin gani hiding in the folds of her gilt, one peeking out with wide, frightened eyes. Christine tousled the boy's hair and gave him a reassuring smile when he peered up to her. His face was so pinched. The bruise on his cheek and jaw had faded to a light yellowish gray. Christine had a strong desire to comfort the boy's malla as well, to hug the emaciated lita who appeared so lost and hopeless, the lita who had saved her life, not once, not twice, but three times. Though the desire to grasp and hug her fiercely was strong, Christine chose instead to reach over and clasp her hand, giving it a firm squeeze. "Do nayat fret," she whispered, "all will end well."

She thought at first Tasta would not respond, but then the frail hand within hers tightened, the squeeze ever so brief and awfully weak.

She prayed she was right, that all would end well for this lita and her child. She couldn't imagine any situation worse than the one they were leaving behind. She scanned the faces of the ganist below them, wondering which would purchase Tasta and her son, which would bid on herself and Rebecca.

Overhead, gray rain clouds were being ushered along on a brisk breeze. The ganis at the podium, sorting through papers, cursed as a snatch of wind almost yanked them from his grasp. Straightening them, he continued to shuffle through, occasionally glancing over with a frown at the pitiful group to be bid off.

At her feet, Rebecca sat enraptured by the beads on the new gilt she'd been given for the bidding. She fingered them delicately, trying to pluck them free. "No," Christine chided when she brought the beaded material to her mouth.

When Rebecca looked up to her with big innocent eyes, Christine felt her heart melt. She could only pray she and Rebecca would find a good home. Keeping Rebecca safe was her top priority—keeping far away from Sam, a close second.

For the first time in weeks, thoughts of the forbidden kiss resurfaced, and she hurried to bury them deeper, to a grave they could never escape. She struggled with the feat, feeling a flush come over her as her breaths quickened.

"Malla," Bixten said, tugging on his mother's gilt. "Neema," he said, pointing.

Christine spotted the hound near the back of the crowd, sitting obediently at Kaltica's feet. There came a tightening in the pit of her stomach at the sight of the troller.

Tasta nodded, then began to cough, the violent hacking fit bringing up blood. She wiped it hastily on her sleeve.

With his face in a tight grimace, the auctioneer motioned to a man behind them, and he responded, shoving Tasta forward to middle stage where she stood dispirited, her shoulders sagging, chin to chest.

"This lita, as yon does note, is in the final stage of genopé rot," the auctioneer barked in an apologetic tone. "But one gani is of sound health. He does only need a few cycle's good supping and he will be one fine gani for chores and such. He can work in yon coarse fields and—aya, one slice," he said, acknowledging a ganis near the front, one short and stout with a round face and the drooping jowls of a bulldog. "One slice, one slice. Do I hear two, then?" the auctioneer intoned with more enthusiasm.

"One round," a deep voice spoke, and the bulldog man, along with the entire crowd, turned to gape incredulously at the ganis who would bid such an exorbitant amount on a dying blacktongued lita and her railed gani.

"One round! One round from one ganis with the hound, then," the auctioneer proclaimed heartily. "Do I hear one round with one slice added? Bidded, then," he added hastily as if afraid to lose the one round procured.

As Tasta and Bixten were led offstage, the auctioneer motioned to Christine. "This lita is blacktongued as well, but, as yon does note, she does nayat own many segs. She does own all her teeth and fine dark locks. She does have woundings, but is meshing nicely. She is malla to one fine babe. As yon does note, one babe does own blazened locks. Same will be worth many rounds when she does come of age. Aya, then, one round," he said, pointing to somewhere near the middle of the crowd. "Do I hear two? Aya, two rounds—three."

"Ten rounds."

A collective groan sounded through the crowd, disappointment at having been robbed of a chance to bid.

"Ten! Ten rounds bidded by one fine ganis with the hound, then! Ten rounds!" The auctioneer's voice had raised two decimals in his excitement.

"Five and ten."

"Five and ten! Five and ten rounds to the ganis on the left, then. Five and ten rounds!"

Christine spotted the second bidder, and her heart turned cold. It was Harvin, standing silent, his arms folded across his chest, his face set grimly.

"Two by ten," Roltin countered.

Such a bid sent the auctioneer into an animated jig. Throwing his arms up, he swept them toward Christine as if presenting a queen. "Two by ten rounds," he shouted shrilly. "Surent overly low one bid for such a fair lita and one blazened-locked lia."

"Three by ten," the scarred troller intoned dryly, his stony eyes glued to Christine. A muted murmur traveled through the onlookers

"Ten by ten."

A shocked silence fell over the crowd. Even the auctioneer fell still. "Ten by ten?" he asked tentatively. "Did I hear ten by ten rounds?"

Roltin gave a single nod.

The auctioneer exhaled loudly. "Ten by ten! Ten by ten rounds bidded! Do I hear five added, then?" he shrilled, pointing an unsteady hand to Harvin.

The crowd turned expectantly to the second bidder, but it seemed his bidding was done. Casting dark eyes to Kaltica, he turned and strode away, shouldering his way through the crowd.

"Bidded by one ganis in the back, then," the auctioneer shouted triumphantly. "Ten by ten rounds!" His face was flushed with excitement. It had turned out to be a profitable day after all.

CHAPTER 29

Christine turned away from Trost's dour frown where he rode along behind the supply wagon, not wishing his foul mood to spoil her good one. Though the breeze was brisk, Sola's smile was bright, the warmth soothing. As the wagon labored slowly along, Christine watched Rebecca where she sat perched high upon the pony's back within the safe circle of Kaltica's arms. Seeming to enjoy her view from on high, she clapped her hands as she practiced the sounds of the alphabet. The consonant of the day seemed to be the letter B.

Across from Christine, Tasta swayed weakly with her eyes shut. She was terribly pallored, yet her lips were rosy, stained with blood. The boy Bixten, to the contrary, abounded with energy. Running alongside the wagon and wielding a stick as a weapon, he attacked imaginary enemies with great gusto, shouting and lunging and twirling as he fended off his foes with unprecedented skill. The hound, Neema, trotted diligently by his side. She had benefitted from a week's good supping, and her coat was beginning to sport a glossy golden sheen.

Christine breathed deeply as she watched the giant trees pass by, trees owning trunks three times the circumference of those of Earth. The leaves, though similar in shape—oak, maple, beech, walnut, birch—were gigantic as well and beginning to turn. In a few weeks they would be brilliant hues of scarlet, orange and yellow. Shortly after, they would begin to fall. The wintered winds would follow.

CHAPTER 30

It had been a long day's travel. Seated on a crate by the fire, Christine enjoyed the remaining warmth of the dying embers, for a nip had surfed in on Sola's wake. Seated on the opposite side of the fire, Penningcole—the timer who drove the supply wagon—fought to keep his eyes open, the mug in his hand miraculously holding its contents despite the unsteady swaying. Besides him, she was the last to remain at the fire, except for the children who sat on the ground playing. Bixten was drawing pictures in the soft dirt with a stick. Squatting beside him, Rebecca raptly studied his artwork.

"He is one bright gani."

Christine started at Kaltica's sudden appearance.

He grinned at her startled expression as he moved closer to the fire, holding his hands out to gather warmth. "He is of one age to begin lessoning once we arrive at Rostivane."

"And what is yon aiming for mine babe and mineself once we arrive at such?"

Crouching down by the fire, he picked up a long stick to stoke more flames to life, prodding gingerly. "One Cas of Rostivane is always in needing of labor litas."

"Surent ten by ten rounds will nayat be handed over for one labor lita."

He looked at her oddly. "The rounds are of little portance. Trost is one brazened troller, but he does own one heart hardened, as any troller must. I did nayat think yon should land in his hands."

"Then I must hand thankings yet again."

He looked back to the fire and Christine had to grin despite herself. It seemed Kaltica had a shy side. She studied his profile in the firelight. He was a striking man with his dark hair and fair skin, both delicate and dominant at once. The golden hound approached and he reached over to scratch her head.

"Yon heart does nayat seem so hardened."

He gave her a sideways glance before turning back to the fire to poke absentmindedly. "Troller's do note many foul things, things would rip one weakened heart to shreddings. And so such must be hardened in order to survive one title Troller." He turned back to her with eyes not shy in the least, these riveting on her in a most unsettling fashion. "Then I did note one lita locked in the jaws of one woodslink, one brazened malla would battle to her dropping to save one babe. I did feel mine heart soften at the noting of such."

Christine dropped her eyes to the hands in her lap. It had been a foolish statement. She cursed her own stupidity, cursed it ten times over as he stood to approach her.

Kneeling down before her, he plucked a chilled hand from her lap to rub it between his own nicely warmed ones. "I do bunker at the ganist quarters of Rostivane. Such is all one troller does need. But I have been aiming to search for one rez on the skirts. I will be in needing of one scullery lita."

Christine moved her eyes to the droopy eyes of the hound, thus spurring its tail to wagging. Kaltica had been kind to Rebecca and herself. She had no desire to hurt him. Pulling her hand from his, she smoothed the gilt at her lap. "Troller Kaltica—"

"Roltin." It surprised her when his hand went to her cheek, his finger tracing lightly along the thin scar. "I will nayat ever bring harm to yon, Christa. This I do swear on Sola." He dropped his hand to her chin to gently turn her face to his—to kind, olive eyes peering longingly, drawing her in.

Gasping, she stood so quickly she nearly toppled him.

He stood just as quickly to steady her by the shoulders. "Do nayat fear this ganis."

"No. Naya. I do nayat. I just—it's been one long sol."

He nodded. "Aya. Yon should get yon resting. The morrow will bring one last long sol of travelings. And it will take us into Rostivane."

CHAPTER 31

She couldn't sleep. The carry was no longer cramped, there being only four occupants. But Tasta's breaths were erratic and they rattled moistly in her chest. There were times when they became so shallow, Christine would prop on an elbow to make sure she still lived. Bixten lie curled like a kitten at her feet with Rebecca sprawled out beside him. Even Neema was deep in slumber beneath the wagon. Christine could see her through the cracks of the floorboards curled up behind one wheel, her legs jerking as she chased some elusive quarry in her dreams. A night flower was in bloom, the fragrance sweet like jasmine, and the rhythmic drone of crickets was lulling. And yet sleep eluded her. It was Kaltica—Roltin, his offer. He had shown nothing but kindness to Rebecca and to herself—but he was still a man. And there had been something in his eyes, a burning not the reflection of the flames he stoked. She would have to deal with him delicately.

Snoring sounded from the closest tent to the left. Their carry driver, Bastian, had lifted one too many mugs of spirits to a good cycle's bounty, as had many of the trollers. Divers were plentiful, wages were good and morale was high.

Somewhere off to the right, a pony nickered softly. A chill had come in on the night breeze, and even though the canvas sides had been rolled down for protection, it had found its way within. Through the seams of the cover, Christine could see the night sky was cloudy, the stars peeking through only on brief occasions.

Adjusting the blankets on Tasta and the children, she then pulled her own to her chin, snuggling deep within.

~~~~~~~~~~

She was roused by the sound of flapping wings. The gosers in the supply carry parked behind them had been spooked. Lifting the hem of the canvas, she peered at the edge of the tree line in time to catch small shapes slinking in the darkness. The foxlike creatures, frii, were tempted by the feathered fowl, but hesitant to venture into camp. Christine peered through the floorboards at Neema and was immediately alarmed. She lie sprawled on her side with her neck bent back at an odd angle. Christine whispered her name, then again louder, with no response.

Slipping from the wagon, she crouched beside the wheel and tentatively reached between the spokes to prod at Neema, feeling the sense of dread peak—till the hound lifted her head to peer around groggily.

Christine chuckled in relief. “What kind of guard dog are you, anyway?”

There came a faint yipping in the distance, and Neema scrambled to her feet with a rumbling growl, then dashed away on unsteady legs. Watching her beneath the wagon, Christine grinned as she disappeared into the forest in off-balanced loping leaps.

She was grasped from behind, her cry muffled by a hand clamping tightly over her mouth. The arm about her waist clamped just as tightly, neatly pinning her arms as she was lifted effortlessly from her feet. The ganis who held her was powerful, and all her kicking and struggling did not hinder his progress as he spirited her into the woods, the terror mounting with each long stride he took.

Her terror turned to panic as a pony appeared before her tethered to a tree, one she instantly recognized. With a snort, it lifted its head high, prancing nervously as they approached.

Without warning, she was upended and body-slammed onto her back, the vicious move knocking the air from her lungs. In an instant, the ganis pounced atop, straddling her hips. Grasping the collar of her gilt, he ripped it open to the waist.
~~~~~~~~~~

She flailed at him, even with no oxygen to fuel her efforts, but he grasped her wrists, pinning them at her ears as he leaned in close. Angry eyes glared menacingly in the darkness.

"I did ask nicely, lita," he sneered, and just as air entered her lungs with a sharp piercing pain, he backhanded her, a blow so brutal, darkness nearly claimed her. The offending hand went to her neck next, clamping tight, and she struggled to stay conscious, prying at his fingers, her growling mere gurgling as he leaned in to latch on greedily, taking forcefully what she would not give willingly—even when asked nicely.

She was only vaguely aware of the whining hound, Neema having followed their trail, vaguely aware of a rough hand groping up her gilt to rip off her undergarment.

Digging her heels into the ground, she clawed at the choking hand, fighting to keep consciousness from leaving her.

It was a battle she did not win.

CHAPTER 32

She came to at Neema's urgent barking. The pressure at her throat was gone, as was the ganis who had placed it there. Rolling to her belly, she pushed weakly to hands and knees.

They were grappling on the ground, two dark forms, a violent writhing display. The pony shied as they rolled near, giving a frightened snort. A wave of nausea assaulted Christine, and her stomach convulsed, sending up its contents, the vicious upheaval nearly sending her back into unconsciousness.

They were on their feet when next she looked, crouched low, circling slowly, their drawn blades glinting in Luna's light. The screaming in her brain was telling her to run, but her body was not responding. She managed to crawl only a few feet before collapsing to her belly.

Through a hazy fog, she witnessed the horrific scene unfold—one ganis down, the other kneeling above him, his upraised blade held firmly in both hands. She tried to scream as the blade was thrust downward, but her voice was lost, pulled down into darkness.

~~~~~~~~~~

The hands that rolled her to her back were gentle, gentler the fingertips which brushed the hair from her face.

"Roltin," she breathed weakly.

His eyes ran the length of her, and when they returned to her own, they were in the face of a man tortured. Wrapping the tattered gilt about her, he scooped her into a tight embrace.
~~~~~~~~~~

~~~~~~~~~~~

The trip out of the woods was much different than that entering. She took comfort in the arms which embraced so tenderly. Clinging to him, she buried her face into his neck as his long strides carried her back to camp, back to safety. She could not keep from trembling, could not catch her breath, could not fight the unconsciousness so intent upon claiming her. Her last memory was of Neema padding proudly by his side.
~~~~~~~~~~~

CHAPTER 33

As daylight filtered through her closed lids, Christine started awake with a gasp. She gasped again upon realizing she was unclothed beneath the covers.

"Lie still," Roltin ordered. "Yon gilt and underclothes are all being mended." He sat in a chair on the opposite side of the tent, his hands resting on his knees.

She brought a hand to her tender face, to her bruised cheek, her right eye swollen nearly shut—then ran her tongue over her swollen bottom lip, over the tender flesh down the center where it had split open.

Roltin's olive eyes watched her closely. "There is bruising on yon face, yon neck," he said. "I did find naya other woundings."

"Becca?"

"Safe," he assured her.

She shifted beneath the blanket and grimaced at the tenderness of an assaulted body.

"Did he force hisself inside of yon?"

She was startled by the bluntness of his question. "Naya."

He nodded, his expression stony.

She looked to his bedding. It hadn't been disturbed. "Is he dropped, then?" she asked, though she was already certain of the answer.

"Aya."

There was a chilliness behind this answer. He was angry. He'd been forced to drop one of his own ganist.

"Yon is blazened-locked."

It was not a question, but a statement. The implications both embarrassed and frightened her. She fidgeted as he drilled her with accusing eyes. "I did think it best to dye mine locks while in travel. I did only—"

"It is said PacMattin did slice the throat of one Loper of Zeria."

"Roltin." Grimacing, she sat up, clutching the blanket to her chest. "Yon can nayat think me to be such, surent."

"I have noted the likeness of such in several paintings—light eyes, fair skin."

"One Loper of Zeria was dropped by fraigens."

"Aya. At Black Pond, the very waters yon band did dive. It is spoken she can still be noted at such."

"Aya," she laughed. "Riding the backs of fraigens. Blow."

"Yon did ride the back of one woodslink."

Christine sighed in exasperation. She studied the troller. His face had an abrasion on the left cheek and his shirt was torn at the neckline. There were small splotches of blood where she had buried her face at his neck.

His eyes were oddly cold as he studied her in return. "Any lita owning blazened locks and light eyes must be viewed by one member of the Zerian council."

"Fine, then," she said with a shrug.

"Such is proclaimed by one Leader of Lors."

"Fine," she said, cursing his strong sense of allegiance.

There came a clearing of a throat from beyond the tent flap—Gaile informing that one campment was near readied to take leave. He handed in Christine's repaired clothing. The hands which had stitched the repairs had surely not been skilled, but Christine was grateful for the attempt.

"We will continue on to Rostivane," Roltin said as he headed out to give her privacy. "The wintered winds draw near. When they cease, I will send word to Zeria."

CHAPTER 34

Tasta swayed weakly, her eyes half-mast. Her face was pallored, and a boil the size of a quarter had appeared on her left cheek, seemingly overnight. Her dark hair was quickly losing its color, fading down to a muddy gray, and her scalp was clearly visible past the thinning strands, giving away several seeping sores cloistered beneath. Bixten leaned against her side, his legs swinging lazily. He eyed Christine curiously, taken aback by her appearance. Becca, too, had distanced herself, puzzled by her mother's bruised and swollen face. She sat on the wagon floor, busying herself with a doll Bixten had fashioned for her of rags.

Eleven trollers on horseback plodded ahead of the carry. The supply wagon brought up the rear with Harvin's pony clopping along behind it. Draped across its back was his body bundled in blankets.

Christine looked down at the plate of goser eggs and crout strips which sat untouched in her lap. It was no use. Her stomach was clenched in a tight knot so that no food could enter. The very sight of it brought a wave of nausea. Dumping the contents of the plate over the side of the wagon, she watched as Neema gobbled it greedily.

"The blogart should nayat have laid hands on one Loper of Zeria."

Christine looked to Tasta, startled by her words. "Tasta, pleadings do nayat call me such."

"Did yon use rock or blade?"

It took several moments for the odd question to sink in. "I did nayat drop one troller! Was Kaltica did such."

Tasta shut her eyes, though the sly smile remained on her stained lips.

CHAPTER 35

Rostivane was a cassing which easily rivaled Zeria in size. Streets of hard-packed dirt turned quickly to cobbled stones, these echoing the hollow clopping of pony hooves as they meandered slowly toward the cas. Their procession drew an occasional curious glance, especially to the body being towed behind. Several people raised their hands in salute to the trollers, and they nodded greetings in return.

One by one, the trollers dropped from the procession, exchanging brief words of parting before going their separate ways. The supply wagon was the last to part ways, turning off down the market street with the bundled body in tow.

"I will be in contact after the winds cease," Roltin called out to Penningcole as he waved in salute.

Three trollers accompanied Christine and Tasta as they continued toward the cas—Bastian driving the wagon which carried them, and Roltin and Gaile sitting high upon ponies. There was a nip on the light breeze which fluttered the foliage on the trees lining the streets, ancient trees whose multiple trunks spanned blocks. They passed a flock of gosers congregating beneath one such tree, this producing a whine from Neema and prompting her tail to sweep vigorously along the wagon's bed. Rebecca was equally excited by the feathered fowl with the long necks. She squealed and pointed a pudgy finger.

A stray hound caught Neema's attention, a jet-black male with two white ears, the ends of these a muddied gray from dragging along the ground. His nose went into the air, taking in Neema's scent, this prompting him to trot alongside the wagon for a short distance. Deeming pursuit futile, he stopped to peer longingly as they trundled away. Neema seemed intimately intimidated by the encounter, her golden coat trembling as she watched the dark stranger watching her.

Rebecca squealed and pointed. She had spotted more gosers paddling about in a standing pool which held a statue center. They were traveling through a small park, one littered with gargantuan maples sporting foliage just starting to turn. There were tables scattered about, one seating a group of timers, their silver hair glistening in Sola's smile. They were obviously in the midst of a passionate conversation, taking no notice of the small procession passing. A separate grouping of tables was occupied by a group of young boys. It seemed they were being lessoned late in the park this fine sol, their books open before them. Their teacher, an older ganis, strolled from gani to gani to peer over their shoulders. Bixten eyed this group with particular interest, and several of the ganies eyed him in curious return.

As they passed near the pool, Christine admired the statue. Carved of stone, a silky pony stood gallant, this larger than life, it's head held high and proud. The rider atop was just as proud, his chin held high, his shoulders back, a splendid cape flowing about him. Wavy hair fell to below his shoulders, and his head was tilted slightly, his eyes cast down at such an angle, it appeared he was watching the wagon in passing.

Christine blanched as the face came into clear view, for it was a face she knew well. The resemblance was immaculate, the angle of the jaw, the set of the serious eyes—the Lor of Zeria, the first ever Leader of Lors, his stoic countenance carved in stone to withstand the elements for segs to come.

Swaying weakly, Tasta motioned to the statue. "Is he nayat eyegrand?" she asked with a sly smile.

"Aya," Christine answered weakly, feeling as if the breath had been snatched from her lungs. "I supposc hc is."

CHAPTER 36

Christine glanced at the three trollers conversing with the bridge guards. It seemed to be a light conversation, the men smiling and laughing—before it turned suddenly serious, the name Trost making its way to her ears on a hushed whisper.

Turning her attention away, Christine studied the splendid cas sprawled out before her on the opposite side of the moat, one rivaling Cas Zeria in both size and grandeur. The stones had a more natural look, the faces rounded like boulders, the color a deep granite-gray. The windows were tall and arched like those of Zeria, and guarded by the same iron bars. And there were similar creepers scaling the walls, the striking trailers of yellow and lime reaching clear to the rooftops. There were more turrets than could be tallied, and countless flags being flaunted, these lining the many roofs and circling the many towers high above. More flying flags spanned both sides of the bridge they were about to traverse. A lilting breeze toyed with these, lifting them to fluttering life on an occasional whim before leaving them to hang listless yet again.

Bixten was enthralled by the cas, his eyes wide as they roved over it. "Is this where I will be lessoned, then, malla?" he asked.

Tasta gave a weak nod. She'd been with fever the last few sols, and was pallored as paste, thus making the rosy splotches on her cheeks stand out like beacons. The abscess on her cheek had ulcerated, and was oozing a yellowish puss. It was just one of many. Several on her scalp had been seeping for days, and Christine had seen her lift her gilt to inspect several on her thighs.

As Christine watched, a thin thread of blood trickled from her nose. This Tasta removed with a sleeve already bearing the markings of many such bloody swipes. Settling back against the wagon boards, Tasta closed her eyes.

Jumping down on thin legs, Bixten ran to the front of the wagon, his neck craning back to see the top of his new school. Neema went to stand by his side, her tail wagging. This prompted Rebecca to do the same. Standing beside Bixten, she craned her neck back and pointed a finger to a soldier on horseback who rode high upon the rooftop.

"Christa Clavin."

Christine looked to Tasta, startled she had spoken. She was startled further by her posture. Though the words had been a weak whisper, she was sitting tall, her shoulders back, her chin held high, appearing almost regal. She was startled especially by the eyes. They were glassy eyes and the whites a sickly yellow, but the dilated pupils seemed to burn with an inner fire which had nothing to do with fever.

"Grand Loper of Zeria, hear mine words."

Christine opened her mouth to protest, but it was plain there would be no arguing.

"Protect mine gani. I do place him in yon care. Mine end draws near."

"Naya, Tasta. We are in Rostivane. They have meshganist."

Tasta gave Christine a chiding look, then the chin, raised so high, tilted further still as she looked to Sola, seeming to revel in the warmth on her face. "Sola is sweet," she whispered as a rare smile formed, one showing gray rotting teeth.

As the wagon lurched forward onto the bridge, Bixten ran to her, clearly frightened by the murky waters they crossed and the creatures they held. She caught him, holding him at arm's length. "Naya," she chided. "Yon must act as one ganis now. Ganist do nayat own such fearings."

Gulping down his fear, he nodded.

His malla hugged him, then placed a tender kiss upon his forehead, the first Christine had ever seen her do such. "Now, go to Christa," she said, riveting Christine with eyes ablaze. "Same does wish to give one hug as well, does yon nayat, Christa."

"Aya," she said, and despite the mounting confusion, she put on a brave smile as Bixten shuffled bashfully into her outstretched arms.

"Hold him. Hold tight," Tasta spoke sadly—and with that, sprang up with surprising agility. Like a lithe acrobat, she hopped onto the seat she had occupied—and dove over the side of the wagon.

The scream caught in Christine's throat as she clutched Bixten to her chest, burying his face in her gilt. There was a splash and shouting, and the trollers leapt from their mounts to peer over the bridge railing. For a moment, it appeared Roltin meant to leap in, but he was quickly restrained by Gaile and Bastian.

"Rope!" Roltin shouted to the bridge guards who were sprinting toward them. "Rope!"

There came a garbled cry from below and Christine threw her arm over Bixten's ears as a horrific screaming ensued, this cut suddenly short.

CHAPTER 37

The room was spacious—the floors tiled in marble, the walls draped in silk. The table was grand as any she had seen, easily twenty feet long, the high-backed chairs lining both sides padded in luxurious ivory leather. The high-arched windows lining one side of the room showed Sola sinking low. In preparation for Luna's arrival, a slender ganis with silver hair shuffled about the room with punk in hand, lighting the many candles which lined the walls.

Christine brushed at a tear as she watched him make his rounds. Numbness had settled over her, mercifully dampening a sorrow deeper than she would have ever imagined. Tasta's had been a tragic life. The indignities she had suffered, the pain endured. She had been a child once, innocent and pure as her own sweet Becca.

Christine looked to where Rebecca was kneeling on one of the chairs, bouncing her doll on the table. She was practicing the letter M, the continuous stream almost sounding as if she was saying the word 'mama'. Bixten sat quietly beside her, his hands folded in his lap. He seemed confused by his mother's absence, his eyes darting frequently to the entrance where the double doors stood propped wide.

Once again, Christine found her eyes drawn to the life-sized mural masterfully painted on the wall. Stepping nearer, she peered up at the blazened-locked lita. She owned an ethereal face, the ivory skin seeming to glow in Luna's bright smile, the eyes shimmering like crystals. She was dressed in an angelic gilt of white trimmed in gold, this flowing gown seeming misplaced considering the woman wearing it surfed the backs of two foul fraigens which skimmed the top of blackened waters. With one foot upon each broad back and grim determination upon her face, she reined in the harnessed beasts whose toothy maws were yawning wide. She seemed unaware of the silky white pony prancing on the far shore, its rider looking with longing toward the one woman destined to elude him.

As Christine's eyes lingered on this man, a vise compressed her chest like an iron fist. A chill raised the hair on her arms, this traveling up the back of her neck and to her scalp. The Lor of Zeria, the very Leader of Lors, the most powerful and revered ganis in all of Atriia. He *was* a handsome ganis, one loved and admired by all. And yet, the thought of falling into his hands brought horror to her heart.

"He owns one pleasant mouth, does he nayat?"

Christine spun, a hand fluttering to her throat. The woman was tall and elegant with snow-white hair wound into a neat bun at the nape of her neck. Though she was older, mid-fifties to sixty, her skin was flawless, the only wrinkles those very fine at the corners of her eyes. Her gilt of ivory clung to a curvaceous figure. She held herself in a regal fashion, her slender shoulders back, her refined chin high. She was in the company of two younger women, both dressed in flowing gilts of buttercup-yellow and both hanging back a respectful distance.

"His eyes are pleasant as well," the woman continued, her gaze glued to the Lor on the pale pony. "Though sad. Some do speak his heart was swallowed into the bellies of fraigens along with one loper."

Christine nearly choked. "Such is blow, surent," she retorted, immediately regretting her hasty reply.

The woman turned to peer at her, the cold, gray eyes conveying that she did not appreciate the tart reply either. "He does only take blazened-locked litas to his bunker from that sol forward," she informed, pressing fists firmly to her hips. "And *that* is nayat blow. It is also nayat blow that blazened-locked litas are in highest demanding since then—especially those fit for pleasuring." Her demeanor softened as a grin formed. "Once was a sol I did own locks that danced. I have been informed yon does as well." Her slate-gray eyes ran the length of Christine, her nose crinkling as if detecting an unpleasant odor.

Christine tolerated the woman's disdainful scrutiny, holding her place as the woman strolled a leisurely circle about her. She held no illusions as to what the assessment would be. Her eyes were bloodshot from crying, her face bruised and swollen, and her lack of appetite over the past week had left her overly railed. And though the gilt she wore was clean, it was stained and tattered, and with many of the repairs on the verge of pulling loose.

When the woman came before her yet again, it was with lips pursed tightly. "It is well yon does own scullery skills," she said with a frown.

Becca tottered up to the stately woman, proudly holding up her new doll for the stranger to admire.

"As Sola shines," the woman spoke, her face breaking into a pleasant smile as she dropped down to the child's level to give her chubby cheek a gentle pinch. "How spellerly."

Becca giggled and hugged the doll close before scampering back to Bixten.

There was an odd glimmer in the gray eyes as the woman straightened to smooth the lap of her gilt with ring-adorned hands. "I will hand ten rounds for yon lia." She frowned at Christine's puzzled reaction. "She will have one better life then yon could ever give. She will want for nayathing." Leaning close, she lowered her voice. "Does yon know how many genopé stones yon can bid with ten rounds?"

"I have naya needing of genopé stones, and mine lia is nayat for bidding."

The gray eyes narrowed dangerously. "Does yon know who I am? I am Sherva Rostivane, sasturn to the very Lor of this cassing."

"It is grand to meet yon, Mine Lita," Christine said, bowing respectfully, "but mine lia is nayat for bidding, nayat now, nayat ever."

Pulling her shoulders back, the woman donned a chilly grin. "Fine, then," she said, motioning to the doors. "Gather her and follow me to one litas' quarters. The gani will be shown to ganist's quarters. Yon do all need lotice dipping."

"Naya!" Christine cried, her heart suddenly racing.

The woman placed her hands calmly on her hips as she lifted her chin. "I do know now why yon face does own such bruisings," she confessed. "Yon does own one spectless tongue, lita. I did hear of the gani's malla," she said, shooting cold eyes in Bixten's direction. "The skewed blacktongue did throw herself to fraigens. Does yon wish to end the same, then?"

Christine gave a quick glance to where Bixten sat wide-eyed. "She was nayat skewed!" she whispered with venom, putting her back to the boy while trying to block his view of Sherva Rostivane, the high-class woman with no class at all. "She had genopé rot! Mayhap after one life of suffering, she did choose nayat to have one dropping to match. And I can nayat be dipped for lotice! Mine skin will burn."

The woman squared her shoulders. "Slige does bite, aya. Such is needed to drop lotice."

"Naya! Mine skin does burn as if by fire! It does blister—does turn brittle—does crack and bleed. I fear mine babe's skin will act the same. She can nayat be dipped!"

The sasturn to the very Lor of Rostivane furrowed her brow. "Naya blacktongue does wish to be dipped, lita. Yon did choose one life so lowly. Now yon must suffer one dipping, yon and yon babe, both. I can nayat set lotice loose on the whole cas."

Christine felt a dangerous flaring in her belly, one she quickly squelched. Squaring her shoulders, she spoke in a calm but firm tone. "I do wish to speak with one Troller Kaltica."

She witnessed an odd darkening of the woman's gray eyes before they narrowed to slits. "Spectless tripe," she hissed, her slender neck craning forward. "I am Sherva Rostivane. Does yon think it wise to speak to me in such tones?"

"Yon must nayat speak in such tones to one Loper of Zeria," Bixten interjected in a tiny, frightened voice.

Sherva swiveled toward him with a scowl. "Loper of Zeria," she scoffed.

Bixten nodded. "Just ask mine malla."

The scowl turned instantly to an incredulous grin. "Yon malla?

Yon malla did throw herself to fraigens, gani. Does yon gest I do speak to piles of fraigen dung, then?"

Christine witnessed Bixten's jaw go slack—and such was the last she saw clearly, for it was as if a thick red shade had been drawn over her eyes. Spitting obscenities, she lunged at the shadowy figure before her, feeling her hands press into the soft flesh of her neck. She was only vaguely aware of people shouting—and completely unaware of time passing.

When her vision cleared, someone was restraining her from behind, and the two buttercups were helping Sherva from the floor. The older woman's face was flushed, her eyes wide as she clasped her throat with trembling jewel-studded fingers. Five ganist were gaping from the doorway—Gaile and Bastian. The other three, she did not recognize. Bixten stood in the far corner holding Rebecca's tiny hand as she looked with bewilderment at all the new strangers. The doll had been discarded at her feet.

"Is yon calmed, Christa?"

Relief swept through her at the sound of Roltin's voice, and she did not struggle as he turned her about to place firm hands upon her shoulders. Kind olive eyes beseeched her.

"One blacktongued bligart is skewed!" Sherva spat in a shaky voice as she adjusted her gilt.

"Roltin, I can nayat be dipped. Mine skin will burn. I was nearly dropped by mine last dipping, as Sola shines! The same might happen to Becca!"

Sherva expelled a high humph. "Yon will nayat need one dipping where yon is headed. Take her to one keeper," she ordered.

"Naya!" Christine screamed, throwing herself into Roltin's arms, clutching fiercely. "I can nayat be keepered again! Pleadings," she blubbered against his chest. "Roggii!"

Roltin pushed her gently away to peer upon her with curious eyes. "Yon has been keepered before?"

Christine lowered her eyes and nodded, her chest hitching as she fought back tears.

"On what accounting?"

"On the accounting that same is spectless!" Sherva spit out.

Roltin shot her a dark look before continuing. "It is spoken one Loper of Zeria was overly spookered by roggii from the sols same was keepered."

Sherva laughed haughtily. "I also am spookered by roggii. "Mayhap I am one Loper of Zeria, then!"

Roltin's face hardened as he looked to the older woman. "And now who is spectless, lita?"

Sherva paled, thus making the fresh scratch on her left cheek stand out.

"This lita will nayat be sent to one keeper." Roltin stated firmly. "And she does nayat need dipping. She has naya lotice, as one babe does nayat. I will have one meshganis sent in to confirm such."

"But—"

"Are mine words made clear, lita," he reiterated, and Sherva drew her shoulders back at the harshness of his tone. She dropped her eyes submissively, and the two buttercups flanking her exchanged nervous glances before doing the same.

"She is only here on loaning," he informed her. "I will be returning for her in a few sols. One allten at most. Does yon think yon can keep from flustings that long, Christa?" he asked with a chiding raise of his brow. There was a twinkling in his olive eyes.

"Aya," Christine breathed, hoping that her own eyes were conveying the gratitude that she felt.

CHAPTER 38

Christine watched the shadows dancing on the ceiling, those cast by the single candle left burning. Her roommate Dahla was afraid of the dark. She was a young woman, late teens, tall and thin with fair skin, dirty-blonde hair, a slight over-bite, and a strawberry birthmark completely covering the left side of her face. She was sleeping on her back this night, a thin halting snore whistling through her teeth.

Though freshly bathed, wearing a new sleeping gilt and lying on a bed soft as down, sleep was eluding Christine. There was a gnawing in the pit of her belly and a vise around her chest. She'd been forced to leave Rebecca at the brooder's quarters. She was to begin her duties of scullery in the morning and early, before Sola stirred, and so had been assigned a bed at the lita's labor quarters, this at the opposite end of the cas from where her babe slept.

Rolling to her back, she forced her eyes to shut, but Tasta's pallid face appeared yet again—the stained lips, the inflamed cheeks, the fantastic flames in her eyes, burning bright as if she was already becoming one with Sola.

Putting a fist to her mouth, Christine tried to stave off the threatening sob. She had not been given enough time with Bixten before he was ushered away. There had only been time for a quick hug and a promise to see him soon—a promise she didn't know if she could keep.

Turning her back to the whistling lita, Christine swiped angrily at a tear as she faced the blank wall, her thoughts turning to the degrading examination she'd been forced to endure—the gloating glint in Sherva's eyes as the meshganis had gone over every inch of her body with nauseating thoroughness—the tight smirk when the meshganis had pronounced her free of lotice. This announcement had not stopped Sherva from standing at the edge of the bathing pool one turning later, her head held at haughty heights, her eyes an ired, icy gray. "This blacktongued tripe has nayat been dipped," she'd proclaimed for all to hear. "There may be lotice in one bath, so yon do all risk infecting." She'd grinned most smugly as the litas had scurried from the pool, disdain darkening their features.

Only one lita had been slow to exit, one thick around the middle and broad across the shoulders. Picking up a towel, she'd blotted at her face as she sidled up to Christine. "Mayhap next chance, yon will do the job proper and throttle till one timered bligart is dropped," she'd whispered with a pert grin. "Yon is brazened, lita—but nayat overly wizened," she added, before climbing the steps to exit.

Thinking back on the words chilled Christine. There would be reprisal for her brazened actions. She had dishonored Sherva Rostivane, very sasturn to the cassing's Lor.

Perhaps dishonored wasn't the correct word, she thought as she scratched at the healing woodslink wounds on her shoulder, now mere itchy dimples. She'd tried to choke the very life from the bligart. Probably would have succeeded if Roltin hadn't been there to pull her off.

The troller was up to no good, and she knew what it was. He would be spending the next few days searching for a rez on the skirts of Rostivane. And that was just fine. She would be his scullery lita, the best damn scullery lita there ever was.

PART II

CHAPTER 1

He lie heavy atop. Soft kisses tickled her cheek, working their way to her lips.

Opening sleepy eyes, she pushed weakly against his shoulders. "No. Wait, Sam," she whispered.

He drew back. "I've waited long enough, Mine Lita."

She tried to clear the fuzziness of sleep from her brain, from her eyes. The voice wasn't right—not soft and raspy. It was deep and rumbling. "Lor Zeria?"

He grinned.

Sherva was right. He *did* own a pleasant mouth.

He leaned into her lips…

Christine came awake with bed sheets plastered to her skin. Kicking them off, she peered over at Dahla who was peering back at her. "Apologies, Dahla," she whispered.

Dahla rolled to face her. Propping on an elbow, she rested her head in her hand. "Lundevons again? That does make ten sols straight."

"Aya," Christine admitted, grateful for the darkness which hid the flush. Dahla's candle was down to a mere puddle, the dying flame floating center.

"I was having lundevons as well," Dahla confessed. "Tavaka was reaching to me from one deep, darkened pit. There was blood on her hands."

"Tavaka is fine," Christine assured through a sigh, "sleeping sound in the next boarding."

"Aya," Dahla breathed, brushing the hair from her eyes. "Yon did speak of Lor Zeria."

"I did?"

"Does yon dream of him, then?"

"Naya!" she snapped, and was immediately sorry for the harsh tone. "Apologies," she whispered. "I am overly wearied."

"Naya apologies needed," Dahla spoke sadly. "It is nayat right what Sherva is doing, the turnings she does make yon labor sol and lun."

Christine sighed wearily. "Ten sols straight now."

"And it is nayat right that she does turn every other lita gainst yon."

Christine rubbed at her forehead. It was true. She supped every meal alone, was forced to bathe in a bowl. No one spoke to her unless to hand orders.

"Apologies, Christa," Dahla spoke as if reading her mind. "I would sup with yon, but…"

"Naya, Dahla. Save yonself this vile vengeance."

"Whilst yon does labor, Sherva does stroll about one cas with yon babe on her hip."

Christine bit down on her bottom lip to keep from cursing.

"Yon should have taken the rounds offered, Christa. She will end up with yon babe on any account."

"She will nayat! I will nayat let her."

"Sherva does as she wishes. It is she who runs this cas, nayat her brathern."

"Bligart!"

"Shh," Dahla warned.

"I do barely note mine Becca," Christine moaned, swiping angrily at a tear. "Mere mounds at midsol and just before bunkering. And I have noted Bixten only once, this from one window as he walked about the courtyards. He is being trained as one stable boy," she wept, throwing an arm over her eyes.

"What of yon troller?" Dahla asked. "Can he nayat lend aid?"

"I've sent several messagings, but—naya answer."

"Sherva," Dahla whispered. Adjusting her pillow, she rolled to her back and pulled the covers to her chin. "I warned she does run this cas."

CHAPTER 2

"It is of grand portance I do get one message to Troller Kaltica. He does board at the ganist's quarters."

"Kaltica?" The guard took the basket she offered, lifting the cloth cover to inspect the contents. His eyes lit at the sight of the scullies.

"Aya," she said. "The number is three-two-two. Send word that one Lita Clayton does wish to speak with him."

He shook his head. "If yon does wish to send word to Kaltica, yon need send word to one keeper."

"Keeper!"

"Aya. He did drop one fellow troller."

"Aya, to save his own throat from being ripped."

"One saker will decide his guilt. But his fating is darkened by genopé, surent." He plucked out a cookie and popped it into his mouth.

"What does yon mean, darkened by genopé?"

"He is accused of stelchering such," he spoke as he chewed. "Ten by five rounds worth found hid in his boarding."

"Naya!"

He swallowed, then lifted the cover to search out his next victim. "It is spoken he did drop his fellow troller when same did threaten to spill word of his stelchering."

Christine felt her heart drop. "Sherva," she hissed.

CHAPTER 3

The enormous fireplace warmed the room nicely. Perhaps too nicely. A fine sheen of perspiration shone upon Gaile's forehead and upon his bald head as he fidgeted nervously. Standing stiffly before the saker, he shifted his weight from foot to foot and wiped sweaty palms upon his thighs. From where she sat at the table, Christine could see he was struggling to keep his eyes averted from Roltin. Roltin's eyes, however, never wavered from his fellow troller.

Christine's heart ached for Roltin. He had been ushered into the room a disheveled mess. A scraggly growth covered his pallored face and dark circles were etched beneath his eyes. No one had bothered to give him clean clothes. Those he wore were rumpled and stained.

The saker, a frail looking man with thinning white hair, shuffled through the papers with long spindly fingers. "Troller Gaile Liticea," he began in a voice deep and resonant, one not matching his appearance in the least. "Yon has labored beside one Troller Kaltica for eight segs?"

Gaile cleared his throat. "Aya. We did serve as Rostivanian battlers for five segs, trollers for three."

"Yon is second in standing beneath Kaltica, is this truths?"

"Aya."

"As first in standing, Troller Kaltica is in charge of collecting and destroying all genopé stones collected from captured divers?"

"Aya."

"Did yon ever note Kaltica pocketing any such stones?"

"Naya."

"But it is possible same might have pocketed such without yon noting."

The bald-headed troller shrugged. "I suppose."

"Has yon noted any actions from Kaltica that did seem odd as of late?"

Gaile fidgeted, and Christine saw him flash a quick glance at Sherva. "Same did take one lita to his tenting," he said, nodding in Christine's direction. He hung his head as a murmur traveled through the room.

"Does Kaltica make habit, then, of taking captured blacktongues to his tenting?"

"Naya. The lita was injured. He did tend her woundings. He did tend to her babe as well. The lita was nayat able to do so her own self."

The saker looked down to the papers spread out before him. "Same blacktongued lita and her babe were bidded off at Toskeena, were they nayat?"

The troller ran his hand over his dampened forehead. "Aya. Roltin and Harvin did bid head to head."

"Harvin being Harvin Trost, one other troller in yon grouping, also under Kaltica?"

"Aya."

"The same later dropped by accused."

"Aya."

"And Kaltica did win one bidding?"

"Aya."

"It states ten by ten rounds," he read, his eyebrows arching high.

A rumbling of male voices reverberated throughout the spacious room, bouncing off the walls.

"Ten by ten rounds bidded on one blacktongued lita?" the saker directed to Roltin.

"I would nayat note the lita fall to Harvin's hands," Roltin spoke in his defense. "He did try to force hisself upon her once alreadied.

"Untruths!" a ganis shouted as he shot to his feet. "Harvin was one honored ganis. He was mayhap spellered by this lita, and for this he was dropped—for Kaltica was spellered as well. Why else bid ten by ten rounds on one blacktongue?"

There were murmurs of agreement from those surrounding him, and Christine felt a flush come over her as all eyes turned in her direction. Across the table, Sherva pursed her lips as she suppressed a grin.

Christine stood on weak legs. "It is truths! Trost did try to force hisself on me!"

"Do nayat hear truths in the blow this blacktongue does speak," Sherva spat, shooting to her feet. "Same is skewed."

"Silence!" the saker barked as the crowd erupted. "Seat yonselfs, litas," he ordered, and they both complied. "Was there naya witness to one battle between the two trollers?" he directed to Gaile.

"Naya. One Lita Clayton only."

"And is it truths same lita did spend that very lun in Kaltica's tenting, and with naya garb?"

Gaile hung his head and nodded.

"Mine gilt was being repaired," Christine defended, her words lost in the angry rumbling of the crowd. She looked to Roltin. His face was ashen—but there was no fear in the olive eyes which scanned the crowd. Only sadness. These accusations pained him, a blade deep in his soul.

The ganis, who was obviously a good friend to Harvin, shot to his feet yet again. "Kaltica was stelchering genopé for the blacktongue," he insisted, pointing a livid finger at Christine. "When this was found out by Harvin, Kaltica did drop him down, then did spend that very lun having his kagege blackened!"

The crowd erupted in a fury, ganist shooting to their feet to yell obscenities at the ganis on trial.

"Silence," the saker ordered, his booming voice quieting the agitated crowd.

"Untruths!" Christine insisted as tears of frustration surfaced. "I did lie injured! Harvin did nearly choke the life from me! Roltin did save me from being dropped! He is one decent ganis! He didn't lay one finger on me! Nayat that lun, nayat ever, as Sola shines!"

"Sherva stood angrily, her chair toppling backward in a clatter. "This lita's foul blackened tongue does speak untruths," she sneered, pointing a long, accusing finger. "Same did sneak down to one keeper near every lun to same decent ganis."

"Untruths!" Christine gasped.

Sherva placed her hand on the woman's shoulder who sat beside her. "Fosteena did follow yon. I did make surent of such. Might Fosteena speak, highest saker?" she asked, and the saker motioned for Fosteena to rise.

Throwing her shoulders back and her chin high, Fosteena pointed a finger at Christine. "Same did sneak by the guards on the tips of toes, like one tippet, then did stick her hands through one food slotting. And by the moaning, it is mine thinking one tripe was nayat holding his hand," she added, grinning pertly as the snickers sounded.

"She's lying!" Christine cried, pounding her palms upon the table and standing to beseech the saker. "I wasn't allowed to visit him! Sherva saw to such! This is all her doing! It was she placed genopé in his boarding. She wants to take my babe from me!" she railed as a dangerous beast stirred in her belly. She felt her lips curl back, her hands clench. "She does own one heart black as genopé. She's a conniving witch! Roltin was kind to me—to Becca. He's a man of honor. He's done nothing wrong!"

"Enough, lita," the saker boomed, pointed a commanding finger to her chair.

Christine battled against the beast in her belly, drawing in its taut leash fist over fist, forcing it back to its haunches. It was a struggle which sapped all her strength. Her wobbly legs buckled, and she sat heavily, watching numbly as Fosteena righted Sherva's chair so she could do the like.

The saker shuffled through his papers, organizing them as the crowd quieted. "One Mas Penningcole, stand then."

At the table's far end, the wagon driver stood, and Christine breathed a relieved sigh. Roltin had a close bond with this ganis. He would have favorable words.

Penningcole rested his fingertips on the tabletop as he faced the saker timidly.

"It is scribed yon did hear speakings one lun while at one fire pit, this between one Troller Kaltica and one Lita Clayton."

Penningcole had attempted to make himself presentable for the hearing. His sparse gray hair was slicked back, his usually stubbly face shaven, his spirit-belly neatly contained in a new blue shirt tucked securely at his waist. He cleared his throat nervously. "This timer was tipping spirits, highest saker. Mayhap mine ears did hear wrong."

"And what did yon ears mayhap hear wrong, then?"

Penningcole looked sheepishly to Roltin, before dropping his eyes to where his fingertips rested. "Mas Kaltica did speak of bidding one rez on the skirts of Rostivane. He did—did ask one lita if she and her babe might come to live at such."

An undulating rumble rippled through the crowd.

"As scullery! As scullery lita," Christine cried. "Tell them, Penningcole!"

"Hold yon blackened tongue," the saker snapped, his patience worn thin. "One troller did nayat bid ten by ten rounds for one scullery lita! It is clear one troller did become spellered by yon. He did stelcher genopé for yon—did drop one Troller Trost for yon. And so, such reasoning set in mine brain, this highest saker, before Sola, does hand down the following ruling."

An older man shot to his feet, his face ashen—a face strikingly similar to Roltin's. "Highest saker, pleadings. Roltin has always been one ganis of honor, one battler brazened, one troller trusted!"

"Aya," the saker agreed, his hardened face set grimly. "And for this reasoning he was placed in one positioning of highest standing. Such standing was abused, such trust betrayed. And so it will stand, at the sixth turning on the early morrow, one fallen troller Roltin Kaltica will look upon Sola's face one final time as she does waken. Same will bow before such to plead forgivings, will bend low to lay lips to malla Atriia. He will then rise to greet five arcing arrows that will end the beating of his blackened heart, one blackened by the spellering of one blacktongued lita."

There came a chorus of approval from the audience, and Christine watched numbly as Roltin's father was steadied by the men who flanked him. Feeling on the verge of faint herself, she moved her eyes to where Roltin sat. He was looking to his father with sad, haunted eyes. The blood had drained from his face and he struggled only briefly as two armed guards hoisted him to his feet. He looked to Sherva lastly, his eyes dripping hatred.

Squaring her shoulders, Sherva gave him an acknowledging nod as she struggled against the tight smile tugging at the corners of her lips. She set her eyes upon Christine, these alight with shining victory—and the creature cloistered deep within Christine was unleashed in an instant.

With a growl, the beast leapt over the table, its readied claws digging into the meek flesh of the older woman who toppled from her chair. The beast was snarling as it lashed out at the person tugging at its mane from behind, driving its elbow backward. The snapping of bone and the howling of a lita momentarily cleared the blur of rage. The sight of blood spurting from Fosteena's shattered nose incited Christine to give Sherva one matching, and so she drove her forehead into the face so near.

The room was in a whirl—ganist shouting, Fosteena shrieking, Sherva gasping. A boot appeared to her right, one housing a blade—and so, as the ganis yanked her to her feet, the blade hilt conveniently found its way into her small palm. She thrust it at him, and he leapt backward, narrowly avoiding the slice meant to gut him wide. "Back, motherfuckers!" she screamed, and the circle of ganist complied most readily.

"Mine nose," Sherva moaned from the floor as blood seeped from between her ring-studded fingers.

With a strength belying her size, Christine yanked Sherva to her knees by the hair and thrust the blade against her throat. "Tell them, you bitch!" she snarled. "You tell them the truth or, I swear to God, I'll rip your fucking throat wide!"

Sherva pulled her hands from her face, blanching at the sight of her own blood. "Did I nayat speak one lita was skewed!"

Christine yanked the woman's head back brutally, digging the blade deeper into the pale flesh. "Do you think I won't do it!" she hissed into the woman's ear. "I did slice wide the throat of the devon

PacMattin and I will slice yon devonous throat without thinking twice!"

"Enough!" the saker ordered, his voice resounding about the room like the voice of God. "What is this talk of PacMattin? And in one tongue so thick I do barely catch half the meaning."

Several ganist surrounding him nodded agreement.

"It was mine aiming to send word to Cas Zeria," Roltin spoke from where he stood restrained by guards, and a hundred heads swiveled toward him, including that belonging to the saker.

"Zeria?"

"For one viewing. One lita is blazened-locked. Such is darkened with socket roots."

There came a murmuring from the crowding ganist.

"Her eyes are light," he continued, "her skin fair. She does own the scarring of one slice across the throat, and her tongue does grow thick at times—as yon does hear with yon own ears."

"What is yon thinking, then—that this lita is one Loper of Zeria?" the saker asked incredulously.

Roltin lifted his chin defiantly at the snickering which ensued. "When I did first lay eyes upon this lita, she was locked in the jaws of one downed woodslink, and one of full sizing, one she did drop with her own hand. Four ganis did swear on Sola she did ride upon the back of such, as if the back of one foul pony."

"Aya, he speaks truths," Gaile broke in. "I also did note her locked in the jaws of such," he admitted, and several other trollers surrounding him confirmed this with knowing nods.

All eyes turned toward her. There was a painful pounding in her chest, a pumping of boiling blood surging through like liquid fire. Squaring her shoulders, she pressed the blade firmly against Sherva's exposed throat. "Aya, I am Christa Clavin, one Loper of Zeria. May Sola strike me down if I speak untruths. And as such, I do pronounce the troller Roltin Kaltica innocent of the acts accused. This bitch," she spat, giving Sherva's hair a less than tender tug, "framed him, did yon nayat?"

Sherva cried out as the digging blade drew blood. "Skewed bligart!" she hissed, her bloodied fists clenching as composure seemed to abandon her. “Yon is spectless as the blasted troller! I am Sherva Rostivane! Rostivane! Sasturn to the very Lor, mine callen the same as this very cassing! Nayaone is spectless to Sherva Rostivane!”

“And so yon did have genopé hid in the boarding of one troller would dare be spectless to Sherva Rostivane!”

“The blogart was deserving of such!”

Removing the blade from Sherva’s throat, Christine put a foot to her back to shove her to the floor. “Bitch!” she spat—before leaping to the table.

“Lita,” the saker spoke in a condescending tone. “Put one blade aside, then.”

“You come put it aside, asswipe,” she challenged, circling the blade’s tip menacingly in his direction. “You would send this honored ganis to his dropping because yon does fear Sherva, yon kagege-less tippet.”

“If I may speak.” A ganis from the crowd stepped forward. “There is one merchanteer at market who does claim to have laid eyes upon one Loper of Zeria. He proclaims most loudly to any will listen that he did sell footings to same when first she did arrive in one cassing of Zeria.”

The saker looked to Christine, his eyes running the length of her where she stood crouched upon the table, wielding the blade before her. “Fetch him, then,” he ordered. “And if this be untruths, lita, yon will stand beside this troller to note Sola rise one last time.”

CHAPTER 4

The crowd parted to let the men through. It seemed word had spread, for a whole throng of people, ganist and litas alike, poured in behind them amidst a chatter of excitement.

Christine recognized the bruin-like ganis immediately. His black beard was longer, reaching halfway down his bulging belly, and with a network of colorful beads braided in as before. A mass of black shaggy curls framed his square face. He took her in with a furrowed frown as one giant paw stroked his baubled beard.

"Socket root was used," Roltin offered.

Christine could feel her heart pounding as the man hesitated. With the passing of time, the beast had slowly slunk back to the deep pits of its lair, leaving her to stand alone in the precarious position it had landed her in. Her very life depended on this ganis, one whom she had met only once, and for mere mounds.

She began to panic as the grains sifted through one by one and recognition failed to dawn. She looked to where Sherva and Fosteena sat nursing broken noses with bloodied cloths. Pointing the blade's tip at the large ganis, she squared her shoulders. "Thought you were going to get a free show, didn't you, moron," she said, repeating the phrase she'd used on the sol she had met him several segs past.

His eyes popped wide beneath the thick brows. "As Sola does shine," he breathed. He dropped to a knee, moving nimbly for a ganis so thick, and bowed his head. "Mine honored Lita," he spoke with reverence—and the room became deathly quiet.

CHAPTER 5

Sola was sinking low. Standing at the window, Christine let the fading smile pull the moisture from her hair. Three stories below, there was activity in the courtyard where two supply wagons were being unloaded beneath two massive oak trees. The leaves had turned quickly since she had arrived in Rostivane. They were a brilliant crimson. Many had abandoned their boughs, and the nip creeping in with Sola's descent said the remainder would not be clinging much longer.

Retreating inside, Christine seated herself before the dressing mirror, frowning at the face frowning back at her. It seemed like a child's—too thin, too pale—certainly not the face of the grand Loper of Zeria. Only in the eyes, so icy blue, did she catch a glimpse of the fierce woman she was proclaimed to be. Her locks, having been treated with fallow sap, were once again ablaze and dancing in Sola's waning smile, the freshly washed curls cascading in luxurious waves to just below her shoulders. The gilt she'd been given was a soft cream, trimmed in gold, uncannily similar to that in the conference room mural, the room where first she'd sparred with Sherva.

"Aya, the grand Loper of Zeria resurrected," she spoke to the reflection.

Spinning in her chair, she took in the room around her, her own spacious, private boarding; the ornate upholstered settee, the huge double king-sized bed. There was a large cubit in the corner, one capable of holding many gilts. The mural on the wall boasted an outdoor park scene with trees and gosers and men deep in conversation seated around tables. It was a room fit for a queen.

The punk bearer shuffled through the open doors of the

threshold, then went to work lighting the candles in the sconces. The guards posted at her door entered behind him to shut and securely lock the double shutters running the length of the windows. The younger of the two seemed nervous in her presence, shooting frequent glances to where she sat at the dressing table. He approached and dropped to a knee, bowing his head. "Is there any other service yon does need, Mine honored Lita?"

"Setkin," the older guard grumbled. "It is nayat yet proved she is the one."

"The Troller Kaltica," Christine interjected. "Can I send word to him?"

The guard kneeling before her fidgeted uncomfortably. "Same remains keepered," he said, "till one viewing."

"Why? He did nothing wrong. And why can't I see mine babe. What reasoning is this, then?"

"Many do think one merchanteer mistaken," the leery guard stated flatly. "That yon is but one blacktongue with one brain skewed."

"But do nayat fret," the kneeling guard added at her open disappointment. "Several members of Zerian council do stay boarded very near at Cas Lazette. One should arrive as early as the morrow."

CHAPTER 6

It was the very room where it had all begun. Lor Rostivane sat at the head of the table. As Sherva, he had a lofty air about him. Tall and thin with watered down orange hair, graying temples, and gray eyes, Christine put him in his mid to late fifties. The two ganist flanking him were most certainly his sons, their features identical—light-blue eyes in narrow faces with pale freckled complexions and orange curly hair. Twelve men in all took up the length of the table, the entire body of the Rostivanian council present for the venerated viewing.

Christine ignored the curious glances thrown in her direction. Her attention was held, in any case, by the mural on the opposite wall, and especially by the man seated upon the pale pony. It seemed his eyes were no longer focused on the lita riding the backs of fraigens. They seemed to be focused firmly on where she was seated off by herself, securely flanked by four appointed guardsmen.

"Cas Rostivane will be ridiculed by the entire region," the Lor grumbled, flashing Christine a scathing scowl. "This over untruths spewed by one bligart's blackened tongue. Zerian council members do travel to mine cassing this very grain to view same skewed bligart, same did draw the blood of mine sasturn, same did threaten to drop mine highest saker. Same should now lie in the bellies of fraigens. In the stead, she does sit here decked in the finest of garb while Sherva, one Rostivane, does lie in wait of one keeper." Shifting to the side, he slid his mug toward the server so she could refill it with spirits. "When this viewing is done with, it will be the hand of Sherva does feed yon flesh to fraigens, lita," he promised, and the other council members nodded agreement.

"She *does* own the coloring," the younger of the sons admitted.

His father turned to him with a scowl. "As do many litas, Acrabe."

"Her neck bears one slicing."

"Aya. And it will bear a second this sol. As Sola shines, mine hand will nayat fail to slice deep enough to finish the deed."

Conversation was cut off as a guard entered the room and approached the table. In the hallway, a stirring could be heard. There was a stirring in Christine's chest as well as her heart sputtered, and a gurgling in her belly as it twisted.

"Of all Atriia! Zeria hisself?" Rostivane hissed under his breath—and Christine felt the blood drain from her face.

The council members stood, and though she knew she should do the same, her legs would not comply. She could only sit and watch as ten guardsmen filed in, five to line the walls on either side of the double doors. She recognized the Zerian insignia—Sola, black as night—engraved into their chest plates.

"One Mas Kynneth Zeria," a voice heralded loud and clear—and Christine nearly fainted with relief. "Brathern to Jerrod Zeria, Leader of Lors," the herald announced as the honored guest strode in with five additional guards on his heels.

He was as she remembered, tall and handsome, his dirty-blonde hair longer, falling well below his shoulders. Assured unfettered strides carried him quickly to the table, his eyes locked on the tall man who was the Lor of the cas. Stopping ten feet shy, he gave a curt tilt of his head. "Lor Rostivane," he addressed. "It is grand to note yon again. It has been segs since last we met, though yon has nayat aged one sol, it seems."

The compliment brought a flourish of flush to Lor Rostivane's pale cheeks. "Thankings, kind Mas," he replied with a tilt of his head. "I do speak for mine entire council when I say we do feel grandly honored by yon presence. We were nayat prepared for one of such high standing. We did expect a lower council member, mayhap."

"The honoring is mine," Kynneth assured him with a pleasant grin. "I did rush straight way at hearing word that one grand Loper of Zeria did crawl from the bellies of fraigens to stand brazened before us."

At this, Lor Rostivane did positively blush, the crimson color on his pale face clashing comically with his orange hair. "I must hand apologies," he stammered with a nervous chuckle. "The blacktongue is skewed, surent. It would be mine grandest pleasure to send same back to such fraigen bellies fore yon very eyes." He directed a glaring glance in Christine's direction, and Kynneth turned to follow his gaze.

On legs weak and wobbly, Christine stood ever so slowly, feeling a hint of satisfaction as the grin plummeted from Kynneth's face. For a few long moments, he did only stand and stare.

"Do I look well, then," she asked, "having just crawled from the bellies of fraigens?"

"Of all Atriia," he breathed at last. He moved closer, his wide hazel eyes clouded with confusion. "How? How, then, does yon stand before me? Yon did dive into waters brimmed with fraigens."

"I did find it overly dark and overly cramped in the bellies of fraigens," she teased. "It did smell badly as well."

He did not seem amused.

CHAPTER 7

The room bustled with commotion. The gilts had arrived, these tailored especially for her, for she had been tediously measured from head to toe so that seamsewers could work laboriously throughout the lun. Two litas stood in the cubit hanging them as they chattered excitedly. Other gifts had begun arriving as well; jewelry, perfumes, flower arrangements, trays of extravagant sweetcakes and scullies in every shape and flavor, dainty boxes of delectable squddy, bowls of fresh fruit piled high. Christine grinned at the sight of Rebecca tottering about the room with a giant seedberry in each hand.

"Bixten, will yon wipe her chin, then."

Grabbing a napkin from the tray, he obliged readily, swiping at Rebecca's puckered, stained lips.

One of the guards at the door cleared his throat. "One Troller Kaltica," he announced.

"Aya. Let him through."

She beamed as he entered. Though a bit thinner, he was shaved and clothed proper, his shoulders back and head high. He approached to take her hand, dropping to one knee before her. Bowing his head, he pressed the back of her hand to his lips, then his forehead. "Mine honored Lita."

Grasping his hands, she pulled him to his feet, and he peered down at her with somber olive eyes.

"Roltin, I must hand apologies for the many untruths I did speak."

He sighed deeply. "I do search mine brain overly to know why yon would nayat claim yon true callen. It is one of great honoring."

She lowered her eyes. "Lor Zeria, he will come for me, surent."

"Yon does hold fearings of him. What thing has he done to cause such?"

A shiver ran through her. "I did watch him slice wide the throat of one lita, his very pleasurer, one who did share his bunker near every lun."

"Aya. I have heard tales of PacMattin's loper," he said, his features hardening. "This ganis would have sliced her throat ten by ten times over."

Sliding her hands from his, she sat heavily at the bureau. There would be no sympathy from Roltin on this matter. He was loyal to the Zerian Lor—to his very core.

"I will be taking mine leave on the morrow," she said. "It is Mas Zeria's wishing to outrun the wintered winds."

"Aya, it is best yon does take leave right off, fore word of yon rising does reach sleeper regions." He knelt before her to recapture her hands. "There are bands in the high-hills of Torabas and RusTassin, those who remain loyal to the callen PacMattin. They hold much hatred in their blackened hearts for one loper did dare drop their honored Lor."

"I'm in danger, then?"

"Yon should arrive at Zeria fore word does even reach the high-hills. Yon will be well protected there."

Over his shoulder, she watched as Bixten carefully picked up a sweetcake from one tray. He admired it with awe, turning it this way then that, before taking a tentative bite. Becca tugged on his shirt and tilted her head back, her mouth thrown wide like a baby bird, and Bixten dutifully obliged, breaking off a tiny piece and popping it in.

"Many Rostivanian battlers will be escorting yon to Zeria, and as many Zerian battlers will be meeting yon halfway. Yon should be safe enough," he said, giving her hands a squeeze.

"The litia's have arrived, Mine Lita," a guard informed her from the door.

She couldn't help but grin. "One grain, then."

Roltin's face softened. "Yon has had many visitors?"

"The ganies did visit earlier. Each one did kneel before me with wide eyes, each wishing for one famed Loper of Zeria to lay hands upon them."

"Aya," he breathed, his expression turning suddenly somber. He gave her hands a gentle squeeze as his warm eyes gently caressed her face. Finally, his eyes fell, as if in defeat, lashes dark against pale skin. Taking advantage of his eyes downcast, she gazed upon him, taking in the dark curls framing his fair face, the straight slope of his nose, the set of his lips—realizing how greatly she would miss this ganis, one who had shown her nothing but kindness from the first sol they met. Leaning forward, she placed a gentle kiss upon his forehead. "Many thankings for all yon has done for me and mine—nipper. I do nayat know how I will ever repay such kindness."

"Yon did save mine life."

Christine scoffed. "Such was only in danger because of me."

Nodding, he gave a soft chuckle.

"Yon will be greatly missed, Roltin."

He nodded, and Christine was certain she saw a subtle moistening of his olive eyes before he stood abruptly, pulling his hands from hers. "The litia's do lose patience," he said, motioning to the hall. He went to Rebecca, giving her a squeeze and a kiss on the cheek, thus spurring her to giggle unabashedly. He spoke briefly to Bixten, telling him he was a bright and brazened gani, then giving a firm hug. At the door, he hesitated, turning one last time to give her a reassuring grin.

She took it in, burning it into her brain, somehow knowing she would never see it again.

CHAPTER 8

News had traveled quickly throughout Rostivane. With curious eyes, Rebecca peered through the curtains of the carriage window at the crowds lining the streets.

Leaning forward in her seat, Dahla peered out as well, her eyes wide. “Aiyee, one babe does stir one crowd. Come Becca,” she said, patting the seat beside her. “Seat yonself next to Dahla, then.”

Outside, the din of the crowd swelled suddenly.

“Becca, do as Dahla speaks. Sit,” Christine ordered, and Rebecca complied with a pout. On the seat beside Christine, Bixten sat as far back as possible, his legs tucked under. Curled in a ball on the floor, Neema rested her head on her paws, her ears twitching, her eyes shifting nervously about the carriage.

It jerked to a quick halt and shouts could be heard outside, the guards barking orders. Across from her, Dahla’s pallor invited her birthmark to stand out harshly. A chant began, this growing louder as others joined in, voices in unison calling for one Loper of Zeria.

“I’m sure all is well,” Christine reassured and, almost immediately, they began to roll again. She ruffled Bixten’s dark hair and he gave a gingerly grin.

“Why must Roltin stay behind?” he asked.

“His hailing is here in Rostivane.”

“He did nayat bid farewell.”

“I am sure he did try.”

“But he did bring Neema.”

Christine had no more to offer, only a meek smile. A surrealness pervaded her at the departure from Rostivane, one very different from her arrival. She was dressed in finery and bedecked with jewels, her hair braided and styled most stunningly, her make-up applied skillfully. Her carriage was fit for a queen with plush wine carpeting and double seats thickly padded under wine-hued velvet. Matching throw-pillows in a paisley pattern of wine, gold, and black were scattered about. Bixten hugged one of these to his chest as, outside, throngs of adoring fans shouted for her attention. In hopes of getting the briefest of glimpses, the masses crowded close, severely hampering the progress of the procession.

Neema shifted and gave a nervous whine.

"All is well, Neema," Christine assured, leaning forward to give the hound's head a pat. But, in her heart, all was not well. She had done what was necessary in order to save Roltin, to save her babe and Bixten. But in return, she was headed toward the one man whom she feared more than any other. A flush dampened her skin at the mere thought of him, making her gilt cling uncomfortably. Closing her eyes, she attempted to slow a heart threatening to hammer its way through her chest. She loathed the ganis to whom she was being delivered, loathed him for the fear he instilled.

"All will end well," she whispered, more to soothe her own nerves than anyone else's. "All will end well."

CHAPTER 9

Sola was sinking low in a sky streaked with orange and purple, her face a brilliant crimson. A crisp breeze was snatching leaves from their limbs and churning those already fallen. Kynneth seemed agitated as he poured over the map spread out on the ground. "It did take nearly two turnings to pass through Rostivane," he spoke with a scowl. "Cassing Looftis will be likened to such, doubtent. Turnings might be saved by traveling round," he said, motioning with his pointer stick.

"It will take four turnings, least, to travel round," one of his men replied. "The back-roads are nayat well kept."

"Mine vote is to travel straight through," another replied. "Send runners ahead with intructings to double the guardsganist, to use battlers if needed to keep the streets clear."

Kynneth nodded. "So be it, then. But if there be flustings at Looftis, we must sider taking this back road through Woroff Woodland in the stead of through one cassing. We have naya grains for wasting. I do think the wintered winds aim to arrive earlied this seg." As if to confirm this, a blustery gust swept a pile of leaves into the air, swirling them into a flurry, before scattering them in all directions.

CHAPTER 10

She was running in a woodland deep in misty shadow. Branches like gnarled fingers grasped at her hair, ripped at her clothes, clawed at her skin. Tears blurred her vision as she stumbled forward, her feet sinking into soggy mush which insisted on hindering every fleeing step. The air she gulped into her lungs was frigid, every exhale sending plumes of vapor billowing. Her whoofing and wheezing were the only sounds—for the forest was eerily silent. The woodland creatures could sense it as well as she. Danger. Save it didn't slither on its belly through underbrush. It was seated high upon a white, silky pony.

She caught herself just in time, grasping hold of a tree to keep from tumbling over the edge of the woodland, it having been neatly sheared by a stone precipice which plummeted to a thread of a river a mile below.

The hairs on the back of her neck told of his arrival, the tingling traveling down to her toes. She could hear the snorts of his winded pony, the pawing of its hooves as it pranced in place.

Every piercing breath she took was painful, the moisture crystalizing on her trembling lips. She dared not turn around.

Stones tumbled over the side of the precipice as she inched closer.

"Christa," he implored softly, the word making her skin crawl…

"Christa."

She came awake in the dark carriage just as a gust of wind whistled by, rocking it roughly.

"Lundevons?" Dahla asked sleepily from where she lie curled on the seat opposite.

Christine pushed the hair away from her forehead, one dampened with sweat despite the plummeting temperature. "Aya." She pulled Becca close, then the blanket as a chill overtook her, one which had nothing to do with the weather.

Outside, a pony nickered softly.

Dahla sighed deeply as she adjusted her own blankets. "It is overly darkened in here. I wish Tavaka was traveling with us. And I wish all the peoples of Looftis will stay in their boardings on the morrow. But I know they will nayat. Every last ganis and lita will be on the streets to note one famed loper. Then we will need to pass through Woroff Woodland, and I so do nayat wish to pass through such."

"Why nayat?"

Dahla hesitated. "If yon does stray and lose yon way, in worgle bellies yon will lay."

"Worgle?"

"Surely yon has heard of worgles, then."

"Naya."

Dahla moaned as a shudder ravaged her. "Devons that do move silent as shadows through Woroff Woodland—half huganis, half beast, long tails and tongues, eyes that do glow as any fraigen's, teeth meant to rip flesh from bone. Many who travel into Woroff Woodland do nayat ever come out again."

Christine kissed the top of Becca's head. "Tot tales, surent."

"Aya, tot tales," Dahla repeated, though with little conviction. "I did often hear of one other tot tale as one litia, this of one blazened-locked battler who would rise from waters blackened."

Bixten stirred where he slept bundled in blankets on the floor beside Neema, mumbling in his sleep. Somewhere in the distance, a night bird gave a warbled trill.

"I can nayat believe the very Loper of Zeria did share mine boarding for near one cycle without mine knowing," Dahla mused. "Yon is truly skilled."

"Was only two alltens."

"Is it truths, Mine Lita," Dahla pressed. "Was it yon hand did slice one neck of PacMattin?"

Christine sighed heavily at the memory; PacMattin throwing his head back to laugh—the fraigen scale so light—like nothing in her hand, a deadly weightless weapon. "Aya."

"Of all Atriia," Dahla breathed. "At least if we do meet up with worgles, I do have the greatest battler of all Atriia by mine side."

Any reply was silenced by a light rap upon the door. It was Kynneth who stuck his head in, his breath showing as he spoke. "Firstsup will be served shortly," he informed them. "We must be off fore Sola wakens."

CHAPTER 11

Rebecca was of a foul mood. Too many turnings pent up in one cover-carry were taking their toll. And Dahla's mood was not much better. She had been right. Every ganis and lita of Looftis *was* present, along with every ganis and lita from every bordering town, and every child and babe and hound and pony. The carriage was crawling at an excruciating pace. From without, frustrated shouts of the guards could be heard over the din. The ponies, unused to crowds of such sizing, pranced nervously, jostling the carriage about.

Dahla's eyes grew wide as the carriage finally ground to a halt. Bixten's did as well, though more from excitement. He braved a peek through the crack of the drawn curtains. "So many," he spoke, mystified. "Yon malla is the most famed lita of all Atriia," he told Rebecca, patting her head like a puppy. Then Bixten jumped, nearly toppling backward as the door was suddenly yanked open.

Kynneth stuck in his head, his face flushed. "The crowds will nayat part," he shouted to be heard over the din. "We did draw blades, even, and still they do nayat budge. I do fear they might charge one cover-carry if yon does stay hid. They do wish to lay eyes upon one Loper of Zeria."

Christine looked to where Rebecca sat on the floor by Neema with her doll in her lap, a look of abject misery on her pouting face—then stood, smoothing the gilt at her lap. "Then they will lay eyes upon such," she said, feeling her heartbeat quicken at the thought of debarking the carriage into the awaiting mayhem.

Kynneth hesitated. "Yon safeness will be at risk. A blade could be cast, an arrow arced."

"Do we have any other choice, then, Mine Mas? Will we sit here on the streets of Looftis till high-hillers arrive?"

He put three fingers to his forehead as if to stave off a headache. "I will seat yon next to one driver, then. Do nayat stand," he ordered. "Keep yon seat."

Gathering up the skirting of her gilt, Christine readied herself for the reaction of the crowd—but was unprepared for the reception received. They did not erupt into an excited uproar as expected. There came instead a collective gasp as she descended the steps using Kynneth's hand for balance. This was quickly followed by a hushed silence which traveled through the throngs in an eerie wave. The disconcerting hush followed her as Kynneth guided her to the front of the carriage and up the steps.

She turned, her intentions to seat herself, and the breath left her body at the sight. From such a vantage point, she could see the mass of people, thousands of them, tens of thousands, crammed tightly together, every face turned up to her, every eye riveted upon the blazened-locked Loper of Zeria.

A cool breeze swept through, fluttering the fabric of the ivory gilt she wore and snatching several locks of hair free from their constraints. A flock of birds swept by overhead, those they called ringlings, black as ebony with colorful markings about their necks like rainbow necklaces. They flew without a caw, swooping low to land in a nearby tree where they situated to stare expectantly as well. As the grains slowly sifted through, the unsettling silence grew deafening. It came to her then, what the crowd—and the ringlings—were anticipating. They were waiting patiently for the Loper of Zeria to address them.

Christine summoned her courage and cleared her throat. "Good peoples of Looftis," she spoke, surprised at the strength in her voice, one ringing loud and clear, slicing through the silence like a foghorn, "many thankings on one greeting so grand. Such does touch mine very heart. But it is of great portance we do reach Zeria fore the wintered winds. Yon must part. Allow mine passing through this grand cassing, and I will be thankful."

A whispering murmur swept through the crowd—until one ganis braved a shout. "Is it truths, then? Is yon one Loper of Zeria, same did drop PacMattin?"

An expectant hush fell over the crowd. She could feel the eyes boring into her.

"It is truths," she spoke. "I did send his blackened heart to blackened waters."

The people erupted. "One Loper of Zeria lives," someone shouted, and others followed suit, the chant gathering strength as it traveled through the throngs.

A surreal aura enveloped her as she seated herself and the crowd parted slowly. They continued to chant and cheer, men and women alike, children running alongside and calling out, dogged until she acknowledged them with a nod—their beloved loper, the lita who had dropped PacMattin, ending his reign of terror—a tot-tale come to life, one blazened-locked battler risen from blackened waters.

"This can't be real," she whispered under her breath as she looked from face to face, each plastered with giddy adoration. It was a dream, the misguided wishful dream of a young woman who was ostracized in real life, shunned by all who knew her.

She gave a nod to a group of children who, like the ringlings, had perched themselves high in a tree for a better view. Many of the trees lining the road were occupied as such. People stood crowded upon parked wagons, scattered along rooftops.

"Not real," she whispered as she acknowledged a boisterous group of gawkers who had climbed atop the base of a large statue. She recognized the stoic stance of the stone ganis, knowing his countenance even before it came into view. It was the Leader of Lors standing tall and proud, his hand resting casually upon the hilt of his sword.

The blood turned to an icy sludge in her veins, the breath in her lungs frigid as the wintered winds. How had the Lor of Zeria reacted to the monumental news? Had he leapt upon his silky white pony the very instant it was imparted? Was he barreling toward them at the very grain?

He was. She was certain. As she looked upon his face, one of stone, hard and unyielding, she was certain of one other thing as well. Even if Jerrod Zeria was some figment of a phantom dream, her fear of him was not. It was all too real.

CHAPTER 12

The night's lastsup of coarse with crout was not sitting well within her belly. It churned and rumbled. Once clear of Looftis walls, they had made good progress, the ponies keeping at a fast clip for most of the sol. But as the shadows began to lengthen, they ventured off the main road onto one less traveled, and the going had been slower, the carriage hitching over the fallen branches and dipping into ruts.

Sola had been sleeping several turnings by the time they made camp.

Dahla was especially quiet as she brushed out her hair in preparation for sleeping. She did not like the fact that camp had been set up on the outskirts of Woroff Woodland. She certainly did not appreciate the fact that, when Sola wakened, they would be traveling through such. It was indeed an ominous forest, thick and threatening. Though bereft of leaves, the monstrous trees were tightly packed, their bare tops swaying in unison to the tune of a gusting wind coming constant from the north. Above them, dark, angry clouds sailed swiftly across Luna's full face.

Bixten poked his head out for the third time to call Neema, and a gust of wind snatched his voice away. He pulled the door quickly shut before it, too, could be snatched from him. "I do fear Neema lost," he said with a frown.

"Naya. She does explore the woodland, surent," Christine assured, trying to hide her concern. Neema was a timid sort, not one to stray too far from safety.

Her concerns escalated as she lie awake listening to the howl of the wind that lun. And so it was, when she detected voices beyond the carriage, she gathered the blanket about her shoulders and slipped out into the blustery night.

"Mine Lita," Kynneth shouted over the wind, "yon should nayat be out."

She gave a nod to the newly arrived rider who appeared windswept and haggard.

"One road through the woodland is nayat well-traveled," Kynneth informed her. "I will send two ganist ahead to clear the way. And one Ralling River will need crossing. It is wide, but nayat deep. It should cause naya flustings."

"Did yon note mine hound in yon travelings?" she inquired of the rider, and he shook his head.

Kynneth put an arm around her shoulder to guide her back to the carriage. "One hound did follow one scenting of frii, doubtent," he assured her. "She will return."

"Is it possible the strong winds did cause her to lose the scenting of camp?"

He shook his head. "Do nayat fret on one hound," he advised. "Yon must rest. We do have one long sol's travel on the morrow. I fear the clouds may open soon and so do wish to place one river behind us before such."

He looked weary, a shadowing of growth on his face, his hair tousled by the wind. Yet there was an excited sparkle in his hazel eyes. He was on a mission of great portance—to safely deposit the Loper of Zeria at his brathern's feet.

Stopping beside the carriage, he eyed her curiously. "What is it, Mine Lita?"

Christine swiped at a few unruly curls being tossed by the wind. "What if—," she began, summoning her courage. "What if it is nayat mine wishings to return to one cassing of Zeria?"

Immediately Kynneth became agitated. He guided her closer to the carriage so it might block the wind. "Yon does rightly belong to one Cas of Zeria," he said, leaning close. "Yon was bidded fair. Yon does need protecting on any account. PacMattin did have many followers."

"I can dye mine locks, change mine callen—"

Kynneth threw up a hand to silence her. “One Leader of Lors will decide.”

She felt the blood drain from her face, her knees weaken.

Kynneth pressed his lips thin. “Why does yon hold such fearing of mine brathern? Was this ganis did try to force hisself upon yon, and mine brathern who did nearly rip mine throat for such. He is one ganis of honor, chosen to lead the Lors for his fairness, his kindness.”

“Is it fair to force me to live where I do nayat wish?”

Kynneth squared his shoulders. “Zeria is the grandest cassing in the whole lower region. There is naya other which can protect yon as well. Besides,” he added, “there are many fatings worse than brooder to one Leader of Lors.”

Christine felt the blood rush back to her face with a vengeance. “What!” she gasped, searching his eyes for a hint of humor. “I will never be such!” she insisted as she attempted to push past him.

Her passage was quickly thwarted by an arm positioned against the carriage. With a jaw clinched tight, he leaned close. “I have noted him, Mine Lita,” he spoke, the icy words pushed past gritted teeth. “One ganis more brazened than any other, one grand Leader of Lors. I have noted him skewed at the thought of yon dropping. He did have yon likeness carved to stone, so to stand before it lun after lun, turning after turning, gazing upon his precious blazened-locked loper.”

Gritting her own teeth, Christine shook her head.

“I have noted him reach out to caress one chilled cheek of stone,” he continued, recreating the act with the back of his hand, “have witnessed him lean in, lips to chilled lips…”

She turned her face away from his so close and, like a child, clapped her hands over her ears.

He quickly yanked them down, his eyes like daggers in the darkness. “When next he does lay lips to those of one blazened-locked loper, they will be warmed and welcoming. As Sola shines, they will.”

She shoved past him to scurry back into the safety of the carriage—jumping as he thumped the door behind her with an angry fist.

"As Sola shines, they will!" he trumpeted over the wind.

CHAPTER 13

Less than one turning after they set out, the rumblings began to sound in the distance. Shortly after, the heavens opened, sending down angry squalls, the huge drops drumming loudly on the carriage.

Bixten peered out the window at the trees passing swiftly by, his face long. Neema had not returned, and Kynneth had informed them curtly that a search was out of the question. Dahla's pale face was also turned toward the window, though it was not one hound she meant to catch glimpse of. Worgles were overly on her brain, tot-tale or no.

Having tossed and turned most of the night, Becca was napping fitfully. Cradling her head on her lap, Christine brushed a russet curl from her forehead, feeling skin slightly warm to the touch. She was cutting a tooth and, unfortunately, no Gum-Numb to be found.

She, herself, was no better off. She had not slept well, her dreams haunted by the man she was being delivered to, he chasing her through dark places which seemed to have no end and no exit. She had only nibbled on firstsup, her stomach still sensitive, but what little she did eat sloshed in her belly as the carriage jostled along the rough road.

A loud clap of thunder sounded and a startled Bixten hurried to Dahla's side, jumping up on the seat to pull his legs underneath him. Dahla put an arm around his shoulder, hugging him close. "Does yon think it safe to cross one Ralling with so much rain that does fall?" she asked of Christine.

"I'm certain Kynneth will nayat put us in danger. If the river is high, we will just have to wait for such to go down."

"Once we do cross such, Neema will lose our scenting," Bixten said with a frown.

"Mayhap nayat, mine gani," Dahla said with a squeeze. "Hounds do own overly strong noses. Do they nayat, Mine Lita?"

"Aya, they do," Christine assured him, though she was afraid they had lost Neema for good. The procession was moving at a fast clip, much faster than the rutted road recommended. Much faster than her stomach appreciated. It was churning. And her brain was churning as well.

Closing her eyes, she stroked Becca's hair and tried to concentrate on deep, even breaths.

~~~~~~~~~~

They stopped briefly at midday while the rain was at a lull. A drenched ganis handed in dried crout, seedberries, and slices of soggy bread. The skies showing through the trees were a grievous gray and a constant deep rumbling warned of more rain to come.

And, indeed, the rains did fall, this through most of the day, intermittent squalls coupled with intervals of light sprinkles, a most miserable day seeming to stretch on and on, dampening the mood of all four occupants of the carriage. Becca was of an especially foul mood, falling often into bouts of pathetic whining. The babe was inconsolable, though they all did try.

A flood of relief swept over Christine as finally the carriage pulled to a halt. "Have we reached Ralling River, then?"

Dahla climbed up on her seat to slide open the shout slot. "Have we reached Ralling River, then?" she yelled.

Christine could not discern the muffled reply of the driver.

"Naya," Dahla relayed dejectedly. "One downed tree."

Christine rubbed at her temples. "Mine head aches," she moaned. "Even with one cover-carry halted, I feel as if mine brain does still rattle within."

"Aya, mine as well," Dahla confessed.
~~~~~~~~~~

With a squeaky palm, Bixten wiped away the condensation from the window, and Christine caught snatches of movement past his head—ganist fastening ropes about the downed tree. She felt badly for them so soaked—and also for the ponies, their thick coats surely saturated through. The rain drummed steadily on the carriage roof and the air was damp and nippy within. She could only imagine what it felt like to be soaked to the skin out in the gusting winds.

This notion didn't seem to bother Bixten. He watched longingly through the hazy window, wishing to go out, no doubt, but knowing better than to ask. He was a smart gani with a gentle way about him. She thought sadly of his malla, of her tragic end. The memory made her think of Roltin, another gentle soul. There was an odd aching at the thought of him, a wounded wondering at why he hadn't bothered to see them off. She pictured his last grin, and it brought a bittersweet smile to her face. With a sigh, she tucked the covers in around Rebecca, grateful she had finally succumbed to sleep.

Dahla jumped as a pony screamed out.

"Aiyee!" Bixten's jaw dropped down as his brows shot up.

"What! What is it, gani!" Dahla cried as shouts and whinnying erupted from without the carriage.

Christine clutched at Rebecca as the carriage lurched forward.

"Aiyee!" Dahla cried, erupting into tears. "Is it worgles, gani? Speak, then!"

"One…one pony did take one arrow," Bixten said, his face gone waxen. "Here." He pointed to his thigh.

Christine and Dahla exchanged glances, the poor girl virtually on the verge of vomiting.

A deafening crack of thunder exploded, and the ponies screamed as the wagon lurched forward, the right wheels hitching over the fallen tree with a violent jolt, landing both Bixten and Dahla on the floor. Rebecca awoke with a startle, and Christine clutched her close as the carriage took to flight, pitching left then right. It sideswiped a tree, then another, then slammed into a deep rut before catapulting over something in the path. The door's window shattered, pelting them with shards of glass, and there came a violent collision with another tree, this throwing Christine and Rebecca to the floor.

Scrambling to hands and knees, Christine thrust the wailing Rebecca at Dahla. “Hold her tight!” she screamed to be heard over the careening carriage, one she feared would rattle apart at any moment. She scrambled onto the opposite seat to slide open the shout slot—only to find the forest thundering past as the frantic horses barreled blindly ahead, their ears laid flat, their necks stretched forward—and with no driver to rein them in.

She sized up the slot, a small opening, but surely large enough that a small person might squeeze through.

She looked over her shoulder at Bixten lying on his belly, his arms thrown protectively over his head. He was squalling like a baby. Dahla had the blanket-bundled Becca clutched tightly to her chest, the babe’s cries muffled against her bosom.

Without a second thought, Christine stuck her head through the square. It was the shoulders proved most difficult. Contorting herself, she pulled one through and, for several horrible moments, struggled with the other, thinking herself stuck. With dogged determination, she wriggled the other through, then grasped the driver’s seat, kicking to wrench her hips through. Elation turned to fear as the wagon bucked over a branch, nearly throwing her from the seat. Raindrop pellets pelted her as she maneuvered carefully to the foot-trough to retrieve the fallen reins.

“Whoa, then!” she yelled, emulating the driver’s gruff call as she had heard it repeated so often. Bracing her feet, she leaned all her weight back, pulling against the runaway ponies. But if they felt her efforts, they did not show it. She barked the order again and yet again, desperate as, directly ahead, the trees began to thin and the Ralling River appeared. There were ganist lined along her banks, ganist she did not recognize sitting high upon ponies. They had built a blockade of branches across the crossing.

Realizing the ponies were unable to stop, the ganist scattered in all directions as the carriage barreled toward them. Christine braced for impact, but in a move unexpected, the ponies veered left, the sharp turn nearly toppling the carriage. It listed precariously on two right wheels before skidding to a grinding halt.

The laws of physics, however, played a cruel joke on the railed carriage driver, for inertia sent her sailing, a flailing acrobat flipping head over heels. It was her back which hit the water first, water so cold it sucked the breath from her lungs. She quickly found it again as she buoyed to the surface, the scream already sounding as her head broke through.

In the clutches of a raging monster, she sputtered and flailed, struggling to stay afloat, fighting against the saturated gilt intent on dragging her under. The current swept her blindly along, impelling her swiftly away from the carriage, away from Becca. Floating debris came within reach, a mass of tangled branches. She grasped it, holding for dear life. She detected shouting, just barely over the roaring Ralling. She was being tracked, strange ganist prodding ponies along both banks.

The tree-lined banks rose suddenly to steep cliffs, the terrain thwarting the ponies' passage—yet there was no thrill of triumph. Clinging to her life raft, Christine rode the raging beast as it sheared its way between cliffs of stone and furrowed through the forest.

The beast spun her around and she peered downriver, squinting against the pelting rain, certain she was seeing two bobbing heads, possibly more, amazed the blogarts had jumped in after her. A cry escaped as she was swept around a bend and white water appeared, the rapids rushing past a cropping of bulging boulders littering the river bed. Kicking frantically, she tried to avoid them, but the behemoth kept its tenacious hold.

Numb fingers were stripped of the raft as it shattered against the first boulder, plunging her into the frigid depths. She buoyed sputtering to the surface and was jetted between two boulders, the dip pulling her under again—then yet again. She struggled for breath, for her very life.

Finally, the river leveled out and, seeming to have tired of toying with her, deposited her neatly onto a pebble-strewn shore.

Here she vomited, heaving river water until her sides ached. It was distant shouts which spurred her to action. Waterlogged and shivering, she dragged herself into the dense thicket of trees.

CHAPTER 14

Rain-saturated wind tore through the woodland as the last patches of filtered sunlight faded to darkness. Huddled within a standing hollow tree, Christine hugged her knees to a trembling chest and bit painfully on her bottom lip to keep her teeth from chattering. She was not alone in the cramped confines, and the other inhabitants—blood-red, long-legged, luminescent spiders—wanted her gone. Though her back burned from several bites, she was loath to leave. Terror consumed her at not knowing what had befallen her Becca and Bixten, but the ganist who accompanied her on the harrowing ride down the Ralling were close, searching, snatches of shouting being carried in on the howling wind. She eyed the brush which she'd hastily compiled to conceal the opening, praying it would be sufficient.

A bolt of lightning struck very near and she stifled a yelp. It was fortunate that she held her voice, for a ganis transpired in the flash of brilliance, slinking from the shadows, his drenched clothes clinging to a powerfully built body. Seeming impervious to the pummeling rain, he slowly swiveled his head, methodically sweeping the area for signs of his quarry. He was a dangerous ganis. She read this in his feral stance, in his hardened features, his cruel eyes, these revealed to her in the series of after-flashes that followed. She held her breath as these eyes skipped over her hiding spot.

In the final flash, he was slinking silently away.

~~~~~~~~~~

Time had no substance as she shivered in a blackness darker than any night had a right to be. Though the rains had passed, the
~~~~~~~~~~

wind was gusting, and it was this fact which kept her within the safety of the hollowed hideaway. She was frantic to find her way back to her child, desperate to know she was safe, but she would most certainly freeze to death exposed to the icy winds. Her saturated gilt, torn and tattered by the monster that was Ralling, would offer little protection.

"Please keep the children safe," she whispered, and felt the moisture from her breath turn instantly to ice crystals upon her lips.

~~~~~~~~~~

She stood on the bank of the mighty Ralling, watching as, one by one, the bodies drifted by. Dahla was first, her body rolling like a lazy log to reveal a face frozen in death, half strawberry red, half frog-belly white, her lifeless eyes wide. Bixten was not far behind, his small form face down, his arms thrown wide. And lastly, the small form of a babe, mercifully face down as well, her red hair fanned out in the waters as she was swept swiftly by…

Christine's head jerked up from her knees. Someone had discovered her hiding spot! She tried to focus, her eyes adjusting much too slowly in the dim and misty morning light. A hound. She could just make out its form as it nosed about the barrier of branches with wet snotty snorts. It let out a whine, and a male voice urged it to silence.

The branches were snatched away and Christine could only shiver helplessly as the ganis squatted to peer within. "Christa?"

"Roltin!"

"Come, Christa," he whispered, extending his hand. Grasping her wrist, he pulled her from the hollow, and pain suffused her as frozen limbs unfolded. Numb legs could barely support her weight as she clung to him, his tight embrace forcing tears to her eyes. "Roltin—mine babe—Bixten," she forced out past chattering teeth.

"Safe. Hush, now," he warned, pushing her away to steady her by the shoulders. "The woodland does crawl with ganist."

The hound let out a bark, and Roltin hushed her harshly.
~~~~~~~~~~

"Neema. She was with you, then."

"She did find mine campment."

"Yon did follow mine carry?"

His eyes dropped shyly. "I—did wish to note yon off safely."

Throwing herself at him, she hugged fiercely. "Roltin, I want to stay with you. Please. I don't want to go back to Zeria."

The arms wrapped around her tightened. "Christa. It is—"

There came an odd, muted thud, and a cry escaped her as she was shoved sideways. She saw it for only an instant—the arrow protruding from her recently evacuated tree—before Roltin was propelling her through the underbrush, dragging her by the arm.

On frozen limbs, she stumbled after him, trying not to go down. A ganis came charging from the right with a burly battle cry, his blade upraised, and Roltin efficiently intercepted him with a sword to the sternum.

Roltin swiveled sharply as three more accosted from the left, the four facing off for mere grains before Roltin engaged, locking blades with the closest. The troller put a knee to the man's gut, then spun him about to intercept the blade of his rushing comrade, the thrust meant for Roltin not only dropping his own man, but instantly instigating his own demise, for Roltin dropped him before his weapon could be withdrawn.

"Roltin!"

He jumped backward as the third ganis took a wide-arced swipe at his mid-section, the blade slicing his sodden shirt. With a growl, Neema lunged at the attacker's ankles, and the ganis kicked her away, a minor lapse in concentration that decidedly dropped him, Roltin bringing him down in two deft moves.

Dropping to one knee, Roltin clutched at his belly.

Skirting around the bodies, Christine tried to offer aid, then gasped his name at the amount of blood seeping between his fingers. He shoved her aside and staggered to his feet as another ganis burst through the bushes—

Christine relaxed as she recognized the Rostivanian insignia, the sword and shield sewn into his soaked coat. With blade drawn and readied, the young man surveyed the carnage.

~~~~~~~~~~~

Holding her upper arm in a bruising grip, the battler plowed through the wiry brambles, hacking at the thick undergrowth with his blade.

"Wait!" Christine cried, craning her head around. Roltin had stopped yet again to lean heavily against a tree, his head hanging, his hand clutching at a shirt soaked through with blood. A drenched Neema stood shivering by his side, her tail tucked securely between her legs as the squalling winds whipped the trees about them.

"Mine Lita, we must keep moving," the battler insisted.

"Naya!" she shouted over a bitter gust of wind which snatched the word away, just as she was trying to snatch her arm away from his tight grip.

She screamed as an arrow struck the battler in the back, propelling him forward, his clutching grip unclasping as he was thrown to the ground.

"Run, Christa." Roltin's voice was weak, his face pale as he struggled toward her.

She did as he ordered—but toward him instead of away. She had almost reached him when the arrow streaked in, a sickening thud sounding as it found its deadly mark. He was propelled forward into her arms, and she crumpled beneath him as he collapsed atop, pinning her to the ground. He struggled only briefly, a gurgled gasping—before falling still, his last breath in her ear, the soft whisper of her name.

With a tortured cry, she threw her arms about him, clutching tight, holding him as she had never dared while he held life.
~~~~~~~~~~~

CHAPTER 15

Neema snorted loudly as she nosed at Roltin's still body. She gave a low, threatening growl, then skulked away as two sets of legs approached, heavy boots plodding through the soggy mush of leaves. Christine closed her eyes, gripping tightly to the dagger confiscated from Roltin's boot, keeping it hidden in the folds of her tattered gilt. A numbness had settled over her, this along with a resolute determination.

"If yon did drop the loper, Boskiel will have yon head," a ganis growled.

"Mine tip did find the blogart's heart from nearly one full long," the braggart boasted. "Even with one eye, mine aim is true."

Christine clutched the hilt tightly in a frozen fist as Roltin was rolled off. She sensed someone leaning close, then a hand cupped her chin, turning her face one way, then the other.

A gust of wind whipped through with a whine, and she struck like a snake, silent and swift, driving the blade into his belly. There came a swine-like grunt and he grasped her wrist, twisting till the blade tumbled. Neema began to bark, this the last thing she heard before the blow—like a brick to the side of the head—plunged her into darkness.

~~~~~~~~~~

Muffled voices pulled her from the dark abyss, these becoming more clear as she slowly resurfaced. There was pain at her left temple, and a pounding in her head like a bass drum. And she was bitterly cold. She lie curled on her side on a bed of soggy leaves, her hands bound tightly behind her, these so frozen she could barely
~~~~~~~~~~

detect them. She tried to wriggle her fingers, but was uncertain if she succeeded.

She opened her eyes to a rain-soaked thicket deep in shadow. What could be seen of Sola's smile through the swaying branches was smothered by thick, roiling clouds dark as charcoal. The Rostivanian battler and Roltin lie belly down less than five feet away. The arrows had been removed from their backs—as had the heads from their necks.

Her vision blurred as the abyss tried to claim her yet again—till movement caught her eye—Neema standing hid in the trees, watching warily. As the hound became aware of Christine's wakening, her tail began to wag—and then she was knocked backward with a yelp, her legs coming out from under her as an arrow pierced her chest.

Christine whipped her head around to shriek insanely at the ganis who stood with bow in hand, her garbled obscenities coated with frozen hysteria.

"Ah, yon is wakened then, lita, grand Loper of Zeria," he intoned, his mocking words dripping with sarcasm. He was grinning as he moved near, a dark-haired man with a patch over one eye and a severely pocked face. "Such does please this ganis—as I do wish to hand thankings for mine sliced belly," he said, drawing his foot back.

Christine absorbed the boot's blow, folding herself around it, this act no doubt saving her several broken ribs.

When he drew his leg back yet again, he was shoved roughly aside. "Blogart! Rounds are halved if she is dropped!"

A gust of wind forced its way through the thick underbrush to where she lie struggling for the breath knocked from her by the brutal blow. "What number rounds are offered for me living?" she stammered through chattering teeth, the words slurring past numbed lips. "Lor Zeria will offer five—ten times the number!"

He answered by stuffing a gag into her mouth.

~~~~~~~~~~
~~~~~~~~~~

She rode in front of the ganis, swaying as the pony picked its way through the saturated forest. The rag in her mouth was saturated as well, by saliva. She fought against the urge to vomit. She was also fighting for consciousness as her body shivered violently. The ganis behind her made no attempt to shelter her within the thick coat he wore. Nor did he offer a blanket to block the buffeting winds. The one-eyed monster who rode ahead of them had one such blanket rolled up behind his saddle, unused and taunting her tirelessly. How long she stared at it, she wasn't certain; hours, minutes, seconds. Time lost all concept in a fuzzy, frozen brain.

She blinked, one which must have been much more, for when her eyes opened they were traveling along the river, the sound of the raging waters like a freight train in her ears. Scattered rain was beginning to fall, drops fat as marbles and with near the same force. She listed to the right, then the left, and the ganis riding behind righted her roughly with an angry grumble.

Her eyes drifted to the woodland on the left, to trees swaying and shuddering in the gusting winds. There was movement within. She glimpsed it briefly, a hunched figure scurrying from trunk to trunk. Half huganis, half beast. Somewhere in the distant regions of her brain, a word was trying to take form. It began with a 'w' and ended with an 'le'. The rest eluded her. But she remembered enough to be afraid. Squirming about, she attempted to alert the rider behind, but he only cuffed her head curtly and warned her to be still.

She focused in on the rider in front, he with the bow slung across his back, he with the blanket going unused. He didn't need to use it. He wore a thick coat, one complete with hood. She'd made this hooded ganis angry—had hurt him somehow. He would never give the blanket up! There had been blood—and grunting pigs—and the kind, olive eyes were closed forever—and danger was lurking to the left. It started with 'w' and ended with 'le'—woodslinkle, wasple, wolfle, waffle. Waffles were delicious—deep craters filled with melted butter. And syrup. Waffles needed syrup. Maple. Maple was good—sweet—and the blanket was not being used. Blogart! The dirty rotten one-eyed rat-bastard had killed Roltin! And Neema!

She would stick him, stick him again if given the chance, stick him like the dirty, rotten pig he was!

She eyed the blade nestled in the boot of the leg just behind her own. It would look nice protruding from the one-eyed monster's belly. She pulled against the cord binding her wrists behind her back. The moisture had softened the leather, giving it a bit of elasticity. With a little effort, she loosened it some more.

A frigid blast of air rolled off the river, snatching her breath away and pelting her with an icy mist. She noticed it then. The blanket ahead—having been buffeted by the wind—had unloosed a lock of auburn hair from between its folds. As she watched, an arm flopped out as well, the small, pale limb bobbing stiffly with the rhythm of the horse's gait.

As if sensing her discovery, the hooded figure ahead twisted in the saddle to grin at her. His face had transformed within the shadows of the hood. One small, black, beady eye leered out. A snotty snout glistened. A loud squealing sounded. Coming from the pig face or her own muted screams, she couldn't discern. She began to gag against the rag, choking as violent convulsions wracked her. The world around her was spinning. Wrestling her hands from the loosened cord, she clawed at the gag with one hand—and fumbled for the blade with the other.

CHAPTER 16

The steady sound of the freight train was chugging through her bumbled brain.

Slowly, she opened her eyes to a turbulent sky, charcoal clouds thick with moisture roiling across the heavens.

She was on fire—burning up. The soggy ground beneath her could not even dampen the fierce fire raging within. A supreme will of effort brought her to a sitting position, then staggering to her feet. Her gag was gone. Her hands were free, but they were useless, dangling like dead frozen fish at her sides. A ganis was lying a few yards away. He was face down, one cheek buried in the mossy mush.

A snorting drew her attention—his pony pawing nervously at the ground. The other pony was farther away near the trees. It was riderless as well. And there was danger in the trees—waffles. But this didn't matter. On stiff legs, she lurched forward, her focus on the pony—the one with the blanket being used after all.

Lava coursed through her veins. She needed to tear her clothes off, but the dangling fish lacked the dexterity. She stumbled upon another dropped ganis, this one face up, his one eye wide and vacant. His torso had been flayed from neck to groin, his innards strewn. And his neck had been sliced for good measure. There was blood on the hair of his chinny chin chin. The waffle had stuck the little piggy and that was fine—waffles were sweet with strawberries. Dahla had strawberries on her face and she was sweet—and Bixten—and Becca—Becca bundled in a blanket.

She focused on the pony, the black pony with the blonde mane, the pony which didn't want her near, for with every lurching step she took, it moved further away. The heavens opened up, the driving drops pelting her, trying to knock her off balance. They instantly turned to marbles of ice, these bouncing off her frozen flesh. Hollow thunks sounded in her head as they collided with her skull.

The pony hurried off into the cover of the trees.

There were waffles in the trees.

Still, she followed.

Naked treetops churned in the storm. Ice marbles dropped all about but with less force, their fall being broken by the branches overhead. One of these branches came crashing down, a limb large enough to kill spearing the ground to her left. The dead fish flopped as she lumbered onward on legs like pillars of ice. She had lost all feeling in these pillars and so was not surprised when one went out from under her and she went down like a felled tree plummeting back to the earth. Soggy leaves embraced her like long lost children. She reveled in the pungent, earthy smell. It reminded her of a different place—a pond—sun dappled like sparkling diamonds. Lazy ducks paddling, lazier turtles sunning. Velvety cattails rustling—clouds like giant white doves soaring high in the heavens.

"Heavens." She was surprised to hear her own voice, surprised further when she was rolled to her back.

A hazy face hovered close, a dark blur fading in and out.

"Hello, waffle," she breathed.

CHAPTER 17

Moaning wafted in from a distant land, low and constant and pitiful. It was accompanied by a horrific throbbing, a painful pounding in her head. As consciousness slowly seeped in, so did the pain—piercing pins and needles in her feet and hands. She moved one foot, and cried out as stabbing pain shot up her leg.

There was shuffling close by, and a shadow crossed her lids. She lifted these lids, blinking her dimly-lit surroundings into focus—a small room, one piled high with clutter. She lie on a small bed, wrapped in a cocoon of blankets. Rocks the size of grapefruits outlined her body. They had been heated, the warmth emanating from them thawing her frozen limbs beneath the blankets.

A different blanket came to mind, the image rising like a wisp of mist from the deep recesses of a foggy brain. This blanket cocooned a body as well, a small body with russet curls and a tiny alabaster arm.

A tortured cry wrenched its way from her parched throat—one cut short as a horrific figure popped into her line of vision. Momentarily, her plight was forgotten at the sighting of a creature so hideous it could barely be conceived as human. He was squat with a body direly deformed, every joint twisted at odd angles. But it was the face which startled her most, one monstrously malformed; a mass of crooked teeth crammed into a mouth too small, sunken eyes set much too deep and hid beneath folds of pale, fleshy flaps of skin that served as a forehead. A broccoli nose was smashed flat so that the oversized nostril florets nearly reached to protruding cauliflower ears which were much too small.

He put a gnarled finger to the toothy maw, and foam flew as he shushed her. “Yons will wakened one babe,” he hissed in a moist voice, each word coated with spittle.

The pounding in her head intensified and the pins and needles stabbed angrily as she squirmed beneath the binding blanket, craning her neck to see where the creature was pointing. She spied the crude crib of boughs against the far wall.

"Mine babe, she does sleep, then?" Her high-pitched voice was strangely muted over the pounding in her ears.

The creature became instantly incensed. Hopping in place, he growled moistly and clenched his fists, pounding them against his thighs in a tight tantrum. "Mineseth! Mineseth!" he hissed, the spittle-foam flying. "Tries to stelcher mineseth babe, this lita will rips yons throated wide, bligart!"

"Lita?" Christine asked incredulously, momentarily losing focus—but it quickly honed back in. "Rebecca!" she screamed, flinging aside the blankets. Several large rocks bounced to the floor, and the waffle did an odd disjointed jig to avoid them.

Christine ignored the stabbing pain as she scrambled from the bed and staggered across the room. With a hoarse cry, she stumbled the last few steps. Catching herself on the crib railing, she clutched tightly as she peered with horror at the child bundled within. The head was all that was visible, the babe's body swaddled as it was. Blackened, mummified skin clung to sunken cheeks and empty eye sockets. The jaw had come unhinged, the tiny mouth wrenched wide in an eternal wail.

A hollow thud sounded in Christine's right ear, a sound both innocuous and ominous at once. It was a sound in need of her attention. With great effort, she forced her eyes away from the long dead babe to find a knife blade embedded in her right hand, skewering it to the crib's rail. At the sight, a bolt of blinding pain shot to her shoulder.

Before a scream could form, a matching thud sounded to her left. Unlike the first, the pain of this second infliction was instantaneous. Throwing her head back, she howled. And not for the pain of two skewered hands—but the skewering of any hope for her beloved babe.

The waffle was growling, the moist menacing sound

reverberating through the room. "Mineseth nexted blade will rips off yons head!" it growled from behind, and Christine heard a blade being slid from its scabbard. "Yons willed nayat stelcher mineseth babe!"

A frightening vision was flung to forefront, her own mummified body sitting eternally in a dark corner of the godforsaken room.

With a hoarse howl, she grasped the rail firmly with two skewered hands and swung the crib around, hurtling it toward the hissing waffle who tried to shuffle backward. The creature toppled with an angry snarl, and the sword meant to behead Christine went clattering across the floor. The waffle shrieked as the crib—with Christine attached—overturned on top of her. She shrieked even louder as the bundled babe tumbled from the crib, its head detaching and rolling along the floor like a warped bowling ball.

Blinding bolts of pain shot through Christine, forcing out screams, the blood-chilling cries reverberating about the room. Her vision cleared for a brief moment to the waffle pinned beneath the crib. She was spitting and sputtering like a wildcat caught in a snare, twisted arms flailing and gnarled fingers clawing at the rail pressed against her throat. The huge florets were flaring as they tried to pull in air, and the folds of forehead flesh had fallen back to reveal beady eyes wide with panic, one set much higher than the other, and both bulging oddly. There was blood splattered on the hideous face—her own, she realized, her pierced hands raining crimson drops. A ringing sounded in her ears, drowning out the sputtering wildcat, and the scene began to fade. As in an old film, the edges turned fuzzy—working slowly toward the center—till all was blackness.

CHAPTER 18

The wicked waffle was dead.

Lying atop the crib which lie atop the waffle, Christine was forced to face closely the face of a monstrosity. As she looked down upon a face unmercifully deformed—one with eyes wide and empty—a sob erupted, wrenched violently from deep within, a precursor to the torrent of sobs which followed, her chest hitching and shuddering. As she wept, anger seeped in, an emotion with which she was far more familiar. Fueled by this fury, she righted the crib, wrenching it to its legs, howling as the wounds in her hands re-awakened with a vengeance. As her tormented body tried to crumple, she gripped tightly to the rail, howling even louder as fresh waves of pain pummeled her.

"Aya!" she screamed, throwing her face upward. "Make me suffer, you fucking bastard! For Becca!" Taking in as much air as her lungs could hold, she screamed for as long as she could—till all that issued forth was a thin, squeaky hiss. Still, she pushed until patches of fog rolled before her vision.

The door burst open, and a cold blast of air buffeted her in the face, forcing her to draw in breath, a sharp painful intake.

The dim outline of a tall figure stooped and entered cautiously, his sword held out before him.

~~~~~~~~~~

They were Zerian battlers, the face of Sola embroidered upon their thick coats. They were drenched and shivering and ill-at-ease huddled within the cramped confines. None dared approach her, the group of eight hovering close to the door as they gaped at the
~~~~~~~~~~

skewed lita skewered to the crib. It seemed they gaped for eternity—or perhaps merely grains.

The trembling had slowly subsided in her limbs, the screaming pain dying to a meager moan as numbness settled in. She knew for whom they waited. He was close. She could feel him. A palpable presence was approaching, one pulsating with power. It was in her head, like a giant drum beating. She lifted her numb gaze to the Zerian battlers, and they fidgeted uncomfortably.

"Is yon—one Loper of Zeria?" one braved.

She sighed heavily. "What do you think, ganis?"

"Why then, Mine Lita, is yon hands so pierced?"

She looked to the impaling daggers. They were beautiful weapons, a matching pair, the hilts dappled with stunning jewels. She drew in breath, pulling it deep within before releasing it as a shuddering sigh. "I must suffer," she whispered, "for the babe."

"But, Mine Lita," he spoke softly, "one babe—one babe is dropped."

The drum in her head beat ardently. "Aya—and so—I must suffer." She felt a fist squeeze her heart, for it was there true suffering endured. Lifting her chin, she faced the men squarely. "As one Loper of Zeria, I do order that yon drop me down and so end mine suffering."

Eight Zerian battlers fidgeted uncomfortably.

She drilled the ganis whose sword haft still rested in his hand. "Drop me this grain, ganis," she ordered.

"I can nayat, Mine Lita," he replied hastily. Shifting his weight, he pointed the blade at the dead crumpled creature. "What is this?"

She could not bear to look at the pathetic being. "Waffle," she replied softly.

It struck her then—the absurdity, and she began to giggle, one which quickly built. Throwing her head back, she laughed heartily, the eerie sound echoing oddly about the room. And as the brave battlers cowered, she laughed harder still, laughter commingled with bitter sobs. Mercy would not be meted at the hands of these cowards. She was forsaken.

She dropped her chin to her chest, noticing for the first time that she wore a man's shirt, one unbuttoned to the belly, exposing an immodest portion of cleavage. She was swollen with milk—and Becca was dead.

She closed her eyes tightly, squeezing out hot tears. The pounding had extended beyond her head. The room was a giant drumhead, a steady, deafening beat. Not so loud, however, she could not hear shouting sound from beyond the door.

Instantly, she sobered, steeling herself as the door was thrown wide and the battlers shuffled aside. Clasping firmly to the crib railing, she faced him as he came before her, a caped figure so very tall his head did nearly graze the ceiling.

He towered before her, water dripping from the slick cape he wore. He had ridden hard. His breaths were deep as his eyes were sharp. They left her briefly, scanning the room, taking everything in in an instant. Lastly, they fell on the twin daggers holding her in place.

"Naya," she warned as he made to move toward her, the word difficult to force out through air thick with power. "I must—" She struggled to clear her thoughts, for they were being overrun by the overpowering presence pulsating through the room, through her very being. "I must suffer—for Becca." She broke at the mention of the name, the wracking sobs nearly buckling her knees, the tears blinding.

She felt him then, behind her, pressing close to slide one arm about her waist. "Yon has suffered enough, Mine Lita," he breathed into her ear—before wrenching the first blade free.

CHAPTER 19

"Daddy." Pain, like a living entity, pulsated through her ravaged body. "It hurts!"

"Ten grains and it is done." He rocked her gently, his warm embrace comforting.

Clinging to him, she buried her face into his neck. "Don't leave me. Take me—take me with you."

"Aya," he whispered, stroking her hair lovingly.

"Mine babe," she wept, burying her face deeper.

"Aya. She does wait," he promised.

"Yes," she breathed weakly.

"Sleep now." Pain screamed out as he laid her down. Leaning over, he placed a gentle kiss on her forehead, then another on one tear-moistened cheek, then the other. "If there is anything yon does wish, Mine Lita," he whispered in a voice which did not belong to her father, "yon need only ask and I will give it."

She opened her eyes to the face of the Lor of Zeria mere inches from her own. "Give me back mine babe, then," she whispered weakly.

"She does wait." It was her father again, his face aglow, radiant with a loving light.

"Don't leave me," she breathed. "Don't leave." Her voice seemed distant, a faraway humming in a dream newly taking shape.

"I will nayat," he promised, a whisper from worlds away. "Nayat ever again."

~~~~~~~~~~
~~~~~~~~~~

The sun was a blistering blaze. It pulled the moisture from her skin. It parched her throat. She drank of the blackened waters, gulping, drowning a thirst which would not be quenched. An ugly undertow tugged at her. She kicked desperately against it, but it claimed her all the same, dragging her downward, down to dark tunnels, scraping her angrily against jagged walls of stone.

The tunnels held death. It drifted eerily wearing faces like the underbellies of dead fish, pale and bloated. A scalped Myurna drifted by, her curvaceous body creped in a crimson gilt. Larid followed, his skull staved in most horribly—then Tasta, morbidly mangled, one arm missing, splintered bone jutting from one leg where it was severed at the thigh. Roltin's head drifted by, his olive eyes turned white with film. The heads of Bocksard, Shyla, and Tallia passed one by one, each in a slow mesmerizing roll. Dahla came next, her birthmark gone pale in death. She was clasping Bixten's small hand, and he in turn clasped a smaller hand, their tiny fingers interlaced.

Christine's screams were drowned out, strangled by thick blackened waters…

With a cry, she sat up in the bed, sending her head to spinning. The room came into focus; dark, windowless—clutter piled against the walls. The waffle was gone. The spot where she died had been cleared, as had the mummified babe, the crib pushed off to one side.

Something was dripping—constant, irritating—a tap in need of tightening. Slowly, her eyes adjusted to the dimness, the only light the smoldering of embers at the fireplace to her right. Situated a few feet from the hearth, a vessel sat catching water dripping from the ceiling. She held up her hands for inspection, each bandaged snugly, thin stripes of crimson bleeding through.

"Rebecca." With the thin utterance of the name, the breath caught in her throat, lodging firmly. She struggled to dislodge it, gasping and hitching until finally it was released as a wrenching sob, the first of many shuddering sobs that followed. When all were spent, she sat weeping weakly.

She was alone, she realized. Alone in the room. Alone in the world that was Atriia. Her eyes moved to the grouping of weapons laid out upon the cluttered table; bows, arrows, swords, daggers. She recognized two of these last.

Numbly, still weeping silent tears, she pulled back the covers to thin legs jutting from a man's shirt. Even as thin as they were, it took great effort to swing them over the side of the bed, greater effort to stand upon feet wrapped thickly in several pairs of slips. The pain seemed distant as she shuffled toward the daggers so captivating her attention.

She reached out to trail her fingertips along them. They were stunning, the masterfully honed blades seeming to give off a radiant sheen in the darkness. Jewels inset on the hilts were giving off a dazzling glow; ruby red, amethyst, turquoise, amber. There was an olive-hued jewel matching closely the color of Roltin's eyes. There was a jewel casting a shimmering refraction of a deep sapphire blue—Becca blue.

The steady plop of water drops echoed about the room. She lifted one dagger delicately, casting a dappling of shimmers along the ceiling and walls—then placed the blade against one slender wrist. She squeezed her eyes shut, the amplified dripping ricocheting in her head like a stray bullet.

A different sound forced her eyes to open again, the scrabbling of tiny feet—not a roggi—a tippet trotting across the wooden table. It seemed impossible that feet so small could produce such a ruckus, like a hundred horses thundering through the room. Seeming to suddenly spot her, it stopped in mid-step to stand stock-still, as if this act would render it invisible.

It bolted suddenly as the door flew open. A fog of chilled air entered, along with a bearded ganis lugging an armful of firewood. Like the tippet, he froze at the sight of her. Behind him, a taller man appeared, the Leader of Lors, his soaked hair clinging to his face. He nudged the man-mouse aside, keeping his eyes glued to her as he carefully deposited a line of dangling fish to the floor. "Mine Lita," he breathed, straightening to his full height. "Yon—yon is safe now. Yon suffering is ended."

She scoffed at this, almost laughed. "I will suffer every grain—of every sol. Becca—" Her voice broke, and she felt her mind do the same. Her body followed suit, a moment of weakness, one which the Lor seized, for he was upon her in an instant, sending the deadly dagger clattering to the floor.

With a growl, she struggled against him.

Grasping both her wrists, he drilled her with hardened eyes. "Yon would take yon own life and leave yon babe with naya malla?"

She grimaced at the pain shooting up her arms—and through her heart. "Babe? Mine babe is dead! Dropped!"

The face hovering so close softened, his eyes searching. "Yon babe is safe, Christa."

"No!" Breaking a hand free from his grasp, she pummeled the liar, a beating which sent pain screaming up her arms and into her boggled brain.

He restrained her with caution. "Christa, she is safe at Cas Woroff—she, one gani, one lita with the marked face."

"Untruths," she wept, ceasing her struggles. "I saw her…" She pictured it—the blanket, the hair blowing in the breeze. "Yon own ganist—same did speak mine babe was dropped."

The man-mouse stepped forward and cleared his throat. "Mine Lita, I think they did speak of one babe on the flooring, one babe long dropped."

"But—I saw her."

With a gentle finger, the Lor slid the hair from her eyes. Trailing the finger down to her chin, he lifted her face to his. "Christa, yon was bit by toskins. Such poisoning can skew one's brain. Yon babe is safe. She does wait in one cassing of Woroff for her malla to return."

There was water dripping somewhere. It seemed so far away. "She does wait?" She felt herself sway.

He scooped her up to settle her gently on the bed, then knelt beside, the corners of his lips curved slightly in a half grin. It *was* a pleasant mouth. It was more than pleasant. It was beautiful, the most beautiful mouth she had ever seen. It claimed her Becca was safe. She believed the beautiful mouth. It spoke again, glowing, golden words spilling out, thick and sweet like honey.

"She does wait, mine Christa."

She fought fatigue with every fiber of her being, unforgiving fatigue which flummoxed her thoughts. She wanted to kiss the beautiful mouth that would speak her Becca was safe, to drink in the honey, to twirl it on her tongue. The mouth moved close and she felt the sweetness on her cheek, warm and comforting.

"Safe," she breathed, this no longer a question.

CHAPTER 20

The shivers would not subside. She was frozen upright, her unlimber limbs set rigidly as she sat the tall pony. The only spare blanket was occupied. She kept her eyes glued to it, trying to blink away the rain. Something had fallen from the folds and was tossing in the howling wind. A babe's cry hurtled past on a strong gust—or perhaps just the cry of the wintered winds. The dripping was constant somewhere beyond the chattering of her teeth. She sputtered and choked on the hot liquid poured down her throat.

"She does need one blasted meshganis!"

She could see the beautiful mouth which spoke, though just barely, her rain-filled eyes refusing to focus. "Mine babe," she pushed out through clinched chattering teeth.

"Shh." He placed a hand of fire on her forehead, this sending her to violent shivers. The dripping seemed overly loud in her ears, louder even than the wintered winds howling as a pack of wolves at a full-faced moon. Shards of frozen rain swirled through the room like a swarm of angry hornets—stinging, stinging…

His hands were blistering her frozen skin.

"Burns," she moaned, the word barely audible over the howling wolves.

He lie heavy atop like a blanket ablaze, molten hands on icy skin, caressing urgently.

"Battle, mine Christa." They were honey-coated words, sticky sweet and warm on her lips.

She threw her arms about his neck, ignoring the pain as she pulled him down, desperate to drink of the sweet warmth. But he allowed her only a small sampling before forcing her away.

"Hannen," she wept, a breathless plea. "Mine pale nipper—mine pony. Danger! Waffles! Wolves! Wildhounds! Woodslinks! Becca!"

He held her tight, constraining her convulsions, breathing warm words at her ear. "Becca is safe, Christa. Safe."

~~~~~~~~~~

She released the breath slowly, a long contented sigh, then opened eyes to embers glowing warmly in the fireplace. A quiver with jetting arrow shafts lie propped beside the hearth, the bow resting adjacent. They belonged to Robin Hood. He lie behind her on the small bed, his breaths long and deep in sleep, the heat pouring from him where he pressed tightly against her. One arm lie draped over her hip, his hand resting lightly upon her bare belly. She was unclothed beneath the blankets, a fact which did not distress her as it might have.

A small movement caught her attention—Mickey Mouse as he went scurrying past. He had saved her life with his clunky clodhoppers.

He stopped midway and stood up to peer at her, his nose twitching, and she grinned at the sight of his huge ears. He returned her grin and waggled his fingers, then fell back to all fours and dashed off.

She closed her eyes, listening to the merry crackling at the fireplace, feeling warm and safe in his arms. All was well. Mickey was keeping vigil, Robin was sleeping soundly, and Rebecca was safe. Becca was waiting.
~~~~~~~~~~

CHAPTER 21

A delectable aroma pulled her from a dreamless sleep. A man sat by her bedside, long legs stretched out, the stool being much too short for his large frame. He was terribly handsome, brown wavy hair falling to broad shoulders, and a half grin raising the corners of a beautiful mouth. Her stomach grumbled, this lifting the corners of his mouth higher yet. The smile carried to his eyes, these glowing bright in the dim lighting.

"Yon did battle brazenly," he said, his deep voice echoing strangely.

Her eyes traveled about the small, windowless room, over the stacks of supplies piled against walls of stone. The ceiling was stone as well and very low. In one corner, giant tree roots reached down like groping fingers.

"What—" The word cracked, coming from a mouth dry as cotton.

He rose, pulling the water flask from the table. "The boarding is built into the heart of one hill," he explained as he poured water into a mug. She grimaced at the pain as he helped her to a sitting position. Holding the mug to her lips, he helped her to drink. "It can nayat be noted from the outer side. We would still be in searching," he admitted, "if nayat guided by the jelt hound."

Christine pushed the mug from her lips. "Neema?"

He nodded. "Pierced by one arrow," he said, motioning to his chest. "But the head did nayat dig deep. She was taken to Cas Woroff with the others."

She felt her eyes moisten at the news. "Thankings to Sola."

He grinned his half grin, and Christine found her eyes oddly drawn to his lips. Only with some effort did she drag them up to the hazel eyes studying her curiously. It came back to her then, his body on top of her, his hands like fire on her skin, his mouth on hers. Feeling suddenly uncomfortable, she quickly scanned the room.

"We are alone," he offered, reading her thoughts much too easily. "I did send Reesal after one meshganis."

She looked at her bandaged hands and winced as she wriggled her fingers.

"It was nayat yon hands did worry this ganis. Yon was bit by toskins, several times over, and did have one strong reacting to such."

She nodded. "The hollowed tree. Mine back."

He frowned. "Toskins are small in sizing, but own strong poisonings. With so—"

"Roltin," she cried out suddenly, the horrid memory flooding in. "The Troller Kaltica! Was he—did I imagine that, as well?" She scoured his face, desperately searching for any signs of hope, but all she received was a stony stare.

"Christa, yon must think on yon babe."

She tried to stifle the sob, one that tangled in her throat. "Take me to her! Take me at once!"

He shook his head. "There will be naya travelings while the wintered winds blow."

"We must! Yon ganist did travel in the wintered winds!"

"Aya. Strong, abled ganist."

"But, mine babe—"

"Is in good care," he finished, stopping her protests short. "Yon is poisoned, yon hands ripped, yon feet froze." His face softened somewhat as her belly grumbled. "And yon is overly railed and weakened. I did make coarse with swill. Mine scullery skills are of limit, but it will fill yon belly."

~~~~~~~~~~

It was rare to catch him sleeping. He'd made a bed on the floor in front of the fireplace, close to the glowing embers. As he lie so
~~~~~~~~~~

peaceful in slumber, it was difficult to imagine why he had instilled such terror in her heart. He had been thoughtful, leaving her to mourn in peace till she could mourn no more. And the hands that spooned the coarse to her mouth had been gentle, her own hands refusing to cooperate with the unwieldy utensil. His touch had been tender as he'd administered to the wounds, unwrapping her hands to soak them in tepid water, then slathering them with salve so to wrap them again.

She listened to his deep and steady breaths, watching as his chest rose and fell. His features in repose were resplendent, the lines straight and strong, the cheeks and chin chiseled. And there was something formidably sensual about his mouth—the way it had downed lastsup with an almost primal relish. His was a mouth designed for devouring.

She willed her eyes away, running them the length of the wall, studying the stelch, the booty the worgle had stolen from her victims. And it seemed there had been many. Chests, saddles, satchels, travel sacks, saddlebags, footings, and clothing layers deep lined the walls clear to the ceiling.

As she assessed the leaning tower of stelch, a furry tippet crept from the shadows, tiptoeing timidly. It pushed to its hind legs, and the ridiculously oversized ears—more befitting of an elephant—raised to high alert. It put its nose to the air and long whiskers bobbed as it sniffed for remnants of lastsup. Dropping to all fours, it folded its ears neatly back against its body and scurried under the table.

With a sigh, Christine rolled to her back, taking in the ceiling of solid stone. It seemed to be a cozy cave of a home, one that held warmth well. If she listened closely, she could just make out a whisper of the wintered winds drifting down the natural chimney. It was obviously a dwelling dug deep.

Once again, her lids grew heavy as a deep weariness seeped in. She rolled one last time, putting her face to the soft glow of the fireplace and the man who slept so soundly before it. As sleep settled over her, she gazed through half-mast lids upon him, the beloved Lor of Zeria, the legendary Leader of Lors. The most powerful man in Atriia was by her side. Kynneth was a bastard, but he was right. She needed protecting. His brathern meant to keep her safe, she and Becca and Bixten. And if there was one ganis in all of Atriia who was capable of such, it was he.

CHAPTER 22

The dark and deserted halls of Cas Zeria were alive with shifting shadows. They fumbled for her as she fled, a flurry of frantic fingers snatching at hair, at her gilt as she stumbled forward. She dared not look back. He was close. She could feel his presence, one thick and oppressive, pressing down on her. He meant to devour her, and in a most primal and unforgiving fashion. Her screams for mercy would go unheeded, for he was the Lor of the cas. And as such, was much more familiar with the different passages. She had come to a dead end, a lavish room designed for banquets. There would be no turning back.

She sought refuge behind a long panel of drapery in the corner where darkness was deepest. With a heart that pounded, she watched the long shadow appear in the threshold, this followed closely by the foreboding figure, he who claimed the title Leader of Lors. He was terribly tall and draped in a cloak which fell to his feet, a dark devon stalking the damned.

He came to a halt just within the entrance, and his eyes—cold and hard as shiny black stones—swept the room. They fell upon the statue, the very fashioned after his cornered quarry. He approached it, a frown furrowing his brow as he pondered on the hardest of stone chiseled to resemble the softest of flesh. Stepping close, he ran a fingertip along one cheek, then over to lips parted prettily. A pained pining etched his pallid features as, ever so slowly, he leaned in with a mouth designed to devour.

No!

Though it was a word uttered only in her mind, the cloaked figure swiveled toward her, his attention drawn as if shouted aloud.

She knew flight would be futile, his formidable frame thwarting any fanciful hope of such. The wall of stone at her back became a splintered block of ice, working thousands of searing shards into her flesh. She shivered at his approach, the strides slow and deliberate—a predator stalking prey.

She closed her eyes against a dream too horrible to bear.

"Christa," he whispered, his words wisping in from fathoms away.

~~~~~~~~~~

With a gasp, she opened her eyes. His was pressed against her to restrain her struggles, his face hovering mere inches away.

"Christa," he spoke firmly, snapping her from panic—and slowly the dim room came back into focus.

He ran his fingertips down her cheek. "Yon is fevering again."

"Naya. I—it was lundevons," she explained, forcing the breathless words past the terrified lump in her throat. She slid her eyes about the room, looking everywhere except into the eyes that would see too much. She saw his bedding had been pushed to one corner. The fire had been fed and was flaming brightly.

"Am I yon lundevon?" he asked.

With a deep sigh, she faced him, a face entirely too close, the smallest hint of mischief playing at the corners of his mouth.

"Yon is short of breathing," he teased. "Did yon flee from one foul lundevon, then?"

That he found amusement in her discomfort was irksome. "I can nayat breathe with yon lying heavy as one shike atop."

An almost full grin surfaced, one fleeting, before his face turned suddenly somber. "Yon does tremble as one tippet," he whispered, his tone turning tender, as was the finger that slid a lock of dampened hair from her forehead. "Yon must know this ganis would nayat ever force hisself upon yon."

The room seemed uncommonly hot as he delved with eyes lit by dancing flames. The air seemed thick and heavy, the breaths difficult to pull in. An unsettling shift in mood had come over him, his hazel
~~~~~~~~~~

eyes turning serious in the flames that flickered. Shadowy silhouettes danced silently about the room as she struggled to draw in breath.

"Did PacMattin force hisself upon yon? Is the babe his, then?"

The question more than startled her. It horrified her. "Naya! Mine Becca does nayat belong to that devon! He did nayat lay one foul finger on me!"

This seemed to be the answer anticipated. "She belongs to Fallier, then."

Shock snatched her breath away and, despite the shame flooding, she could not force her eyes away from those lit with an impassioned intensity.

It was he who looked away first. Pulling back, he seated himself on the edge of the bed. "It was yon thinking I did nayat know of yon affair with Fallier? It was clear yon did lie hid in rolled tenting." He gave a halfhearted grin at the look on her face. "I did come in search only for show. I did note yon flee to one carry of one fraigen dropper. It was yon wishings to be with Fallier," he said, a pained shadow briefly veiling his face, "and so I did allow such. But nayat ever again," he swore, his eyes turning cold. "As Sola shines, if Fallier does ever again make attempts to come near yon, I will slice his throat ear to ear."

A chill coursed through her as visions of another throat flashed into her memory, one pale and slender. He had taken Myurna's life without hesitation, had sliced her throat wide and stood watching, stone-faced, as she'd drowned in her own blood.

Struggling for breath, Christine tried to blink back the tears. "Yon does know he lives, then?"

His expression remained icy. "Was this Lor did send for one meshganis. But I will reclaim the life I saved if ever he does—"

"Please, Mine Lor, do nayat harm him!" Frustration flooded at a voice so thin and trembling. She felt hot tears slip from the corners of her eyes, though this did not warm the cold eyes piercing her. "He will come for me. As Sola shines, he will. But yon must send him away. I do nayat wish to lay eyes upon him, nayat ever again."

Leaning close, he grasped her face between two palms, holding her gaze firmly. “Did Fallier force hisself on yon?”

“Naya!” she swore with a vehemence which left no room for question.

He pulled back, his face hardened. “I will nayat allow Fallier to bring harm to yon again.”

“He did nayat! He would never bring harm to me! It is yonself will do such, should yon harm him.”

The line of his jaw flexed and his eyes flashed as he leaned close, pressing hands into the mattress at either side of her shoulders. “The blogart did allow yon to fall into the hands of one devon.”

She tried to steel herself against his proximity, one entirely too close. “As was mine fating. So same devon could be dropped by mine hand. Was such nayat how the tale was told, then?”

“Aya,” he breathed, his manner softening. “Only then would one battler return to waters blackened,” he recited, his eyes pouring over her face. “I did with mine own eyes note such. So—how is it yon does nayat lie in the dried dung of fifty foul fraigens, mine dearest Christa? How is it yon does, in the stead, lie neath me on this bunker?” It seemed his own words brought to his attention their intimate position, for his fire-lit eyes dropped to her lips, only to drift back dark and smoldering. His mouth hovered dangerously close, terrifying and tantalizing at once.

“Naya!” she snapped as he leaned in, the frantic word stopping him short.

He scoured her face with eyes that blazed. “Yon lips do speak naya, mine Christa, but yon eyes do speak differed.”

She narrowed the eyes of which he spoke. “Lay lips to mine, Mine Lor, yon will find them colder than any stone carving.”

His reaction was subtle—fleeting surprise—then there was only pain in his hazel eyes as he pulled away. Rising, he moved to brood before the dancing fire.

Immediately, she regretted revealing her knowledge of such intimate indiscretions. She sat up, resting her bandaged hands in her lap and her feet firmly on the cold stone floor as dizziness doused her. “Apologies, Mine Lor.”

“The blood does run through yon body, lita, is cold as any

fraigen's," he spoke to the flames. "Mayhap such is mine answer, then. I did, with mine own eyes, note yon jump into waters brimmed with the foul creatures. Yon did nayat surface again." A dark look over his shoulder warned off any attempt at denial. "It is spoken there are those can shift their form."

Christine brushed aside a dampened curl with the back of a bandaged hand. "Does yon gest I did shift into one fraigen, Mine Lor?"

"Mayhap. And mayhap yon did shift into one tippet, as well, so to hide within the walls of Zeria, so to lope upon its Lor."

"Naya. Was Kynneth di—" She felt herself sway—and immediately he was at her side.

He laid her gently down, pressing his palms to her cheeks, then her forehead. "Fevering," he whispered, his frown laced with worry.

~~~~~~~~~~

Hidden amongst the reeds, she lie in silky waters, eyeing the ganis on shore. He sat tall and valiant upon a white pony, its mane whipping in the gusting breeze. He was the Lor of Zeria, his legs long, his shoulders broad, his posture regal where he sat on high. He searched the waters, his eyes roving over the glassy dark surface.

"Come forth, mine Christa," he spoke in a deep, commanding voice. "Do nayat fear this ganis." His pony dropped its head to paw the ground, snorting nervously. "I have brought one gifting, mine Christa."

The gift he spoke of knelt beside the pony, his head bowed—Sam, his hands bound behind his back.

The Lor dismounted and drew his blade. Grasping a fistful of hair, he lifted Sam's head. Her gifting had been horribly beaten, his face swollen, his nose broken and bloodied.

"Come, mine Christa."

He meant to slice his throat, to rip it ear to ear. She tried to shout to him, but her toothy maw would not cooperate. Propelling with her tail, she slid through the reeds, a silky slithering—though her body turned cumbersome as she lumbered onto shore.
~~~~~~~~~~

"Aya, mine Christa. Come and sup," he said as he drew the blade across his throat…

She came awake with a moan. Her body was soaked, the sleep-shirt clinging. A raging fire consumed her. She was strangling, struggling to pull breath into scorched, soot-sodden lungs. He sat over her, worry etched plainly on handsome features.

"Mine Lor," she croaked, her breathless words stinging a blistered throat. "Please don't harm him."

He shushed her as he adjusted the rag draped across her forehead.

She grasped his wrist, clutching it tight. "Do nayat harm him! Promise me!"

"I will nayat harm him."

"Swear it! Swear it on Sola!"

"As Sola shines," he promised. He fumbled with the sweat-soaked shirt, peeling it over her head, the cool air hitting her dampened skin causing painful bumps to surface. The sensation was unsettling, as a body covered in scales.

"It is truths, Mine Lor. I did shift into one fraigen." She moaned as the cool cloth made contact with her shoulder and slid down one arm. The heat in the room was distorting the air, warping his face. "I will nayat sup on mine brathern. I will starve first. I love him." Somewhere in the distance, she thought she heard the giggle of a small child. "Becca?"

"Aya, Christa," he spoke, his voice distorted as well. "Battle for yon Becca. Battle, mine Christa."

~~~~~~~~~~

Cold.

A shiver ravaged her, rattling reason.

She opened her eyes, allowing them to adjust to the darkness. The last remnants of embers were glowing warmly at the fireplace. There was movement in the darkness. Roltin came into her line of
~~~~~~~~~~

vision. He held several blankets. One by one, he shook them out before draping them over her. They had been warmed by the fire. He leaned in to place a palm against her forehead and cheeks, his touch warm against her clammy skin, his olive eyes warmer yet.

"Roltin," she whispered as the warmth of his gaze traveled through her like a gentle wave. "Becca is safe." She ran her tongue over lips dry and cracking. "Bixten—Bixten is bright. Ten by ten rounds. Ten by ten. Your heart—is warm."

He leaned closer to place a kiss upon her forehead, and she closed her weary eyes.

PART III

CHAPTER 1

Looking over the rim of his glasses, the meshganis sized her up where she sat propped upon the bed. "I did nayat think yon would be so railed," he said while carefully measuring out a spoonful of white powder. Peering through spectacles which magnified his eyes comically, he dumped it into the mug at hand and stirred briskly. "One spoon-filled at firstsup and one at lastsup for one allten," he directed to Lor Zeria. "I do think the worst of fevering over with, but this will make certain."

He added the pouch of powder to the other supplies accumulating on the table; loaves of bread and dried goods, toothbrushes and soap, clothing, lungilts, slips and footings, ointment and bandages for her knife wounds, a salve for her cracked and peeling feet, this the only telltale signs of frostbite. If the meshganis was correct, the toskin fevering had saved her toes, maybe even her life.

She took the mug handed her by the meshganis, wincing as she tried to grasp it with uncooperative fingers—till the Lor of Zeria stepped forward to help guide it to her lips.

"Yon has done well in yon tendings, Mine Lor," the spectacled meshganis spoke. “The stitchings are holding well,” he directed to Reesal, “and there is naya infecting. But yon must allow the lita to use her hands, lest they mesh stiffly.”

“Christine drank down the bitter liquid, wiping her lips with the back of a bandaged hand. “How many sols till I am well enough for traveling?”

The meshganis peered sternly over his spectacles. “Mine Lita, yon must nayat travel till the wintered winds have ceased.”

“But yon did travel in such.”

“Aya. And such was one difficult task at least. Even within mine cover-carry, the winds did find their way into mine ten layerings of garb and into mine very bones.”

The carriage driver standing before the fire with hands outstretched, turned and nodded adamantly, his beet-red face amply communicating the dangers of the whipping winds.

“Then I will put on twenty layers.”

“Yon ears did hear the wisened words of one meshganis,” the Lor of Zeria spoke sternly. “We will wait till the wintered winds cease.”

Christine drilled him with an annoyed glare which he absorbed with a stately grace.

Dratsum cleared his throat. “It seems yon does have enough supplies to last through ten segs of wintered winds,” he said, looking at the walls piled high with stelch. “This—devon yon does speak of—”

“Worgle,” Reesal corrected.

The meshganis scratched his temple. “Mine good ganis, worgles are nayathing but tot-tales.”

“Aya? Speak such to the ten by ten ganist dropped, then,” Reesal said, motioning to the stelch.

“That many, then?”

Lor Zeria nodded. “Least.”

“And it did drop so many loner?”

“There are naya signs of others,” Reesal informed him. “Though a more thorough searching will be carried out once the winds cease.”

Putting his hands on his hips, the meshganis surveyed the stelch lining the walls. "Are such tales truths, then. Was this worgle half huganis, half beast."

"One nose reaching ear to ear," Reesal said, demonstrating on himself. "One eye here, the other there."

"I must note such a creature," Dratsum insisted.

"The foul thing does lie bundled in the entrance," Reesal replied with a shudder.

The meshganis rubbed his hands together. "I will note such first thing as Sola wakens." Taking his glasses off, he began to clean them with the hem of his shirt. "And this railed litia, same did drop the very worgle did drop ten by tens of ganist?"

"Need I remind, this railed litia is one Loper of Zeria," Reesal intoned. "Same did drop one devon PacMattin."

"Enough on this," the Lor of Zeria ordered. "It seems one famed loper's lids do grow heavy."

"Aya. Chouster leexer will cause such," Dratsum informed them. "She will sleep well this lun."

~~~~~~~~~~

The low drone of male voices pulled her from sleep yet again. A thin fishy gruel was spooned to her mouth, then her bandages were changed as she sat in a stupor—then her teeth brushed. Through sleepy eyes, she studied his face up close while his attention was focused intently on the task at hand. He was freshly shaven, his skin smooth and flawless save for the faintest of scars just under the edge of his chin, an older scar—a mishap as a boy perhaps.

"Ahhh," he said, prompting her to open her mouth wider so he could reach the teeth in back.

While his eyes were on her mouth, hers went to his, noting teeth even and very white. Guilt gnawed at her at the coldness with which she'd treated the Lor now tending to her with such diligence.

She rinsed with the water he offered, then spit into the bowl held under her chin.
~~~~~~~~~~

As he settled her back on the pillows, pulling the blankets to her chin, she had to remind herself whom he was beyond the walls of stone—the Lor of Zeria, the very Leader of Lors, extremely powerful, extremely dangerous.

As was becoming a ritual, he brushed the hair from her forehead so to place a goodnight kiss, his warm lips lingering. As he pulled back, she met the eyes of the most powerful ganis in all of Atriia, and very possibly the most handsome man on any world. Especially appealing was the mouth with the semi-grin, one which said he was most content in his role as care-giver without speaking a word. Despite her greatest efforts, she felt her heart soften the tiniest of bits.

~~~~~~~~~~

A high whistling pulled her from a deep, drug-induced sleep. Slowly, the dream faded—a sandy pony with sky-blue eyes galloping across an amber field where knee-high grass swayed in a gentle breeze. Rolling to her side, she fluffed her pillow, then settled back into it, allowing her eyes to adjust slowly to the dimly lit room.

Four ganist were laid out side by side before the fireplace. The snore coming from the meshganis was comical, a halting pig-like grunting as air was pulled in, followed by the classic high-pitched exhaling whistle. From the opposite end of the line-up, Lor Zeria wadded an article of clothing and tossed it, striking Dratsum on the shoulder. The meshganis stirred, smacking his lips before rolling to his side. A triplet of pops sounded from the smoldering embers—then the room fell quiet.

Their eyes met in the darkness and he gave her a half grin. With sleep tugging at her, drawing her lids down, she burrowed deeper into the covers.

A shadow crossed her vision as he placed another blanket atop, one warmed by the fireside. He had risen so silently. He was uncommonly stealthy for such a large man.

Squatting beside the bed, he delicately plucked a curl from
~~~~~~~~~~

where it had fallen across her eyes, depositing it neatly back to its proper place. "Is yon in need of water?" he asked, his voice a low, warm whisper. There was a faint hint of spirits on his breath, just one of the many other 'essentials' brought in on the carriage.

Before she could answer, a high-pitched, drawn-out tooting sounded from the direction of the meshganis, the breaking of wind so comical, Christine could not contain the giggles. Lor Zeria's eyebrows shot up, then he too broke into a contained chuckle, a bassy rumbling deep in his chest.

Sleep, like an iron anchor, was pulling her under. She fought to keep her eyes open, for it seemed, once again, she had become transfixed by the mouth put so close. "Speak the words, again, Mine Lor," she breathed dreamily as she snuggled into her downy pillow.

"What words, Mine Lita?" He seemed especially relaxed as he crouched beside her with one arm resting casually upon the bed. "It be yon wishing, I will speak them ten by ten times over."

Despite her efforts, she felt her heart soften a smidgeon more. "That mine babe is safe."

Even in the darkness, even in the sleep-filled state, she caught the slight stiffening, the fleeting flinch of features. As if the iron chain had been snapped in two, the anchor was gone. "Mine babe!" Her heart was racing as she struggled to sit up.

Placing firm hands upon her shoulders, he kept her in place. "She is safe."

She searched his eyes in the darkness, desperate to read them. "You're lying!"

He put a finger to her mouth, pressing firmly to silence her. "She is safe, Christa, as Sola shines," he swore. "But Meshganis Dratsum, he did inform—there are whisperings. It is being spoken she was born of the seed of PacMattin."

She felt relief flood through her. "I do nayat care what untruths are spoken."

"There are many did think PacMattin one devon, as would be any babe born of his seed."

"Is she in danger?"

"She is closely guarded, but she will nayat be rightly safe till behind Zerian walls."

By the fireside, the meshganis mumbled something and smacked his lips in slumber.

"The ganist who did capture me, were they after Becca?"

With a sigh, Lor Zeria sat on the edge of the bed, the small bunker groaning beneath his weight. "On this matter, I am still in searching. I am thinking it was nayat high-hillers. Word of yon returning could nayat have traveled such longs so quickly. The ponies bear Toskeenian brandings, but many ponies are bidded at such. Was anything spoken between them, any callens?"

As quickly as the anchor had vanished, it reappeared, tugging ardently. Slowly, a recollection surfaced through the murkiness. "Boskiel."

He repeated the name, trying it out on his tongue, though it seemed it was unfamiliar.

Leaving him to his thoughts, she burrowed deeper into the covers. The potent white powder was pulling her from consciousness, each breath drawn deeper than the previous.

She could only wonder sleepily at the fingertips caressing her cheeks, like velvety moth wings fluttering along the curve of her chin, the bridge of her nose, over the swell of parted lips. She was drifting—drifting on a serene sea so soothing. A warm, wayward wind whispered her name like wafting music, a lovely lilting lullaby. Slowly, she slipped under.

CHAPTER 2

There was no blood left in her face. It had all drained to her toes. Gnashing her teeth, she kept her mouth clamped to constrain the cries which craved their freedom. The beads of sweat on her furrowed brow joined together to run a jagged trail down the side of her nose. She opened her eyes to drill the torture master with a grating glare. The urge to beg the Lor to stop was overpowering. She fought this urge with every ounce of willpower she could muster. He was watching ever so closely, the bastard, watching with talcar eyes, waiting for her to buckle. She would not waver, would not whimper, would not give the blogart the satisfaction of seeing her crumble.

"Yon is brazened, Christa," he whispered, all the while inflicting pain as she had never known before.

A strew of profanities came to mind in response, but she held her tongue, trying to concentrate on deep, even breaths. It took a certain cold and callous breed to be capable of inflicting such excruciating pain with such calculated thoroughness. In the days since the meshganis had left, the Lor of Zeria had played her caretaker without complaint. On this day, however, his true character had come to surface. This was the Lor she remembered, the same would throw one litia into one keeper, there to suffer for weeks on end, the same would slit wide the throat of one lita who had just, mere turnings earlier, pleasured him in his bunker. The cold, heartless bastard was ripping her flesh and grinning as he did it.

She felt her eyes well, felt a hot tear slip free to trace a torrid trail down a bloodless cheek. She cursed the watery weakness.

"Breathe, Christa," he instructed. "Yon is doing well."

She'd been holding her breath, and they were too quick and

shallow when she resumed. The fact that she was panting like a hound didn't thwart his mission, however. With sadistic glee, he applied even more pressure, extending her fingers fully until her nails made contact with the table, until gray orbs floated before her eyes.

Finally, the pressure was released, this near sending her to collapse.

"Now fist it," he instructed from across the table where he sat so casually, seeming not to care that her dampened hair clung to her forehead and cheeks, nor that she was quaking from head to toe.

The thought of making a fist was very appealing, as was the notion of punching him with it right in the nose. Instead, she tried to comply, fighting to quell the quaking. Intense pain traveled up her arms, then downward, twisting her belly and weakening her legs.

"I can nayat." She confessed in a voice so weak and wobbly, cursing the moisture sliding from the corners of her eyes, twin tears of betrayal.

He closed his large hands over hers, assisting in the torture, slowly forcing her fingers into a tight fist, watching her closely all the while, scrutinizing her pain with cool curiosity.

When finally he released her hand, she pulled it to her belly, cradling it as it pulsated with pain.

As he reached across the table, summoning her other hand, she pulled her shoulders back abruptly. "Yon and PacMattin are nayat so differed," she said, feeling satisfaction at the subtle shift in his posture. "PacMattin did also find pleasure in the pain of others."

His shoulders drew back. "Meshganis Dratsum did give strict instructings."

"Aya, and yon is overly eagered to carry out such. Mayhap next yon can rip mine nails free one by one. Such should give yon pleasure for many turnings."

Reesal cleared his throat from where he stood warming himself at the fireplace. "I am thinking to tend the ponies."

"Aya, Reesal," she intoned acidly, "you should tend to such. This way the great Leader of Lors can torture me to his very heart's content!" She glared at Reesal as he snatched up his jacket and gloves. As he hurried out the door, a rush of cold air entered, chilling her dampened body.

Chillier still was the look on the face of the torture master. Resting his forearms on the table, he leaned in close, drilling her with eyes that flared. "Does yon think I gain pleasure from yon pain, Christa?" He stood abruptly, sending his chair flying backward. Two long strides took him to the fireplace where he snatched up the broadax—and for one fleeting moment she thought he meant to lop off the offending hands.

"With every grain yon does suffer, I do yearn to chop one cursed creature into ten by tens of tiny bits!"

He meant to do it. She could see it in his flashing eyes, in the tight clench of his jaw, the rigid line of his stance. His breaths were much too deep as he contemplated on the intended deed. He shifted the ax in his hands, testing the weight in a tight grip.

"Mine Lor," she spoke from her spot at the table, "I must hand apologies. I do nayat think yon does find pleasure in mine pain, as Sola shines. Was mine pain did speak such."

"Yon hands must be stretched. Meshganis Dratsum did give strict instructings."

"Aya. And I will follow such," she promised.

~~~~~~~~~~

He put the ax to use none-the-less, the hollow thunks reverberating about the stone walls as he destroyed the babebunker of boughs with controlled conviction. She could only sit and watch, guilt hacking at her brain with every swing of the ax, and weighing heavy in her heart.

It would weigh heavy upon her late into the lun as she lie listening to him rummage through the stacks of stelch. Reesal slept close to a fire flaming brightly, this methodically rekindled by the offending babebunker so radically reduced to kindling.

Her words had offended the Lor. He'd been quiet throughout the
~~~~~~~~~~

day, the sparkle gone from his hazel eyes as he went through the routine of caring for an invalid. She was puzzled at just how deeply her words had wounded him, puzzled further by the vise gripping her chest so tightly, by the painful lump lodged in her throat as she fought back tears.

She tried yet again to fist her hands beneath the covers, grimacing at the pain, forcing them, forcing them further, then shuddering a silent sigh as she relaxed them. She would continue with the exercises throughout the lun, for the pain in her hands she did understand. It was the other, that which gripped her heart, she did not.

CHAPTER 3

Lor Zeria was diligent in her daily rehabilitations—three times per sol and one turning per session. She never did again accuse him of finding pleasure in her pain, though there were times when she was not as cooperative as she could have been, even attempting on occasion to wile her way out of such exercises.

She was to find, however, the Leader of Lors was not so easily manipulated. Only once did she manage to persuade him, complaining of a severe headache, a fib for which she paid dearly the following session, one which lasted twice as long and which nearly landed her on the floor in faint.

Though the two ganist lacked skills in hunting, they did well for themselves, bringing in crouts and fowl and other small game, not an easy feat, for all were sheltering from the winds. They took turns swilling at the Ralling River and preparing meals. Despite winds awhirl with icy river mist, they kept their battling skills sharpened, returning drenched but revitalized. Lor Zeria spent many turnings putting pen to parchment, taking record of the stelch. Time was also passed playing tookets, a game which involved the tossing of painted stones and the tallying of scores.

Because her injuries prevented her from performing all but the most simple of tasks, Christine was forced to spend much of her time idle, a fact which did not benefit a brain allotted far too much spare time to pine. Mental anguish converted to physical pain, her entire body aching with the longing for her beautiful blue-eyed Becca. Her arms ached to hold her, her ears to hear the sweet giggle, her nose to breathe the pure essence, her lips to kiss the plump cheeks. Such aching would bring on sudden tears during the day, and even during the night, pulling her from sleep. She would lie awake, staring at the piles of stelch, counting the grains sift through one by one and hoping that the tippet might appear, the one thing which seemed capable of lifting her spirits. Often, she would spy him as he crept from the stelch pile to scamper beneath the table, there to scavenge the crumbs she had purposely scattered.

Though the sols passed slowly, each seeming to last an unbearable eternity, they did pass, one by one, each bringing the wintered winds closer to an end.

CHAPTER 4

She stood close to the fire, reveling in the warmth emanating from the large stones. She pulled the blanket tighter about her shoulders, an act which pained her, though she was grateful she could grasp it at all. The numbness in her fingertips had gradually been replaced with a biting tingle. The nerves were repairing themselves. It was a good pain, one not near as debilitating as the other which consumed her, that of her pining. She sighed as she listened to the wintered winds howling faintly beyond the chimney, wondering if they would ever end.

The clatter of tookets stones rolling along the table sounded one final time.

"Blast it all! Does yon think it wise, then, to best yon Lor three times over, ganis?"

Reesal chuckled. "Apologies, Mine Lor. Next game I will toss mere four stones to yon six. Mayhap then yon will chance one winning."

Sounding like a caged animal, the Lor of Zeria growled, then slid his chair back to stretch long legs. "I am done with tookets."

"Yon does nayat take well to defeating, Mine Lor," Reesal chided. "What says yon, Mine Lita," he directed to Christine, "tookets? It will take yon brain from other things."

Christine shook her head. "Naya. Mine head aches. Apologies, Reesal."

"I think it is yon heart does ache. Do nayat fret, the winds will end soon enough."

"Not soon enough for me."

Lor Zeria sighed as he set aside the mug of spirits to pick up the leather-bound journal resting at the table's edge. "More stelch does need going through this lun," he announced as he leafed through the pages

Reesal swirled the spirits in his mug. "Will yon ever be done going through such?"

Lor Zeria frowned. "By mine counting, I have gone through the belongings of ten by ten ganist, with half still to be done."

Reesal whistled through his teeth. "More than I did think."

The Lor held up the journal, examining the binding in the firelight. "This ganis, Axermme, did travel to Woroff with his lita and two gans to bid ponies."

"Does yon think all four dropped by one worgle, then?" Reesal asked.

Lor Zeria nodded sadly.

"Axermme?" The word was weak, but it drew the eyes of both ganist instantly.

"Aya," Lor Zeria affirmed. "Does yon know this callen?"

Christine nodded, then brought her fingers to her temples to massage as the throbbing instantly intensified. Shuffling numbly to the bed, she crawled in, pulling the covers to her chin.

CHAPTER 5

Christine barely registered the many people crowded about the room, so focused was her attention on the lita standing before her. She was having difficulty breathing past the anxiety lodged high in her throat. How she had awaited this moment, sol after sol, turning after turning, grain after grain, yearning, pleading for the winds to cease. Yet she could not get her legs to work. It was Dahla. She seemed so thin where she stood cradling the bundled babe. And so pale, dark circles etched beneath haunted eyes. And Bixten seemed ill at ease, hiding behind Dahla, peeking around her skirt like a frightened puppy.

It was Lor Zeria who finally moved forward to take the tiny treasure. "As promised, Mine Lita," he whispered as he transferred the bundle to her arms.

"Mineseth! Mineseth, mineseth!" Bixten sprang from behind Dahla, spewing spittle-coated words—for Bixten had transformed into a worgle. Two daggers materialized in its hands as it lunged at her. It was halted in mid-flight, however, Dahla lopping its head off in one deft stroke—for Dahla had transformed into Roltin. He never saw the arrow that arced in from behind, the impact propelling him forward. No sooner had his body hit the floor, then the crowd moved in, pouring over him, a swarm of roggii come to life.

"Christa," Lor Zeria commanded, shouting to be heard over the sound of rioting roggii. "Yon must think on yon babe."

Tearing her eyes away from where roggii were ravaging Roltin, Christine peeled the blanket from the babe's face, and the mummified skull toppled to the floor, bouncing away till it was apprehended by pouncing roggii.

Christine looked up as a gentle hand was placed upon her

shoulder. “Antiva?” she spoke numbly, for it seemed the Lor of Zeria had transformed as well.

Antiva’s face was pale and sad. “I do miss yon scullies overly,” she confessed, her chin trembling as she fought back tears. “I do miss mine sasturn. And Trenden and Triden. It is their birthingsol.” She began to cry, and then to shriek, spinning in circles as roggii attacked, leaping at her, seeming to converge from every direction. She flapped her arms, swatting at them as they scrambled up her gilt—then collapsed in a heap, her shrills muffling as she disappeared beneath the writhing mass…

Christine opened her eyes to a ceiling of stone, her breaths ragged, the gorge rising in her throat. She forced it back down as she forced back threatening tears. The headache that she’d fallen asleep with was still pounding at her temples, and the stench of cooking food was cramping her stomach. She could hear Lor Zeria, still rummaging through the sickening stelch pile. He spoke to Reesal, summoning him to come note.

Reesal rose from where he stooped stirring stew at the fire. Stroking his beard, he inspected carefully the contents spread out upon the table. “Lita garb.”

“Aya, and here,” Zeria said, pointing to one article.

“What is yon thinking, then?” Reesal asked. “One lita did travel with babe?”

“It is mine thinking one babe was nayat yet birthed. Note the dricloths.”

Christine kicked the covers away at this. Rising on wobbly legs, she went to investigate the articles strewn out; lita’s undergarments, a make-up pouch, a small hand flector, a gray gilt with purple trim. There were several small baby blankets and a pile of cloth diapers, the dricloths too clean and white to have ever been used.

Reesal stroked his beard. “Same babe from one babebunker?”

The Leader of Lors nodded.

“Does yon think one lita was keepered here till one babe was birthed, then?"

"The foul devon did likely rip one babe free," Lor Zeria surmised.

Christine shuddered, this only exacerbating the throbbing at her temples. She swallowed down the rising gorge as she pulled the blanket tighter about her shoulders.

"One worgle did most likely think yon with babe as well," Lor Zeria spoke unexpectedly, turning to Christine. "Yon was swelled with milk."

She felt the heat rise to her cheeks.

Reesal nodded. "Yon should give thankings to Sola only yon hands did end ripped."

She felt gnarly knuckles knead into her knotted belly, forcing the bile back into her throat. Putting the back of her hand to her mouth, she ran her eyes over the horrid heaps of stelch, over the cruel stone walls that seemed to close in with every passing grain. She hated the cramped, dark room and the ghosts it held, hated that she was being forced to stay against her will. There were no locked doors, no giant roggii, but it was one keeper all the same. Once again she was a prisoner, and once again, it was at the hands of the Lor of Zeria.

Reesal held a hand up to silence them, then bent down to carefully pick up a boot. "Blasted tippet," he muttered as he hurled it overhand. His aim was true, targeting it in mid-flight and sending it tumbling across the floor. Landing on its back near the hearth, its huge ears unfurled to lay flat on each side as its tiny feet twitched.

With a snarl, Christine leapt at Reesal, pummeling his chest and spitting obscenities.

She caught sight of his face through the haze—the wide-eyed dumbfounded expression—and then she was fleeing out the door and down the narrow entrance tunnel, past the stacked firewood and the bundled worgle, past the startled ponies and into the turbulent storm. She gasped frigid air into her screaming lungs as the raging winds slapped her in the face like a stinging palm. Saturated with river mist, the wind whipped her hair and drenched her gilt, entangling it about her ankles as she stumbled forward. She went down, her cries drowned out by the whining winds as pain ricocheted up her arms to her pounding temples. Moisture blurred her vision—tears of pain, of anguish—and the fist clinched her belly, forcing up a vile liquid that burned her throat and nose—then again, the angry fist twisting till there was nothing left.

She struggled against the ganis who lifted her so effortlessly, pushing against his chest, then pummeling at his back when he clutched her close. "No!" she cried. "I won't go back there. I won't stay! You can't make me! Take me to Becca! Take me to mine babe, right now! Right now, you bastard—you fucking bastard!"

She buried her face into the warm, sheltered crook of his neck and there she wept for the tiny tippet with the elephant ears. She wept for the lita whose babe was ripped from her belly, wept for Axermme, his wife and twin sons. She wept for Roltin with the kind olive eyes. She wept unabashedly with the longing for her Becca, and for Kyle, the most patient man on the world that was Earth, a world she would never see again—a man she would never see again. She wept for a mother she would never see again, a sister. She wept at the thought of the pain she had caused them—and so many others. It seemed the list was endless. It seemed the tears were endless as well.

CHAPTER 6

Lying on the small bed, she listened to the cozy crackling at the fireplace. The cathartic release of tears had not only alleviated her headache, it seemed to have cleansed her very soul. A peacefulness had settled over her as she shamelessly shed tears while he rocked her like a child. She couldn't remember when exhaustion claimed her, bringing on sleep mercifully free of dreams. She had not been wakened for lastsup. He had even foregone her nightly meshing session, a first for the regimented Leader of Lors.

She glanced to where he lie sleeping on a pile of blankets before the fire with Reesal stretched out beside. With a soft sigh, she pulled the blanket to her chin. She was wearing nothing beneath. Only vaguely did she recall the saturated garments being peeled away. Modesty had not been forefront in her mind at the time, but now, fully rested, the thought of the Leader of Lors disrobing her brought heat to her cheeks. It hadn't been the first time. He was obviously quite familiar with her body parts.

She ran her hands over the swell of full breasts. The tenderness had dissipated over the past weeks. She was grateful for this, yet saddened she would no longer be breast-feeding Becca. It was just as well. It was time.

She ran her hands down to rest on her belly. Thanks to bed rest, three meals a day, and constant confounded idleness, she had filled out a bit.

She turned her head toward the table where the toothbrush and water sat readied. Gathering the blanket about her, she slipped from the bed and padded quietly to seat herself.

A task which had seemed so simple in the past took extreme

effort as she willed her hand to grip the tiny brush, to perform the strokes just so. When completed, a fine sheen of perspiration graced her brow. She wiped it away with a trembling hand while eyeing the other contents on the table; the pile of unused diapers, the lita's beauty case, her hair brush and mirror.

With a quick glance toward the sleeping ganist, Christine tentatively picked up the latter.

The face peering back at her in the darkness was not what she expected. It was not the face of a hardened woman, one who had suffered harrowing hardships, one who had dropped one devon, one blacktongue, one woodslink, even one waffle. The girl peering back at her looked young—fifteen, maybe sixteen—with a mass of curls framing a pale face. She lifted her chin, running fingertips lightly over the raised scar.

"It can barely be noted."

She jumped, surprised she had not heard him stir.

"The devon did least make one clean slice." He placed an object upon the table, a crude cage fashioned of twigs and twine. The trembling tippet was crouched within, his eyes wide and frightened.

The Lor grinned at her expression. "One tippet was stunned only. Though one leg is wounded."

Christine blinked back tears. "I need hand apologies to Reesal. One tippet, it did—when I meant to take mine life, it did stop me."

"Then one tippet will be treated as the very highest of Lors," he teased. Moving behind, he pulled her hair free from the blanket, then picked up the hairbrush belonging to the lita long dropped.

"I can do it," she insisted.

He nodded and handed over the brush—then straddled the chair beside her, sitting uncomfortably close.

Securing the blanket with one hand, she began to brush with long measured strokes.

He watched her hand performing the simple task. "Yon grip grows stronger," he said, the sweet scent of spirits drifting to her on his breath.

"Aya."

"Two new scarrings to add to yon many."

She nodded, keeping her eyes on the tippet as she brushed. He was trembling where he sat dead center of his cage, his breaths overly quick and shallow—as were her own.

"Most battlers do nayat have as many to boast." The Lor wrapped his long arms about the back of his chair, hugging it close. "It is spoken yon did laugh in the face of PacMattin when he ripped yon throat wide."

She paused in mid-stroke, only briefly, before resuming. "I do nayat recall such," she replied, knowing he knew the lie even before she finished speaking it.

He stayed her hand, pulling the brush from her grasp so to run his thumb along the scar on her palm. Bringing it to his lips, he placed a gentle kiss upon it. He was too close. And there was an odd glimmer in his eyes, one unrelated to the reflection of flames dancing there. She flinched as he put a finger to her cheek, gently tracing the fine scar there.

"PacMattin?"

She nodded, afraid to use her voice, lest it be trembling. An uncomfortable crawling sensation traveled down her arms and legs as the fine hairs lifted. Her heart was pounding painfully. It began to race as he slid the blanket from her shoulder so his fingertips could gently examine the twin dimples.

"Woodslink."

She nodded, then struggled to pull in a difficult breath. She didn't realize that her face had drifted toward the tippet cage, until he gently guided it back.

"Is it truths yon did drop one full-sized woodslink?"

Her eyes tried to wander to where Reesal slept, but the man leaning so close softly spoke her name, drawing them back. "It did mean to drop mine babe," she explained.

The flames in his eyes flared. "Christa," he breathed, the sultry whisper of her name on his lips startling her. She gasped as scalding hands came up to cradle her face. "With both hands skewered, yon did best one creature did drop ten by tens of ganist. With yon throat sliced wide, yon did laugh in the face of one devon. Yon did drop one woodslink, did dive into waters brimmed with fraigens—yet yon does fear this ganis."

It was true. She hated that it was, hated that fear squeezed the air from her lungs at his nearness, that she trembled as one tippet at his touch. There was something dangerous in his flaming eyes. He longed to lean into her lips—and he did not struggle with indecision for long.

"Was yonself did spur me into such waters," she lashed out, her stinging words halting him. "The thought of yon lips on mine. I would rather end fraigen dung."

She watched his eyes, waiting for the fire to fizzle and die, waiting for him to pull away as the pain seeped in. She was not prepared for him to lean closer yet, nor for the flames in his eyes to flare.

"Yon fear does speak, Christa. Do nayat fear me."

Even as he spoke the words, she feared him more than ever. Her trusty weaponry of words had not wounded him in the least, not even a measly scratch. A miserable misfire and with him hovering so near—the hands on her face searing, the eyes on her lips yearning. She cursed the confounded quaking she couldn't quell. "Will I be yon pleasurer, then—as Myurna was?" she fired—but once again discovered she had missed her mark. He leaned in, and though she meant to unload yet again, it was too late. Both barrels were empty.

It was a kiss which did merely tease, he drawing sweetly on her bottom lip, the sensuous savoring sending shivers through her. When he pulled away, the fire in his eyes had grown to a dazzling inferno. Like a moth, she was drawn to it, even knowing that danger lurked within.

He caressed the scar on her cheek with his thumb. "This ganis does also bear scarrings," he breathed. "When I did think yon dropped, was one blade in mine heart thrust deep." He leaned into her cheek, a molten mouth placing sensuous kisses along the scar, and a shudder shook her as he moved to that on her neck to do the same, lifting her chin as he worked his way across with slow seductive purpose. A moment of panic seized her as his feverish mouth dropped to the scars on her shoulder.

"Mine Lor, I—"

Her words quickly drew his lips to hers where they caressed most tenderly. "Sola did bring yon back to me, mine Christa," he breathed huskily. "It is fating."

"Mine Lor—"

"Jerrod," he corrected between gentle kisses.

She could taste the sweet fruitiness of spirits on his lips. "Jerrod, I—"

He silenced her in an instant, a devouring which dizzied. The room became a blur as her head whirled, any resistance muted by a mouth that knew no mercy. She could hear nothing above the thumping of her heart. It drowned out any pathetic voice of reason whispering in her ear, drowned out the warning siren sounding in the distance. She was not privy as to how her hands found their way beneath his shirt, but they were there, gripping his back, their plight to hold her blanket in place forgotten. As it slid from her shoulders, goose bumps surfaced, so pronounced they were painful. Electricity was alive within the room, lifting the hair on her arms, sending a tingling down her scalp. A shock shot through her where their mouths were melded, like a jolt of current, and she pulled away with a gasp.

Either he didn't feel it, or he didn't care. His chair toppled over as he scooped her up and carried her to the bed, showering her face with kisses as he lay her gently down. He took her in boldly as he stripped himself in mere grains, yanking the shirt over his head—then the tie at his waist.

She was trembling as he settled himself atop, a ganis ablaze, his flesh blistering where it pressed against her own, his breaths scalding where they mingled with hers, his fingertips burning trails where they caressed at her temples.

"Christa," he whispered, "do nayat fear me."

He was reading her well. Fear raged through her—mixed with feverish desire. She ran trembling hands up his back and to his neck, pulling his mouth to hers, thirsting for the fruity elixir, drinking it in, rolling it on her tongue, moaning at the sweetness. She let out a disappointed sigh as he pulled away much too soon—and then a cry as his scalding mouth dropped down to one nipple—a most savage attack, the rapturous ravaging forcing out whimpering gasps as she writhed beneath him. There was no pain in the hands which gripped at his head so to guide him to another in need of equal fervent attention.

A shudder commenced when finally he released her, this turning to shivers as his mouth slid back to hers. Running his fingers into her blazened locks, he unleashed a fresh onslaught of savagery upon her lips which sent her brain to reeling.

Even with senses swaying, she was acutely aware of that which waited below, primed but patient. She longed to feel him inside, ached for him. And perhaps her mouth told him this without uttering a word, for he shifted his weight, pressing into soft flesh, this ending the kiss most abruptly as she arched against him with a breathless gasp.

With a growl, he reclaimed her lips, the weight of him crushing as he pressed deep. She moaned against his mouth as he began to move, then louder, and louder still as each gliding stroke seemed to guide him deeper yet. But the Leader of Lors was nayat meting mercy to the moaning lita pinned piteously beneath him. He was a master at doling out torture with methodical precision—and it was sweet torture, indeed, each slow sensual stroke pushing out muted moans.

The Lor torturing her was on fire, his flesh unnaturally hot, his mouth a scalding tempest, pulling the oxygen from her very lungs. Digging her fingers into his back and her heels into the bed, she struggled to escape the mouth so greedily consuming her—and only reluctantly did he relent, pulling back to slather her face with kisses—yet all the while exacting sweet torture as only a master could.

As she clutched at his shoulders and struggled to pull in air, he calmly traced a path along her jaw-line to her ear, nibbling the lobe—before sliding to her cheek so to tickle it with his tongue. He lapped the tip of her nose like a hound, then chuckled, his fruity breath mingling with her harried huffs.

It came upon her without warning, a searing shock wave surging through. She struggled against it, clinging to him, clenching her teeth as it shook her like a ragdoll, jarring her bones, rattling her brain, shattering her senses.

It abated just as quickly, leaving her weak and vulnerable, completely at the mercy of the Lor intent upon torturing her. He chuckled at her ear and she shuddered as a tingling traveled to her toes. Goose bumps followed, and he traced them with soft fingertips, up and down her arms, up and down her thighs, exercising patience—but not for long.

He kissed a heated trail to her lips, gently coaxing to them to part as he began to move yet again. Every nerve in her body was leaping, every muscle quivering. Her trembling hands traveled up his back to the nape of his neck, caressing, welcoming the delectable devouring, tasting him, savoring. She welcomed the sweet torture as well, opening herself to him, reveling in every torrid stroke. It was pointless to resist. Any sense was lost in the sensuous kiss of the Leader of Lors. Hazy smoke filled her head, thick and roiling.

She turned away from his kiss with a cry, clinging tightly as another furious wave ripped through. She was in the clutches of the raging Ralling yet again, being swept away by a churning frothing beast, spitting, sputtering, kicking, fighting desperately to stay afloat.

Wrapping long, powerful arms around her, the Lor clutched her close, holding her head firmly above the surface—though the deep rumble of his laughter seemed to come from fathoms below it.

As he lay her spent body gently down, she could still hear the Ralling, though it was distant—a million miles away. Her head felt light, her limbs heavy. Her breaths were shallow, her eyes shut.

He waited most patiently, the Lor of Zeria, though one part of him was undeniably anxious to resume. He was hovering close, his deep, steady breaths moistening her lips.

Slowly, she dared to open her eyes.

There was no grin tugging at the corners of his mouth. The man planted deep was delving deeper still with eyes alight with blazing victory. Lacing his fingers into her hair, he gently massaged her scalp. "I have noted him, Christa," he spoke softly, "in mine dreaming."

She tried to clear the haze from her brain, one starved for oxygen. "Him?" It was a breathless word, for her lungs were sorely depleted of oxygen as well.

He dropped his mouth to her ear, the moist breath sending a shattering shudder through her as he whispered. "Our gan."

She let out a moan as he began to move again, his momentum building quickly to a more stringent stride. The fingers gripping his back dug in deep as the small bed rocked beneath them. A siren was sounding—high, insistent, the blatant blaring breaking through the roaring of the Ralling—and she began to struggle against him, a feeble attempt which went unheeded.

Slipping an arm beneath her shoulders, he held her tight as he latched onto her neck, a ravenous vampire sapping her strength, thwarting any resistance as his momentum continued to mount.

She struggled to find her voice, but all that issued forth was a breathless mewling, thin and warbled. A blinding, deafening urgency possessed the Leader of Lors. He had become the raging river—ruthless, relentless, tossing her hopelessly, battering her body, forcing out hoarse cries.

A snapping sounded, a splintering of wood, and she thought for an odd moment that he had broken her—till the bed at their feet dropped to the floor as two legs buckled. The remaining two quickly followed suit, bringing the frame to the floor with a jolting crash.

He was chuckling as he pushed up to grin down at her—then grew silent at the look on her face.

She pushed against unyielding shoulders, slapping at them when he wouldn't budge. "We can nayat!"

"Shh, Christa—"

"I can nayat birth another babe!" she forced out breathlessly. "It will mean mine dropping. He will nayat fit past mine hips, as Sola shines, he will nayat!"

He studied her intently, his own breaths deep and labored. "Yon lia—"

"Same would nayat pass through! I…" She struggled for breath as she struggled for the right words. "One meshganis did slice mine belly to pull her through!"

He shook his head.

"I swear on Sola! I do bear the scarring!"

An odd expression came over his face. He had seen it, then. She was not surprised. He had attended to her most thoroughly while she lie in fever.

Still, he hesitated. "Yon would be dropped if such were truths."

"Aya. And so I will be if I become big with babe again. The meshganis did make this very clear."

Vulnerability suffused her as he held his place defiantly. If he decided her fating must be met, she would be defenseless against him. And he was close—very, very close.

She struggled to get her fuddled brain to work. "This ganis would nayat ever force hisself upon yon. Yon did speak the very words, Mine Lor."

CHAPTER 7

She stirred the coarse absently in the bowl set before her. Seated beside her at the table, Reesal was doing the like. She was uncertain of how much he had heard. Certainly far too much. She cursed her own stupidity. With every move she made she cursed it, for hers was a body tender, a heart torn. How easily she had given in to him. She'd fancied herself impervious to his advances, but he'd proven far more dangerous than she ever dreamed. It was his infernal mouth. She could feel the heat of it still. She shivered at the very thought.

She glanced yet again to where he stood staring into the fire, tall and brooding, a position he'd managed to maintain for several turnings straight. She cursed the cave which kept her confined with the confounded creature, cramped together turning after turning, sol after sol. She cursed the wailing winds, her cries faint yet constant beyond the walls of earth and stone. She cursed her own weakness.

She looked to the bed broken in a heap on the floor, four legs splayed out—and a tear born of frustration slipped from the corner of her eye. She had truly tried to keep him at bay, had lashed out at him with the most powerful weapon she owned—her tongue, a stinging whip, and he hadn't flinched. It had been a foolish notion to believe she could keep such a beast at bay.

As if hearing her thoughts, his eyes left the fire for a brief moment, drawn to where she sat sulking. Her heart stopped. Her breathing stopped as well, so that she might hear him clearly. The beast was speaking with feral eyes, and the message was chilling. She had only just begun to face the consequences of her foolishness. He had sampled her flesh and would not rest until he was fully sated.

She dropped her eyes quickly to the coarse in her bowl, feeling her face grow flush. With a trembling hand, she scooped a spoonful and placed it in her mouth, feeling her stomach clench at the mere act. She forced it down, not bothering with the formality of chewing, then scooped up another. She needed to eat. She would need her strength if she was to battle the beast. And she would need to arm herself, to gather together what little weaponry remained in her meager arsenal. She would have to use it well. One grenade, if placed correctly, could do an enormous amount of damage—and this was a battle she could not afford to lose.

~~~~~~~~~~

Therapy on her hands that sol was more difficult than usual. It was not the pain. This seemed tolerable as of late, her fingers flexing further, her grasp gaining strength. It was his touch, his fingertips seeming to caress where they met her skin. And his eyes seemed to caress just as brazenly. The small room seemed especially cramped and stuffy, making it difficult to draw in breath. Shortly into the first session, her stomach was in knots. Her trembling hands turned clammy, as did her body, the gilt sticking to her back. And her heart was pounding so loudly she feared he may hear it—for he was leaning especially close. It took every ounce of her strength to keep from fixating on the mouth hovering so near. It beckoned to her, whispering of slow, smoldering kisses. And he knew she was weak. He could sense it, could probably smell it. The caged beast was biding his time—waiting for night to fall.

~~~~~~~~~~

Night fell much too quickly.

His eyes were upon her from across the table, shamelessly assaulting her as she tried to force down the meal Reesal had so diligently prepared—roasted fowl, the woodland bird they called fleecins, likened to pheasants. He had been fortunate enough to discover the nest tucked deep into a hollowed log. He had added ringroots and coneroots and pickens, allowing them to simmer in spirits and spices the entire day, this filling the room with savory scents. A jar of jeeters had been opened, a great delicacy, a rare root that cost many rounds and was reserved for only those owning the highest of standings. It was a meal fit for a Lor, one which seemed to be lost on the Lor present. Though he ate as if ravenous, Christine was certain he tasted nothing, overly focused as he was on the dessert sitting across from him. She tasted nothing as well, though she ate to keep her eyes down and her hands busy. Aware of the tension, Reesal curtailed his usual idle chatter. The only sounds were the scratching of the tippet in the cage and the scraping of utensils upon plates.

Only when the Lor pushed his plate away to lean back with mug in hand, did Reesal clear his throat. "What does yon think, Mine Lor? Tookets this lun?"

"Aya. But only one or two rounds. I do have plannings for later."

His brazened words lifted her eyes from her plate to where he sat grinning devilishly. "Aya," she huffed, tossing her napkin to the table as she tossed a glare across it. "There is still much stelch to be gone through."

He chuckled as he swirled the spirits. "Aya, stelch," he agreed.

CHAPTER 8

She struggled to stay awake, her brain and body weary from a day of constant worry. She listened to him sort through stelch, whittling the pile down piece by piece. She watched the tippet devour the jeeter she had given him, turning it round and round in his tiny paws as he nibbled at the edges, whittling the delicacy down bite by bite. She watched Reesal lay out his bedding before the hearth, watched as he stoked the fire till it blazed—watched as the flames devoured its fuel, whittling it away to warm, glowing embers.

~~~~~~~~~~

Even before her eyes opened, she knew he stood over her. She could feel the heat of him like a bonfire blazing, could feel the prickling of static electricity beneath her blanket. There was minimal light, the fire having reduced its meal to mere ashes, and so he was but a dark figure looming ominously at the foot of the bed. With it collapsed to the floor as it was, he seemed to tower to the very ceiling.

Pushing the haze of sleep from her brain, Christine fumbled for the grenade and pulled the pin with hands that shook. "So, yon would drop me down, then, for yon own pleasuring. Go on, then, Mine Lor," she challenged. "But when the deed is done, yon seed planted deep, show mercy on this lita and slice her throat wide. Yon is well practiced at slicing the throats of yon pleasurers, is yon nayat?"

He dropped to his knees, then to all fours, turning feral in an instant. "I can nayat plant seeds with mine tongue, lita," he growled—then whipped the covers aside.
~~~~~~~~~~

Like a predator on prey, he crept upon her, dark and deadly. Frozen in fear, she was unable to fend him off, unable to flee. She could only quiver as whiskers prickled against soft inner thighs, the velvety tongue lathing, working boldly toward a tender feast.

And the ravenous creature did feast to his heart's content. Powerless as a lamb in a lion's clutches, she writhed beneath him, crying out, a pathetic bleating which did only prove to incite him further. With claws digging in, a ruthless ravaging ensued, a rapturous onslaught, one rendering her weak and helpless, completely at the mercy of a most merciless beast.

~~~~~~~~~~

He lie curled about her, purring contentedly, his breaths warm against her neck. Soft fingertips caressed absently, a gentle stroking where they rested at her belly. There was a painful lump lodged high in her throat as she tried to stave the tears of frustration. She had lost the first phase of the battle miserably. It had been a complete slaughter, her convictions crushed by one scandalous sentence. So foolish. So reckless. So very dangerous. Playing with fire, a delicate moth flitting in and out of flames.

It had been a grueling test of willpower for the Leader of Lors. As he'd settled his weight upon her, she had felt all too clearly the testing of such will. And yet she had not denied him his goodnight kiss. She had welcomed the divine devouring, her fingers caressing the nape of his neck, stoking the fire even further, one perilously close to erupting into a blazing inferno.

And then his will had weakened. "Christa," he'd pleaded against her lips. "I will be careful."

"Becca was born of careful," she'd informed him, before selfishly pulling his lips back to hers.

He shifted his arm, his fingertips dropping low to lightly trace over the scar, one very fine, and certainly not large enough for one babe to pass through. She sensed a seed of doubt take root, drawing
~~~~~~~~~~

her closer to danger.

She would rip it up by its roots before it could burgeon. She must.

~~~~~~~~~~~

He crept upon her yet again in the early morning hours, returning to a feast unfinished, a stealthy hunter in the blackness, a prowling beast insatiable. She didn't even bother with the grenade pin, or with ripping anything up by its roots, for her fingers were busy—laced into his hair as they were, kneading—needing.

Basking in the warmth of a sultry sun, she drifted drowsily, undulating on a lazy sea, the waves swelling and dipping, a gentle succession on an endless ocean. Their lapping on a distant shore was a soothing lullaby which rocked her—rocked her…
~~~~~~~~~~~

CHAPTER 9

She kept her eyes on the bowl before her, any appetite far removed. The famished creature which had crept upon her in the night had sapped her of strength, leaving her weak and listless, a delicate injured moth, its powdery wings sadly singed.

It sat across the table, eating firstsup with ravenous relish, devouring as a creature starved, its nightly prowling having evidently only worked up a greater appetite.

She was painfully aware of its eyes upon her, smoldering eyes of an infernal beast. She tried to suppress a shudder, tried to lift the spoon, but she hadn't the strength. It was useless. It knew. It smelled her weakness—would feed on it. If she didn't fight with all she was worth, it would consume her.

~~~~~~~~~~

Tookets stones tumbled across the table. "Aiyee," Reesal boomed. "It does seem yon luck has turned, Mine Lor. That does make five rounds straight."

Zeria chuckled, the bassy rumble resonating about the room. "Aya, mine luck has turned," he agreed, and she could feel his eyes shift in her direction.

Seated before the fire, she pretended to be unaware, continuing to filter fingers through damp hair. Though effects of the previous night still lingered, much of her strength had returned throughout the day. The cleansing of her body had helped greatly. Though nothing more than a cloth dunked in a heated pail of water, it had been refreshing to wash away the grime—and perhaps some of the shame. The shampoo had been heavenly. And though her appetite was still
~~~~~~~~~~

in hiding, she had managed to force down a good portion of lastsup, the leftover fleecin now a heavy lump in her belly.

She looked to the cage sitting close to the fire. The tippet was grooming himself, his ears spilling about his feet as he bent himself in half to gnaw a spot on his belly. Even this could not produce a smile. It was drawing near, the time when Reesal would lay himself down. Not long after, the hungry beast would begin to prowl. She felt a tightness in her chest at just the thought, a fluttering in the pit of her belly, a quickening of breath. Would she have the strength to defend herself this night? Her arsenal was not having much of an impact, for it seemed her foe was gaining in strength with every passing grain. His presence filled the room, pulsing with a life all its own. It was stifling, smothering—sensual.

Plucking up her most recent Lor-assigned project, Christine tried to concentrate on the trying task, pinching the tiny needle between thumb and forefinger, guiding it through the fabric one painful stitch at a time. It was to be a doll, one fashioned of rags and other materials scavenged from the stelch pile. A gift for Becca. She yearned for her babe, a pining physically painful, every muscle in her body seeming to ache at the mere thought of her. He had given Becca back to her and had sworn to protect her. But at what price?

She moved closer to the fire as a shiver crept over her. Wafting down the chimney of stone was a whispering of the whining wintered winds. How much longer would they last? And caged as she was with such a creature, how much longer would she?

~~~~~~~~~~

She watched the shifting silhouette on the blanket draped for privacy, watched as he scrubbed with the cloth, washing broad shoulders and long arms. She was transfixed by the tall figure, the Lor of Zeria, the revered Leader of Lors bathing in a bowl. He was accustomed to pool-sized baths with steaming water and fancy soaps, to the finest of sup served on heaping platters, the finest of
~~~~~~~~~~

boardings with double king-sized bunkers.

She dragged her eyes away to Reesal's still figure. He slept soundly before the fire, his breaths deep and steady, had been thus for hours while Zeria sorted through stelch.

She envied his deep sleep. She was afraid to close her own eyes, afraid the creature would creep upon her unawares while her defenses were down. She pulled the covers to her chin, feeling a chill which had nothing to do with lack of heat. The room, one insulated with stone, held warmth well enough.

Her eyes drifted back to the silhouette, watching as he dunked his head into the bowl. It was a sight which forced a grin to her lips—a grin which quickly became a grimace.

She felt hot tears well yet again as they had been with frequency throughout the day. Her emotions, fragile as a moth's wings, were being ripped asunder. She could not control them any more than she could her racing heart, one not racing in fear, but something entirely else.

Lost. She was lost in her lusting for the Leader of Lors, wandering from the safety of the path despite the dangers lurking. A ravenous beast wandered the woodland, licking chops in anticipation of a divine devouring, and she was running straight into his snare, willingly so.

CHAPTER 10

The savage beast had finally finished feasting. Sated, he traveled upward with hot, tickling kisses along her belly, a trip which evidently fueled his hunger yet again, for he was ravenous as he came upon her breasts, giving each in turn fervid attention as she gripped at a back of supple steel.

The climb to her lips had the same effect, for the mouth which captured hers was hungry indeed. Sighing weakly, she ran her fingers into his hair—and a cry escaped at the mask her fingers encountered, this muted against melded lips.

He pulled back to peer down at her with eyes black as coal. "Aya," he breathed, the word raspy and thick. "Remove it, if yon must."

She awoke with a gasp, and the arm draped across her waist tightened. Rolling in his arms, she clambered clumsily atop of him, clutching him close, needing to hold tightly the man who was not her brother.

"Yon is safe," he spoke, the deep rumble of his voice vibrating through her. He slid his hands beneath her lungilt, gliding his fingertips along her back, this bringing to mind the first intimate caress of the fraigen dropper, the man who *was* her brother.

With a shuddering moan, she began to place frantic kisses upon his cheeks, showering the face of the man who was not her brother. She moved quickly to his lips, and he parted them readily at her prompting. She kissed him with gluttonous greed, needing to taste the man who was not her brother.

With a trembling hand, she reached between them, sliding it brazenly into his sleep pants, needing to caress the man who was not her brother. And then she was sliding downward to place urgent kisses upon a chest which held no leering fraigens, down further still to fumble frantically with tangled ties. With these, the Leader of Lors did offer kind assistance.

With muffled moans, she devoured him shamelessly, a sumptuous savoring. She was quaking at a feast so exquisite, silky soft upon her palate. In desperation, she had become the hunter. A consuming hunger drove her. It would be fed, and the Lor of Zeria, the ganis who was nayat her brathern, seemed all too willing to offer himself as prey.

CHAPTER 11

The fire had been amply fed. It burned hot as it feasted, the flames licking high. Christine hung the shirt on the makeshift clothes rack, spreading it out to dry next to the other, and Reesal came up beside her to aid in maneuvering it closer to the fire. Plucking up a dricloth, he began to scrub at his wet hair. “This ganis is one blasted blogart,” he grumbled under his breath.

She looked to where the Zerian Lor sat shirtless at the table, tipping a mug while dabbing at a wound over his shoulder with a bloodied cloth. “Yon should thank Sola yon did nayat take off his arm,” she said. “It doesn’t seem wise to practice battling skills out in the wintered winds.”

“It is that or turn skewed,” Reesal growled. “This stone boarding does grow more cramped with every passing turning.” He turned to his Lor with a frown. “One more mug,” he ordered.

“This is three alreadied. One more, I will be on one flooring.”

“Four it is, then,” Reesal insisted. “And pour this blogart one as well.”

~~~~~~~~~~

Reesal took the blade she held readied and snipped the last thread. As he stepped away, she moved in to closer inspect his handiwork. The stitches seemed sound, six neat x’s just above the left shoulder blade. Just to the right of this fresh wound, there had been another, the scar sitting between his blades. She felt an uneasy stirring in the pit of her belly at the sight of the wound which had landed her in the keeper. She had meant to drop him that lun, one which seemed as a very distant dream. She shivered at the
~~~~~~~~~~

remembrance of swarming roggii, a living nightmare. Those twenty sols had been her darkest.

“Does yon think mine stitchings will hold, then?” Reesal asked. “I am nayat skilled as one meshganis, but yon hands did mesh well enough.”

“Aya,” she whispered, her knees suddenly feeling weak. “They will hold.”

CHAPTER 12

She didn't have to see them. She could smell them—a foul stench, putrid urine-soaked fur. She could hear them, dozens, hundreds, all chattering angrily as they swarmed about the cot. Pressing her back against the keeper wall, she shivered in the darkness. "Mine Lor," she whispered weakly, parched words pushed past cracked lips. "Pleadings."

The door was thrown wide, spilling blinding brilliance along the floor—and the roggii scattered, whipping wiry tails as they shrieked shrilly.

Light radiated about him, from within him, an ethereal being of beauty—her savior. She fell to her knees, shielding her eyes, unable to gaze upon such brilliance. He gathered her into his arms, only to lay her down, gently pressing himself atop, the purest of warmth ending her shivers instantly. Then his mouth was upon hers and she drank readily of the pureness, quenching instantly her dying thirst…

She opened her eyes, blinking away the grogginess, and pushed weakly against the thief who would creep upon her in the night to steal a kiss as she slept. He pulled away to peer down at her with eyes lambent in the darkness. His fingertips at her face caressed as he studied her. Though not as bright as in the dream, there was an aura about him, glowing warmly.

"Yon tossed me in one keeper," she accused, her words husky with sleep.

A small grin surfaced as he gave a nod.

"Roggii did nearly drop me down. Why did yon nayat just throw me to fraigens? Such would have been more merciful."

"Many did insist I do the very deed," he spoke softly, the

fragrance of fruity spirits on his breath. "Such was nayat yon fating. Mayhap the battling of keeper roggii did give one frailed litia the strength needed to battle the largest roggi of all."

His demeanor took a turn then, the grin fading as serious eyes scoured. "Yon can nayat hide from fating, mine Christa," he stated firmly. "Yon may try, but in the end, it will take its rightly claim."

She wanted to drop her eyes from those delving so deep, but he forbade it. It was not the stone walls of one keeper which surrounded them, but she was his captive all the same, helpless and trembling. There were no roggii to rip her flesh. Her foe this time was much more ruthless, one which would rip her to shreds while she pleaded with him not to stop.

Her heart was racing when he leaned into her lips, a deadly kiss, slow and demanding, one which forced back any frail words of refusal, one which forced her nails to trace light trails up and down his back, one which forced her knees to part so he might position himself snugly in between. She melted beneath him, a pathetic puddle of a trillion tender tears destined to lay trails far from the path of reasoning. With fluttering wings aflame, she soared high, knowing full well a fall would follow, a fatal fall forthcoming.

She was forced firmly back to Atriia as Reesal shot up from a dead sleep with a sharp intake of air. Clutching his throat, he spit and sputtered.

The Lor of Zeria chuckled as he pushed up to forearms. "Lundevons, Reesal?"

Shaking the sleep from his head, Reesal looked toward them sheepishly. "Apologies, Mine Lor," he stuttered. "I did—I was—" He cocked his head. "Does yon hear?" he asked, a strange grin surfacing.

"There is nayathing to hear, ganis," Lor Zeria teased. "Go back to sleeping."

Reesal's grin turned quickly to a full-fledged smile. "Aya. Nayathing to hear, Mine Lor. The wintered winds have ceased."

CHAPTER 13

The cave was in constant commotion, ganist coming and going, carrying out the stelch piece by piece. They had converged by the dozens within turnings of the ceasing of the wintered winds, obviously just as anxious for them to end as she had been. Christine was not blind to the reverent attention of these ganist, some stealing discreet glances when they believed her attention was turned, others ogling openly. They had all come prepared and with purpose. The stockpile was to be loaded onto several travois carriers harnessed to ponies so to transport the stelch more conveniently through the dense woodlands.

But it was the Leader of Lors who was assigned the duty of transporting the most precious of the stolen items.

Riding in front of him, Christine surveyed a forest ravaged by the wintered winds. Naked trees stood stark against gray skies, their branches dripping with icicles, giant fingers groping for the forest floor. Many of these fingers had broken free to litter the floor along with the many broken limbs. The ponies picked their way nervously around these obstacles, their hooves sinking into sodden ground.

And the wintered winds had left a bitter chilliness hanging in the air. It was frigid in Christine's lungs, every exhalation a misty plume. She tucked the blanket securely about the tippet cage held in her lap, then pulled it tightly about her own shoulders. She leaned back against the Lor behind her, welcoming the warmth pouring from him, feeling secure in his embrace. At last, he was taking her back to Becca as promised, back to her babe.

~~~~~~~~~~

They met up with the carriage at the river's crossing where it had all begun, save safely on the opposite side. This was fortunate, for the swollen river raged, drifts of bobbing debris and frothy foam rushing by on a deadly current.

It was an elegant carriage, the white body panels etched in elaborate gilded trim and adorned with golden lanterns. With silky coats of chestnut brown, a team of four ponies stood hitched, their heads held high and ears perked forward.

Two lita escorts waited within. Though they sat primly with hands folded in laps, their eyes were bright, their faces flushed. "Mine Lita," they spoke in unison, nodding as she entered.

"Was that he, then?" one asked breathlessly as soon as the carriage door was closed. She leaned to the window, eyeing through the curtain. "It is!" she squealed. "Same is more eyegrand even than one stone carving!"

"Rialla," the older lita scolded, though she was practically falling off her seat to get a look for herself. "Of all Atriia! It is, then!" she exclaimed, and they both tittered unabashedly.

Letting the curtain fall back into place, they eyed her curiously. "Yon does own far less segs than was mine thinking," the older lita confided.

Rialla nodded agreement, then gasped, slapping a hand over her mouth. "Is that one tippet?"

"Where, then!" the older woman screeched, lifting one foot high, then the other, her wide eyes frantically searching the floor.

Rialla giggled behind a cupped palm. "Really, Hilfra," she chastised. "There, in one caging," she said, pointing to the seat beside Christine.

Placing a hand over heart, Hilfra sighed her relief.

"His callen is Hopper." Reaching down, Christine repositioned the cage, pushing it safely to the back of the seat. The tippet was trembling. He thought himself hidden, though it was only his face buried in shavings. "His leg is injured."

"One tippet does own one callen?" Rialla asked in astonishment.
~~~~~~~~~~

She looked to Hilfra with eyebrows raised, and they both broke into a barrage of giggles.

"Apologies," Hilfra offered through a suppressed grin. "I have nayat ever heard of such, one tippet with one callen. We do nayat aim to be spectless."

"Oh, naya," Rialla stressed. "We do nayat. We—" She squealed suddenly, her hand slapping over her mouth yet again. "Hilfra, one scarring," she pushed out past her fingers. "There, crost one neck!"

Hilfra leaned down, then further until Christine feared she might topple from the bench. To avoid this, Christine lifted her chin a tad, and Hilfra gasped, throwing a hand to her chest. "Ear to ear! It is truths, then. Yon is one Loper of Zeria!"

Rialla bobbed her knees, her pale cheeks blotched with flush. "And yon hands. Is that truths as well, then? Were both ripped by one foul worgle?" She shuddered at the very thought.

Christine offered her hands, and the two litas squealed, turning each over in close inspection.

"Mine babe? Is she well, then?" Christine asked, and instantly the two escorts sobered.

"Aya," Hilfra offered. "Though we have nayat laid eyes upon her. She is closely guarded."

"Closely," Rialla stressed, folding her hands in her lap.

Hilfra became agitated, her mouth turning down in a deep frown as she wrung her hands. With eyes cast down, she shook her head ruefully. "It does pain mine heart that PacMattin did force hisself upon yon!"

"Devon!" Rialla hissed.

"Untruths!" Christine barked, causing both heads to pop up at attention. "The babe is nayat his!"

"Naya?" Hilfra gasped. "Oh, Sola is sweet!"

Both litas became animated once again, clapping hands and thanking Sola profusely.

With a sigh, Christine scooted back to rest against the plush velvet cushions. Placing the doll on her lap, she hugged it close and gave a silent prayer for the carriage to roll.

~~~~~~~~~~~

She heard the first muffled shouts almost immediately upon exiting Woroff Woodland, lone voices hailing the Leader of Lors, invoking the Loper of Zeria. These lone voices very quickly began to multiply until many could be heard chanting in unison—throngs lining the road, braving the bitter cold for a brief glimpse, forcing the procession to slow as they drew nearer to the cassing.

"Of all Atriia," Rialla marveled as she peeked through the curtain.

As Christine struggled to hold back tears at a pace so excruciatingly slow, she stroked the doll she'd put so much sweat and tears into, knowing that every stitch she sewed brought her a few seconds closer to the day when she would hold her babe. Becca was close. And the nearer they drew, the stronger the need to hold her. There was a tightness in her chest which made it difficult to breath, a tightness in her throat which made it difficult to swallow—one in her stomach which made her want to heave. She wanted to scream at the blogarts to get out of the way, to scream at the two escorts who seemed to drivel on endlessly about absolutely nothing.

She tapped on Hopper's cage, and he poked his nose out of the shavings, his whiskers bobbing as he sniffed the air. Realizing that no food was forthcoming, he pulled his nose back under and fluffed up the shavings to bury himself deeper.

Pulling the blanket up over her shoulders, Christine did the same.
~~~~~~~~~~~

CHAPTER 14

The murmuring crowd grew silent as they entered the room. This barely registered to ears attuned to her child's voice only. Her eyes did barely register the procession of heads that bowed as she passed, for they were busy scanning.

Dahla stood center, separate from the crowd, smiling shyly. She was cradling a swaddled bundle to her chest. Bixten broke from her side at a trot. Throwing his arms about Christine's waist, he hugged fiercely. "Neema is here," he chirped excitedly. "She was injured, but she is fine now."

"I know, mine gani." She knelt to peer into brown eyes brimming with adoration. She tousled his hair, and he grinned shyly. "I did miss mine Bixten," she crooned, holding him at arm's length. "Did yon take good care of mine Becca, then?"

He nodded proudly, looking over his shoulder to where Dahla stood. Her face seemed pale, her birthmark stark in comparison.

Christine felt the blood drain from her own face as she stood, felt her breaths grow shallow, her feet anchor fast.

And so it was the very Leader of Lors who moved forward to take the bundle from Dahla. Gingerly, he transferred the tender treasure to Christine's trembling arms. And as the blanket slipped away, Christine's breath caught at the sight, her knees nearly buckling.

Becca's skin was not brown and shriveled. It was an inviolate ivory. Blazened locks softly framed a flawless face. Dark lashes fluttered as she stirred in sleep—then came to rest once again against alabaster cheeks.

Christine pulled her close, placing a kiss on one such cheek, savoring the dewy skin against her lips, then pressed the babe to her breast, embracing the weight of her, the warmth of her. She felt a tear slip free to trail alongside her nose—tasted the saltiness on her lips.

The room about her came into focus at last—the people, so many, so silent, all watching, taking in the treasured moment. The Lor of Zeria was watching as well, so close, so tall—so handsome. She found her eyes drawn to the most sensual mouth she had ever seen.

He leaned down to her, and she up to him, ignoring the murmur that passed through the room as their lips met. She savored the lips that were savoring hers as if a hundred pairs of eyes were not riveted raptly upon them. It felt right in his arms with Rebecca tucked between, safe in her arms at last. The lips on hers had spoken the golden words. She caressed them lovingly, attempting to show her gratitude as only a kiss could.

CHAPTER 15

Becca slipped a square of froma between the bars and Hopper snatched it up. Scurrying to the opposite corner, he sat on his haunches, turning the morsel round and round in tiny paws as he nibbled.

Sneaking up from beneath the table, Bixten stuck a finger in while Hopper's attention was turned, stealing a touch on his furry back before he could scamper safely to center cage. This amused Becca enormously. She clapped her hands and gave a squeaky squeal, and Neema wagged her tail, her nose held high to catch the tippet's scent.

Christine and Dahla exchanged grinning glances. "The tippet is barely able to move," Dahla teased.

"One more bite and he will surent burst," Christine laughed.

"Ten sols straight. I did think the two would tire of one tippet by now."

"Ten and two," Christine corrected with a sigh.

Dahla grinned. "Lor Zeria must be in search of the finest cover-carry in all the land, surent, one dappled with jewels and trimmed in jelt, the finest of fabrics to sit upon, the finest of wheels to travel yon safe to Zeria."

"How can yon be so surent one cover-carry is what he is in search of?"

"As one team of ponies did arrive two sols past," she reminded her. "Six grandly Cleerian ponies. Jelten Cleerians at that. I have only noted the like in picture binds."

Christine looked pensively toward the fire. "I do nayat think it would take so many sols to find one cover-carry. He did nayat even inform he was taking leave."

Dahla gave a knowing nod, looking to the children captivated by the caged tippet. "I have heard he may also be in search of jewelwear," she sang with a sly grin. "The finest can only be found in Smetkin, a good three sol's traveling. Only the finest of jewelwear for the most eyegrandly of litas." She gave a giggle behind a slender hand.

Christine looked about the opulent boarding—a far cry from the cramped cave that had served as her abode for six long alltens. The floors were polished marble, the walls draped in velvety fabrics of olive and gold. The trays from lastsup still sat upon the ornate table. Though now only remnants remained, they had been delivered heaping with baked goser smothered in a cream sauce, sugar-glazed pickens, bread with assorted jams, and an arrangement of sweetcakes for dessert. A fire blazed brightly, one in the main room, another in the bedroom, these tended to diligently every few turnings. And to thwart any undue visitors, four armed guards stood stalwart just outside the doors, battlers with barrel chests and broad shoulders. She and the children were dressed immaculately in the finest of garb and footings, and a lita was sent daily to tend to hair and nails. A harpist sat just within the entrance vestibule, plucking out a celestial melody, and shalia arrangements filled every corner and every unoccupied table top, their sweet fragrance permeating the room. Several elaborate displays stood nearly eight feet tall.

As Christine admired these, Hilfra shuffled in with yet another large display, an amazing spray of orange copes mixed with trailers of purple ivy.

"Aiyee," Hilfra exclaimed as she made room along one wall, sliding aside two smaller arrangements to squeeze it in. "Yon will nayat guess who did send these," she said with a wry grin, her cheeks rosy with flush. "Lor Zeria hisself," she answered before they could respond. "Same will be returning on the morrow. One grand guestive is in the planning," she announced, clapping her hands at such exciting news. "Scullery has been advised to prepare shike flays and jeeters." She smacked her lips at such a succulent menu. "Seamsewing is to work through the lun as well, yon gilt made special, Mine Lita," she directed to Christine—then screeched, throwing her hands to her cheeks and performing a jostling jig, the third such elicited response in as many turnings. "Gani! Aiyee! Of all Atriia!" She thrust her hands onto her hips and pursed her lips indignantly, her annoyance directed at Bixten who was holding the tippit cage up to her nose with a devious grin. "Why does it bring yon such pleasure to torture this lita?" she huffed as she stormed haughtily from the boarding.

"Bixten," Christine chided, though she was having trouble suppressing a naughty grin of her own.

CHAPTER 16

A tongue was lapping at her cheek—her nose—lips. "No, Neema, down," she groaned, wiping her mouth on the back of her hand. Neema's nails clicked across the marble floor, coming to rest at the table.

Rising up on one elbow, Christine tried to clear the sleep from her eyes. "Bixten?"

He sat in the darkness, the glowing embers from the fire offering little light. With his elbows propped upon the table, he rested his chin on a hammock of interlaced fingers as he gazed upon the tippet.

Sliding from the bed, Christine pulled a chair up beside him. "Lundevons, Bixten?"

He shook his head.

She tousled his hair. "Can yon nayat sleep, then?"

He gave a ragged sigh. "Is yon mine malla now?"

Christine turned to the tippet. He was rummaging through his straw bedding in search of missed morsels as if actually still hungry. "Bixten, I can nayat take yon malla's place. But I will act as yon malla when yon does need me to do such."

He nodded, wiping at an eye with his fingers. "The lita did speak mine malla ended fraigen dung."

Christine bristled. "That was naya lita. That was one bligart with one heart black as lun."

Bixten looked to her, his eyes brimming with tears and hope. "Is mine malla with Sola, then?"

"Aya." She put her arm about the small boy, pulling him close to place a kiss upon his head. "When yon does feel the warming of Sola's smile, that is yon malla's embrace, holding tight."

He nodded quietly. “I am going to one Cassing Zeria?”

“Aya. Yon and Neema, both.” She reached down to pat the hound’s head, spurring her tail to wag. She had healed nicely. Not even a scar to boast. “Yon will begin lessonings at such—reading, scribing, numbers.”

“Battling?”

“Aya, that as well.” She ran her fingers through his dark hair, smoothing down a cowlick. “Is it yon wishing to become one battler one sol?”

“One troller,” he confessed, “so to ride beside Roltin.”

Her heart dropped, someplace vast and cold. “Bixten—”

“Roltin did speak I was bright and brazened,” he whispered as if to himself. “Mine fallar did only call me one blasted tippet.”

A chill assaulted her as her heart leapt back into her chest with a riled resurgence. Sliding an arm across his shoulders, she pulled him close. “He can nayat bring harm to yon, mine gani, nayat ever again.”

In a move unexpected, he threw his arms around her, hugging fiercely. “I do know!” he cried. “Thankings. I did wish to do the very deed mineself,” he swore, clinging tight. “Mine very self!”

~~~~~~~~~~

It had not taken much to coax Bixten back to bed. Reaching out, she stroked his hair, and he smacked his lips at the touch. She grinned, even as sleep tried to claim her. A scent sifted into her drifting state, a masculine mixture of campfire smoke, horses, and polished leather. She stirred at the thumping of Neema’s tail at the foot of the bed, then drifted awake as a form settled on the mattress beside her.

Raised up on one elbow, he was gazing down upon her, a ganis fresh in from riding, his hair tousled by the wind, his jaw shadowed with stubble.

“Mine Lor.”

He placed a finger to her lips to silence her, his eyes motioning
~~~~~~~~~~

to where Becca and Bixten slept at her side. Fingertips like feather tips caressed along her lips, then skipped over to her hair. Pulling a lock to his nose, he breathed in deeply, closing his eyes to better savor the fragrance.

"Yon did take leave with nayat one word," she accused, but he was not interested in talk. There was a sparkle in his eyes as he leaned in to shower delicate kisses about her face, and a hint of pleasant fruity spirits on his breath.

Behind her, Bixten shifted and mumbled in his sleep.

She spoke to him in a hushed whisper. "Did yon find what yon did search for?"

His wandering lips slid to nibble at her own. "Aya," he breathed.

Emboldened by the company of two sleeping children in her bed, she slipped her hands to the back of his neck, caressing as she returned his nibbles, this the only prompting needed for a mouth designed to devour. He partook masterfully, a delicate delving, one she savored as heat spread through like Sola's smile. There was a yearning ache as he pulled away to peer down at her with lambent eyes.

With a sigh, she pulled him down again, and the dutiful Leader of Lors complied most readily.

CHAPTER 17

Her face was beaming radiantly. Running fingertips along lips still tender, she grinned at her reflection in the mirror as she reflected back on the lun's events. Two sleeping children in her bed had almost not been deterrent enough for the lusty traveler.

"I have nayat ever noted one gilt so eyegrandly," Dahla said as she admired Christine's reflection. "Every eye of every ganis will be firmly planted on yon this sol."

Christine adjusted the sleeve of the gorgeous gilt, one of cream coloring with delicate trimmings of cocoa and mauve. It was stylishly sequined and beaded. Like a pleasurer's gilt, it sat low on the chest, save with a bit of bouffant fabric sewn along the bodice hem to spare a lita's dignity. Her hair was pulled up into a regal bun, this secured with a sheer net studded with tiny sparkling jewels. Wisps of curls had been plucked free to softly frame her face.

"Of all Atriia," Hilfra exclaimed as she bustled in with a gift box in her hands. "It is as if yon does wear the face of Sola her very self."

"Her very self," Rialla agreed, entering close on Hilfra's heels.

"Quickly, quickly, then. Guests do alreadied arrive," Hilfra urged, handing the box to Christine. "A gifting from one Lor of Zeria," she informed, clapping her hands like a child.

They gasped in unison as Christine lifted the lid to unveil a stunning necklace, rows of dazzling green gems nesting in a webbing of finely spun jelt.

~~~~~~~~~~
~~~~~~~~~~

She greeted the guests one by one, graciously offering her hand to all did approach. And it seemed the line was endless, many ganist and an occasional lita of high standing, all leaning low to lay lips upon a hand manicured, bejeweled, and scarred. Though protocol curtailed inquiries, most studied the injury with interest, many even turning her hand over to observe the exit scar. A humbled Lor of Rostivane was among the inquisitive guests, his two gans by his side. With flaming ears and cheeks, he pressed lips to her hand.

"I can nayat speak enough of how pleased I am that yon is safe, Mine Lita, as well as yon precious babe. And I can nayat hand apologies enough for the actions of mine sasturn," he spoke candidly, his flush seeming to grow a shade darker with every word he uttered. "Same has been duly keepered," he promised.

The sons flanking him nodded agreement, their cheeks splotchy and their light-blue eyes studying her curiously.

With a face turned nearly purple, Lor Rostivane moved on to the esteemed Leader of Lors, clasping his shoulder in the Atriian greeting of ganist. "Lor Zeria," he greeted with a nervous chuckle before leaning in to his ear. "I did hear tale of yon special gifting for this fine lita. Well done."

Lor Zeria gave a nod. "One courtyard," he informed amiably. "One turning of six and ten."

"Aya. We would nayat miss such."

"Special gifting, Mine Lor?" she asked as the next guest stepped in to take her hand.

His only reply was a contained grin.

~~~~~~~~~~

Sola's radiant face was just beginning to dip. She'd been working resolutely to pull the chill from the air since the ceasing of the wintered winds, so to induce latent leaves to form on limbs. Her work had paid off. It was a grand sol—warm and breezy, the trees fluttering with new life—a perfect day for a grand presentation of the grandest cover-carry in all the land. Each and every guest had piled out to the courtyard to join with the many townspeople already
~~~~~~~~~~

assembled, for it appeared as if every ganis and lita in the cassing was in attendance. It was a peculiar sight, those decked in finery mingling with those in common garb, but an animated buzz of expectation united them. A battlean on ponyback policed the large crowd of onlookers, as did many set upon foot. It was an occasion not meriting full battle armor, and so mere meshed metal lay draped upon broad shoulders and lengthy swords sheathed at their sides.

Christine had never felt more like a queen. Surrounded by a veritable garrison, she sat high upon a velvet-lined throne sitting high upon a covered platform. The Lor of Woroff sat by her side, appearing resplendently regal in a robe of royal-blue edged in snow-white fur.

He reached over to pat her hand. "Fine fingerrings, Mine Lita," he complimented with a stately nod as he twirled the tip of his goatee between thumb and forefinger.

"Many thankings, Mine Lor." She held up her hands to show off the eight rings, one on every finger. "Yon is overly kind to have gifted so many."

"And yon is overly kind to have worn all gifted." He nodded toward the necklace. "And such a fine neckring I have nayat ever noted. The Leader of Lors did well. But it does nayat compare to that yet to be gifted."

She trailed her fingers along the webbing of gems at her neck as her eyes trailed to where the Leader of Lors stood in conversation with Kynneth and Reesal near the stairs of the platform. "He has been kind to me," she admitted.

"I may nayat be as pleasing on the eyes," Lor Woroff teased, "but I can be kind as well. Is yon surent yon must return to Zeria? Yon is most welcomed to stay here, if yon does wish."

"Lor Zeria does hold claim to me."

He chuckled, reaching over to pat her hand. "Yon is one Loper of Zeria, Mine honored Lita, higher in standing even than one Leader of Lors. He has naya claiming on yon."

Christine frowned as she fingered the rings. She looked to the Leader of Lors—just as he looked up to her, grinning handsomely. "I am free to stay?"

The rise in volume told of his gift's arrival, the horse-drawn carriage rounding the corner of the cas as it headed for the courtyard. Trundling past the crowd, it turned every head. Though it was not drawn by six Jelten Cleerians, but by two broad-chested ponies, both mottled gray. Lor Zeria approached it with Reesal and Kynneth close behind, all greeting a cover-carry not grand in the least, one not white and gleaming with gilded trim, but matte black, the windows decorated with nothing but an iron grill.

Four men were shoved from the carriage, their hands bound behind their backs. Their clothes were filthy and tattered, their faces bruised and swollen.

Despite Sola's warm smile, goose bumps shot up her arms. "What is this," she breathed, the words lost in the murmur of the masses.

The Leader of Lors planted his feet firmly before the four men. "There she sits," he declaimed for all to hear, sweeping an arm toward her. "One Loper of Zeria, the very yon did risk yon only lives to lay hands upon. Cast yon eyes upon her, then, and beg forgivings."

Christine numbly perused four men she did not recognize, three dark headed, one gray.

It was the older man who spoke first. "Was high rounds did lead this ganis to lend hand in yon hunting," he confessed in a tone not apologetic in the least. Neither were his eyes apologetic. They were shooting daggers.

Lor Zeria stationed his fists staunchly on his hips. "Five by ten rounds is worth yon dropping, then? Spill where I can find Boskiel, and mayhap I will nayat spill yon blood."

"I do nayat know Boskiel," he sneered. "Was Rellec did hire me, he dropped by one bligart." He directed a scathing glare toward Christine. "As was mine only gan. Yon may remember him, he with one eye."

Christine tried to find her voice, but the ganis addressing her was impatient.

"It was nayat enough to rip his throat. Yon did rip his belly, did pull his innards out from in. I would hunt yon again, even with naya rounds offered, so to rip yon blasted throat wide. Yon is one devon, as is the blasted babe pulled from yon loins."

The slice came quickly, the blade drawn and dashed across his throat so deftly, she missed it entirely. He seemed to have missed it as well, for he continued to leer for many long grains before his eyes popped wide. He collapsed to his knees, and before his face could meet the dirt, Lor Zeria tipped his blade at a different throat.

"Has yon any words, then, for one honored Loper of Zeria?"

The man fidgeted, glancing down to where his cohort flopped about. "I do nayat know Boskiel, as Sola shines. Was Rellec did hire me as well. High rounds did lead this ganis to devonry," he admitted, turning remorseful eyes toward Christine. "Apologies, Mine Lita."

"Wisely spoken," Lor Zeria said—before he ran the blade through his heart with a nimble hand.

The scream tangled in her throat, as did the legs in her gilt, preventing her from springing to her feet. There was a ringing in her ears as she gripped the arms of the throne. She spun to implore Lor Woroff, but the words were jumbled behind the jammed scream.

In her distress, she did not see the third man meet his demise. Her reeling senses cleared just in time, however, to grant her full witness to the fourth throwing his face to the sweet smile of Sola one last time.

CHAPTER 18

She fixated upon the feeding flames. Though she stood close to the hearth, a chill pervaded, and though the flames licked high, the room was drearily dark. The cloying scent of wilting shalias was nauseating. She could hear the children frolicking on the bed in the adjoining room, though their laughter seemed distant to ears still ringing.

"Mine Lita," Hilfra whispered behind her—a third or fourth attempt. "Allow me to help yon off with yon gilt, then."

"Did yon note his face," Christine spoke to the flames, "the last?"

"Naya, Mine Lita."

"A boy. No more than a boy."

It was some time before she realized Hilfra was no longer present. She had slinked silently away.

~~~~~~~~~~

The room grew darker and colder with his entering. The others quickly cleared away, shutting themselves within the adjoining bedroom. She felt him approach to hover behind, leaning close, his breath chilly upon her cheek. She shrank at the icy hands that touched upon her shoulders, and he quickly drew them away.

"Christa, yon is safe now. We can travel to Zeria with naya flustings."

She searched in the vastness that was emptiness, rooting for a shred of sanity. "I will nayat be traveling."

She felt him stiffen behind her. "Those ganist did aim to drop
~~~~~~~~~~

yon and yon babe."

"Aya. Many thankings, Mine Lor. I am safe now, safe to stay where I do please."

"There is still danger. What of Boskiel? He did offer high rounds for yon and yon babe. He may be one solist. And what of high-hillers? Does yon wish to fall to their hands?"

"I'll take my chances."

He leaned down to her ear, sending a chill through her as he spoke. "We leave for Zeria on the morrow."

It was Dahla who spoke in her ear next, whether grains or turnings later, she was not certain.

"Mine Lita, we must prepare for travel. The bathing room is readied. We must—"

"There will be naya traveling," Christine replied.

"But, Mine Lita, one Lor of Zeria—"

"One Lor of Zeria need run blade through mine heart next. Only dropped will this lita be traveling with such."

~~~~~~~~~~

He stalked into the room like a riled wildhound, his hackles raised and teeth bared, sending the others scurrying from the room like frightened tippets. "Turn when one ganis enters, lita," he snarled in a tone that implied she best comply.

Still, she could not pull her eyes away from the entrancing flames. "Yon should address me as *Mine* Lita, Kynneth."

Grasping her arm, he spun her around. "It seems yon is nayat yet readied for travel, *Mine* Lita."

She looked up into eyes dark and challenging. "It is mine wishings to remain at the Cas of Woroff."

He grinned, pulling his shoulders back. "Is it, then?"

"In case yon does forget, I am one Loper of Zeria, of higher standing even than one Leader of Lors. He has naya claiming on me."
~~~~~~~~~~

His jaw tightened. "Yon would turn on mine brathern for he did drop those would drop yon? Yon should fall to his feet and lay lips to same!"

She gave a humph, one which near transitioned to a sob. She held it back, an effort which left her body trembling—as well as her voice. "The sol he did drop one pleasurer straight from his very bunker, I did know he owned one heart cold as any devon's."

He craned toward her, his eyes flashing. "If there was ever one throat in all of Atriia deserved of ripping, it was PacMattin's loping bligart!" He pulled his shoulders back to stand tall before her. "Sutter was PacMattin's loper as well," he spoke in a calmer tone. "And one foul as the devon hisself. Both did own one tasting for huganis flesh. Was yonself did cause PacMattin to sup on Sutter." He nodded at the look on her face. "His ears for taking in untruths," he quoted, "his lips for passing such on." His infuriating grin popped neatly into place. "Sutter does hide his shammered face in high-hills. But I am surent once he does hear of yon rising from blackened waters, he will be overly eager to meet with yon again. I am certain he will be eager to meet yon sweet lia as well. Is such yon aiming, then?"

She forced down the gorge rising in her throat. "I do aim to keep her from the hands of all devons. That includes yon brathern."

His eyes narrowed to slits. "Mine brathern is one Leader of Lors, chosen for he is one ganis of honoring. He did swear on Sola to keep yon from harm, and so he will—with his very life. The ganist dropped did hunt yon and yon babe. And I do nayat think they did mean to throw yon one guestive."

"There are keepers for such! They were but hired ganist lured by rounds! The one barely more than a gani! They did nayat even stand before one saker! Naya, was the grand honored Leader of Lors did hand down sentencing, then carry out same with his own hand!"

He straightened to his full height, squaring his shoulders. "The honored Leader of Lors did also swear on Sola nayat to bring harm to Hannen Fallier." He grinned deviously at her reaction. "But I did nayat," he warned, his grin vanishing. "The blogart did stelcher yon from one Cas of Zeria. His head should have fallen segs ago." He nodded, pleased to have captured her full attention. "Same is very close this lun, just without the walls of Woroff, he along with thousands of others, all traveling in from distant cassings to note one famed Loper of Zeria. It would be one shammering if stelcherers were to set upon him so to rip his throat wide for the few slices in his purse. With a gathering of such sizing, it is difficult to control stelchering—*Mine* Lita."

She tried to swallow down the lump, to blink back the tears. "Kynneth," she implored even as a tear escaped, making a mad dash to her chin, "was mine fating to be stelchered by Fallier, so to be brought before PacMattin—so to bring about his dropping."

He traveled the length of her with talcar eyes, taking in the gilt reflecting the glow of the fire, the neckring shimmering in the flickering flames, the bejeweled blazened locks

His face softened. "When first I did note yon—yon was decked in ganist garb." His fingers went to the neckring, running a tickling trail over the gems. "Is it truths one fraigen scale was used to slice PacMattin's throat?"

"One fraigen scale handed me by Fallier. Was his fating to be there, as much as it was mine own. Please do nayat harm him."

His hand lifted to her chin, tilting her face to his. "We take leave on the morrow—Mine Lita."

CHAPTER 19

The grandest cover-carry in all of Atriia transported them away from the cassing of Woroff—white paneled sides with gilded trim harnessed to four gallant Jelten Cleerians, their silky coats shimmering in Sola's smile as if spun from gold. Boasting bridles and reins studded with jewels, they tossed manes the color of cream and snorted at a crowd that cheered and chanted. A battlean of armed guardsmen performed their job efficiently, clearing the path so the grand procession could make its way through the melee unhindered. Bixten sat wide-eyed, hugging tight the tippet cage upon his lap. Neema sat at his feet, looking more timid than the tippet. Sitting beside Bixten, Dahla looked proper in a gilt of soft lilac with peach ruffles, her blonde hair wound neatly in a bun at her nape.

Christine stroked Becca's hair. The child clinging to her new ragdoll and to her malla's side wore a definitive pout, had been wearing such since the sighting of the carriage, the memory of the last ride being far too fresh in the babe's mind. The child was not impressed by the opulent cab, the plush buttoned seats upholstered in white and gold velvet, nor the padded walls lined in golden silk.

Dahla put an arm about Bixten, rubbing his arm. "Do nayat fret, mine gani," she crooned. "This traveling will be much differed from the last, surent. Many battlers do ride on all sides and the very Leader of Lors does lead one way."

Christine breathed a hollow sigh. The very Leader of Lors had come to visit that morning dressed for travel—had pulled her aside into the bedroom—had fallen to one knee to grasp her hand, pressing it to his forehead, then to his mouth, caressing it with his lips before placing a dazzling ring upon her finger. The gift had elicited an eruption of tears, certainly not the response anticipated, for he stood to look down upon her with lips set thinly.

"Bandi stones are the rarest of all," Dahla said, admiring the ring. "When one ganis does offer such, he is offering his heart. I have nayat ever noted one of such sizing."

It was indeed beautiful, a square-cut diamond with a bluish hue. And it was hard and cold as the heart of the man who had gifted it. Christine slid off the ring she'd been fingering, offering it out to Dahla. "One gifting."

Dahla's eyes popped wide. "Naya, Mine Lita, I can nayat!"

"Surely yon would nayat refuse mine gifting. Mine feelings would be overly harmed at such."

Dahla's hand was trembling as Christine placed the coveted jewel into her palm, folding her fingers around it.

PART IV

CHAPTER 1

Eubreena turned Dahla to the flector. "Open."

Dahla opened her eyes, and the surrounding litas giggled at the amazement that lit her face. "Of all Atriia!"

"Did I nayat speak Eubreena was skilled," Christine said, and the litas gathered around the flector table nodded affirmation.

Tavaka leaned in to hug Dahla's shoulders. "Yon does look eyegrandly, Dahla!"

Eubreena beamed. "On the morrow, I will show yon how to paint yonself," she promised. "It is overly simple. One thin coating. It must be thin. Let it dry, then one added."

Tears began to pool in Dahla's eyes.

"Naya tears, Dahla," Eubreena warned. "Such will streak the paint."

Christine witnessed the sleeping Becca transferred to yet a different lita's arms, Tressa beaming upon the cradled babe before bending to place a kiss upon an ivory cheek.

Ryla approached the group and cleared her throat. "I have been called down," she announced in the lofty tone of one pleasurer. "Mineself, Sheilla, and Tiatra to one Mas Zeria."

“Fetch them, then,” Eubreena said with a sigh. “Give me ten mounds to prepare.”

“She is the most spellerly babe in all of Atriia,” Tressa said as she transferred the babe to Christine’s arms.”

As the audience of litas dispersed, Eubreena corked the vial of freshly mixed face paint and handed it to Dahla. “Only three pleasurer’s this lun,” she quipped, looking around to be sure she wasn’t overheard. “Kynneth must be overly wearied.”

Dahla giggled behind one hand, though her eyes never left her reflection.

“Yon would think the ganis put in charge of one entire cassing would have more portent matters to tend,” Christine chided as she rocked her babe. “I mineself have requested to speak with him on several occasions, and all go unheeded.”

“Kynneth is doing one fair job while his brathern is away,” Eubreena defended as she began to prepare her working area. “More so than Dashingten. The blogart could barely run cas scullery, much less one entire region. Same near fell to waste whilst they were away. Yon does note how many sols our Lor does spend trying to mesh his mess.”

“One full cycle thus far,” Tavaka admitted.

Eubreena nodded. “Last I did hear, he was in Cassing Tazziele, as such does battle over boundaries with Seritar.” Pulling out a fresh palette, Eubreena began daubing patches of color upon it. “From there he is to travel upperly to Cassing Emoclew. Same is on the verge of overthrow.”

“Aya,” Tavaka acknowledged, observing as Eubreena began to blend together the different colors, skillfully creating three different shades to match the gilts of the three different pleasurers. “I have heard the other litas speaking of such. Lor Emoclew’s brain has skewed with aging, yet those who do gest he step down do end up with naya heads.”

“Aya,” Eubreena agreed. “He has ten and two gans, but none dare cross him. But our Lor will sway him, doubtent. He is skilled at bending others to his will.”

Dahla slid the vial of face paint into her pocket, then slid herself from the stool. "Yon can stay to aid Eubreena if yon does wish, Mine Lita," she spoke to Christine. "Tavaka and I will put Becca to bunker," she offered as she gently took the sleeping babe. "Come, Neema."

Eubreena moved aside so the hound could squirm from her hiding place beneath the dressing table, then watched as she padded obediently away, her nails clicking upon the tiled floor as she followed on Dahla's heels. Brushing her hair back, Eubreena shook her head. "I have nayat ever noted one as timid."

Christine watched the hound keeping close pace with the two young women. "Does yon speak of one hound, or of Dahla?"

"Both," she admitted with a laugh. "Mayhap Dahla will nayat be so shammered of her face, now she has paint to hide her birthing mark."

"Aya. Many thankings, Eubreena. She is a good litia. And she is fitting well here. She and Tavaka, both."

Eubreena nodded. "It was kind of yon to send for her friend."

"I had naya choosing in the matter. I did tire of the constant moaning."

Pulling a key from the drawer, Eubreena unlocked the jewelwear box and began to sort through necklaces and earrings, laying several delicate pieces gently upon the table. "And what of yon, mine dearest Christa? Is yon fitting as well, then? Is yon done with the bind scribers, least?"

"Auggh, naya," Christine groaned. "Near three turnings every sol. How many counts must I speak the same tale over and over again? They do want every detail—what I ate this sol, what I wore that, every word spoken. I can nayat remember such things. And the bind painters are worse yet—what coloring was this, what sizing was that?"

Eubreena turned to her suddenly, gazing down with misty eyes, a deed she had been repeating with some frequency since her return. "They must be certain all is truths before inked to parchment." Gripping her by the shoulders, the large woman pulled her close, squeezing tight. "Yon words scribed on parchment, yon likeness carved to stone. Mine wee Christa, barely the sizing of one litia," she crooned, before pushing her to arm's length. "Yon did drop PacMattin, did drop one woodslink." She grasped her hands to gaze upon the scars, running her thumbs along them. "One foul worgle. And now yon is to be brooder to the very Leader of Lors."

Christine gave a dramatic gasp. "Eubreena, I have—"

"Naya aimings of such," Eubreena finished for her as she resumed arranging the table for the lun's work. "It is mine guessing one certain Lor has aimings of such. Why else is one boarding being prepared crost from his very own?"

"*Two* boardings are being prepared. One for Dahla and Tavaka, and one for Becca and mineself. He knows I am flustings and does wish to keep close eyes on me, is all."

Propping her hands on her hips, Eubreena shook her head. "Why is it the one should be informed she is to be brooder to the Lor of Zeria, is the only one in all of Atriia who is nayat?"

"All of Atriia has nayat spoken to the Lor of Zeria on this matter as I have."

Eubreena checked over her shoulder before sliding open the top drawer, then digging to the bottom for the pleasurer's charts. Leafing to the last page, she then sidled closer to point to the symbol in the top right-hand corner—a black medallion on a red ribbon, the honor of Sola. "This is yon symbol."

"Mine! Yon is keeping track of mine lita's cycle?"

"Shhh," Eubreena warned, peering about. "I have been handed instructings to do so," she said with a devious grin. "But yon must nayat speak of such," she added hastily, "lest I do lose mine tongue."

Ryla returned with Sheilla and Tiatra in tow, all three dressed in their revealing pleasurers gilts cut high on the arms and low at the chest. They were three of the newest prized pleasurers, all with deep red hair, light blue eyes, and fair skin. They gave an honorable bow of their heads to Christa.

"Mine Lita," they chorused.

~~~~~~~~~~
~~~~~~~~~~

Kynneth lie propped up in his gigantic four poster bed, a sheet draped across his hips and a mug of spirits in his hand as he greeted his guests one by one. His grin instantly vanished at the sight of Christine.

"Blast it all," he snarled, the liquid sloshing from his mug as he slammed it on the night-stand.

"If I could have one word, Mas Zeria," she spoke hastily.

He shot up from the bed, clasping the sheet at his hip as he made for the door in long angry strides.

"I am content at the lita's quarters," she blurted before he could order her out. "I do nayat need one private boarding. And the boy Bixten—I am pleased he is lessoning, but could he nayat at least visit? He—"

"Blogarts!" Kynneth shot out at the two guardsmen. "I did speak three pleasurers would enter, nayat three pleasurers and one loper!" Pointing a finger down the hall, he ordered his guards gruffly away. "Send two ganist who will note one blasted loper when one does pass before their very eyes!"

The pleasurers cowered as he turned to glower at them. "Out!" he shouted, and they hurriedly complied, shuffling past him without a word and leaving a cloud of pleasurer's scenting in their wake. Slamming the door behind them, Kynneth stalked toward her. "And what of *yon* guardsganist, lita? Did yon slip past them as well?"

"I did also mean to speak of such," she said, wringing her hands nervously. "Must guardsganist stand over me every grain of every sol? I do—"

"Yon *did* sneak past them, then, loping as one pleasurer." He moved close to hover over her, his eyes flashing. "One grand Loper of Zeria, loping yet again? Mayhap I should have their heads removed for they did fail in their duties." His eyes sparkled at her reaction, then raked the length of her. "Yon is nayat even decked as one pleasurer. Blinded blogarts!"

Christine retreated a few steps to gather her thoughts, but he quickly moved in, backing her against the bureau. "Does yon think it spectful to lope on this ganis?" he asked, the spirits pungent on his breath.

"I did nayat aim to be spectless. I—"

"Yon does give away every gifting handed by mine brathern. Now yon would turn away one private boarding as well? Such does shout spectless, lita!"

She dropped her eyes to his chest, one sparsely surfaced with light brown hair, then over to a scar which ran from under his left arm to his collar bone.

"Our labor litas do boast the grandest of jewelwear," he lambasted, "the finest of garb. They sup on sweetcakes from the lower regions, globeberries from the upper. They boast shalias in every corner. Our pleasurers are nayat even kept as well!"

"I—I have naya needing of so many giftings."

"Will yon give away Fallier's gifting as well, then?" he asked, the question drawing her eyes back to his in an instant. "One fine pony indeed—pale-coated, light-eyed." He acknowledged her reaction with a knowing nod. "I am thinking it best to send such away. The stone-yards in Alabas are always in needing of strong ponies, for such do nayat last very long at such heavy laboring—four, five segs at most fore they drop."

"Kynneth—"

"Mas Zeria," he corrected, stepping closer yet. "Fallier is one blasted blogart! Same was warned nayat to come near Zeria, so he does bid one boarding on the skirts, then does send giftings! I'm of one mind to go mine very self and drop the spectless blogart!"

"Yon did swear on—!"

He grasped her wrist in a tight fist. "Do nayat mistake this ganis for his brathern, lita! If Fallier does step foot within this cassing, I will take his head in one sifted grain! *This* I do swear on Sola!" He whipped the sheet off, flinging it aside, freeing his hand to grasp a fistful of blazened locks. "I am gladdened yon did lope to mine boarding, lita, so I might lesson yon in spects. Does yon think it spectful to pull away from mine brathern's every touch, to keep yon eyes cast down to his feet when he speaks?"

She fought to free the breaths trapped in her throat, blocking any haughty rebuttal.

He leaned close, pressing himself against her. "When he returns, yon will turn yon face to his, as such," he demonstrated, wrenching her head back. "When he leans to yon lips, yon own will welcome his, as such," he said, leaning in, his mouth closing over her own closed tightly.

With a growl, she shoved him away. "Blogart!" she spat, wiping her mouth on the back of her hand. "Do nayat mistake this lita for yon tripes!" she gasped, the escaping breaths tumbling out at once.

He chuckled. "There is naya mistaking such. Mine tripes do own welcoming, wide-opened lips—as well as legs," he added with a smirk.

"They do also own wide opened brains!"

He laughed as he raked his fingers through his hair, brushing it back from his face. He was laughing still as he strolled back to the bed to lie out in his smug nakedness. Stretching to the bed-stand, he retrieved his mug. "Have mine empty-brained tripes sent back down, then," he ordered.

"And, Lita," he called, stopping her at the door. "If yon does wish to keep one pony, I gest yon does keep any giftings the Leader of Lors does send to his precious loper."

Keeping her eyes on the door, she rubbed her bruised wrist. "I would like permission to visit the stables early on the morrow."

"Granted, Mine Lita. I will inform yon *new* guardsganist."

She looked over her shoulder to a ganis lounging with not one shred of modesty, one wearing nothing but a mocking grin. "I do nayat wish mine guardsganist punished—or yon own."

He brought the mug to his lips, sampling its contents and smacking his lips. "Hmmm. Yon does nayat wish mine guardsganist punished, and I do nayat wish mine brathern punished." He replaced the mug upon the night-stand to fold his arms across his chest. "Will he return to lips wide opened and welcoming, then?"

Christine bit her lip to hold back the invectives, choosing instead to nod in answer.

"And legs?" He grinned smugly. "Yon can nayat be one brooder with yon legs closed tight."

She whirled to face him, keeping one hand firmly on the door handle. "Yon brathern and I have spoken on this!"

He gave a dubious chuckle. “Aya, one babe pulled through yon belly. Does yon think us blogarts, lita?”

“I do swear on Sola!” She struggled not to drop her eyes from his face, for it was becoming increasingly evident the conversation was stirring excitement.

“Yon has naya shammering, lita. And as yon does note, I have nayan as well, so I gest yon get yonself gone. Send down mine tripes. They may nayat have much by way of brains, but least they do own curves to boast.”

Christine pulled her shoulders back indignantly. “Aya, as well as blazened locks and light eyes, the very coloring of one Loper of Zeria. And all three at that.”

His grin only broadened at the jibe. “Mine brathern’s favorites,” he informed her smugly. “I now sider it mine duty to keep their skills honed since he will naya longer be doing such. He will now have the Loper of Zeria, her very self, just crost the hall in her own fine, private boarding.” He laced his fingers behind his head as he lounged back against the headboard. “Yon should find it to yon liking,” he assured her. “It does hold one of the grandest bunkers in all of Atriia, one with four overly *sturdy* legs,” he stressed, the mocking grin growing to a full-fledged smile.

Christine felt the blood drain from her face. “Reesal!” she growled as she stormed from the room.

CHAPTER 2

"Yon is so tall." Christine pressed her cheek against the pony, hugging her about the neck, then chuckled at the warm breaths at her hip as gentle lips explored her pockets. "Ahh, does yon search for this?" she asked, producing a slice of sweetstalk.

The stable boy stopped cleaning the stall to lean on his rake. "Luckied Lita does like yon. She does nayat take to most. But—yon must nayat treat her with sweetstalk."

"Luckied Lita," Christine repeated, trying the name out on her tongue. "I like yon also, Luckied Lita." She scratched her forehead and the pony closed her eyes, leaning into it, pressing her chest against the stall door as she savored the caress and the sweetstalk at once. "Why should I nayat treat her?"

"She has been gifted to Christa Clavin, the very Loper of Zeria," he boasted.

"The very Loper of Zeria? Well, she must be one special pony, surent, to be gifted to such, the most famed lita in all of Atriia."

"Aya. And she is trusted to mine caring. I am surent one loper would be angered if her gifting was to fall ill from sweets."

"Mmm." Christine nodded. "Yon must nayat anger the Loper of Zeria. Same does own one horrid temper."

He scratched his chin. "I have heard such. Has yon noted her then, within one cas?"

"Mmm, aya. She is blazened-locked, like mineself."

He nodded. "But much taller."

"Taller?"

"Aya, as tall as any ganis. And owning the battling skills of same."

"Aya, one fierce battler, surent."

"It is spoken she did drop one full-sized woodslink."

"Is it?"

"Aya. She did sit its back, just as I might sit this pony," he said, stroking the pale silky flank. "She does ride the backs of fraigens as well."

"I have heard such."

"And it is spoken she did—did take off PacMattin's…" With an embarrassed grin, he motioned to his privates, "before she did take off his head."

"I have heard as much," she admitted. "I gest yon does take special care of her pony, lest she does take off yon head as well. Or worse," she added, motioning low.

The gani, one owning dark hair and fair freckled skin, paled considerably. "It is spoken she owns one face horridly scarred."

Christine's hand fluttered to her cheek. "Horridly?"

"And her hands as well—by one worgle. Three fingers ripped clear away—yet she did still lift one babebunker over her head, so to smash the foul creature's brains."

She held her hands up to wriggle her fingers. "Naya, I do still own all ten."

The gani glanced at the two grinning guardsmen standing off to one side, then back to her, taking in her hair and eyes. "Is yon—" He blushed at the possibility.

She gave a grin and nodded.

The young boy dropped to one knee in an instant. "Apologies, Mine Lita," he said, bowing his head. "I did nayat know. I—I did think yon would be—"

"Taller?"

He lifted his eyes bravely and nodded, his cheeks splotched with flush.

She motioned for him to stand, so to look into brown eyes abovc the level of her own. "How many segs does yon own?"

"Four and ten, Mine Lita."

"And yon callen?"

"Earltin. I—I have been caring for Luckied Lita every sol," he stammered, "brushing her, feeding her. Her water and grains, I do keep fresh."

"Well, Earltin, yon has done one fine job. She looks well kept. Yon will keep yon head for now."

The boy grinned shyly, his face turning redder yet.

"However, yon duties as her caregiver will naya longer be needed every sol. I will be here on many to take over such."

He glanced to where the armed guards stood stoic. "Will yon be riding as well, then? And will yon guardsganist need ponies for escort?"

"Riding?"

The boy nodded. "Luckied Lita is well-trained, and to all three—bit, leg, and voice."

"Aya," she said, stroking the silky neck. "Aya, I will be riding. Though I will need lessoning."

The boy seemed surprised, his brows shifting high as an incredulous grin formed.

"Well, I have only ridden the backs of fraigens and woodslinks," she spoke in all earnestness, checking the gani's grin in an instant. "But, as I do note nayat one fraigen or woodslink here to be rid, one pony will have to do."

The boy frowned, then scratched his head. "The ganies do have riding lessonings every other sol. Mayhap yon could join."

"Aya, mayhap I could." Christine grasped the pony's halter to place a kiss upon her muzzle. "I will be riding yon, Luckied Lita," she informed her, scratching the forehead between two sky blue eyes. "Luckied Lita is one good callen. Yon did birth yon nipper, then, with naya flustings. I was worried."

"She has nayat been weaned from her nipper long," the boy informed her. "She did call for same near three full sols after arriving."

"Ahhh, does yon miss yon nipper?" she crooned, combing fingers through her silky mane. "Did yon birth one, or two like yon malla?"

"Yon does know Luckied Lita, then?"

"I did raise same from one nipper."

"Does yon know how she was ripped, then?"

"Ripped?"

"Aya. One scarring here to there," the boy said, motioning on himself from navel to groin.

~~~~~~~~~~

Christine sat in her bunker, propped back against pillows filled with the softest of goser down. It was a sturdy bunker, indeed, with legs thick as tree trunks towering to the ceiling. The four immense posts were intricately carved with shalias and draped in sheer swags of cream-colored chiffon. The entire room was similarly adorned towards a lita's taste—a bureau matching the bunker in wood stain and design, a mirror framed in jelten shalias sitting pretty atop. A luxurious chest lounged at the foot of the bed, storage for extra blankets and the many dolls and stuffed animals gifted to Becca. A six-foot vase displayed a spray of purple shalias in one corner, their delicate scent sweet on the air. The cubit was overflowing with tailor-madc gilts and footings, and twenty some-odd bottles of scenting oil sat upon the bureau along with a jewelwear box, this overflowing with jewelwear sent from all over Atriia to the beloved Loper of Zeria.

Putting a hand to her mouth, Christine nibbled at her nails.

The beloved Loper of Zeria had been thoroughly examined in the sturdy bunker not two turnings earlier, the two meshganist going over every inch of her body with a nauseating thoroughness. They had been especially interested in the many scars, leaning close to study them—taking precise measurements of all—asking endless questions. And blasted Kynneth had been right there by their sides with his arms folded across his chest, invading her privacy with no signs of qualms. All had carefully scrutinized the scar in question, leaning close, three heads hovering side by side, each in turn tracing a finger lightly along its length. They didn't appear convinced by her
~~~~~~~~~~

account of how she had acquired it. The fact that she could not even provide the callen of the meshganis or the cassing from which he hailed only managed to garner further suspicion.

"The ripping was stitched by one skilled meshganis, surent, but naya babe was pulled through," the older meshganis had stated. "One lita would be dropped if such were truths."

"Aya, such was mine thinking," Kynneth agreed.

"Aya," the younger meshganis added as he scribbled notes on a tablet. "Though I have nayat ever seen one scarring placed such."

"I can show one other," she'd said.

A rustling drew her attention to the cage on the night-stand—Hopper rummaging through his bedding in search of missed morsels of bread crust. His search being unfruitful, he hobbled to his water bowl and propped on the rim to drink.

His drink was cut suddenly short at the light rapping on the door, this sending him to diving beneath a mound of straw bedding. Neema came awake as well, scurrying to her feet.

"Aya. Enter."

Reaching down, Christine softly stroked Neema's coat as the guards marched in to shut and secure the shutters. She watched as the hunched and hooded figure shuffled in behind them, toting his oil can. As was ritual, he attended to the sconces that lined the wall first, extinguishing each, then topping them with oil. One in particular seemed to give him difficulties on this sol. He fiddled with it for several mounds, adjusting the wick before moving on to the lamp seated on the night-stand. She watched as he lifted the glass, setting it carefully aside.

She checked the guardsganist who, having finished with their own task, stood waiting in the doorway. Their backs were turned and they were in discussion.

"What is yon callen?" she whispered to the ganis so close.

He hesitated in his work, glancing briefly to where the guardsganist stood conversing. "Grayson," he whispered back as he tilted the oil can.

"How does yon know Fallier?"

Though she could only see a portion of his profile past the hood, it was enough to see his lips pull into a tight grimace.

Replacing the glass, he adjusted the flame down.

"Can yon message him?"

"Is yon nayat finished yet?" a guard barked from the door.

Lifting his oil can, Grayson shuffled from the room, his pace much quicker than when he had entered.

With a sigh, Christine slid down under the covers and rolled to her side to watch Becca sleep. The meshganist and Kynneth had not returned after filing out to head for the stables. Had it been enough to convince them?

No. Not Kynneth.

Never Kynneth.

CHAPTER 3

"Bixten! Mine gani!"

"Christa!" He ran to her, throwing his arms around her waist to squeeze tight. "One Loper of Zeria," he announced proudly to the group of ganies assembled in the stables. "And this is Neema, mine hound." He knelt to hug Neema about the neck, then giggled as she licked his ear. "Where is Becca?"

"With Dahla. I am here to be lessoned in pony riding."

"As am I!" He jumped up to bounce excitedly. "This is mine riding cap," he said, pulling it from his pocket and pulling it down over his ears. "It fits tight so the wind will nayat claim it. And this is mine gani-grouping," he said, pointing to the group of ten ganies who stood in a tight pack, gaping at her. "This is one Loper of Zeria," he repeated as if they had all forgotten his previous proud announcement. "Jacond, come," he said, motioning frantically, and one gani separated from the others to stand shyly beside him. "This is mine friend Jacond. Note," he said, pointing to the boy's arm. "I did cause such bruising. And, here," he said, rolling up his sleeve to reveal a bruise of his own. "We are being lessoned in battling!"

Christine couldn't help but beam at his bright eyes, his flushed face. It seemed he had grown a few inches, as had his hair. She pulled off his cap to tousle this last. "And what of reading and scribing?" she asked.

"Aya. Mine lessoner does speak I am bright at such. Roltin did speak I was bright. Does yon remember?"

His riding instructor was approaching as he spoke, leading two ponies, and Earlton followed, lugging two saddles.

"This is Mas Renner," Bixten piped. "Mine riding lessoner. This is one Loper of Zeria. Mine friend," he boasted, clasping her hand.

"Those are her guardsganist. She does nayat need such, surent. She is the most skilled battler in all of Atriia. She did drop PacMattin. She did drop one woodslink and one worgle. Note her scarring," he said, lifting her hand for all to see.

"Mine Lita," Mas Renner greeted, giving a reverent bow of his head—though he didn't appear overly impressed by the raving accolades. He was a rugged sort, tall and solid, his face shadowed with stubble and etched with lines. His dark hair was graying at the temples and managed to appear mussed even though clipped short. He was not much for formalities.

"I have been informed yon is to be lessoned. Gather round, then," he said, motioning to the ganies. "We begin with saddling."

CHAPTER 4

Thunder rumbled in the distance.

In the mirror, Christine watched the pleasurers practicing the zalt across the room where the table and chairs had been pushed to one side. It was a dance originating in the upper regions, one with which they were unfamiliar and so were practicing until the very last moments before the guestive was to begin. Decked in colorful gilts and dangling jewels, they stepped in prim time to the lilting music of the harp. With shoulders back and chins held high, they each held the hand of an imaginary partner as they went through the motions. After sols of lessonings, Christine knew it well—take ten steps, twirl under your partner's arm, face your partner and step forward to grasp his hands and curtsy, wait as he leisurely strolls around, take his hand and begin again. Ten steps, twirl under his arm—

"Done," Eubreena said as she clipped on the last earring. "Lor LaRosse will be spellered, surent.

Christine sighed. "Thankings, Eubreena. Yon is truly skilled. I do look readied to greet guests the entire lun, when, truths be spoken, I am readied for mine bunker only. I am thinking to send word that I am nayat well."

Eubreena tapped her lightly on the nose. "Kynneth will nayat take well to such," she chided. "LaRosse is one most honored guest, the first Lor from the upper regions to ever visit this cassing. He did bring many guests and did travel many longs. Kynneth does wish to treat them with spects."

"Kynneth can lay lips to mine backside."

"Christa," Eubreena scolded. "There is nayat one lita of this entire cassing would nayat take yon place. It is spoken Lor LaRosse is pleasing on the eyes. Overly eyegrand," she stressed, her brows arching high. "And it is spoken his cassing is ten times the sizing of Zeria. I can nayat picture a cassing of such sizing. *And*, he did gift globeberries," she said, plucking one such from the heaping bowl on the dressing table and popping it into her mouth. She let out a moan, her eyes rolling back in her head at the savory sweetness.

"Mine nose is leaking," Christine groaned. "It will nayat stop. Surent Lor LaRosse will tire of hearing me blow it the entire lun." Christine pulled a wadded hanky from her pocket to demonstrate, honking loudly.

"Yon is reacting to the sallen trees. Many do have flustings with the like. Here," Eubreena said, rifling through a drawer to pull out a small vial. "Serin. In one turning, yon nose will be cleared." Measuring a portion into a mug, she added water from the pitcher and handed it over, waiting with hands on hips till Christine downed it. "Now, let me note those nails," she said, inspecting Christine's hands briefly. "Auggh, yon has been tending to ponies again," she accused, pulling open the drawer to rifle for the nail cleaner.

"Aya. I did ride two full turnings. This sol does mark one cycle, so mine lessoning is done with. And I did nayat even leave one courtyard. The ganies do travel through Zeria and even beyond the walls. I've done nayathing but ride in circles."

"Kynneth does have good reasonings for such, surent."

Christine looked to where Becca sat propped on Dahla's hip. As usual, a group of litas surrounded them, each waiting their turn to lavish the babe with attention. Becca giggled as Tressa tickled her belly and leaned in to kiss a rosy cheek. "I will miss noting Bixten," Christine said with a frown. "I did ask for visitings. I am nearly the gani's malla. But—Kynneth is one foul blasted blogart."

"Christa Clavin," Eubreena rebuked. "Lita's do nayat use such foul words. Ganies are taken from their mallas for lessoning. It has always been such. Now—where is mine nail filer."

"Such thinking is skewed. One gani so young does still need his malla."

"Ganies of such age are proud to leave their mallas and begin lessoning. And yon should wear hand slips while riding."

Christine watched the large woman skillfully shape her nails, filing one after the other in mere grains. Once finished, she plucked a nail buffer from the drawer and went to work shining each nail in turn as she hummed along with the music.

"Will yon paint mine nails next?"

Eubreena's brow furrowed. "Paint?"

"In mine hailing, litas do paint their nails."

Eubreena quit her busy buffing to frown at the palette setting on the table.

"Nayat with face paint, silly." Christine pointed to the nail buffer, tapping on the blue handle. "Paint that hardens, as such. It can be any coloring. It's called nail polish."

Eubreena peered at the buffer's blue paint. "I have nayat ever heard of nail polish. How many segs does it last?"

Christine laughed. "It might last a few sols. When you wish to change colors, you use polish remover."

Eubreena frowned. "Like fallow sap?"

"Aya. Like fallow sap. Mayhap stronger," she added, dabbing at her nose with the hanky.

Dahla came shuffling over with Tavaka by her side. They were quite the pair, Tavaka just as shy and awkward as Dahla. But even with her oversized nose and gapped teeth, she was beautiful in her own way. Her hair was dark and her skin was fair and her smile was sweet. With every passing day, she seemed to become more at ease at her new home. And she seemed to enjoy her job as market lita, one of several in charge of purchasing goods for the lita's quarters, be it beauty supplies, cleaning supplies, clothing, food.

"Mine Lita," Dahla addressed Christine, rubbing Becca's head where it rested upon her shoulder. "Becca grows wearied. Will same bunker with me this lun?"

"Aya," Christine said with a sniffle. "There is to be zalting after lastsup, so I will be in late. And have Neema bunk in yon boarding as well," she added as thunder rumbled yet again. "Same is spookered by storming. Be warned though, she may try to climb into yon bunker."

"There is one good chancing we might all end in one same bunker, then?" Tavaka admitted with an embarrassed grin. "I am also spookered by such."

"Aya, she is," Dahla admitted, shaking her head. "Sorry as it might seem."

"Aya," Tavaka said, smiling sweetly. "Nearly as sorry as being spookered by darkness." She concluded this statement by sticking out her tongue, and Dahla swatted at it with a giggle.

Eubreena inspected her handiwork, tugging on the sleeves of Christine's pale lavender gilt, then adjusting the necklace at her chest. Plucking a blue bottle from the table, she pried out the cork, and dabbed scented oil beneath both ears. "Right, then. Now yon is readied to speller the Lors."

CHAPTER 5

He was much younger than expected. Mid-twenties. Wide of shoulder, narrow of hip. And wise to his good looks. His hair was long and dark, his eyes sky blue. And he owned a resplendent smile which produced remarkable dimples. And he was brazened as any ganis, giving full account of his many broone hunts, showing off the scars of a mauled arm and the neckring of broone claws, the very which had inflicted the wounds. The pleasurers hung on his every word and flirted shamelessly when he passed close, batting lashes and plumping bosoms.

But he only had eyes for one lita—one famed Loper of Zeria. Aiming to please, Christine lavished him with avid attention, if for no other reason than it seemed to irritate Kynneth considerably. She obligingly sampled the globeberries he had transported as 'one special gifting for one special lita', even allowing him to pop several into her mouth. She sampled the globeberry spirits at his insistent prompting, a sweet and mild wine pleasing to the palate. She readily showed the scars when requested, going so far as to slide the gilt from her shoulder so he and his fellow comrades might closely inspect the twin markings of woodslink fangs.

Kynneth did wish to treat them with spects. And she intended to do just that.

~~~~~~~~~~

The rumbling of thunder seemed strangely distorted in her ears, this throwing her off balance. She tried to concentrate on the steps of the zalt, but the room was behaving oddly, seeming to stretch on forever one moment, then turning terribly cramped the next. She
~~~~~~~~~~

laughed giddily at the dizzying sensation. "Mine Lor, yon globeberry spirits are quite deceiving," she said, having to concentrate on every word. "Weak on mine tongue, but strong in mine belly."

He smiled, the dimples popping into place. They brought to mind a different dimpled man—one from a very different world. Taking her elbow, he gently guided her back on course.

"Apologies, Mine Lor, I am new to the zalt."

His incredible blue eyes were sparkling like jewels. "Yon has been overly busied for zalting, Mine Lita. Dropping devons, battling worgles—" He brought her hand to his mouth to kiss the scar, before continuing on with the lengthy list of accomplishments. "—swimming with fraigens, riding the backs of woodslinks. Did yon use one saddle for such?"

She laughed heartily. "Naya, I did wrap mine legs around the foul beast, locking mine ankles tight." She leaned close to his ear. "I do own very strong thighs."

This time it was he who laughed heartily. "Yon skills own naya limits, Mine Lita."

"Yon is overly kind, Mine Lor," she said with a curtsy, before he routed his way around her to retake her hand. "And you must call me Christa. If nayat for yon kindly guidance, I would surent zalt out the very doors." She threw her head back and hearty laughter pealed forth with a dazzling echo.

He chuckled and beamed down on her with laughing blue eyes. "Mayhap I *should* zalt yon out the very doors, mine spellerly Christa."

She laughed. "And into yon boarding, Mine Lor?"

A mischievous sparkle lit his eyes. "Into mine bunker."

They laughed in unison—throaty, unfettered. Thunder, muted by thick stone walls, rumbled softly in the background.

"I'm so glad yon did travel these many longs, Mine Lor. I have nayat laughed so much in cycles."

"Yon must call me Val," he insisted, steadying her as she performed her twirl. "And yon must come visit mine cassing. LaRosse is as grand a cassing as yon will ever note."

"Aya, I must," she agreed with a tipsy curtsy.

"I will take yon broone hunting," he promised as he strolled around her. "But yon must make promise nayat to jump upon its back."

"Oh, must you take all the fun out of it." As they took the mandatory ten steps, following closely the couple ahead of them, she caught sight of Kynneth. Though he stood in conversation with a group of ganist, he was watching her closely. She twiddled her fingers at him and giggled. "Wheee," she chimed as she attempted another twirl, the act sending her head to spinning. Tripping over the curtsy that followed, she fell into her partner's arms and he pulled her close with a deep chuckle. "Oh my, slow dance it is, then," she mumbled, hugging him close. "Mmm, Kyle," she sighed, sliding her hands up to his shoulders and resting her head upon his chest. "I'm so glad you're here."

"May I stelcher one lita, Mine Lor?"

"Noooo, Kynneth," she groaned, holding tight. "Go away."

Lor LaRosse chuckled. "I do think one lita does wish to stay."

"And *I* do think one lita has been tipping spirits when mine head was turned," Kynneth replied.

Pulling away, she jammed her hands onto her hips. "Yon head has nayat been turned away from me one blasted grain this entire lun, Mr. Nosey!" She cocked her head haughtily, an act which sent her staggering into the Lor of LaRosse. Grabbing him about the waist, she hugged tight. "Ready mine cover-carry and mine Jelten Cleerians at once, Mr. Nosey Pants," she ordered, the words slurring oddly. "I have been invited to visit one grand Cassing LaRosse."

"The only thing yon will visit this lun is yon grand bunker," Kynneth replied, extending his hand.

"Mmm, mine bunker." Clutching tighter to the Lor, Christine giggled. "Will yon zalt me to mine bunker, Mine Lor?"

"I will drag yon to yon blasted bunker by yon blazened locks if yon does nayat turn loose this grain," Kynneth warned.

The man in her arms stiffened. "Mas Zeria—yon words are spectless."

"Aya," she intoned tartly, holding tight as her legs grew weak.

"Mayhap it is *yonself* does need lessoning in spects, Kynneth," she spat, and the entire room seemed to take a collective inhale, one which was not let out again. The music stopped, the instruments trailing off one by one, leaving the silence to echo strangely in her ears.

"Aya, mayhap," LaRosse agreed, prying her away.

It was fortunate someone came up from behind to hold her steady. The room was spinning, the faces blurry, so many huddled close—and not one of them breathing.

Kynneth stepped close to the young Lor, putting them nose to nose. "Will yon lesson me in such, then?"

Lor LaRosse pulled his shoulders back as his men moved to his side. "Let us nayat forget who does hold one standing of Lor between us."

"Yon may own one higher standing, Mine Lor," Kynneth retorted as Zerian guards moved in to surround them. "But let us nayat forget in which cas yon feet stand planted. Yon is one guest at one Cas of Zeria only."

"Aya. As is one Loper of Zeria. Does yon treat every guest as spectless, then?"

Christine rubbed at her forehead. "I'm not a guest. One Cas of Zeria is mine blasted keeper! And Kynneth is one big, fat, blasted roggi!"

The collective inhale was released at last in a unified rushing whoosh of air.

"I will treat yon with spects," Kynneth directed to Lor LaRosse as if she hadn't spoken, "I will allow yon to leave this cas with yon head still sitting upon yon shoulders. Is such nayat spectful?"

CHAPTER 6

Her eyes were closed as she rested her head upon his chest—a slow dance, their ballad the soft lapping of waves upon the shore and the cries of gliding gulls overhead. She could smell the saltiness of the sea, could feel the warm sand between her toes and Sola's warm smile upon her back. And she could hear Kyle's heart beating strong and steady. She wanted to see his face. Needed to see it. But when she opened her eyes, there was only a ship on the far horizon. Kyle was on that ship. It was sailing him away—and he would not be returning.

A gust of wind lifted her hair as the sea began to churn. A bolt of lightning shot down to the sea, followed by a crack of thunder. A storm was brewing. The wind began to howl, whipping her hair and yanking the tears from her eyes as she tried to keep sight of the listing ship between the rising swells. Roiling thunder-clouds formed in an instant, and just as instantly, a sheet of rain descended from them, further stirring the surging sea. Christine closed her eyes as the mouth of the sea yawned wide and the ship was pulled under, swallowed whole…

Christine's eyes flew open at the crack of thunder that shook the bed, her heart beating a rapid tempo in her chest as rain rattled the shutters like angry fists.

"Kynneth!" She sat up, and the room turned black as she was doused with dizziness. She rubbed at her temples until, slowly, he came back into focus, his face hard in the flickering lamp light, his eyes glassy and dark where he stood at the foot of the bed. Even with his distance, she could smell the spirits.

He threw a bundle to her lap.

She eyed it warily. "Kynneth, I'm so sorry. I—I must hand apologies."

"Open," he demanded coldly.

Swallowing hard, she rubbed at her forehead as she studied the package, a mere folded cloth. Lor Zeria had presented her with just such a package several segs past. On that occasion, it had been the locks of the murdered Myurna folded within.

She clamped a hand over her mouth as her stomach turned queasy, the rattling shutters seeming suddenly muted. Kynneth was presenting her with the dark locks of the murdered Lor of LaRosse. She was most certain.

"Open it," he hissed.

With unsteady hands, she lifted one fold, and then another. It *was* a mass of locks—blazened locks—her own, the very PacMattin had clipped one by one as she'd stood naked with a throat sliced wide. As Myruna's, they had been fashioned into a wig

"He did order every pleasurer did enter his bunker to wear yon locks."

She could do nothing but shake her head as tears welled.

"He was nayat the same after yon did dive into blackened waters, and he has nayat been the same since yon did rise from same. He can nayat think straight. He can nayat note untruths when they are placed before his very eyes, can nayat hear untruths when they are spoken clear. Yon will send him to the pale pony as yon did mineself. He will send the meshganist to Fallier to inquire about such scarring—as did I. Fallier will send them to Meshganis Tieslen. And when they return with Tieslen's reply—mine brathern will hear truths where untruths were spoken."

"It is truths, Kynneth! As Sola—"

"But I have made it mine duty to be certain mine brathern will nayat ever note yon pale pony, that Fallier will nayat ever send his meshganist to Huyetti, and Meshganis Tieslen will nayat ever speak foul untruths again."

Another flash of lightning illuminated the room, followed by a crack of thunder that seemed to rattle her brain. Of a sudden, her breath was gone. The room was spinning, or perhaps just her head.

She blinked several times, trying to refocus. "Kynneth, I will nayat send him to the pony, as Sola shines!"

"Aya, yon will nayat, as there is naya such pale pony to be sent to."

She clutched her head, trying to steady it.

"Will yon zalt me to mine bunker, Mine Lor?" he mimicked in a high girlish voice.

"Kynneth, I—I didn't mean it! Was the serin! The serin did react with spirits!"

He shook his head sadly. "Eight heads lost on accounting of serin, then?"

"Eight heads!" Scrambling from under the covers, she knelt upon the bed, steadying herself as the room turned fuzzy, the rattling shutters all but muted by the pounding of her heart.

Propping one foot casually upon the trunk, Kynneth held up one fist. "I did take the pony's head mineself," he said, popping up one finger. "Fallier's head has surent fallen by now," he said, popping up a second. "The head of Lor LaRosse will fall on the morrow. The sorry blogart has challenged me to battle," he said, popping up a third. "And ganist are in travel to Huyetti as we do speak. Meshganis Tieslen." He popped up finger number four. "His lita," he said, adding the thumb. "His gan." He brought up his second hand to proffer up a sixth finger. "And his litar," he said, popping up a seventh.

"Naya." It was a feeble word pushed out on a weak whimper.

"And mine spellered brathern can nayat note untruths about one babe, as well."

She looked to him, confusion shrouding a whirling brain.

"It is clear she does carry the blood of PacMattin." He popped up finger number eight.

A lightning flash lit his face for an instant, followed by a crash of thunder, this catapulting her from the bed toward a door that lay hidden in a fog of gray. She fought viscously against the man she could not see through the haze—he who would block her from finding her babe—biting, scratching, spitting, snarling. Glass shattered as they crashed into the bureau, then the night-stand.

He wrestled her to the bed, using his weight to pin her and pinning her hands with his own as she gasped for breath.

"Put it out, yon blogarts," he yelled to the guards who stood gaping in the doorway, and they hurried in to stomp the fire where the oil lamp had fallen to the runner of carpet.

"Mine babe! Bring mine babe!" she screeched at the guards.

"Out!" Kynneth countered, and the guardsmen complied most readily.

"I am one Loper of Zeria!" she screamed to their retreating backs, rushing to get the words out before the cowards could pull the door closed behind them.

Kynneth struggled to hold her in place, his breaths ragged, his nose and lip bloodied—as were four furrowed welts along his neck. He was restraining her with a grin, one which quickly turned to a grimace as he examined the teeth marks on his arm.

"Bastard! I'll kill you! I'll kill you if you hurt Becca!"

"I will nayat harm yon babe," he promised between deep breaths. "But yon will birth mine brathern's in return."

"Aya! I will, then!"

"Yon will tell him truths about yon scarring."

"I will tell him truths!"

"What truths?"

"Naya babe was pulled through! Kynneth, pleadings, do nayat harm mine babe! Do nayat harm Fallier or the Tieslens!"

"It is too late for Fallier," he stated flatly, bending his neck around to wipe his bloodied lip on the shoulder of his sleeve. "Same did meet up with pony stelcherers this lun, ten and two foul devons." He shook his head woefully.

A sob erupted, one which shook the entire bed, one which sapped her strength in grains, leaving her weak and feeble. It seemed the storm had weakened as well. The rain on the shutters had petered to a mere pitter-patter, and the rumble of thunder was rambling away.

He put his mouth to her ear to shush her. "It is nayat too late for the Tieslens," he whispered

She forced back a choking sob. "Spare them, then. Please."

Realizing her fight was gone, he released her wrists to prop himself on his forearms, hovering close. "Is it yon wishing I send riders to turn mine ganist?" he asked, his eyes cold and glassy in the darkness.

"Aya. And—and try to turn the—pony stelcherers as well. Pleadings, Kynneth." She placed her trembling hands upon his back, sliding them to his shoulders. "It may nayat be too late."

A wry grin slowly surfaced. "Done, then." He called to the guardsganist, issuing orders to turn back all battlers sent out.

When the door was pulled shut, she slid her hands to his neck, caressing gently. "And Lor LaRosse. Yon must call off one battle."

His eyes had warmed considerably. They roved over her face, drifting slowly down to her lips. "He claims I did shammer him. I do nayat wish to drop the blogart."

"Yon could hand apologies."

His eyes slid back to hers. "And seem as one tippet?"

"Naya." She slid her legs apart so that he might rest comfortably between them—and witnessed a glimmer appear in the glassy eyes. "Yon would seem as one ganis owning one kind heart, one who does nayat wish to drop one Lor so young." She caressed the back of his neck gently. "All do know yon skills with blade. Yon could best the Lor easy. And all do know yon heart is kind. That is how I know yon did nayat drop mine pale pony."

He sighed, the smell of spirits heavy on his breath. "Bidded off," he admitted. His eyes narrowed suspiciously. "I may have tipped spirits overly this lun, but mine brain is clear enough to know when one blazened-locked lita is loping as one pleasurer—so to bend mine will." He grinned at the look on her face, then pulled a blazened lock to his nose, breathing in deeply. "One grand Loper of Zeria—the most skilled loper ever to walk the face of Atriia. How far will yon lope this lun, then? Will yon wrap yon legs about this beast and lock yon ankles tight?"

She started at the words. "Was everybody in the boarding loping on me, then?"

"Yon did purposely speak every word loud enough to goad this ganis."

She decided against defending her actions. He didn't seem to care that serin was at fault.

He ran a tickling trail down her cheek with her own lock. "If yon does wish apologies handed to one Lor of LaRosse, then mayhap yon *should* wrap yon legs about this beast," he advised.

A rumbling resounded in the distance, staggering across the heaving heavens, causing the bed to vibrate beneath them. "As I am well practiced at wrapping mine legs around woodslinks," she retorted, "what is one added?"

He chuckled as she pulled her knees up about his hips, locking her legs around him. Running his fingers into her hair, he leaned in to place a kiss on one tear-stained cheek. "At last then, yon legs are wide opened and welcoming," he said, shifting to place a kiss on the opposite cheek. "Now—what of yon lips?"

CHAPTER 7

"Mine Lita, yon is injured!" Dampening the corner of a napkin in the water pitcher, Dahla gently rubbed at Christine's cheek, then began to carefully dab at her lips. "Of all Atriia," she breathed, sounding close to tears.

"The blood is nayat mine," Christine said, pausing in her rocking so Dahla could administer to her. The thought of Kynneth's mouth on hers brought a lump to her throat. The taste of his blood and spirits mixed, the gloating in his glassy eyes as he'd pulled back from lips wide opened and welcoming.

She looked down upon the sleeping babe resting in her arms, needing to drink in the beauty, needing to flush the foulness from her memory.

"More here," Dahla said, scrubbing at her neck.

Christine closed her eyes, but this only brought the image to forefront—Kynneth leaning into her neck, his hot mouth sending a shudder through her.

Neema snuffled at the scorched carpet, then shifted to the shattered tippet cage, nosing through the spilled straw bedding.

"Hopper," Christine whispered.

"Tavaka is in search. It did slip under one door, surent." Dahla moved to the bureau to right the jewelwear box, then knelt to retrieve several pieces of scattered jewelwear at her feet. "Apologies, Mine Lita," she sighed as she carefully lifted a delicate neckring from the floor. "I did hear yon call out. The guardsganist would nayat allow me to leave mine boarding."

Neema padded over to sniff the shattered water-bowl.

"Naya apologies needed. I did think mine babe in danger, but—she is safe." Christine kissed the babe's head, breathing in of the pureness, hoping it might expel the vulgar image replaying in her mind—Kynneth leaning in again, his eyes challenging, his kiss so terribly tender, lasting an excruciating eternity—until the wide and welcoming lips had twisted in a tortured sob.

She clapped a hand over her mouth.

Dahla paused at the bureau. "Was it Fallier did this?" she asked suddenly. "Did the foul devon try to stelcher yon again? Is this why guardsganist were sent to his rez in the lun?"

Becca began to squirm in her sleep. Christine quickly loosened her grip. "How does yon know such?"

Even though the lighting was low, Christine saw the color rise to Dahla's cheeks as she fidgeted at the bureau. "One of mine guardsganist, Darris, he owning locks of yon blazened coloring, we have become—" she gave a shy smile, "close. He did inform they were being sent to where Fallier does board."

Christine felt her heart begin to race. "And—have they returned?"

"Naya." Dahla put her hands to the flat of her stomach. "I should nayat fret," she said with a frown. "Darris is one skilled battler. I have watched the courtyards from mine boarding on many sols." This memory instantly turned her frown, but it quickly reverted. "But it is spoken one fraigen dropper does own one blackened heart as well as one blackened tongue. I do hope there was naya flustings."

Christine brushed at the tears with a numb hand. "He does nayat own one blackened tongue or one blackened heart. He's a fine ganis. One of the finest," she said, struggling to push the last word out past the lump in her throat.

"He did land yon in PacMattin's hands," Dahla said with a shudder.

"As was mine fating! I don't want to hear you speak ill of him, is that clear!"

Dahla nodded, her eyes dropping to the floor. Kneeling down, she began to carefully sift through pieces of the broken oil lamp.

Christine sighed as regrets for her outburst surfaced. “What number guardsganist were sent, then? Did yon guard speak of such, Dahla?”

“Naya, Mine Lita.”

Christine resumed her rocking, hugging Becca close. “Ten and two, no doubt.”

CHAPTER 8

"Is she supping yet?" Eubreena asked.

Christine looked beyond her own reflection to that of Dahla's. She sat alone at the table with her hands folded in her lap. As she hadn't bothered with the face paint, her birthmark stood out harshly against pallored skin. Dark circles were etched beneath eyes puffy from crying. She was watching Becca, though she needn't have bothered. Ten other litas were watching her as well, following her about the lita's quarters as she tottered about. "Very little," Christine replied. "What does go down, comes back up."

"Hmm." Eubreena glanced in Dahla's direction. "She is overly railed."

Christine nodded. It had been ten sols since ten battlers had limped home, all nursing injuries. Two more had arrived slung over the backs of ponies. "Any word on Fallier?"

Eubreena bristled at the name. "Still in hiding. One tippetly blogart should be drying in fraigen dung!"

"He did only defend hisself. Any ganis would do the same."

Setting the hairbrush aside, Eubreena separated a blazened lock at Christine's temple. Dividing it into three parts, she began to weave them with nimble fingers. "Battlers were sent to his aid and he did send two back with ripped throats. How does one mistake Zerian battlers for pony stelcherers?"

"Aya, how then?" Christine asked. "Unless Zerian battlers did sneak in like stelcherers."

Eubreena glanced to the door where two guardsmen stood stoic. "Kynneth has every reason to nayat trust the ganis. The blogart did stelcher yon once, did near get yon dropped, and now does wait brazened on the skirts of Zeria to stelcher yon again!"

"I have told yon, he did nayat stelcher me."

"Thousands did travel to the walls of this grand cassing to lay eyes upon one grand Loper of Zeria, and all did heed the wishes of one Zerian council and return to their hailings. All save one faceless blogart." Tying off the braid, Eubreena moved to the opposite temple to repeat the process.

"He is nayat one blogart—and he owns one face."

"Well, he best keep same hid far from Zeria if he does wish to keep such."

In the mirror, Christine witnessed Dahla dab at an eye with a wadded hanky. "I've tried to speak to Dahla, but—she's angered that I defend Fallier."

Eubreena's fingers wove the strands expertly. "I have tried to speak with her also, but she does nayat seem to take comforting from mine words as well."

Christine nodded. "She does at least have Tavaka to speak with."

"Aya." Eubreena looked to the window where Sola's smile was dimming. "Same should have returned from market by now," she said, her brow furrowing. "The turning is late."

In the mirror, Grayson shuffled through the double doors. Christine watched the hooded figure in the mirror as he traveled the perimeter of the room with punk in hand, lighting the sconces which lined the walls. If there was anyone within the cas who might have knowledge of Fallier's whereabouts, it was he. She glanced to the doors where her guardsganist stood forever vigilant. As she scowled at them in the mirror, they stood to sudden attention, bowing their heads as Oscarn came bustling in.

Spotting Christine at the dressing table, he waddled over in portly penguin fashion while pulling a hanky from his pocket to pat brusquely at his bramble brow. Stopping several feet shy, he gave a brief bow. "Mine Lita," he huffed, "Mas Zeria does wish yon presence."

~~~~~~~~~~
~~~~~~~~~~

She tried to concentrate on even breaths as she approached the table. The conference had obviously been long and trying. The ten ganist who stood at Christine's entrance wore faces drawn and haggard. The girl didn't stand. She sat stiffly at the table with her head bowed, her eyes cast down. Her cheeks were splotched with flush, her hair disheveled.

"Mine Lita," Kynneth greeted, bowing his head, and the others followed suit.

"Mas Zeria," she returned with a tilt of her head, "honored members of one Zerian council. Saker Odium. Tavaka," she added lastly, and the girl erupted into a sob, one which she quickly swallowed down, her face drawing into a tight grimace at the taste.

"One Tavaka Hassidy does wish to address yon, Mine Lita," Kynneth spoke.

"Apologies," the disheveled girl choked out, keeping her eyes cast down. It was clear she meant to speak further, her mouth attempting to form the words, but a high-pitched squeaking was all that exited.

"What one litia does wish to speak, is she hands apologies for loping," Kynneth informed her. "She was caught passing parchments to one ganis at market, drawings of Cas Zeria, yon boarding circled."

"Was Sherva! Was Sherva!" Tavaka wept, her lips pulled taut across gapped teeth.

Christine's breaths instantly tripled, for the air had turned suddenly thin. "Sherva Rostivane?" she spoke breathlessly. "Same is still keepered, is she nayat?"

"As long as Sherva Rostivane holds life, she holds power," Saker Odium informed.

"I have drawn up parchments," Kynneth said, motioning to papers spread neatly on the table, "informing of Sherva's devonous plotting against one Loper of Zeria and demanding she be dropped. It does need yon marking."

Christine felt her knees weaken. "I—I do nayat think such is needed."

Kynneth pointed an accusing finger at Tavaka. "Sherva did send one litia to drop yon, to drop yon babe."

"Naya," Tavaka moaned, shaking her head. "I would nayat ever do such!"

Saker Odium scanned the papers laid out before him and pulled out a single sheet, running his finger down the page till he pinpointed the desired passage. "'I was to stay close with Dahla,'" he recited, "'so to stay close to one Loper of Zeria.'"

"Aya! To send back messagings—the placing of her boarding, the timings of her outings! I would nayat harm her," she swore, her face twisting, "nayat for any number rounds!"

"And how does yon think Sherva Rostivane did aim to use such messagings?" Kynneth intoned acidly.

Tavaka wrung her hands as her mouth tried to form words of explanation, the nostrils of her oversized nose flaring as she struggled to pull in air. Finally, she dropped her chin to her chest. "When it was found out I was being sent here, I was forced to visit Sherva in one keeper." Burying her face in her hands, she began to weep. "I do have two sasturns at Rostivane."

Christine placed her palms flat against a stomach tight with knots. The thin air in the room had turned frigid, rendering her body numb. And so was her voice when she spoke. "What is her sentencing, then?"

CHAPTER 9

Sitting at the bureau, Christine watched Dahla in the mirror where she lie upon the bed stroking the babe who slept soundly beside her. Her face was pale and swollen with crying, the birthmark dark as ink in comparison. "I can nayat make any promises," she spoke to the litia, before turning her attention back to the letter she was scribing. Reading over it one last time, she placed the bandi ring in its center, then folded the parchment neatly in half, then in half again and again, securing the ring inside.

The tap on the door sounded, and when invited, the guards entered as they did every sol with Grayson close behind. While the shutters were being pulled shut, draping the room in shadows, Grayson was attending the four sconces upon the walls, snuffing out their flames and refilling them with oil. Lastly, he approached the lantern on the bureau where she sat readied.

She waited until the guards slipped from the room, before she slipped the folded paper toward him. "Fallier," she whispered.

There was only a brief hesitation, he glancing toward the door, before he secreted the paper into his pocket and shuffled from the room.

"Guardsganist," Christine spoke before they could pull the door shut behind him. "I do wish to speak with Mas Zeria at once."

~~~~~~~~~~

She stood at the threshold, hesitant to cross it. It was not his boarding, but one she had never entered before—the library. The
~~~~~~~~~~

bindboarding, as they called it. He was seated at an impressive desk, doing exactly what she had been doing not ten mounds earlier, putting pen to parchment.

"Enter then," he said, not bothering to look up from his work.

"Mas Zeria," she greeted, tilting her head in a bow, though he did not lift his eyes to note such. "I do wish for mine guardsganist to enter as well."

With an amused huff, he nodded. "Fine, then."

Even with two guardsganist as escort, she felt her heart plummet to her stomach as she entered, felt her skin turn clammy. While Kynneth was preoccupied with his penning, she peered about the large room, taking in the massive desk of highly polished wood, the shelving comprising one wall, fully stocked with leather-bound binds, the fine marble statues—one standing by the entrance, a bare-footed boy brandishing a practice sword—another in the far corner, a woman appearing demure even though she wore not one stitch of clothing.

The mural upon the wall stole her attention in an instant, as it did her breath. As Kynneth continued to dip his pen, making slow careful strokes upon parchment, she studied the chilly scene. It was Black Pond, her dark waters gleaming in Luna's light. An empty raft floated in her center, its perimeter lined with torches burning high upon staggered poles.

"Ten sols and luns we did gaze upon such."

She started at his words, unaware he had laid aside his pen.

Pivoting his chair to face her, he lounged back, placing his arms upon the rests. "Was mine brathern's thinking yon might crawl back upon one rafting and push yonself to shore. I did think him skewed. All did think such." His eyes ran down her length in a strange seductive fashion. "It seems he was right all along."

"I am here to ask for the sparing of Tavaka's life," she blurted hastily, then jumped as he leaned suddenly forward.

"If we do nayat drop one loper, the walls of Zeria will be brimmed with the like." He motioned to the mural, continuing on his previous thought. "Where did yon go, Mine Lita?"

She looked back to the silent scene. There were no fraigens to be seen, but this only seemed to make the waters that more dark and ominous. "To my own hailing, kind Mas."

"So—yon did swim to shore in waters brimmed with fraigens? Why is it nayat one eye did note yon crawl from waters blackened?"

"I don't know. I am only asking that you put off Tavaka's sentencing till our Lor does return."

He grinned, shaking his head. "Does yon think mine brathern will spare one litia? He would have dropped her down right off. I did least seat her before one saker. I will show Dahla the same fairness."

"Dahla?" The heart in her belly began to flip-flop wildly.

Lacing his fingers behind his head, he lounged back in the large chair, the leather squeaking beneath him. "Dahla is also from Rostivane. Mayhap Sherva did hire her as well."

"She swears she knew nothing."

"She must be keepered till she can go before one saker."

Christine looked to her guardsganist, then back to where Kynneth lounged as if not a care in the world. "Might I speak with yon loner?"

He shrugged. "It be yon wishing," he said, motioning for the guards to step outside.

As soon as the door was closed, he lifted one foot, motioning to his boot.

She wrenched it off, heaving it across the room, then the other. "Yon can nayat keeper Dahla! Kynneth, pleadings!"

In answer, he leaned over the arm of the chair to rifle through the parchments on the desk. Separating one from the others, he held it up before her. "One invite from Lor LaRosse to one honored Christa Clavin. He does insist yon visit his grand cassing. He has offered to send his entire battlean as escort."

"I do nayat wish to visit such."

He nodded. "Such was mine thinking." He slid a different parchment toward her, the very he'd been inking, then pulled the pen from its holder. "Yon has handed thankings for such inviting, but has declined such. It will need yon marking," he said, holding the pen out to her.

"Dahla is nayat one loper," she insisted as she snatched the pen from his hand and bent to scrawl her signature.

"Yon can nayat be certain of such." Lifting the parchment, he blew on the fresh ink. "Such strange markings," he remarked as he studied her signature.

"I am certain. I am also certain she is with babe."

This statement did not spawn the reaction she'd anticipated. He merely nodded. "Keat. One fine battler dropped by one foul fraigen dropper."

"One fine battler does nayat lope as one pony stelcherer."

Replacing the signed parchment to the desk, he leaned back in the chair, resting his hands upon his thighs. "Fallier did drop two ganist that lun, both skilled battlers, both with kinsganist demanding he be punished."

"Yon should fall to yon knees and lay lips to his feet for he did spare ten added ganist one same fating." Lifting a hand to her temple, she massaged ardently. "I did return to Zeria against mine willing, did swear to birth yon brathern's babe, did mark the request for Sherva's dropping, and this," she said motioning to the parchment just signed. "I have done all yon has asked!"

"Lower yon tongue, lita."

She adhered to his warning, softening her tone, though the hushed words pushed through clenched teeth rang loudly. "What else does yon wish from me, yon blasted blogart!"

He leaned back with smug swagger. "I would rip free the tongue of any other lita for less. But then—I would nayat again have the pleasure of feeling it slip between mine lips." His eyes did not reflect the grin that popped into place. "Reesal does claim it owns other skills as well—of mine brathern moaning till walls of stone did near crumble down upon his head. Mayhap this ganis does also wish to know such skills."

He frowned at her expression, then rose from his seat, arms akimbo. "How often must I speak the words, Mine spectless Lita. Treat this ganis with spects, and I will do the like. It is only truths I do wish from yon tongue."

He moved to a wooden chest seated against the wall beneath the mural, and carefully lifted out its bulky treasure. Depositing it on the floor, he rolled it out from wall to wall. Slowly, he traveled the length of the woodslink skin, counting the slashes as he went. "Six, seven, eight. Nine here," he said, pointing to the fatal wound at its crown.

He looked to her, his eyes running her length. "Face me now and speak truths. If untruths be spoken, one litia Dahla will be keepered this very turning."

"Fine, then," she replied, wiping her sweaty palms on the skirt of her gilt.

Kynneth nodded, seeming pleased at her eagerness to cooperate. "Were these nine rippings done by yon own hand? Did yon drop this woodslink loner?"

"Aya," she spoke without hesitation, lifting her chin defiantly.

"And are the tales truths? Did yon sit upon its back? Did yon wrap yon legs about the foul beast?" His eyes sparkled wickedly at the notion.

She squared her shoulders and returned his grin. "Aya."

"Did yon laugh when PacMattin sliced yon throat?"

"Aya."

"Did the devon force hisself inside of yon?"

"Naya!"

"Did yon slice his throat with one fraigen scale?"

"Aya. The very Fallier did place in mine hand."

"Is Fallier yon litar's fallar?"

For the first time, she hesitated. Closing her eyes, she took a deep breath. "Aya."

"Did Fallier force hisself inside of yon?"

"Naya."

He studied her for a few long moments. "When Fallier stelchered yon, did the blogart let you fall to the hands of one woodslink, one did break both yon arms?"

"Was mine own faulting."

"So the answer is aya?"

"Aya! Just as you let me fall to the hands of one worgle!"

He stiffened, the sting showing briefly in his eyes before they dropped to her feet.

Immediately, she regretted her outburst, especially as his hands lifted oddly to undo the top button of his shirt. "Apologies," she offered. "Mine blasted tongue." She watched nervously as his fingers worked their way down, freeing the buttons one by one. "Perhaps it would be best to rip it out."

Pulling the shirt from where it was tucked at his waist, he unfastened the last remaining buttons, then slid it from his shoulders to drape it neatly over the back of his chair.

"Did yon drop one worgle loner?" he continued with his questioning as he slid open one of the many desk drawers. Removing a wooden vessel, he set it upon the desktop, then delicately lifted the lid to extract a dazzling dagger, one of two—both of which she immediately recognized.

She swallowed down the lodged lump as she took a tentative step back toward the door. "Aya."

"With two hands skewered to one babebunker?" He tilted the blade, admiring the finely crafted weapon.

She eyed it as well, feeling a frosty chill as his grip tightened about the jewel-encrusted haft. "Aya."

"By this very blade?"

"Aya," she breathed, the fear mounting.

"As such?" Placing his palm upon the desk, he then drove the blade through the back of his hand till it struck wood beneath with a dull thud.

Christine threw a hand to her mouth as the scream tangled in her throat.

With a growl, he wrenched the blade free, wiping it on his shirt before placing it back into its silk-lined vessel as delicately as he had removed it. "And with hands so skewered, did yon order Zerian battlers to take yon life?"

She watched as he retrieved his shirt, wrapping it snug about his hand before one drop of blood could spill. Blinking back tears, she searched for her shaky voice, one which came out at a much higher register than previously. "I—I was bit by toskins, mine brain skewed."

"Yon brain skewed." He looked toward her, his eyes cold and challenging. "It is spoken yon does hail from fraig lairs. Is such where yon did dive when yon jumped into Black Pond?"

She took a deep breath and a hard swallow before answering truthfully. "Aya."

"Aya," he repeated as he resumed walking the length of the woodslink skin, his good hand stroking his chin as he studied it. She was struck by the way he moved, his posture similar to his brathern's. Though of a thinner build, and not quite as tall, he was every bit as dangerous.

Wide-stepping over the slinkskin, he moved close to stand before her. "Yon hailing does lie in fraig lairs, then?"

She resisted the urge to shrink back from him hovering so close, struggled to keep her face tilted up to his, to keep her breaths steady. His eyes were as any talcar's, dark and cold, missing nothing. "It lies beyond them," she whispered.

"Beyond." The talcar eyes moved oddly to her hair, then languidly along her features, dropping lastly to her lips.

She drew in a deep breath. "Is yon done with yon questioning?"

"When mine lips were on yon own, did it turn yon belly?"

She baulked at such a question, dropping her eyes to his bared chest as if to find the answer there. "I did answer all questions with truths. Spare Dahla one keeper."

"Yon did nayat answer mine last."

"Pleadings do nayat keeper Dahla." She braved her eyes back to his. "The litia is timid as one tippet. She is afeared of the dark, even."

His pressed his lips into a thin line and gave a curt nod. "Fine, then. But I will be keeping close note of her."

She breathed a jagged sigh of relief. "Fine. And pleadings do nayat harm Fallier."

His jaw tightened. "Keep yon promise to me and I will do the like. But the blogart best keep his distance from Zeria. And yon best nayat try to message him again, is this clear."

"Message?"

He raised his hand before her face, not palm out to silence her, but the other way round so that she might admire the ring displayed on his little finger, one resting on the first knuckle, it being too small to slip beyond. The bandi stone was glinting as coldly as his eyes. "I do think this belongs to yon, Mine Lita. Just one of mine brathern's many giftings yon has chosen to give away."

He grinned at her stunned expression. "Did yon think we did nayat know of how Grayson aided Fallier in yon stelchering? The sorry blogart was lured by high rounds. He did beg for his life, and mine brathern did spare such—being the fair and honored ganis he is. Where is yon honoring, that yon would put Grayson's life at risk yet again?" He moved his hand closer, proffering the ring, and she slid it off with a trembling hand.

Slipping his hand into his pocket, he pulled out the parchment, shaking open its folds to peruse its contents. "Scribings from beyond fraigen lairs, Christa?"

She nodded numbly.

"Can Fallier read such scribing?"

"Aya."

"Does he hail from beyond fraigen lairs as well?"

She hesitated, uncertain of how to respond to the question truthfully. "Naya. He hails from Atriia."

"What does it read?" he asked, giving the paper a shake.

"I did ask him to find mine pony. That is all. Please do nayat harm him."

Crumbling the parchment into a ball, Kynneth tossed it to the floor. "If yon does try to message him again, I will rip his throat wide."

"I will nayat, as Sola shines. And Tavaka. Pleadings do nayat—"

He raised a hand. This time, palm out. "Sherva's loper does rest in the bellies of fraigens this lun."

"But—" She slid her hands to her stomach. "Her sentencing, it—" A quaking hand fluttered to her mouth at the coldness in his eyes.

"I did guess yon would try to spare one litia," he shared as he cradled his wrapped hand to his belly, showing the first sign of discomfort. "Yon is overly skilled at bending mine will, lita. The loper needed be punished."

She shook her head as the tears formed. "She was just a litia."

"I did show mercy. Her neck was ripped fore she was tossed to fraigens."

She felt herself sway as the room turned fuzzy.

Instantly he was upon her. Drawing her close, he pushed her face into his shoulder to smother the sob. "It needed be done. In yon heart, yon does know such to be truths—as I do in mine own."

Finding her strength, she struggled against him, shoving him away. "Don't speak to me of yon heart," she sobbed. "Such a thing does nayat beat in yon chest!"

Fire leapt in his eyes as he grabbed her by the wrist. "What is this, then!" he growled, forcing her hand to his chest. "Feel how quick it beats!"

In an instant, her sobs turned to bitter laughter. "One woodslink on the flooring did once own one beating heart, as well—one cold and empty as yon own." She wrenched her hand from his grasp with a snarl. "I would rather *its* touch to yon own. Aya. There's your answer, then. It *did* turn mine belly. Just the thought of your lips on mine—the thought of your touch—makes me want to—"

Clutching at her stomach, she managed to stumble only a few feet before her actions loudly shouted the word intended. And as she stood by the door, hands on wobbly knees, retching and spitting vile remnants from her mouth, Kynneth tossed his bloodied shirt upon the floor, strolled back to the desk, plucked the blade from its box with his injured hand, and drove it through his other with equal conviction.

CHAPTER 10

Christine awoke yet again and reached out in the darkness. Becca stirred at her touch, then smacked her lips before falling still.

She wiped at the tears which had leaked out in sleep, dampening her pillow. She could see it still, the face from the dream—Tavaka as she had seen her last—pale and frightened, her blue eyes rimmed in red, pleading—begging—the face of her nightmares for ten luns straight.

She heard it then, and recognized the sound which had pulled her from troubled dreams—the whine of a hound. In the darkness, she could just make out Neema where she crouched cowering in the corner, her shiny coat trembling.

Following the hound's gaze to the foot of the bed, Christine discovered the reason behind Neema's quivering coat, a discovery which forced the air from her body in a jagged exhale. She squeezed her eyes shut at the sight of the woodslink slithering onto the bed, squeezed them tighter still as it slid between her legs, forcing them apart. As its weight settled heavy atop, she felt the soft hands at her face, caressing softly, felt the flicking of its forked tongue against her cheek.

"Chrisssssstaaaa," it hissed, its breath warm against her ear. "Wrap yon legs about this beassssst…"

She was gasping as she awoke. Kicking and flailing, she struggled to dislodge the burdening beast. Clamping a hand over her mouth, she moaned as the phantom weight slowly evaporated.

Becca stirred beside her, tumbling to her back with a mumble.

As in the dream, Neema whined. Christine spied her by the cubit door, her golden coat trembling—and followed her gaze to the foot of the bed.

She squelched a scream against her palm as a figure separated itself from the bedpost. “Kynneth!”

He put a finger to his mouth to silence her, then pointed to the stand near the door where the tray of lastsup sat untouched. A small shadow hobbled from the plate and leapt to the floor, an unsteady landing which sent it scrabbling to regain its footing. Righting itself, it hobbled to the door and slipped beneath.

“Hopper.”

He looked back to where she sat clutching the blanket to her chest. “Lundevons?”

She sighed. “Is there something yon does wish, Kynneth?”

His eyes moved about the room, stopping at the low-burning lamp upon the bureau. “I did just receive grand word. Sherva has been dropped and fed to fraigens.” He looked to where Rebecca slept soundly, then back to her, his eyes lowering to where her gown sleeve had slipped from her shoulder.

With a shaking hand, she snatched it back into place. “How very kind of yon to come straight way to inform me of such.”

He stiffened at her tone.

“Please leave,” she asked, running a palm across her forehead. “I am wearied. Ten luns now I have nayat slept.”

“Fine, then,” he said, turning his face away, looking to the door crack which had lured the tippet through. “Dahla has been keepered,” he added flatly. “I did think yon would like to know such as well.”

She brought her hands to her stomach.

“She did come to mine boarding, did beg to have word. She did carry one blade hid in her gilt.”

Christine shook her head slowly. “Dahla?” she asked incredulously.

“I will allow yon to speak with her one last time, it be yon wishing.”

Scrambling from the bed, she hurried toward him—till he halted her with two hands up, both bandaged securely. “Take caring, Mine

Lita," he warned. "I would nayat wish yon belly to empty itself again."

She swallowed the lump in her throat lest this prediction come true. "Kynneth, I did nayat mean it, what I spoke that lun!" She tried to move closer, but he pointed a finger of warning to hold her at bay.

Throwing her hands over her face, she rubbed at her forehead, trying to knead sense into her boggled brain. "Dahla has nayat been sleeping well, either. She can nayat sup. First Darris—then Tavaka. Her brain is skewed. She—she does carry one babe! And she is nayat but one litia, eight and ten segs only."

Refusing to look at her, Kynneth looked instead to where Neema cowered by the cubit. "Same did aim to draw blade on this ganis."

"I did also draw blade on one ganis! Yon brathern! The very Lor of Zeria! Same did find it in his heart for forgivings."

He looked to her then with a face cold and unyielding. "Does yon forget? Such a thing does nayat beat in mine chest."

She threw herself at him, holding tight, though he stood stiff in her arms. "Mine words were spoken in anger! Yon does own one heart, one warm and kind. All of Zeria does know such." With her ear pressed to his chest, she could hear the heart of which she spoke beating fast and strong. She swallowed hard, a lump which was surely her pride, then slid her hands up his back to his shoulders, then to the back of his neck, attempting to pull him down to her lips.

He pulled back with a frown. "Yon would lay lips to one does turn yon belly, so to spare one litia?"

"Kynneth—"

"Does yon truly think Dahla would come to mine boarding with blade in hand?" he scoffed. "There is more chancing one tippet would do the like," he said, motioning to the door crack. He nodded at the look on her face. "I did warn yon to speak to this ganis with spects."

Turning Kynneth loose, she stepped back and tried to steady herself in a room which still seemed to be spinning. "Wait. Dahla is nayat keepered?"

"Nayat of yet," he said as he adjusted his clothing. "Though this may be differed in short."

“You blasted—” Biting her lip, she adjusted her lungilt, pulling both sleeves back up. “Why might it be differed?”

“I did also receive grand word from mine brathern. He will be returning within one allten. Same does travel sol and lun, for he can nayat bear to be away from—” he glanced at her sideways, “his hailing one grain added.”

CHAPTER 11

Hid beneath the bunker, she held her breath and held tightly to the cord in hand. The tippet was wary of the cage situated just inside the door, circling it several times in its limping gait before creeping nearer. With whiskers waggling, it sniffed the stick propping up the tiny door. Was the smell of froma which enticed its head inside. Holding its nose high, it sniffed, stretching his neck toward the amazing aroma. Spooking suddenly, it withdrew its head to skitter beneath the bureau.

Releasing her breath slowly, Christine loosened her grip on the pull cord. The blasted tippet was too smart for its own good. It had already escaped capture on two previous occasions, once when it spotted her crouched beside the bed, and once when Becca had stirred in sleep just as she was about to pull the cord. That had been three luns past, all of which she had spent lying beneath the bunker in waiting.

She tightened her grip on the cord yet again as the tippet crept from its hiding spot. But it simply skirted past the cage to disappear under the door.

"Blast it all!" Rolling to her back, she rubbed at a bruised hip bone. The blankets and pillow she'd dragged beneath the bed were not enough to keep her comfortable on the hard wooden floor.

"Yon best be back, you booger." Fluffing the pillow, she positioned herself on her side so to better keep an eye on the door crack, then pulled the blanket to her chin.

~~~~~~~~~~
~~~~~~~~~~

She smelled the roggii before she saw them, their stench pulling her from a drifting state. Clutching at her belly, she clamped down on her lip as a wave of cramping agony engulfed her. As the contraction built to a crushing crescendo, a high-pitched squeal escaped her, echoing about the stone walls of the keeper.

Roggii answered with high-pitched squeals of their own. They were on the opposite side of the door, dark shadows scrabbling to thrust snouts through the food slot. Incited by fresh blood, they began to squeeze through, four and five at a time, scratching and clawing, contorting to pull themselves through.

Trembling in the darkness, Christine pressed her back into the stone wall, listening to the woman on the floor scream, her pain ricocheting through the room, through her brain. Yet, try as she might, Christine could not get her hands to clamp over her own ears. They would not cooperate, as they were busy clutching at her stomach. She could feel the woman's pain as if it were her own, the cramping of a belly stretched tight. She and the woman on the floor cried out in unison—not at another contraction, but the searing pain of rodent teeth ripping into flesh.

Christine cried out again as the door was flung wide, then shielded her eyes from the brilliance flooding in. Shrilling at the intrusion, the roggii scattered in all directions, colliding with each other and with walls in their frantic flight to escape the spilling light.

It touched harshly upon the body on the floor. The woman's belly was not swollen with babe. It was a mere crater, her innards having been ripped free by feasting roggii. A soiled and tattered gilt clung to a broken frame, arms and legs angled oddly as if dropped from ten stories high. Her eyes were wide and filmy and her birthmark was no longer visible, this blackened by blood long since dried.

The grating of hinges sounded as the door was pulled shut, draping the body in blackness once again.

Painful bumps traveled Christine's body at the sliding sound. Something had entered, something dangerous, something darker even than the blackness that surrounded her. Floorboards creaked as it moved toward her…

She came awake gripping the blanket with clammy hands where she lie curled beneath the bunker. They were by the door—two roggii sitting quiet in the darkness. They crept forward, one then the other, the floorboards creaking oddly. Instantly she feared for Becca—then remembered the babe was bunkered with Dahla, as was Neema, so as not to frighten the tippet.

She blinked, attempting to clear eyes fuzzy with sleep. Obviously her brain was fuzzy as well, for it was not roggii crouched silently in the middle of the room, but something far more dangerous. She didn't have to see the owner of the boots. She could feel him by the painful prickling along her skin. Her heartbeat tripled instantly.

Clutching the blanket to her chin, she closed her eyes, willing herself to waken from a lundevon even more horrid than the one before—till the creaking of floorboards forced them open yet again. The boots moved to the bureau and the darkness of the room lifted the slightest of bits as the lighting was adjusted up, bringing to life a slew of shifting shadows.

She fought to control erratic breaths, to keep from shivering in a room turned suddenly frigid. It was certainly a dream. The Leader of Lors was not expected back for at least another five sols. Preparation for his returning was in the beginning stages—a grand guestive with feasting and music. Guests had not even begun to arrive.

She jumped at the deep voice that spoke her name, the word compelling a hand to clamp over her mouth. No amount of searching could find her voice. It was buried. And not only beneath a hand clamped tight, but deep beneath a strangling fear.

The squeak of leather sounded as he lowered himself into the chair. She watched as he pulled off one boot and dropped it the floor.

"In every cas I did visit," he began, his deep voice resonating throughout the room, "tens by tens of litas did throw themselves at these footings." Pulling off the other, he cast it aside. "As many did offer to meet in mine bunker near every lun." The squeak of leather sounded again as he lounged back. "The one lita I *do* wish to share mine bunker, does lie hid neath it."

She wiped at a tear, then found her voice, one tiny and frightened. "Mine Lor, it is nayat yon I do hide from."

He shifted again. "Naya?"

"Naya. One tippet, it did escape." She cringed as he shifted and his shirt fell to the floor by his boots. "I—I do lie in hiding to capture same. Does yon note one caging by the door?" She flinched as he shifted again. There came the unhitching of a buckle, then the sliding of a belt through loops, before it too was added to the pile.

"Will yon come out, then?"

"I—one tippet might return. I do need to capture him before roggii do the like. With his limping, he is overly slowed and I—" She nearly shrieked as he stood.

Moving to the bed, he sat himself upon it, and his slipped feet disappeared as he laid himself down, his weight settling into the mattress above her. "I will wait, then."

She rubbed at a clammy forehead with numb hands. "Mine Lor, I do fear one tippet might fall to flustings."

His weight shifted above her. "I have waited over three cycles. What is one more turning?" He shifted yet again, and the draping bedcovers disappeared as he pulled them over himself. "I did have many long turnings for thinking in three cycles," he continued. "Mine region did lie in flustings, yet every grain of every mound, mine thinking was of yon," he confessed. "Yon blazened locks. Yon skin. Yon scenting. I do smell it now."

She squeezed her eyes shut, forcing twin tears to slide to her ears. "Mine Lor, one tippet—"

"Was yon scenting did give yon away when yon was hid in mine cubit."

His words thrust her instantly back to that moment, one segs in the past. She had cowered in his cubit on that fateful lun, her heart threatening to leap through her chest, just as it was doing as she cowered beneath his bunker.

"I will set one cage in every boarding of this cas till one tippet is captured," he promised.

She swiped at the tears. The air beneath the bed seemed thin, forcing her to breathe rapidly, forcing her heart to pump painfully. She felt light-headed. "I do nayat note Bixten enough," she blurted suddenly in a voice shaky and thin.

"One gani? I will make arrangements on the morrow. Yon will note him every sol, it be yon wishing."

She gave into the tears. It seemed there was no choice. "Mine pony," she wept.

"I did hear of yon pony falling ill. Christa—do nayat fear this ganis. I do only wish to lay eyes upon yon. Only then will they close in sleeping this lun."

"Tavaka," she blubbered.

He shifted above her. "The litia did lope for Sherva Rostivane. I fear Dahla may have been hired as well."

The fear she held of the man above her instantly vanished as a different fear surfaced. Scooting from under the bed, she stood to smooth her lungilt. "Mine Lor, I—" The sight of the man laid out upon the bed near sent her diving back under. He hadn't covered with the blankets. They lay unused behind him. And he'd slid off the rest of his clothing without her knowing. He was long of leg and wide of shoulder, a body sculpted as if of stone, a face almost too handsome to gaze upon. A dangerous spark lit his eyes as they roved over her face in the lamplight, then down to the blazened locks spilling over her shoulders. "I—I am most certain Dahla is nayat one loper."

He patted the bed before him. "Come."

"I am most certain. Mine lia is in her care this very turning, as I am that certain."

"She will have one chancing to speak before one saker."

"She will surely fall to fainting before same. She is timid as any tippet."

"She will be treated with fairness."

"She is with babe."

His eyes dropped to her waist, then slid dangerously back to her eyes. "Come," he repeated, motioning to the bed. "Mine eyes grow heavy. We will speak of this on the morrow."

She hesitated, then hiked up her lungilt to climb aboard. "She is only one—"

Instantly he was upon her, pulling her beneath to lie heavy atop, his breaths hot and moist as he began to shower her face with kisses. The scents of travel were still upon him, ponies and leather, dust and dew.

"Yon scenting is sweet," he spoke against her cheek, "as is yon skin neath mine lips. But is yon sweet taste I did think on most," he said, moving to her lips, caressing them gently. "Mine tongue did taste yon in every morsel did pass mine lips," he breathed as he sampled the taste he craved. "In every sip."

When she turned her face aside, he nibbled her earlobe before dropping to her neck, this sending a shiver through her and forcing out a breathy moan. "Mine Lor, you said—yon did only wish to lay eyes upon this lita."

He caressed her cheek with his lips. "Forgivings, Mine Lita," he spoke in earnest, "I did speak untruths." He slid his mouth to her ear. "I will know yon sweet taste this lun."

She gasped as he stripped the lungilt deftly over her head, then attempted to strip her of her undergarment, realizing that he wasn't referring to her lips at all.

The strike stung her palm. She gasped at its deliverance, then turned mute, the heaped apologies jumbling in her throat. If it stung his pride, he did not betray such. He was searching, his eyes probing as only they could do, peeling away the layers one by one till he was deep inside.

He looked away, his eyes moving to where his latest gifting stood grand, the regal vase of shalias reaching clear to the ceiling twelve feet above. Beside it, on the floor, displayed boldly before the hearth, another gifting lay prone, this from a different Lor. His eyes lingered on the broone hide for several long grains.

"Yon did manage to cause grand flustings whilst I was away," he said before removing himself from her, then from the bed. Retrieving his clothing, he began to redress.

Pulling the covers to her chin, Christine scooted back against the headboard.

"Unsettlings are being stirred in the upper regions, this headed by one Lor of LaRosse. Same has all but proclaimed battlement on one Cas of Zeria—and those would defend such." He pulled his shirt over his head.

"Battlement?" She swallowed hard to down the lump. "Why would he do such?"

Grabbing his belt and his boots, he stood to gaze upon the broone hide. "He does claim one honored Loper of Zeria is being held gainst her willing." He glanced at her sideways.

She shook her head. "Untruths."

"Is it, then?"

She closed her eyes, a long blink—then opened them quickly at the bloody image of Dahla's eviscerated body. "Aya. It is untruths, Mine Lor. I did nayat aim to strike yon. I—I'm still groggy with sleep. And I did nayat aim to cause flustings with Lor LaRosse. I will message him this very turning."

"LaRosse does insist on speaking with yon face to face."

"Then I will do so."

He nodded. "It is in planning. LaRosse does refuse to return to Zeria, so there must be travelings. Panzine, or mayhap Lazette."

"I will travel, then. I look forward to such. I have nayat been beyond one courtyard for cycles. I feel keepered." She tried to backpedal at the look on his face. "I mean—I am treated quite well. But at times, I do feel such. It will be good to travel."

Moving to the door, he paused with one hand on the knob, peering down at the cage by his feet. "Sleep well," he said, looking back to her. "I do have one special gifting on the morrow."

He grinned at the look on her face. "Do nayat fret. I am surent yon will find this gifting more pleasing than mine last."

CHAPTER 12

She gave a cry, half fear, half elation as the pony picked up speed, a gait she'd never reached within the Zerian courtyards. The grassy fields seemed to stretch on forever, spurring the spunky pony to even greater speeds. Finally, fear winning out, she reined in the pony to a trot, then a walk—finally a halt. Having survived such a harrowing sprint, she put a hand to a tickled belly and began to giggle, a combination of relief and euphoria.

Circling his pony back around, the Lor of Zeria stopped abreast of her. He was amazingly handsome in his riding garb—thigh-high boots over tight-fitting pants, a loose blue shirt tucked in at the waist. He grinned widely, a sight seldom seen, then chuckled at her giddiness.

Reaching down, she patted the silky neck of the tawny pony. "She is most grand, Mine Lor," she spoke breathlessly. "Many thankings. And many thankings for a much needed outing," she added, throwing her face to Sola's warm smile.

His own pony snorted and lowered its head to paw at the grass. "Yon is quite welcomed, Mine Lita," he laughed, pulling on the reins as his pony pranced. He looked ahead to the spanning of woodland in the distance where Sola was just beginning to dip, then over his shoulder to the many guardsganist who flanked them, then beyond to the Zerian walls they had left behind. "We must head back fore word is spread we are about."

"Fine, then," she said, turning her pony skillfully about. "Race yon," she challenged before spurring the masterfully trained pony to an instant gallop with the slightest pressure of heels and knees combined.

~~~~~~~~~~

Pony hooves clopped lazily on cobbled stone. Holding loosely to the reins, she swayed to the leisurely gait of the beast beneath her, reveling in the caress of Sola's smile upon her back. "Was mine gilt did slow me down," she said, tugging on the stretched skirting.

The Lor of Zeria, sitting tall and proud where he rode by her side, grinned over at her. There was a sparkle in his hazel eyes. "Does yon gest I did nayat win fair?"

"Naya, just that pants would be more practical."

"Ganis garb? I do nayat think such would be proper."

She frowned. "Next outing, yon can don one gilt then, and we will note who wins." She gave a respectful nod to a group of ganist riding in the opposite direction, they nearly toppling from their saddles as recognition dawned.

"I will have mine seamsewers work on one riding gilt—for yonself," he added with a grin. "It is nayat one garment called for overly."

"Why is that?" she asked. "Why is it only ganies are lessoned in the riding of ponies? Why nayat litias?"

He shrugged. "Litas do travel by cover-carries. It has always been such."

"And reading and scribing?"

He gave her an odd look.

"Does yon think litias nayat wise enough to learn such?"

"Litias have naya needing of such skills."

"One bind is being scribed in mine honoring, and I can nayat even read such."

He nodded pensively. "I will have yon lessoned, it be yon wishing."

"Aya. It is mine wishing." She nodded to a group of ganist standing at the entrance of the trellis-way. Word had obviously traveled fast, for it seemed they were waiting to catch a glimpse of one Loper of Zeria. A lita stood amongst the ganist, holding the hand of a small litia. The woman threw a hand up to shield her eyes,
~~~~~~~~~~

struggling to catch sight of the loper past Sola's smile. "And if Becca is to hail in Zeria, I do wish her lessoned as well," she said, smiling at the stunned lita and giving a wink to her lia. "I do wish every litia of Zeria to be lessoned, every lita, it be their wishing. What harm could come from such?"

He seemed to ponder on this, but gave no reply.

Her pony snorted and shook her mane. "Eubreena did inform me that Kynneth has been sent out."

The Lor nodded. "Flustings on the skirts." He acknowledged another group of loitering ganist with a tilt of his head. "Shike rezlers battling over boundaries."

"Did he speak with yon of Fallier?"

His jaw flexed.

"I am most certain Fallier did mistake the battlers for pony stelcherers."

He gave a nod, though it seemed to have an angry edge.

"He is one honored ganis, Mine Lor. He did only defend hisself."

"He will have one chancing to speak for hisself before one saker. When one honored ganis comes out of hiding," he added.

CHAPTER 13

The lessoner flashed another card to the group of litas seated around him. “Nuh, nuh, nose,” he enunciated, turning the card over to reveal the profile of a ganis with a pronounced nose.

Eubreena’s nimble fingers barretted a braided lock into place before she paused to ponder the next card—three circles forming a triangle. “Muh, muh, malla,” she said, giving a nod as the card was turned to reveal a lita cradling a babe.

Her brow furrowed at the next card—a spiraling circle that dropped down to a single line.

“Guh, guh, gani,” Christine reminded her.

“Of all Atriia! I did know such.” Eubreena deftly fastened two more barrettes before stopping to study the next card—a square with an x inside connecting the four corners. “Zuh, zuh, Zeria,” she whispered, then smiled proudly as the card was turned to reveal the outline of Zeria with its crimson flag flying, the ebony face of Sola sitting center. “I did nayat ever think I would note one such sol,” she mused, eyeing the large group of litas present—pleasurers, labor litas, brooders—all focused intently on the lessoner.

“And why nayat?” Christine asked. “Litas do own brains bright as any ganis. The litias will be joining the ganies very soon in their lessonings, in reading and numbering.” Looking to the mirror, Christine ferreted out Becca where she sat planted on a chair amidst the litas being lessoned. She was nibbling on a seedberry scullie as she watched the flash cards with keen interest. “I would nayat be surprised if litias do lesson more quickly than ganies.”

Leaning in suddenly, Eubreena placed a kiss upon Christine’s head. “I do nayat care if yon did rise from the deeps of blackened waters. Was Sola did send yon down to such—so yon would know where to send one devon PacMattin." Blinking back tears, she quickly fastened the final two jewel-studded barrettes, then grabbed up Christine's hand to press them against her cheek.

Christine laughed at the uncommon show of affection. "Yon is in good spirits this sol."

"And yon has one new fingerring," she said, admiring the purple stone. "From one Lor of Zeria, naya doubting."

"Aya."

"I do know of more giftings to come this lun," she sang, the Cheshire cat grin reaching ear to ear. "At one guestive. And I do think I know why yon is being overly gifted." She leaned in close. "Only six sols till yon brooding allten, Mine Lita."

Christine snatched her hand away. "Eubreena, pleadings!"

Eubreena clapped her hands. "I do also have one gifting for yon, Mine Lita." She squealed with excitement as she pulled a tiny vial from the drawer. "Note," she said, prying out the top to reveal a miniature brush.

Christine felt her jaw drop at the sight. "Nail polish?"

Eubreena beamed as she pulled up a chair and took her hand. "Made by Tulls his very self, the most skilled painter in all of Atriia. Nayaone does know paint better than he." Leaning close, she made the first slow stroke.

"Oh," Christine gasped, "it's amazing!"

"The coloring of Luna's very smile," Eubreena said as she made a few more cautious strokes. And, indeed, it was—a sheer, shimmering silvery-white. Eubreena stopped between strokes to study the next card. "Puh, puh, pony," she said, smiling as the lessoner turned the card over to reveal a silky pony with a flowing mane. Becca seemed especially impressed by this card. Setting the cookie in her lap, she clapped sticky hands to show her appreciation for such grand entertainment. "Yon has been pony riding near every sol since our Lor's returning," Eubreena said with a wry grin.

"Aya. And Bixten did join this sol as well."

"Yet again?"

"Aya. Three sols in turn. I have noted him more these three sols than the last three cycles."

Re-dipping the tiny brush, Eubreena began to paint the second nail with an air of coolness. "Mayhap Kynneth did nayat wish to pull one gani from his lessonings three sols in turn. Mayhap same did nayat think the Lor of our cas would approve of such. It is most difficult to take the placing of one of higher standing, to try to make his choosings in the stead of yon own."

"I do nayat wish to speak of Kynneth and his choosings. Was he did choose to slice Tavaka's throat, nayat his brathern. Was he did choose to keep Dahla in constant fearing of one keeper. The poor litia can nayat sleep, can nayat sup." She glanced to where Dahla sat at the back of the room, looking frail and listless.

"He does only wish to keep yon safe, Mine Lita."

"I fear for her babe."

"Many litas do have flustings during the first cycles of brooding. It will pass soon enough.

Christine offered up her second hand with a scowl. "The blogart does own naya heart."

"One gifting this lun does come from same blogart with naya heart." Eubreena paused in her painting to view the next card. "Suh, suh, Sola."

"He can take his gifting and stick it where Sola does nayat smile. It is grand our Lor did send him away on duties. I hope such does keep him away for many segs."

Eubreena gave an exasperated sigh. "Yon is overly harsh on Kynneth. It can nayat be easy to be brathern to the most honored Lor of Atriia."

"He thinks he is Sola's gifting to litas."

"Sola's gifting?" The large woman blushed as a giddy grin formed. "Mayhap so. Every lita in this boarding does near fall to one flooring in faint with his very passing." She studied the card being shown. "Huh, huh, hound."

Becca broke into an excited babbling chatter at the picture of the silky hound, sending the surrounding litas to giggling.

Christine bristled. "When he passes close, I do only wish to empty mine belly to one flooring."

Eubreena gave a disapproving frown. "Spects, Christa," she

whispered. "Fuh, fuh, fraigen." This card instantly darkened Eubreena's mood. She was dolefully silent as she polished off the last few nails.

Christine studied her as she painted. "Has there been word on Fallier?"

Eubreena shook her head, then bent to gently blow on wet nails.

"Cuh, cuh, crout," the lessoner spoke.

Becca gave an ear-piercing squeal and clapped her hands at the picture of the furry creature, this prompting more chortles from the litas. Eubreena, however, did not seem amused. "Why does yon hold caring for one blogart did force hisself on yon?"

For the second time, Christine felt her chin drop. "He did nayat!" She looked to the litas who were side-glancing at her, and lowered her voice. "Who did speak such untruths? Was it Kynneth?"

Eubreena shuddered. "Naya lita would lie willing with one ganis as foul."

Christine pulled her hand away and her shoulders back. "He may nayat own one face as fair as Kynneth's, but he does own one heart ten times as fair. Was yon honored Kynneth did try to force hisself on this lita, nayat Hannen."

At Eubreena's paling, Christine instantly regretted such a divulgence. "Eubreena, I—"

Shooting to her feet, Eubreena clapped her hands. "Lessonings are done with," she barked. "We must prepare for this lun's guestive."

CHAPTER 14

The crier thrust out his chest and pulled in a breath. "Christa Clavin, honored Loper of Zeria."

An excited murmur resounded and the crowd parted at her entrance. There were many faces she recognized, many more she did not, the heads bowing with reverence as she passed.

He was standing at the end of the room, a legend hisself, one Leader of Lors—honored, humble, a half grin gracing a handsome face. It was a peculiar sensation, as if walking the aisle toward an awaiting groom. Except he wasn't looking at her as a groom might a bride. There was something odd in his eyes, something dangerous lurking deep within. Her heart began to thump, the beat growing stronger the closer she drew. It was racing like a spurred pony by the time he took her arm, escorting her to a wall hidden behind canvas. Motioning to the canvas cover, he addressed the crowd. "One gifting to one honored Loper of Zeria," he announced, then gave the signal.

The crowd gasped as the canvas was dropped, then erupted into applause at the life-size mural revealed, one masterfully painted, the colors bringing to life the enormous woodslink—its head thrown back, its jaws gaping wide, its many hands flailing as it attempted to rid itself of its unwanted rider. Seated high upon its back, the lita's gilt was tattered and bloodied, her blazened locks wild and windswept. Yet her face was alight with giddy radiance as she wielded the blade. Grasped firmly in two hands, it was poised high above her head, a deadly arc forthcoming.

"It is—quite grand, Mine Lor." She searched his eyes, trying to decipher why they were making her so uneasy. They were veiled, as if to hide a secret they didn't wish to reveal. Holding tightly to his arm, she allowed herself to be led to a second canvas-draped wall, steeling herself as the veil was dropped.

The crowd gasped, some litas giving a frightened yelp. She might have yelped along with them had the sight not pulled the air from her lungs. The woodslink skin had been stretched over a frame that spanned the entire length of the wall. The skin had been cleaned and polished, the black and gold scales gleaming on the behemoth—on every hand, every finger. It was the three dimensional head that was most startling, the glaring eyes, the jetting fangs.

As the murmuring died, a chant began, a lone voice amidst the crowd, this quickly joined by others until it resonated throughout the room—the hailing of one Loper of Zeria, a chorus of admiration.

She felt a flush come over her, and looked to the Leader of Lors for guidance. There was a disturbing sparkle in his eyes as he grinned down upon her.

He held up a hand to silence the crowd. "The grandest gifting is yet to come," he spoke, motioning to Reesal.

Separating from the crowd, Reesal approached. He was carrying a large silver platter complete with silver domed cover.

Her heart began to race. It was the proverbial silver platter. Whose head was the honored Leader of Lors serving up this lun? Was it the worgle's, stuffed and preserved for all eternity? Or was this Kynneth's gift? The very thought brought endless possibilities. Was it the head of Lor LaRosse? Sam! Her vision began to fade as a gray fog filled her brain. Her hearing began to fade as well, muted by a strange buzzing in her ears.

She nearly collapsed as Reesal lifted the cover.

"Oh—god!" was all that came out, before she threw herself at the honored Lor of Zeria, burying her face at his chest and clutching tight to keep on her feet. From a million longs away, she could hear litas screeching at the sight.

Wrapping long arms around her, the Lor held her firm. "They did find him hiding in one scullery," he spoke, a low rumbling that seemed to fill the entire room and her entire being. "He did near drop five scullery litas fore he was captured."

The surrounding crowd thought his words funny. She thought

different. She looked up to the mouth that spoke them. It was a dangerous mouth, one designed to devour. And there was something in his eyes. They were devouring as well, and just as dangerous.

She looked back to the platter where Hopper sat trembling in his cage, feeling as if she were looking at a reflection of herself.

Hooking her elbow with his own, the Lor cleared his throat. "One Lita Clavin will be greeting guests for one turning only, then will sit for one grand feasting. Dancing will follow, but one Lita Clavin and mineself will take our leave before such. We do have more—pressing matters to tend to," he said, glancing down at her with a sly grin.

His grip on her arm tightened as she nearly collapsed. She did barely hear the raucous rallying of the crowd past the ringing in her ears.

~~~~~~~~~~~

Seated at the bureau, she watched as Hopper rummaged through the fresh bedding, sorting through the pieces of straw, intent on finding just the right size and shape to drag into his sleeping corner. He seemed quite content to be back in his cage.

Her eyes lifted to the lita in the mirror. She was dressed as a queen, a gown of mint silk and coral-colored lace. The hair was beautifully coiffed by the hands of a master, the entwined locks interlaced with silky ribbons and sprigs of dainty ivory shalias. The face was pale, the eyes haunted. She barely remembered greeting the guests, a turning which had come and gone in mere grains. Nor did she remember the food which passed her palate. The strong mug of spirits she had borrowed from a fellow diner had broken her numbness for a few grains—until the Lor at her side had slid it from her reach. That she *did* remember, and the way he had downed his meal like a greedy glutton. And she remembered the remarkable mural—her eyes drawn to it time and again. What was most remarkable was that it was not a work of fantasy. It was herself seated high upon the beast, her legs wrapped round tight, her face alight with euphoria as she prepared to deliver the fatal blow.
~~~~~~~~~~~

Twirling the ring on her finger, she faced the haunted eyes. "Calm yonself," she spoke to the mirror. "Yon is the very Loper of Zeria. Yon did best the beast of all beasts. You can handle this one as well."

Hopper stopped his rummaging at the sound of her voice and unfurled his ears. Beady, oily eyes watched her curiously, his whiskers waggling. Suddenly he dove beneath the bedding, and Christine shot to her feet at the turning of the door handle. He hadn't wasted any time.

His stature sent a bolt of fear through her, his head barely missing the top of the entryway as he stepped inside.

Pushing the door shut, he leaned back against it, his eyes roving her length. "Least yon is nayat hid neath one bunker this lun."

She pushed a loose lock from her eyes and looked to his feet, hoping to hide the fact that the very notion had crossed her mind. "Mine Lor, I—I do fear the flay did sour mine belly. I am nayat feeling well."

"Goser was served, Mine Lita."

She rubbed her sweaty palms on the skirting of her gilt, the silky material cool and slippery to the touch. "I did mean goser."

He shook his head, then stood from where he leaned against the door, this simple act nearly forcing out a scream. Stumbling back, she bumped against the bureau, her hand nearly toppling the tippet cage.

He seemed horribly tall where he stopped several feet shy. And his eyes did a horrible thing, dropping to the floor at her feet, then working languidly upward. As they passed her knee region, she wondered oddly if he could hear them shaking beneath the gilt. "Did yon like yon gifting?" he asked at last, his eyes sliding up to meet hers.

She nodded meekly. "Aya. Many thankings, Mine Lor. I am pleased to know the tippet is safe. And the wall painting—it is quite grand."

"Tulls is truly one gifted painter, is he nayat?"

She ran her thumbs along her polished nails. "Aya, he is that."

"Was Kynneth did think to mount one slinkskin."

She nodded. "Yon brathern is overly kind."

His eyes fell to her waist, then to her knees, lingering till she was certain he must hear them.

"Yon need remove yon guestive garb, Christa."

She felt the air catch in her chest. "Mine Lor," she began, trying to keep the tears at bay, "I am nayat readied. If I could have one added cycle. I—"

Her heart fell when he shook his head. "It can nayat wait."

"But, I have six more sols."

"We must leave this lun, Christa. We do have the blanket of Luna to hide neath. Also, one cover of one guestive. With so many carries coming and going, what is one added? We will be returning fore it is known we have gone."

"Gone?"

He nodded. "Don travel garb. We will take leave for Cas Lazette in one turning. Lor LaRosse will have his blasted face to face."

PART V

CHAPTER 1

She was dressed in rumpled travel garb, her hair wound in a simple bun at her neck. Though her nails were still painted, her face was not. To make matters worse, the smell of tippet urine was clinging to her gilt, the cage having leaked onto her lap. After three sols of non-stop travel, and with one babe who was not happy about such, and one nursemaid vomiting up every tiny morsel of food she managed to force down, she imagined she looked quite miserable.

Still, LaRosse smiled ear to ear at the sight of her. It was a dazzling smile with perfect teeth and dimpled cheeks. It seemed travel had not unhinged him in the least. He appeared clean-shaven and well-rested, an amiable sparkle in his bright blue eyes. "It is grand to note yon again, Mine Lita," he said with a bow of his head. He toned down his smile as he gave a nod to the Lor at her side. "Lor Zeria. At last me meet, then."

"Yon has ten mounds and ten mounds only," the Leader of Lors huffed gruffly.

Lor LaRosse motioned to the many Zerian battlers who had filed in behind them. "I do hardly think Christa can speak her own words with one entire Zerian battlean at her side."

"Yon will address her as Lita Clavin."

Lor LaRosse nodded humbly. "Of course. Mine apologies. We did agree only Lazettian guardsganist be present, and so they are," he said, motioning to the ganist lining the walls of the room, at least fifty in all.

"So they are." Lor Zeria motioned to his ganist who began to file back out. "Nayat one grain over," he warned. He stopped at the door and looked to her, giving one last nod before throwing a scathing glance at Lor LaRosse. He motioned to the time keeper, a thin, spectacled timer who immediately turned the hourglass. Still, he paused in the doorway. He was tall and handsome, even with three days of growth upon his face. His stance seemed poised and confident.

"The grains are falling, Mine Lor," LaRosse informed.

The Leader of Lors glanced to the hourglass, then pivoted on his heel, and the double doors were pulled to behind him.

~~~~~~~~~~

"Mine honored Lita."

She took the hand offered, then the chair, seating herself at the table and crossing her ankles to one side.

He took the chair beside, then reclaimed her hand, holding it warmly in his two as he leaned close. "Lend ears, Mine Lita," he spoke in low tones, his blue eyes turned deadly serious. "Yon is being held gainst yon willing."

"Mine Lor—"

"Pleadings, hear me now," he interrupted. "I have put many lives at risking for a mere ten mounds."

She looked down to the hands that dwarfed her own, then back to serious blue eyes. He gave a dubious grin, the dimples popping into place.

She sighed wearily. "Fine, then."

"Yon and yon babe must return with me to one Cassing LaRosse. Its walls can keep yon just as safe as those of Zeria, save
~~~~~~~~~~

its Lor will nayat force hisself upon yon."

She pulled her hand from his. "Lor Zeria has nayat ever done such."

"Nayat yet," he insisted. "I do know his like. He and his brathern," he said, his eyes hardening. "Both do think they are above Sola. Only one honored Loper of Zeria is fit to carry on their callen."

She rubbed sweaty palms on her gilt, this stirring the scent of tippet urine.

Seeming not to notice, he recaptured her hands, leaning in with a hushed secret. "Truths be spoken, there are many think the Zeria bratherns have naya seeds to plant. Nayat one babe between them. One Zeria bloodline will come to an end, this be truths, and one cassing will claim one new callen. Zeria will be naya more."

She looked to the door through which he had exited. "The Lor of Zeria can nayat fallar babes?"

"But he will try, Mine Lita," he swore, squeezing her hands tightly. "Yon is being keepered at Cas Zeria for this very reasoning, is yon nayat?"

He nodded with a tight grin, not waiting for a reply. "At Cas LaRosse, yon will be treated as one guest. And if it be yon wishing to leave mine cassing, such will be yon choosing. I do give mine word on Sola." He raised her hands to his lips to deliver a tender kiss to each in turn. "Was these hands did drop PacMattin, one devon on Atriia. We did all fear him, Mine Lita. The way he did use genopé to band foul blacktongues. The way they did sneak under the cover of Luna as one pack of foul roggii, slipping into cassings, into rez's, into bunkerboardings, ripping throats of those deep in sleeping—ganist, litas, tots, babes. Such was nayat battlement. Such was slaughterment." He squeezed her hands warmly. "Yon has earned spects, Mine Lita. I will nayat allow the blogarts to treat yon with less."

"Mine Lor, I—" Her eyes were drawn yet again to the double doors and to the guards lined along either side of it.

"They can nayat hear, Mine Lita," he promised, leaning close.

She swallowed hard, trying to free her voice so to speak the words gone over in her head for three sols straight. "Was the serin.

Serin and spirits mixed. I—I did have one bad reacting to such."

"If yon does fear for one gani, do nayat," he pressed. "I will have him safely traveled to mine cassing, he and one hound, both. And I know yon is close to yon aide. She is free to come as well, it be her wishing."

Christine pulled her hands from his to wipe at the moisture forming on her forehead. The room had turned uncommonly hot. Folding her hands in her lap, she leaned in to him. "Does yon wish to lose yon head?" she whispered low. "He is one Leader of Lors."

Her whispered words seemed to strike a nerve. "*Yon* is the only reasoning he does own such standing in the stead of mineself," he replied coldly.

"Ah, now I note," she said, leaning back. "Yon does think yonself more deserving of one title Leader of Lors."

He grinned and dropped his chin to his chest, nodding in defeat. "Yon has found me out, Mine wizened Lita."

"So, with one honored Loper of Zeria by yon side, mayhap yon will claim his title."

"Such title should be mine. Mine cassing is ten times the sizing of Zeria, and I do lead the grandest battlean in all of Atriia. Why does yon think the Leader of Lors did travel yon here? He does fear mine battlean, as well he should."

"I do nayat wish battlement on mine behalf."

He waved this away. "Lor Zeria is wisened enough to know he could nayat ever win such. Every upper Lor is with me on this matter." He glanced toward the hourglass. "Grains are sifting through quickly. Speak one word, Mine Lita—one word and yon will be on yon way to mine grand cassing. We will go broone hunting together. And I will nayat mind if yon does leap upon its back."

Christine nibbled her bottom lip as she eyed the hourglass. "And—is one honored Loper of Zeria the only lita fit to carry on one callen LaRosse?"

A full-blown smile broke out, one with dashing dimples. "I do have five brooders, Mine Lita, with two litars and four gans between them. And with one more babe soon to be birthed. Such is one Lor's duty—to carry on his callen." He leaned in to pluck her hands from her lap, bringing his dimples much too close. "As Sola shines, mine dearest Christa, yon will be mine honored guest only."

His eyes were an amazing color, a genuine pleading blue. She closed her eyes against them so that she might think more clearly. A glimmer appeared in the darkness. Hope had a color. It was the same shade as Atriia's first nail polish—a shimmering, silvery-white. And it had a texture, as silk sheets sliding along her skin. Hope had a smell, fresh and clean, like fields of cotton basting in warm sunshine. But there was a taste on her tongue, one not so pleasant. Rusty metal. She had clamped down too forcefully on the inside of her lip.

Suddenly the glimmer became a silver platter. She opened her eyes quickly before the cover could be lifted. Her heart hammered as she leaned close to face his blue eyes squarely. "There is one ganis," she spoke, the words tumbling out breathlessly, "one Hannen Fallier. I wish him protected."

His eyes grew wide. "Fallier? One fraigen dropper?"

"Aya."

"Same dropped by fraigens?"

"He was nayat dropped. And I wish it to stay that way."

He squeezed her hands. "He is welcomed at one Cassing LaRosse. He may board with yon at the very cas."

"Naya! He will board on the skirts. On the skirts of LaRosse. He will need land to raise ponies. I do nayat wish him harmed, nayat for any reasoning. Will yon swear to such?"

The timekeeper cleared his throat. "Ten mounds," he announced, and motioned to the guards at the doors.

Lor LaRosse grinned. "I do swear on sweet Sola."

CHAPTER 2

He sat silent upon the still pony, his face pale in Luna's light, his eyes dark and troubled. Luna's luminous smile reflected upon water like black glass and upon fifty pairs of eyes peeking just above the shiny surface. How long had he been waiting? Turnings? Sols? Segs? His ganist had long since abandoned the grassy banks, leaving him to stand lone vigil.

"Does yon think I take pleasure in yon pain?" His bassy voice reverberated through the room, bouncing angrily against stone walls, causing a pack to tumble from the stelch piled high. The disturbance flushed out a tippet which scurried to hide under the babebunker.

"Naya, Mine Lor, I do nayat. As Sola shines, I do nayat. I—I must suffer—for the babe." She clutched tightly to the railing of the babebunker, fighting faint as pain pounded through her body like a beating drum.

"Yon has suffered enough, Mine Lita." He had slipped behind, his words warm against her ear.

Through blurring tears, she tried to focus on the blades which skewered her hands, for there pierced a pain she did comprehend. It was the other, that which pierced her heart, she did not. She pulled in a deep breath. "Speak the words again, Mine Lor."

His mouth at her ear sent painful goose-bumps down her arms as he whispered. "She *was* safe."

"Was?" Christine peered into the babebunker—where a large silver platter rested. Reaching around her, the Lor lifted the lid, so she might gaze down upon the sleeping babe presented like a basted goser, dressed in bunting and surrounded by heaps of roasted coneroots. Her skin was a crisp caramel color, her hair a mass of frizzy singed ringlets. Her Becca-blue eyes were craters of charred black soot…

She awoke, gasping as she searched for Becca in the large bunker. She found her sleeping soundly beneath the covers, her arms wrapped about her rag doll.

Rolling to her back, Christine fought to slow her racing heart, to allay her labored breaths. It was a dream. Only a dream. She was safe within the walls of Cas Banzine, she and Becca and Dahla.

"Does yon dream of him?"

Christine turned her face to the chair by the door where Dahla sat in the darkness, the bucket cradled in her lap. "Dahla, is yon ill?"

"I can nayat remember when last I was nayat," Dahla replied glumly. Repositioning to a more comfortable spot, she rested her head back against the cushions. "Did yon note his eyes?"

Instantly, tears formed. "I do nayat wish to speak of him."

"I did fear for the life of LaRosse and any did stand in Zeria's way to such."

"Dahla, pleadings."

She *had* seen his eyes, had stood before him with her hands curled into tight sweaty fists, had handed pathetic apologies, had started to choke when the words jumbled in her throat.

And he didn't utter one word. Not one. But Dahla was right. His eyes spoke volumes. They held deadly intentions when they riveted on LaRosse. It was fortunate Reesal and his fellow ganist took the initiative to escort their Lor from the room, though it had been forcefully.

"Does yon fear yon did choose wrong?"

Christine sighed. "Naya. I am rid of Kynneth. Finhap. You don't have to fear one keeper any longer, Dahla. Mayhap now yon can sup and yon babe can grow strong."

"Yon did lay tears from Lazette to Banzine, near one entire sol."

Christine closed eyes puffy from crying. "I—when I left Zeria, I did think I would be returning to such. I'm worried about Bixten. Lor LaRosse has promised to have him escorted, but I fear there will be flustings. And I did nayat hand farewells to Eubreena, to Tressa, to anybody. I miss them alreadied."

Dahla tapped the side of the wooden bucket with her nails. "And what of Zeria's Lor? Does yon miss him as well?"

"For Sola's sake, Dahla! Nayat one added word."

Dahla fiddled with the bucket handle. "How much longer till we reach one Cassing LaRosse?"

"I don't know. Five sols. Mayhap six or seven. Mayhap one allten. The crowdings grow with every cassing."

Dahla sighed wearily. "Why does Lor LaRosse insist on traveling through the cassings in the stead of round?"

Christine pulled the covers to her chin. "He does wish all to note one honored Loper of Zeria by his side."

With a yawn, Dahla rubbed at one eye. "Such does nayat seem safe for one honored Loper of Zeria."

CHAPTER 3

"Such does nayat seem safe, Mine Lor," Christine shouted over the crowd. As it was, the drummers and trumpeters who preceded them could barely be heard over the deafening din. The crowd was becoming increasingly unruly, those furthest away trying to push their way closer. A ruckus broke out, shouting and shoving undulating through the crowd. A lita screamed as a group near the front was shoved into the road, breaking through the chain of guardsganist. The battlers escorting her fought to rein in their panicking ponies before they could trample the scrambling bodies.

"Blogarts," Lor LaRosse swore under his breath.

Seated between the Lor and the driver, Christine attempted to contain her fears. It was the worst crowding the procession had experienced. Being the third day of travel, word had traveled for three days as well, luring throngs of eager onlookers to the streets of Chaspia. The many Chaspian guardsganist lining the streets and the countless LaRossian battlers escorting the carriage on ponyback were insufficient to contain such masses.

She looked out over the crowd as another pushing wave swept through, sending more unwitting victims tumbling into the streets. The team of ponies shied and hitched forward as the driver wrestled with the reins.

Lor LaRosse threw his arm about her shoulders, pulling her close. He was shouting to his ganist, trying to be heard over the chaos. Up ahead, a pony screamed and reared up, its rider somersaulting backward, his drum tumbling after. Screaming sounded as the riderless pony then plowed into the crowd.

Lor LaRosse shot to his feet, shouting at his ganist to clear the road. Bedlam had spilled into it wearing faces of fear and fury mixed, a melee of shouting and shoving. The battlers surrounding the carriage were being crowded, as was the carriage itself. It began to rock with the struggling of the crowd, thus provoking the team of ponies to panic. They lurched forward, sending LaRosse back to his seat in an undignified manner. Screaming sounded from beneath trampling pony hooves and from beneath the carriage as it hitched over those unfortunate enough to have fallen within its path.

As the team hurtled forward, plowing through the sea of bodies, Christine closed her eyes against the petrified faces. She gripped the bench, her nails digging into the underside like talcar talons.

It was a lone voice which prompted her to open her eyes again. They had cleared the main crowd and the driver had the team back under control, moving at a good clip through the cleared streets, any onlookers safely lining the sides. A LaRossian battler had pulled up alongside the driver, and was urgently imploring that he stop the cover-carry.

"Gone!" he yelled, motioning frantically back to the carriage. "One babe! She is gone!"

~~~~~~~~~~

Christine gripped tightly to the back of the chair, barely registering the faces which surrounded her. She nearly collapsed as Lor Chaspia swept into the room with an escort of embattled battlers. "We did find yon babenoter," he announced. "She is injured, but nayat badly." He pointed to his forehead. "One swelling here and some bruising."

"Mine babe!"

She felt her heart sink as he shook his head.

"She claims one door was ripped from one cover-carry, one babe from her arms."

Closing her eyes, Christine leaned heavily on the chair as her knees weakened. "I must note her."

"She is being questioned further, but—"
~~~~~~~~~~

"I will note her!"

The Lor of Chaspia motioned to the guards. "We will find yon babe, Mine Lita, as Sola shines."

Christine didn't bother to wipe at the tears, needing every ounce of her strength to hold insanity at bay. She was in its grips, its claws embedded deep. She felt the talons dig deeper as Dahla was ushered into the boarding, her face ashen and twisted in fear. Clutching at her belly, she hurried to Christine, throwing herself at her feet.

Pulling her up, Christine shook her roughly till she stopped blubbering apologies. "Did yon note who took her, Dahla!"

Dahla grimaced as she shook her head. "I was dragged from one cover-carry into one crowding! So many faces, all shouting. So many hands, pushing, pulling. I was screaming, Mine Lita, begging! But—she was gone!"

Putting her arms about the quaking girl, Christine held her tight. "Yon must calm yonself, Dahla. Think of yon own babe. They will find mine. Lor LaRosse is in search. He—"

Dahla clutched her tightly. "Lor LaRosse is one brainless blogart," she wept. "They did speak it, even."

Christine pushed her away, holding her at arm's length. "Who? Who did?"

Dahla's face twisted as she fought back tears. "They who did drag me from one cover-carry."

CHAPTER 4

Her fists were clenched tightly as she paced before the table. "You said I could leave if it was mine wishing!" She swiped at the tears. "It is mine wishing to return to Zeria at once!"

LaRosse leaned upon the table, tapping his fingers as he watched her. "If the Zeria bratherns did take yon babe, I will have both blogarts thrown in one keeper."

She whirled on him. "You should thank Sola it *was* the Zeria bratherns! It could have been solists—or Sutter!" She slapped a hand over her mouth at the thought.

LaRosse ran the tips of his fingers along his forehead. "I must hand apologies, Mine Lita. I did nayat know the extent of yon faming. I did place yon in danger. When we get yon lia back, we will travel round all cassings to LaRosse."

"Naya, we will nayat! I am leaving for Zeria this very turning!"

Leaning heavily on the table, he hung his head between his shoulders.

"I will ask Lor Chaspia for battler escorts so I will nayat need yon own. And—"

"Yon will nayat be returning to Zeria."

She stopped her pacing to face him. His eyes were dark and dangerous as he glared across the table.

"Mine Lor, I am yon honored guest, am I nayat?"

"Yon must nayat give in to the blogarts. Yon must order her returned."

"They will only claim they don't have her! I will never see her again!"

"The whole upper battlean will descend upon them, this be

truths."

"And I will still nayat have mine lia!"

"All of Atriia will note their honored Leader of Lors for what he really is. If he did stelcher yon lia, he will nayat only lose his title, he will lose his very head. He and his brathern, both."

She buried her face in her hands. "I am most certain was his brathern's doing. Was a mistake to leave Zeria. If I do nayat return, I will nayat ever note mine Becca again."

He thumped the table with steely fists, then skirted around it, kicking the chairs from his path. Grasping her by the arms, he held her in a bruising grip. "I will nayat let fearing send yon running back to the blogarts!" He motioned to the guardsganist.

She yanked from his grasp as his ganist flanked her. "Will yon keeper me in mine boarding, then? You're no better than they are!"

He nodded, his lips set grimly. "On the morrow, when sleep has cleared fearing from yon brain, yon will note that I am right on this."

~~~~~~~~~~

Christine sat staring at the door, forcing herself not to beat on it with the chair till it shattered to bits and pieces, willing herself not to throw herself on the floor to scream and shout beneath it. She could hear Dahla weeping where she lie upon the bunker with her face buried in a pillow, could hear Hopper scratching in his cage. They were distant sounds, drifting from somewhere beyond her point of focus. The smells were opposite—strong, cloying; the shalias displayed throughout the boarding, the dinner sitting untouched upon the tiny table. She looked down upon two heaping trays—goser smothered in froma sauce, glazed ringroots, layerleaves drizzled with seedberry dressing. A large number of rounds had been handed for jeeters smothered in a rich cream sauce. No expense had been spared for one honored Loper of Zeria.

A single swipe of her arm sent the trays to the floor, splattering it with vegetables and sauce. Instantly, the door was thrown wide with two guards within the threshold.
~~~~~~~~~~

"I was careless," Christine intoned coolly as they assessed the cause of the commotion.

Dahla was assessing it as well, pausing in her lamenting to push up from the pillow with puffy eyes. Plopping her face back down, she resumed where she'd left off with renewed fervor, her muffled weeping amplified tenfold.

Slowly, it faded.

~~~~~~~~~~

Her breath caught at the sound of the latch. She ignored the two guards who appeared, stepping in to stand on either side of the door. It was the scullery litia who claimed her focus, the same who had delivered the trays. She was young and slender, her blonde hair pulled into a neat bun at her nape and secured under a hairnet.

"Apologies," Christine handed as the litia surveyed the mess. "I've been clumsy. If yon will bring me one bucket and rags, I will clean mine mess."

"Oh, naya, Mine Lita! I will clean it," she insisted, pulling a rag from her pocket. Hiking up her skirt, she squatted to right the plates, then began to carefully scoop up the food.

Christine took a napkin from the table and dipped it in the water bowl.

The girl seemed flustered, her face flushed. "Mine Lita, pleadings, allow me. Yon will ruin yon grand gilt."

Christine glanced down at the finery she wore. "Aya. Yon Lor did lend me such. I will remove it. Here, Dahla, help me off with it," she ordered, offering her back to Dahla. "Give us a few mounds, kindly guardsganist," she addressed to the guards. "I've made quite a mess and do insist on aiding this litia."

Exchanging nervous glances, the guards hurried from the room, pulling the door closed.

As Dahla slipped the gilt from Christine's shoulders, the confused scullery litia straightened to smooth the front of her own gilt. "Mine Lita. I will clean it. I—"
~~~~~~~~~~

"Dahla, do nayat place it on one bunker," Christine chided. "It will wrinkle. Just—put in on yonself till I am done."

Dahla did as ordered, quickly slipping off her nightgown, then slipping on the grand gilt.

The scullery litia stood nonplused, staring as Christine aided Dahla, fastening the buttons up the back. "Pleadings, Mine Lita," she stammered, "yon does nayat need to aid me. It is mine duty as—"

"Now," Christine said as she faced the young litia, "yon must lend me yon own gilt."

Even more color flooded to the already inflamed cheeks of the fidgeting scullery lita. "Mine own?"

"Aya. Yon can nayat expect me to clean in mine underclothes. And I will need yon hair netting as well."

The girl tried to reply, but all that came out was a jumble of stuttering gibberish.

Christine pointed to Dahla's discarded nightgown. "Yon can don Dahla's lungilt. Dahla, hand the litia yon lungilt, then."

"Naya, Mine Lita," the girl spilled out, finding her voice in a rush. "I do insist on cleaning this mineself!"

Christine placed her fists calmly on her bare hips. "Does yon know who I am?" she asked, feeling an odd mixture of power and shame at abusing such.

"Aya, Mine Lita," the litia said with a bow. "One Loper of Zeria. I am honored to clean yon mess."

"I do insist on cleaning mine own mess, and I do insist yon lend me yon scullery gilt to do so. It would be spectless to refuse me such."

Dahla went to the mirror to adjust the regal gilt she wore and to arrange her hair, twisting it into a bun. "Yon should nayat be spectless to one honored Loper of Zeria," Dahla suggested as she secured the bun with hair pins. "I have noted heads removed for less."

~~~~~~~~~~
~~~~~~~~~~

The guardsganist never gave her a second glance. They were too busy checking in on the Loper of Zeria, she standing at the bureau gazing upon one caged tippet with her back conveniently turned. Her babenoter was laid out on the bed as ordered, her face buried in the pillow—trying desperately not to lose her head.

~~~~~~~~~~~

"Does yon know who I am?" Christine asked of the cart pusher when they had safely rounded the corner.

"Wha—what?" The word was muffled, for the woman's mouth was full as she peeked around the cart. She was a tall lita, even by Atriian standards, broad of shoulder and no waist to claim.

"Is yon stelchering sup?"

"Uh—" The lita gulped down the mouthful, nearly choking in the process, pounding on her chest with a large fist to dislodge it. "Only what was nayat supped!" she swore, using the hem of her apron to wipe away any further evidence. "Such is nayat stelchering, surent!" She scoured Christine from head to foot. "Who is yon, and why is yon wearing Carnita's garb?"

"I am one Loper of Zeria, and Carnita was kind enough to lend me her garb."

The lita appeared confused. "One Loper of Zeria. But—yon is so…." The giantess looked down upon her with a disdainful frown.

Christine jammed her hands on her hips. "I may nayat be tall as some may think, but such does nayat keep me from riding the backs of fraigens when Luna's face is full. I am of one mind to ride such this fine lun."

"But—Luna's face is nayat full this lun."

Christine raised reproachful eyebrows. "I am of one mind to ride, be her face full or nayat. Where is the nearest fraigens to be found, then?"

The round face broke into a quizzical frown. "Uh, the ponds near Doxin, mayhap. But such is a good three turnings traveling."
~~~~~~~~~~~

“Fine, then. Is there a door leading to one courtyard that is nayat guarded? I do nayat wish to have to explain mineself to the blogarts.”

The lita scratched her head. “There is one at the seamsewer’s boarding. It does lead to the drying lines, but there is a route round the fencing.”

“Very well, lead me to such, then. I will need to ride the back of one pony before that of one fraigen.”

~~~~~~~~~~

“Does yon know who I am?” she asked of the sleepy stable boy.
~~~~~~~~~~

CHAPTER 5

As the blanket of Luna was beginning to lift, gently being pulled away by Sola, Christine slowed the pony to a walk, patting at a neck slick with sweat. The mare snorted, an exhausted wet sound, her nostrils flaring and sides heaving. She approached the camp with caution—three carries parked in a tight triangle—pulling the riding cap down a bit further and adjusting the stable boy's shirt so that it wouldn't betray her curves.

She reined her pony to a halt as a dark figure stepped from the shadows with an arrow notched and readied.

"Who goes there?" a man barked.

Christine cleared her throat, preparing it for a deeper register. "Greetings, kindly Mas. I do need water for mine pony."

The ganis kept his arrow aimed. "Sola has nayat yet wakened. Has yon been stelchering in the lun?"

"Naya. I am in traveling to one Cassing RoonEster on urgent matters."

"Is yon loner, gani?"

"Aya."

The man lowered his bow. "It is nayat safe to travel loner. The crowdings draw stelcherers. We did travel from Doxin to Chaspia to note the Loper of Zeria, and did near get our ponies stelchered for the flustings."

"Her callen is Christa Clavin. Her lia was stelchered in Chaspia."

He nodded with a sigh. "I did hear such. I fear one babe is lost. I am thinking solists. Mine lita does think high-hillers, PacMattin's kinsganist. I pray she is right."

"I pray she is wrong!"

The man shook his head. "If she falls to solists, she will be dropped. They claim she was born of the seed of one devon."

"Then I pray yon is wrong as well. Has yon noted other travelers headed lower, Zerian ganist mayhap?"

"There are many travelers, some headed lower, but most upper to note one Loper of—one Lita Clavin."

"Zerian footings are like naya other. Boots that sit high above the knee."

The man shook his head. "I do nayat recall noting such."

"Who is it?" a woman spoke, moving from the wagon to stand beside the ganis.

"This gani is traveling to RoonEster," the man informed her.

The lita stepped into the breaking dawn. She was round of face and round of belly. She pulled the blanket tighter about her shoulders, then placed a hand upon the swell of babe, rubbing absentmindedly. "Yon ride is readied to drop, gani. Come. I'm bout to prepare firstsup. Sit and rest yon pony."

"Many thankings, kindly lita, but I can nayat. It is most urgent I do reach RoonEster."

"Yon pony will nayat go much further," the woman warned.

"Then yon must lend me yon own." Christine pulled off the riding cap and pulled the tie from her locks, freeing them to dance with Sola's dawning smile. "Does yon know who I am?" she asked.

~~~~~~~~~~

She slowed the pony to a walk, leaning forward to pat a slimy sweaty neck. The gelding snorted and shook its head, flinging globs of foam. Its head was hanging low and Sola was sitting high, her smile hot on Christine's back.

As she approached the moving carry with caution, Christine tugged on the collar of the gani's shirt, pulling it higher to protect the back of her neck, then waggled her fingers at the two youngsters who were observing her from the back of the covered wagon—what
~~~~~~~~~~

Atriians called a cloth-carry. The older gani, one owning seven or eight segs, scurried to the front to inform the driver of approaching company, then scrambled to the seat beside him.

The driver was a big, bearded ganis—broad-shouldered and barrel-chested. He eyed the heaving pony as it pulled up beside his team of two. "Yon pony is rid hard, gani. Any harder, it will fall to the ground."

The younger gani peeked round his fallar from the back of the carry. His inquisitive eyes were Becca-blue and lined with dark lashes. She grinned at him even as her heart twisted. "I am on urgent matters. I must reach Cassing RoonEster as quickly as possible."

The man pointed ahead. "Two turnings at full pace, though I am betting yon pony will nayat make two mounds."

"That is why I must use one of yon own."

His eyebrows shot high as he delivered a humored huff. "Does yon aim to stelcher one? I would think again on such," he said, stretching his leg forward so that she might note the blade handle protruding from his boot.

"I would think again as well," the gani seated beside him spoke, motioning to his own smaller boot complete with smaller blade haft.

"I do nayat aim to stelcher. Only to borrow."

"That will be most difficult," the man informed her, "as I do nayat aim to lend."

The boy at his side shook his head adamantly. "We do nayat aim to lend."

She eyed the boy, drawing her brows down in a frown. "Aya, gani. Mine ears work well enough."

The younger gani thought this rebuff amusing. He tittered timidly, till his brother turned in his seat to glare.

"I am nayat so surent yon ears do work." The burly ganist massaged the reins with his thumbs. "As yon does still ride beside in the stead of on yon way."

"I am giving mine pony a rest, kindly Mas, as yon did gest." She patted his sweat-sodden neck. "Has yon noted other riders headed lower, ganist with boots to here?" She motioned high on her thigh.

"Naya. But I did only join this road one long back."

"Why is yon nayat headed upperly to note one famed Loper of Zeria?"

He gave an annoyed humph. "We did note same in Chaspia, though we did hardly get one glimpse, and mine ganies were near trampled for the flusting. Ten and two others were trampled," he informed her with a shake of his head. They were luckied they were nayat dropped."

"Nayan were dropped?" she asked, feeling a sense of relief as he shook his head.

The gani beside him sat up proudly, thrusting out his chin. "Mine fallar did bid one lock of the loper. He did hand one full round for such. Show him fallar."

"A lock from Lita Clavin?"

The man scratched at the chin beneath his beard, then pulled the necklace from where it hung hidden inside his shirt—a miniature glass vial dangling from a finely-woven leather cord. Within the vial, a coiled strand of hair danced with Sola, glimmering in her smile.

Squinting against the bright light, Christine leaned in for closer inspection. "One single strand?"

He tucked it back inside his shirt. "It did come from the loper's very head," he grumbled. "One merchanteer did swear on such."

"One full round for one single strand?"

"I was nayat the only bidder," he defended. "Many others did bid the like."

Christine eyed the team of silky chocolate ponies. They were fresh, not a sweat mark to be noted. "How much does yon think one entire lock would bring?"

He gave a cynical chuckle. "Ten by ten rounds, doubtent."

The gani beside him nodded. "Ten by ten, least."

"Least," the younger boy chirped, then giggled behind his hand, his Becca-blue eyes sparkling in Sola's smile.

"I will nayat ask near as much," she promised, pulling off her cap. "One pony will do."

CHAPTER 6

The cassing of RoonEster was much quieter than when she had seen it last. The streets weren't jammed so that no one could move. Nobody was shouting, nobody pointing, nobody chanting her name. Nobody gave a second look to the young gani on the tall chocolate pony. Nobody gave it a second thought when he inquired of Zerian travelers at the blacksmith, at several stands at market—the blade merchanteer, various food venders.

It was the gani at the pony stables who sent her hurtling toward the cassing of Voghn. They had been there, ganist in high boots, trading out wearied ponies for fresh. She was a mere six turnings behind them.

~~~~~~~~~~

She slowed her pony to a walk. He was wearied, his chocolate coat turned black with sweat. Sola was wearied as well. She was sinking low, pulling the blanket of Luna over Atriia as she drifted into slumber. Christine was also wearied, though there would be no slumbering for her. The aches and pains were wearing, but her exhaustion did not stem from wearied limbs, but from a brain weary with worry—fear for her Becca, fear of LaRosse coming up from behind, fear of flustings ahead. Dark clouds loomed on the horizon. They would hide Luna's face and rain would muddy the way. The road would be dark and slick. And more and more trees were beginning to appear along the roadway. Though not a woodland by any stretch, certainly ample enough cover to hide stealthy stelcherers.

She reached down to fondle the hilt of the knife, a gifting from the gani. She had used it to cut a lock of her hair before sliding it
~~~~~~~~~~

into her boot.

The lowing of a shikes drew her attention to the tree-studded fields. For several longs, she'd been riding the fence which contained the shikes, their noses to the ground as they grazed. Only a few bothered to lift their heads as she passed, eyeing her as they chewed their cud. A rez was forthcoming, and as Sola closed her sleepy eyes and the chorus of crickets began, Christine turned onto the drive, headed to the lights in the distance.

The smell of shike dung grew strong as she passed the garden; seedberries and pickens climbing up wooden trellises, rows of layerleave heads, ringroots and coneroots, tall stalks of coarse, these towering above her head despite the fact that she was sitting high upon a long-legged pony. Just beyond the garden, an orchard of suva trees graced both sides of the lane. The home and barn lie just beyond.

Stopping in the shadow of a suva tree, she stood in the stirrups to pluck a fruit, devouring it in mere grains before stelchering yet another. As she savored the sweet flesh, she listened to the distant rumble of thunder and contemplated on the most inconspicuous route to the barn—but hopes of stelchering a pony were dashed as two braying hounds charged her.

The hounds' owners were waiting on the front porch as she approached—two ganist, one holding a lantern, the other a blade. A stout woman pushed her way between. "Of all Atriia! He is but one gani."

"Naya, I am nayat," she said as she pulled off her cap.

~~~~~~~~~~

"Damn it!" She slowed the pony's pace as the rain picked up. Pulling the hood over her head, she pulled the drawstring tight. The Sherklees had been kind enough to lend the black coat along with Midlun, the black pony. It was a fine coat, made of shike's skin treated with water-repelling oil. But even swill oil was no match for a rain driven with the force of bullets.
~~~~~~~~~~

She swore as a sodden squall whipped past, snatching the curse from her mouth and the hood from her head. As she fumbled to replace it, a jagged streak of lightning split the darkness, followed by a thunderous crack.

The pony shied beneath her. Whipping his head, he fought against the reins, rearing and spinning, hooves slipping and sliding—finally losing his footing on the slick road.

She rolled away from the flailing hooves as the pony floundered in mud, then struggled to her feet alongside him. Her lunge for the reins merely spooked him further. He reared up, knocking her to the ground, nearly trampling her as he took flight in the stormy night.

"Blast!" she shrieked as another flash of lightning showed Midlun's hindquarters pumping madly as he thundered away. She beat her fists against her thighs as rain pummeled her. "Blast yon!" she cried, turning her face upward. She quickly turned it down again for fear the driving drops might knock her senseless.

She sucked in rainwater mixed with tears, then struggled to her feet, crying out as her boots slipped in the mud yet again, nearly landing her back on the ground. Regaining her footing, she pulled the hood tight over her head and leaned into the rain, trudging forward.

When he regained his senses, Midlun would turn and head for home. She was certain.

~~~~~~~~~~

She sat shivering beneath the massive tree, one of many situated close to the road. Lighting split the sky with a jagged streak, and rolling thunder rumbled in its wake. Without warning, Christine's face twisted.

Pulling her legs up, she hugged her shins, hanging her head between her knees. It was Becca. She could hear her tiny giggle in the raindrops. It was tearing her apart. Sweet, sweet Becca. She was not spawned of a devon's seed. She was an angel, an angel on Atriia.

She wept her name, then again and again. The solists were the devons, sitting high upon ponies so to better look down their noses
~~~~~~~~~~

on those beneath, all the while pointing crooked fingers of judgment.

"Yon is the devons! Yon is the blasted devons!"

She shivered, a blend of chills and chilled soul.

~~~~~~~~~~

Opening her eyes, she lifted her head from between her knees, straining to hear. Becca was crying, the exhausted echoing cry of a child sitting alone in the darkness.

Struggling to her feet, she spun in place, trying to discern from which direction it drifted. "Becca! Mommy's here. Mommy's here, mine babe!"

The clouds had covered Luna's face completely, draping Atriia in blackness. Reaching out with both arms, Christine took tentative steps. "Don't cry, Becca!" It occurred a song might calm the babe.

"Fret nayat, mine fairest babe. Stave yon tears, mine fairest—"

"Mine fallar did bid one lock of the loper's lia."

Christine frowned at the young boy sitting tall upon the wagon seat. He was holding a single strand of hair pinched between thumb and forefinger, twirling it so that it glistened in Sola's bright smile.

"Did you say lia?" she asked in a voice that quivered.

The boy nodded. "He did hand one round for such," he boasted proudly.

His father fidgeted on the seat beside him. "Same did come from the lia's very head."

"Her very head," the boy repeated.

Christine looked to where the youngest boy hid behind his fallar, peeking around his shoulder. His Becca-blue eyes were lined with lashes, long and dark.

Christine tried to clear her jumbled brain. "One round for one strand?" she spoke numbly.

The older boy nodded. "Two rounds for one neckring," he said, pointing to his father's neck. The neckring was but a thin lace of braided leather attached to a dangling bauble.
~~~~~~~~~~

She near fainted at the sight. “One tooth!”

The large ganis rolled his eyes. “I was nayat the only blogart to bid such. Many did the like. Two rounds for one tooth, five for one toe, ten for one finger.”

“Ten for one finger,” the boy beside him chimed in.

Clenching her fists, she screamed at the boy. “Mine blasted ears work, gani!”

The worgle put a finger to its mouth to shush her, then pointed across the room to the crib. The wintered winds were howling as she approached the babebunker of boughs, spinning round the room in a whirlwind. Her brain was spinning as well, her body shivering as her frozen feet shuffled across the floor.

“Oh, sweet babe,” she sighed as she leaned over the rail.

Her ivory skin had been violated. It was ripped and bloodied. Her hair was gone, every last strand snipped away, as had been every finger, every sweet toe. Her baby teeth had been pried from her mouth. Her Becca-blue eyes were still intact. But they saw nothing.

Swathing her broken babe in blankets, Christine cradled her to her chest, humming a lullaby as she walked in lazy circles in the darkness.

He appeared before her in a glow of light, tall and beautiful, brown flowing hair, sad hazel eyes. He reached forth his hands, beckoning for Becca, and she proffered the babe without hesitation. “Speak the words, Mine Lor,” she begged as she fell to her knees before him. “Speak the words and I will give anything, mine body, mine soul—mine heart.”

She closed her eyes, waiting to hear the golden words. But it was a different voice which replied, one raspy and raw.

“Do nayat offer yon heart, Christa. Such belongs to me.”

He stood above her, powerfully poised and savagely scarred, his dark hair whipping in the winds, his torso eternally ensconced in the embrace of a foul fraigen. She leapt at him, clawing, striking, shrieking. “Is mine to give and I will give it! I will give it!”

"And I will take it."

The words halted her attack, for they were spoken by the beautiful mouth. She fell into his arms, her breaths labored, her hands throbbing from the pounding. "Aya, Mine Lor. Take it. Take mine heart."

"I *do* own one heart, lita, does yon feel it?"

She stiffened, for it was Kynneth she clung to, and she did feel it. It was strong and steady—like the pounding of pony hooves…

She came awake gasping.

Scrambling to her feet, she fought to regain her bearings. The rain had slowed and the clouds had thinned, allowing Luna's smile to filter through. Midlun was returning. She could hear his hooves muted by mud.

Scrambling into the road, she threw her arms wide.

~~~~~~~~~~

It was not Midlun, she realized too late, but a different dark pony, one complete with dark rider. He was dressed in black so to better sneak about in the lun stelchering that belonging to others. And he was not loner. Three more riders rounded the bend behind him, each leading a riderless pony—one of which was Midlun returning after all.

They pulled to a halt at the sight of her, nervously searching about, twisting their necks, twisting in saddles while slipping blades from boots. It was the ganis in the lead who spoke first, he with the ridiculous Pebbles ponytail bobbing on top. "What goes here, gani?"

The coat on her back was heavy with water, as were her boots. Even if there had been anyplace to run, she would not have gotten far. But there was nowhere—and no desire. A desperate sense of urgency consumed her. "I was in search of mine runaway pony," she said, motioning to where Midlun stood saddled and muddied. "But I note yon kindly gentleganist have returned him to me."

Pebbles chuckled and looked to his comrades. "Such is overly
~~~~~~~~~~

fortunate. As we have been in searching of one pony's rightly owner, have we nayat, kindly gentleganist?"

They grunted and nodded, sneering to reveal gray teeth. One rider gave a tug on the rope of the pale pony he led. "I have been in searching of one rightly owner of this one, as well," he said with a nasty grin.

The ganis next to him dug into his pocket to pull out a purse. "I am in searching of one rightly owner of these slices," he said, shaking the purse to prove it full. "Has yon noted him, one timer with one bearded chin? He did walk with one limp."

She shook her head, ignoring the swine-like snorts. The rain had settled to a fine drizzle. She wiped the moisture from her eyes, then motioned in the direction from which they'd just come. "Mine carry does lie lowerly, nayat one long distanced. Mine fallar will be pleased to hand over payment for his pony's safe returning."

"Will he now," Pebbles said, leaning back in his saddle and slipping his blade back into his boot. "We did just come from lowerly, and I did nayat note one carry. Did yon?" he asked of his comrades, and they snickered and shook their heads.

"It is hid in the trees. Mine fallar does fear stelcherers. He speaks they are foul devons, foul as foul can be. Fouler even than pony dung," she added with a shudder. "Fouler than the beetles do sup on same. Fouler than—"

Pebbles held up his hand to silence her, then leaned down. "Yon fallar is overly wizened, gani," he said with a tight grin.

"Aya. He will be grateful to have Midlun returned. He will surent hand over several slices for such a kindly favor."

Pebbles pulled a sack from his coat pocket and jangled it. "Mine purse is brimmed with slices alreadied. And five more of the like in mine saddle bags."

"Six purses brimmed! Yon is richly. I did think mine fallar richly, but he does only carry five brimmed purses."

Pebbles perked up in his saddle. "Does he now?" He motioned to his ganist. "Hagis, bring one gani his pony, then. We must meet this richly fallar."

CHAPTER 7

It felt good to have the pony beneath her again, even if traveling at a snail's pace, and even if surrounded by stelcherers—Hagis front and left, leading her pony, Pebbles to the right, his leg mere inches from her own, the others trailing close behind.

Pebbles looked to her, his eyes roving from head to toe. "Yon and yon richly fallar do travel loner, gani?"

"Aya."

"To note the most skilled loper in all of Atriia, doubtent?"

She shifted in the saddle. "Aya."

He spit into the mud. "Every blogart in Atriia does travel from the ends of every region to note one blasted scullery lita. Where is the skill in donning false locks so to blast drunken blogarts? Any tripe could do the likc."

"Yon sasturn *has* done the like," Hagis directed to Pebbles with a gravelly chuckle, and Pebbles shot him a scathing scowl.

Christine looked down to where her hands gripped the saddle horn. They were prune-wrinkled and fish-belly white. "Same did convince many ganist she was Myurna, one pleasurer they did know well."

"The blasted blogarts were tipping spirits! I have noted the loping bligart. Same is overly stunted," he said, his nose wrinkling. "And railed as one coarse stalk. Yon does own more curves to boast."

She adjusted the sodden coat and wiped the rain from her eyes. "Even railed and stunted, she did manage to drop PacMattin."

He stiffened in his saddle and spit a saliva stream. "Nayat fore she did work his kagege. She is skilled at one thing and one thing only."

The giant of a man he called Hagis put a hand to his groin. "Mine kagege does wish to know such skills," he sneered, and his fellowganist snickered snide agreement.

She fought to keep her eyes facing forward. "I have heard she did rip off his kagege."

Pebbles grumbled under his breath. "As he lie sleeping, the tippet. But his seed was alreadied planted deep."

Despite attempts to refrain from responding, a derisive humph escaped. "Two inches is nayat so deep," she mumbled under her breath.

He turned to glare.

She straightened her shoulders. "The babe is nayat his."

"Why, then, gani, did his kinsganist reclaim her?"

She felt her prune hands tighten on the saddle-horn. "PacMattin's kinsganist?"

He grunted and leaned close. "High-hillers, gani. *They* are the most skilled lopers in all of Atriia, nayat one railed litia." He chuckled with contempt. "They did snatch one lia under her very nose, *and* that of Lor blasted LaRosse. The grandest battlean in all of Atriia could nayat stop them. And," he stressed, holding up one finger, "they did stelcher one lia in Sola's full smile. Therein does lie skill, gani."

She fought to keep her teeth from gnashing, to keep her jaw unclenched. "How can yon be certain was high-hillers?"

He sat back in his saddle with swagger. "We did just spend three sols in same's company. They were in needing of our own skills, were they nayat, gentleganist," he asked, and the others grunted agreement. "We do know the back-roads of this region better than any," he bragged, "and," he emphasized, raising his chin high, "we do move in one lun as if made of it."

"As if made of it," the others chanted, a mantra delivered in proud unison.

Urgency pulsed through her veins. Despite clothes soaked with chilled rain, heat spread through till she was certain she must be glowing in the lun. She shook with the effort to contain her dire desperation, to control her shallow breaths.

"In Sola's full smile," she said. "They are truly skilled lopers, the most skilled in all of Atriia. What are their aimings for one lia?"

"What is *yon* aiming, mine fairest gani?" Pebbles reined his pony to a halt and turned to smile horridly.

Snickering sounded, and still she contained herself, merely wiping the misty moisture from her eyes so to better size up the four ganist who had stopped to surround her.

Pebbles pointed an accusing finger. "Yon did speak untruths, gani. Yon did speak one long. One long has come and gone."

She shifted from one face to the other, each eliciting different degrees of repulsion. Pebbles' was of the highest degree. She wanted to leap at him, to scratch his face to shreds, to rip out his hair by his Pebbles ponytail.

She took a deep breath and let it out slowly. "Mayhap two longs."

Pebbles raised his eyebrows. There was something off about them. They were perfectly shaped and arched like a lita's.

"There is naya richly fallar, is there, gani? He leaned back smugly in his saddle. "Yon was riding loner and did lose yon pony. It is nayat wise to ride loner in the lun, knowing stelcherers might be about? Stelcherers *are* foul, gani, foul as foul can be. When they come crost one gani sweet as any lita, they do wish to use one as same."

The others snickered and grinned, modeling teeth of mush.

Pebbles put his hand into his lap, his fingers caressing something hidden. "If yon is one good gani, we might even leave yon pony. What says yon?" he asked, a wide grin surfacing. "Will yon be good?"

Christine looked to each of the sneering, leering faces, then down to the pale, prune-hands. She nodded. "Aya. I will be good. I do wish to keep mine pony."

~~~~~~~~~~
~~~~~~~~~~

She brushed a mixture of rain and tears from her eyes. Spinning slowly in place, she took in the foul faces of the four men surrounding her in a tight circle. A leering Hagis was most eager, his hand rubbing at his crotch, his tongue licking at his chops. He was terribly tall, towering over the others. “Start with this, then,” he said, rubbing himself suggestively.

“Naya,” Pebbles said, placing his hands on his buckle. “Start here.”

“Four at once,” she countered, continuing to pivot, taking in four faces frowning in befuddlement.

Hagis scratched at his chin. “Four at once?”

“One, two, three, four,” she counted, pointing to each crotch in turn. “Sola will be waking soon. We do nayat have all lun. Yon will leave mine pony, does yon swear?”

They did all swear, and with great conviction.

Hagis was the first to act, unbuckling with urgency and dropping his pants. “What is yon waiting for, blogarts,” he bellowed. “Yon did hear one gani! Four at once!”

Two more scrambled to comply, both wrestling to undo belts. Pebbles was last, he not nearly as tall as Hagis beside him. His ponytail bobbed as he unbuckled. “Mine ganispole does alreadied feel yon tongue,” he said as his rain-sodden pants dropped about his ankles, his excitement at the event to unfold disgustingly evident.

She moved close to him, looking up into his eyes as she took him firmly in her hand. “Does this feel like mine tongue, blogart?”

He took a startled breath as the edge of the blade met his flesh.

“Does yon know who I am?” she asked, feeling no shame whatsoever. “I am one malla would do anything to get her lia back, even lay hands on yon foul ganispole.” She grinned as she nodded. “If yon ganist do move one finger, I will rip it free—as I did PacMattin’s.”

There was panic within his manicured eyes, and rightfully so.

“What?” Hagis whined, taking a few hobbled steps toward them. “What goes?”

“Do nayat move,” Pebbles ordered. “Do nayat move one finger, nayat one of yon! One Loper of Zeria does hold blade to mine kagege! If she rips it clear, I will do the like with yon own!"

He drew in a high breath as she pressed the blade deeper, his arched eyebrows shooting higher. He not only shaped them, she saw, but wore eye shadowing as well. She believed it was blue. "Order yon ganist to the ground on their backs," she instructed.

"On yon backs, blogarts!"

She waited patiently as the blogarts complied, all mumbling obscenities as their bare bottoms hit the cold mud.

"Now put yon hands behind yon own. If yon does speak truths, mayhap yon will keep yon ganispole this fine lun."

His was breathless when he spoke. "What truths does yon wish to hear, Mine honored Lita?"

"Is mine lia safe?"

"Aya, as Sola shines!"

"Where is she headed? What back road do they travel?"

"They do nayat travel back roads. They—" He gasped as she pressed the blade deep.

"You spoke of back roads!"

"They did travel here by such," he admitted in a much higher pitch. "But such are now crowded with battlers in searching, so they do travel by cloth-carry, loping as fallar, malla, and three gans. Yon babe's locks have been clipped and colored. She is decked in gani garb—as yonself, Mine Lita. As Sola shines, they do travel this very road while battleans do ride right past!"

She nodded, keeping her eyes closely on his. "Yon has aided me well. I will leave yon kagege in place for now. But if yon does try to follow me, I will be more than pleased to finish what I have started."

He screamed as the blade sliced in—a small parting gift—then crumpled to the ground, his hands cupping his crotch. Those on their backs followed suit, clutching themselves and screaming as if she'd sliced them as well.

A surge of adrenaline raged through as she jumped upon her pony. Whooping and hollering, she scattered their rides, then sat high upon her own prancing ride to laugh at the four men wallowing like swine in mud. Throwing her face to the heavens, she howled and hooted. "Yon is nayat made of the lun, blogarts! Yon is made of pony dung! Pony dung!" she yelled as she dug in her heels.

CHAPTER 8

The morning was muggy. Christine slowed her pony and moved off the road as the battlers barreled by, their ponies flinging mud. They were Chaspians, emblems of gold and purple wings embroidered on their vests. They were the third such procession to pass her by in less than one turning. The blogarts would barrel right past the carry as well, that which held her precious lia.

Leaning forward, she patted Midlun's neck, and he twisted his hanging head around, eyeing the gani who would ride him so hard and so long. His mud-stained coat was soaked through with sweat. Her own mud-stained clothes were soaked as well, for even though Sola had wakened, her smile was smothered by gray clouds.

"Alright, Midlun, I get the message" she said, pressing in her heels. "Nayat much further, boy. I see fencing ahead."

The fencing held several small ponds and shikes scattered about. It also seemed to hold no end. Countless turnings had passed before she spied a pony tethered to a tree, and two children, both with poles in their hands. Though the pond had enticed several gosers to its surface, it was not there their lines were cast, but into a patch of yellow wild-flowers close by. Set back a ways off the road, a rez could be seen in the distance beside a field of coarse stalks.

Pulling up to the fence, Christine waved. "Are crouts biting this sol?"

They looked to each other, before shaking their heads.

"Has yon tried dung beetles?"

Putting his pole aside, the boy stood and brushed off his pants. "We did try dung beetles and coarse worms," he said as he moved closer. Stopping back from the fence, he eyed her warily.

"Mayhap it is too early for crouting."

"Has yon been rolling in mud?"

She smiled. He was a young gani, two and ten segs, maybe less. His sasturn threw her pole down and ran to stand beside him. She was a few years younger with mussy brown hair and big brown eyes.

"Mine pony did slip and throw me," Christine explained. "He is overly wearied and limping, and as I am on urgent travelings, I need trade for a fresh one," she said, motioning to the pony tethered.

The boy looked to her muddied pony and shook his head. "Is yon skewed?"

"It's a fair trade," she said, leaning forward to give the pony's neck a pat. "Midlun is grand as one pony can be when he has nayat been traveling through the lun."

"Yon *is* skewed to travel in the lun. Stelcherers do travel in such. And this road does crawl overly with the like—to stelcher from those traveling to note one loper."

She shifted in the saddle. "One Lita Clavin?"

He pulled his shoulders back. "Same's cover-carry did travel past this very fencing nayat one sol passed," he stated proudly.

The young girl nodded vigorously. "With LaRossian battlers in escort."

"Aya," the boy said, pointing up the road. "Many travelers and carries did follow."

"And what of lowerly?" Christine asked. "Has yon noted carries headed lowerly as well? One cloth-carry, mayhap, one holding one ganis, one lita, and two or three ganies—one but a tot?"

He frowned and shook his head. "Naya cloth-carry. But we did just note battlers headed such."

"Aya, many battlers," the girl affirmed.

Midlun snorted and raised his head, and the gani lifted his chin to peer over the fencing as a group of ponies appeared in the distance. "More!" He clambered onto the fence, waving fervently as they whisked by. Despite this valiant effort, the battlers didn't bother to return his greeting, nor even to glance in his direction.

"LaRossians! Did yon note! LaRossian battlers!" he cried,

watching till they rounded the bend. "I will be one battler one sol," he vowed as he jumped from the fence, feigning a sword fight.

"As will I," his sasturn boasted, jabbing at her brother with an imaginary sword of her own. "I will be the grandest lita battler in all of Atriia, grander even than one Loper of Zeria."

Christine looked longingly toward the pony, itching to be on its back and on her way. Pebbles was a pig, but he was right about one thing. Her lia had been snatched right under her very nose while she'd sat cowering with her eyes closed. She rubbed at her forehead. "Aya, the grandest battler of all Atriia."

"Aya," the girl-child agreed, completely oblivious of facetiousness. "One devon did slice her throat wide, yet she did only laugh in his face, then slice his own." She gave a swift swing of her imaginary blade across her brathern's throat, then laughed heartily as he staggered about, clutching at his neck.

"And what of one worgle of Woroff Woodland," the boy barked, then immediately assumed the posture of the creature. Hunching over, he stumbled about in a disjointed manner, his legs crooked and arms flopping. "Mine babe! Mine, mine," he hissed, then shrieked as the Loper of Zeria attacked him, pushing him to the ground. There he writhed and squirmed, spitting and kicking as he was pummeled from above.

"Yon has been practicing such," Christine said, clapping her hands.

Grinning, the siblings stood to brush off their clothes.

She eyed the rested pony. Sliding from her own, she climbed the fence to lean against the top rail. "What of one woodland woodslink?" she prompted, and they obediently assumed their roles, the gani dropping to hands and knees, the litia hopping aboard his back. He reared to his knees, pawing at the air and swinging his head, hissing and snapping as he attempted to dislodge his rider. But he was no adversary for the tenacious loper with her legs wrapped tight, she who drove the blade home time and again.

The creature collapsed to the ground, and the Loper of Zeria dropped to her knees to bury the blade in its hideous head. Throwing her face to the heavens, she gave a throaty, triumphant victory howl.

Christine clapped her hands. “Well done. But what of her woodslink woundings? She was bit twice fore she did drop it down. Here,” she said, sliding up her sleeve and holding out her arm, “note the scarrings, then.”

Brushing off his clothes, the boy moved nearer to study her forearm with a frown.

“And here,” she said, sliding the shirt off her shoulder.

“Nayat so close,” the boy warned, shoving his sister back when she tried to step up beside him for a better view.

“And here,” Christine said, holding out her hands. “Worgle woundings, pierced clear through,” she said, turning them palms up. “And here,” she said, lifting her chin high. “Does yon know the callen of the devon did put this scarring crost mine neck?”

The boy studied the scar, then her eyes, then the lock of hair she pulled from beneath her cap—giving it a wiggle before stuffing it back under. He seemed to struggle for the answer—though eventually it found its way to his tongue. “PacMattin?”

~~~~~~~~~~

The LaRossian battlers had diverted down a side road, one leading them wakerly and away from her babe. The freshly turned mud told her this. It also spoke of a carry, the impression of wagon wheels imparting its direction most decidedly. She followed when they turned sleeperly, headed toward the mountain peaks in the distance, to where high-hillers hailed.
~~~~~~~~~~

CHAPTER 9

A fog had rolled in with Luna's blanket, as had the overpowering pungent smell of rotting leaves and the musk of wet earth. The lun was chilly, the ground soggy, drenching her clothes where she lie loping on the covered wagon parked in the middle of the field. Hidden in the shadows of the clumping of trees, she spied on the two figures seated about the campfire, both draped in blankets. Through the fog, it was impossible to tell if they were ganist or ganies or even litas. She was certain of one thing only, there was no tot within sight. Whether one lie sleeping within the carry was another matter entirely.

On hands and knees, she locomoted to a different tree, one closer and with a better angle for loping. She could just make out the low drone of a man's voice as he stood to toss more wood upon the fire before retaking his seat.

She considered the odds of making it safely to the small standing of trees closest to the carry without being spotted—and decided they leaned in her favor. Pulling the knife from her boot, she readied herself, taking deep measured breaths—then ran hunched over, a distance ten times further than it had appeared. She kept her eyes on the two figures as she ran, but it was only a pony which spied her, turning its head and snorting.

Dropping to all fours, Christine crawled to the tree nearest the carry, then stood, pressing her belly against the bark, fighting to catch her breath without making noise. Her heart was hammering, painful in her chest, loud in her ears. Her body was quaking, the adrenaline bordering on toxic in a body deprived of food and sleep. It was affecting her sleep-deprived brain as well, one which seemed to be pulsating in her head. It was playing tricks on her, sending false messages to her ears in the form of a child's giggle. The laughter faded into the distance, melding into the haunting warble of a night-bird.

She peeked around the tree toward the carry, now merely a stone's throw away. All was quiet, save the rampant beating in her ears and the rumblings of an empty stomach. She could not see those at the fire past the carry. But she could hear them. One hacked, then spit.

The bobbing of a lantern light appeared suddenly. As it rounded the carry, she clutched tightly to the knife and pressed her cheek into the bark, holding her spot and her breath, listening as the soggy footsteps drew nearer. They stopped a short distance away, close enough that she could hear the lantern handle squeak as it was set to the ground, close enough that she could hear the stream of urine hitting the earth, along with a relieved sigh.

She fought to keep from exhaling a relieved sigh of her own.

"Yon should have ripped it free at yon chancing."

She whirled, thrusting the knife toward the dark figure who was keeping a safe distance. Though Luna's smile was clouded by fog, it was shedding ample enough light to reveal a ponytail sitting high upon his head.

It bobbed as he gave a sinister chuckle. "As if made of it," he spoke, the last word barely reaching her ears before she was struck from behind, the blow sending her face first to the moist earth—and into darkness.

CHAPTER 10

She was riding upon the mighty Ralling River, the sounds of roaring constant in her ears. Clinging to the snaggle of branches, she fought to stay afloat, kicking and gasping as frigid water slapped her in the face.

A muted voice chuckled. "Yon should have ripped it free."

"No! Down, Neema!" The hound was lapping at her face as she slept, a wet slobbery tongue at her cheek, her nose, ear. And it seemed Neema detected goser on her breath. She began to lap at her mouth, her tongue delving in.

Christine swatted her away, and a muted voice chuckled.

"I did ask nicely, lita."

"Shhh."

"'Fret nayat mine fairest babe.

Stave yon tears, mine fairest babe.

All Atriia, she will surent save.

All Atriia she will surent saaaave.'"

Despite Eubreena's lulling lullaby, Christine couldn't stave her tears. Nor could she save all of Atriia, try as she might. She couldn't even save herself from the woodslink squeezing the life from her as soft fingertips caressed.

The gani was watching, his Becca-blue eyes wide.

"'Close yon eyes, mine fairest babe.

All Atriia, I can nayat save.

All Atriia, I can nayat saaaave.'"

"Shhhh."

"No, Neema. Down!"

The roaring was constant in her ears, the groping monster

yanking on her legs, trying to pull her under. She kicked to stay afloat. She couldn't see the shore through the fog. But it was there. It was there. "Help!" she sputtered, spitting the bitter liquid from her mouth. "Help me!"

"Shhhh."

She could hear the roggii, hundreds, thousands of filthy tails slithering like snakes upon cold, hard stone. They were incited by fresh blood.

"Pleadings, Mine Lor—"

"Shhh," he whispered. "She is safe."

"The babe is nayat his!" she swore.

"I did ask nicely," Harvin sneered.

Becca-blue eyes were watching.

Eubreena tried to comfort the child with a soft song.

"'Close yon eyes, mine fairest babe.'"

"Down, Neema!"

"Shhhh."

"Feel how quick it beats!" Kynneth hissed.

"Do nayat give yon heart, Christa," Sam warned.

"The babe is nayat his!"

"Fate will take its rightly claim," Lor Zeria promised.

The ponytail was bobbing. "Yon should have ripped it free!"

"No, Neema, down!"

"And legs?" Kynneth asked with a sly grin

"That belongs to me," Sam vowed.

"I did ask nicely."

"As if made of it," Pebbles' voice was muted.

"'Close yon eyes, mine fairest baaabe.'"

Eubreena's song was fading.

"I will give mine heart!"

"Shhh."

"It is mine to give!"

The waffle was dancing a jig. "Mineseth! Mineseth!"

"Yon should have ripped it free."

"Close yon eyes. Close yon eyes…"

~~~~~~~~~~

"Open yon eyes."

She tried to comply, moaning at the pain.

"Open yon eyes, Christa."

She put a hand to her forehead, then slid it around to the back of her head, wincing at the tender lump.

"Christa."

"Becca!" Christine sprang to a sitting position. Grabbing her spinning head, she took in her surroundings. A low-burning lantern showed a canvas-covered carry cramped with travel supplies. It also showed Kynneth where he sat upon a crate, his legs set wide as he lounged back against a water barrel.

"Good to note yon again, Mine Lita." Though his tone was frigid, there was fire in his eyes, a reflection of the lantern burning.

"Kynneth, mine lia!"

He shook his head. "Ask LaRosse. He is in charge of her caring, is he nayat?"

She struggled to hands and knees, then scrambled between his parted legs, throwing her arms about his waist. Hugging tight, she pressed her ear to his heart. "Apologies, Kynneth! I should nayat have gone with LaRosse!"

He put his hands upon her head, his fingers stroking the damp tangles. "Was high-hillers," he informed her. "We were on their heels, but—they have taken to the woodland."

Christine squeezed him tighter still. "Return her and I will return to Zeria! As Sola shines!"

He sighed deeply. "High-hillers do know the woodlands better than any," he confessed, his fingertips stroking. "If we do nayat find her quickly, she is lost."

Clutching at his back, she buried her face into his chest. "What does yon wish from me, Kynneth? I will give it! I will give it!"

Sliding his hands into her hair, he lifted her face to his, bending
~~~~~~~~~~

low to gently caress her lips with his own. There were spirits on his breath and fire in his eyes.

"It this want you want, then?" she breathed against his mouth. Slipping her hands behind his neck, she clung with desperation, offering no resistance when his tongue slipped between her lips—nor when his hand slipped into her pants to caress a chilled buttock.

"I was one bligart," she whispered, the words muffled by his mouth.

"Aya." His breaths were heated against her lips, as was the hand that kneaded below. "Yon can nayat run from fating, Christa."

"Aya, I know this now." She moaned as he slid his other hand into her pants, there being a second cheek in need of warming. "Bring back mine lia, and I will face mine fating, as Sola shines."

Without warning, he pushed her roughly away. "Naya," he snapped, his eyes as harsh as the hands which gripped her arms. "Yon will face yon fating first," he swore.

She gave a gasp as she was flung over his knee, then a cry as he yanked down the pants to expose the buttocks he had warmed so nicely. The blistering palm struck repeatedly, the blows forcing out several yelps—before she could bite down on her lip to smother the cries of pain and humiliation.

When he shoved her off his lap, she quickly scrambled back, grasping his hand, kissing the scar that matched her own, then pressing it against a cheek damp with tears. "Yon is right! Yon is right to be angered. I deserve to be punished!"

"Take off yon shirt," he ordered, his words as breathless as her own.

She didn't hesitate to lift her hands to the buttons of her shirt, her quaking fingers fumbling their way down.

His eyes dropped to where her chest was heaving, and though he didn't ask nicely, she pulled her binder down—and then his head.

It was an offering he didn't refuse, latching on as one suckling babe, his hands slipping back into her pants to massage stinging buttocks.

She massaged at his scalp. "LaRosse is one blogart," she gasped breathlessly. “Yon was right to stelcher mine babe—before devons could do the like.” A moan escaped at his sudden release, his mouth sliding to lavish her other nipple with the same avid attention. She clutched at his head as he latched on, a mouth hot and hungry. Throwing her head back, she squeezed her eyes shut, forcing out twin tears. “I know—know yon will nayat harm her. Yon heart is kind.”

She cried out as he pushed her away with a snarl. He put a hand to his belt, releasing it from its buckle in one quick jerk. “Drop to yon knees before me, lita,” he commanded.

She hesitated, nodding as twin tears made a dual dash down her cheeks. “Is this mine fating, then?” she whispered weakly.

He slid his feet to an even wider stance, leaning back against the barrel with a stony grin. “Yon would do anything for yon lia, would yon nayat—even lay hands on mine foul ganispole?”

She stared for several long moments as his words sank in.

He nodded as his grin broadened. “Nayan do travel through one lun as do stelcherers.”

“As if made of it,” she whispered numbly.

He nodded. “Foul devons. But if anybody was to find yon, I knew it would be they.” He ran his eyes languidly down the length of her where she stood exposed and vulnerable. “One did near lose his kagege for his flustings. I trust yon will be more gentled with mine brathern’s.”

She swallowed down the strangling lump. “Yon brathern’s?”

He nodded. “It does hold the very fating of the Zeria bloodline—as does yon belly.”

She pressed her hands against a stomach in knots. “Therein does lie mine fating, then?”

He replied with a stony grin. “All yon need do is lie on yon back and open yon legs wide. Is such so hard, then? And as yon lia is headed to the high-hills as we do speak, I gest yon does open them quickly. This lun even.”

His grin vanished at the sound of shouting and approaching pony hooves. “This turning even.” He motioned to where her shirt lay open. “Fix yonself,” he ordered. “Yon fating is arrived.”

CHAPTER 11

Try as she might, she could not look him in the face. She kept her seeping eyes firmly upon the crest on his coat, the red and black Sola with striating rays.

It was difficult enough being confined with him in the carry, one not nearly large enough to accommodate a man of his stature, and certainly not large enough to accommodate his presence. It filled every cranny, every crevice, leaving room for little else, including air to breathe. With damp gani's garb plastered to a body weak and trembling, she struggled for breath as she stood before him.

"Does yon wish to address yon Lor?" Kynneth asked, he having kept his seat upon the crate.

She nodded as she struggled to fight back tears. "Aya—apologies," She swallowed hard as the words jumbled in her throat. "I—I was one bligart to go with LaRosse."

"Is yon addressing his footings, then?"

"Kynneth," the Lor spoke softly, "will yon leave us."

She near crumpled to the floor at the sound of his deep voice, one deeply wounded. Burying her face in her hands, she listened as Kynneth took his leave, fighting the urge to scurry out on his heels. Never before could she remember feeling so vulnerable—lack of food, lack of sleep, lack of air—all had her head spinning. Her legs were rubbery. She was certain they would not hold her much longer.

The wagon floor groaned beneath his weight as he moved close. Still, she kept her face safely buried in her hands, ashamed of the tears, ashamed of a body quaking as one tippet cowering before one woodslink. She wanted to run like one tippet, to scramble screaming from the carry and into the woodland, into the high-hills and down the other side, running to the very ends of Atriia. Instead, she did only run a sleeve under her nose. "Mine Lor, I—"

He put his arms around her, pulling her close, squeezing tight as any woodslink, forcing out a barrage of tears.

She pressed her cheek against the damp fabric of his coat. "Yon has always been kind to me, Mine Lor," she wept, "always kind. I should nayat have left, and I will nayat again, nayat ever. I can nayat run from fating. I know this now. I know this."

He ran a hand into her hair, caressing—till his fingers happened upon the lump. "Yon is injured," he said as he pushed her to arm's length.

"It's nothing." He was horribly handsome where he stood in his low-cut coat and high-cut boots. Too handsome to gaze upon without feeling shame. And with the most beautiful mouth she had ever seen. She reached up to run trembling fingertips along it, and, as his brathern, he was receptive to her advances, leaning down as she did up. Slipping her hands behind his neck, she sampled the sweetness, breathing feathery sighs against his molten lips as they caressed her own.

Her sigh had a different pitch as he pulled away, one of desperation. Clinging to his neck, she caressed his cheek with moist lips. "Mine lia."

"We will find her, as Sola shines."

She traced kisses to his neck, nuzzling. "Aya, I do know this," she breathed as she slid her hands inside his coat. Pulling the shirt from his pants, she ran her hands beneath, tracing fingertips along his back.

"Christa—"

"Sit for one mound," she said, guiding him backward toward Kynneth's crate. "Yon battlers have been riding hard for sols. Yon must nayat send them into the woodland wearied."

She lifted the coat from his shoulders, and he helped to slide it off, draping it across the water barrel before lowering himself to his brother's trusty crate.

"While yon ganist rest," she said, lifting one of his boots and sliding it off, "yon and I will nayat." She slid off the other and cast it aside, then went to work on her own clothing.

He leaned back against the barrel, sitting as his brathern had, his long legs in a wide stance. With hands resting upon his knees, he watched as she unbuttoned her shirt for the second time that lun, pulling it off, then the binder beneath.

Suspicious eyes slid to hers, delving deep as she loosed the drawstring on her pants. "I am wearied of hiding," she explained, sliding everything off in one deft move. Stepping from her garments, she slid them aside with her toes, then slid into the vee of his legs. "I am readied to face mine fating, Mine Lor."

He was not nearly as receptive as his brathern, merely placing his hands upon her hips to hold her at bay. His suspicious eyes slid down low and his fingertip followed to run a questioning trail along the scar.

A prick of panic surfaced. "It was untruths, Mine Lor, what I spoke. Naya babe was pulled through." She nearly choked on the words, the thought of her sweet Becca near buckling her wobbly knees.

Before she could collapse, she climbed upon his lap and wrapped her legs about his waist, locking her ankles tight. "I was but a tot," she lied between frantic kisses to his face. "Did get hands on mine malla's crout blade. One meshganis—" She kissed his locked lips with urgency. "—one meshganis did stitch same, that is all."

His beautiful mouth did not respond as she had hoped. He turned it away so that it might speak an unsavory word. "Untruths."

If his lips were not responding to her advances, part of him most certainly was. Seated on his lap, it was impossible to conceal. The small pale hand that slid to manipulate his belt was trembling.

He grasped it, his fist like an iron manacle about her wrist. "Christa! Does yon think this will make me search harder for yon babe? It will nayat! I will search to the ends of Atriia."

"I know this, Mine Lor," she said, pulling her hand free so to unfasten his belt.

He grimaced as the pale hand slipped inside his pants to slip the fate of the Zeria bloodline gently out. "Christa," he warned, as she nuzzled into his neck, softly nibbling as her hand softly stroked.

"Yon was right," she sighed against his neck, "fating will take its rightly claim." She buried her face into his neck, hiding her tears—and her fears, for though the Lor of Zeria was resisting her advances with valiant chivalry, that within her trembling hand was completely without honor.

With a growl, he fisted his hands into her hair, wrenching her face from his neck. There was a snarl twisting the beautiful mouth and darkening the hazel eyes to feral black—the face of a creature fighting his most primal of instincts.

As she slipped her hands behind his neck, lifting to slip upon her fating with a shuddering cry, any resistance from the Leader of Lors instantly slipped away.

~~~~~~~~~~

She grasped at a back slick with sweat and arched against him yet again, an undignified squeal escaping through clenched teeth. Dropping back down to the unyielding boards of the carry, she fought for breath, for her very consciousness as the greedy beast sought out her lips.

"Wait! Wait!"

"Shhh," he breathed into her mouth before closing over it.

There was no resisting such a creature, one denied for too long and demanding atonement. With steely arms wrapped firmly about her, he assailed her with a demented urgency, the rocking carry moaning and groaning as loudly as she. A stack of tent poles overturned and clattered near her feet, and a bundle of coarse stalks followed. Something unseen rolled along the wagon bed, coming to rest near her head, and the creature shoved it aside without breaking stride. He was bent upon sealing her fating this time, even if the carry collapsed to the ground in a broken heap. And there was a good chance it might do that very thing. It was coming apart. Fog was seeping through the cracks, through warped floorboards, through canvas seams.

"Wait!"

"Shhh."

She wrenched her face away from him to find Kynneth had crept
~~~~~~~~~~

back in. He was seated upon his crate, leaning casually back against the water barrel, rocking with the rhythm of the wagon. He smirked when she spied him.

"Bastard!"

"Shhh," the woodslink hissed in her ear.

There was movement in the crate beneath Kynneth. She blinked her eyes, trying to focus through the fog. It was her babe peeking through the slats, her hair dyed dark and clipped short like a gani's.

"Close yon eyes," she gasped, her lungs near depleted of air. "Close yon eyes, mine babe!"

A groan escaped her as Pebbles appeared beside Kynneth, materializing from the shadows to stand shrouded in fog. "As if made of it," he hissed.

"Of dung!"

The woodland woodslink was squeezing the life from her as deceptive fingertips caressed. She dug in heels, dug in fingers, raking nails along its slick back, but the frenzied beast was feeling no pain.

"Please!"

"Shhhh," it hissed.

"I did ask nicely, lita," Harvin sneered, then latched on greedily, taking forcefully that which she refused to give willingly.

She clutched at his head. "Close yon eyes, mine babe! Close yon—get away, Neema, god dammit!

But it wasn't Neema lapping at her face. Pebbles was on all fours, hovering over her. He trailed his tongue to her ear, dipping it inside, then lapped at her lobe. "Is it planted deep enough for yon, Mine Lita?" he whispered.

With a growl, she slapped him away. "Fuck you!" she screamed, digging in heels.

"I have noted him, Christa," the Leader of Lors whispered in her ear.

"Mineseth, mineseth!" The worgle was dancing in the swirling fog, a jig of anger, tight fists pounding against squat thighs.

"Naya, one babe is mine," a raspy voice countered, "as is yon heart." He sat upon the crate, his long legs set wide—as his two predecessors. The fog was not thick enough to hide the ghastly scars marring his face and neck, nor those in his eyes—the deepest wounding of all.

She closed her eyes against his pain, focusing on her own, one merely physical and far more sufferable. With frozen fingers, she clutched tightly to the tangled mass of branches, bobbing on the surface of the savage Ralling as it swept her deep into the woodland. But, as fate would dictate, she lost her grip, and the beast took full advantage, pulling her under again and again, only to shoot her back to the surface, spitting and sputtering and gasping for breath. The raging behemoth flung her against boulders, a painful pounding, bone-shattering, flesh-ripping.

She cried out, kicking and flailing, bucking against the slick beast, but it only gripped tighter, holding firm till her struggling ceased. Only then did it relent, gently laying her bruised and broken body on a pebble-strewn shore.

She hadn't the strength to open her eyes, nor did she wish to. She knew what rested between her legs, a beast lying latent, one far from finished in securing her fating. Soft fingertips caressed her face as hot breaths did her ear.

"So claimed," it whispered.

CHAPTER 12

Bacon.

She could smell it wafting in through the haze of sleep. Bacon and eggs. Toast with butter, crispy hash-browns fried with onions, orange juice, fresh-squeezed with pulp. She sighed, then shifted, then groaned at the pain of a battered body. Grimacing, she moistened dry lips with the tip of her tongue, wondering at the tenderness. She wondered also at the feather tickling her cheek.

"Did yon sleep well?"

His words opened her eyes in an instant. She lie on her side beneath a thin blanket, as did he, facing her, caressing her cheek with the petals of a flower. With a groan, she rolled to her back, but he was instantly upon her, his weight settling heavy atop.

"Mine Lor—"

"Shhh." He put a finger to her lips. "Yon will waken her," he whispered.

She followed his gaze to the bundle laid out beside the crate.

Sola's breaking smile was filtering through the canvas, throwing beams of dappled light upon the babe curled on her side. Her chubby arms were curled around a lumpy doll and her lips were parted, showing that all her precious baby teeth were still intact. Her hair was not so fortunate. It had been clipped short and dyed dark, the black ringlets framing a face of inviolate ivory.

"Becca." She clamped down on her bottom lip to thwart the threatening sob.

"The blogarts left her in one woodland," he whispered as he caressed her cheek with his lips. "The tippets did run, but they will be hunted," he promised. "I will rip their throats wide and toss them to fraigens mine very self."

He would not be tossing anyone to fraigens, she knew, not unless it was his blasted brathern. But she didn't care. She didn't care that it felt as if someone had used a bat on the back of her head to hit a home run—or that it felt as if the same bat had assualted her insides. Her eyes were resting on an angel on Atriia. She clamped a hand over her mouth as her chest hitched in a silent sob.

"Shhh," he breathed against her ear, "she is safe."

The words drew her eyes from the sleeping babe. She needed to see it, the mouth would speak such golden words. Sliding her fingers into his hair, she pulled it down, thirsting for the sweetness. She opened her lips wide, warmly welcoming he who would give back her precious angel, and without even the slightest of prompting, she opened her legs wide as well, and the Lor of Zeria, the very Leader of Lors, accepted her welcome graciously, slipping inside without the slightest of hesitation, as if returning to his own sweet home.

~~~~~~~~~~

Becca giggled and squirmed as her malla burrowed into her neck with loud, sloppy kisses. Pulling back, Christine growled and snarled and snapped at the flushed child sitting on her lap, then swooped into the opposite side like a frenzied animal, attacking her neck with kisses till the babe squealed.

Pulling away, Christine drank in the choked giggles, the crinkled nose, the wide, unreserved smile revealing a mouthful of baby teeth. "Okay, ready?" she asked when Becca had somewhat recovered. "One, two, three."

Holding to her tiny fingers, Christine lowered the child backward till she was hanging upside down, her short-clipped hair brushing against the wagon's floorboards at her feet. With her tummy so exposed, there was no resisting sloppy raspberries. Becca screamed and squirmed as she was attacked with fervor.

"One, two, three," Christine counted, then hefted her back to a sitting position, laughing at her flushed cheeks and dizzy eyes, and the mussy hair standing on end as if she were still upside down.
~~~~~~~~~~

She tried to ignore the commotion without the wagon, the procession of battlers increasing in numbers with every turning of travel. Peeks through the canvas revealed not only Zerians—but Chaspians, RoonEsterians, Vognians, Banzinians, Rostivanians, Woroffians, Cleerians, Lazettians, and many more she did not recognize—all banded together to escort the famed loper safely back to Zeria. By midsol, the ground shook with the pounding of a thousand hooves.

As Sola was dipping low, her flushed face casting streaks of lavender and cerise across the skies, the ground quaked as an avalanche of ponies descended from all sides, halting the procession. She didn't need to see their insignia to know they were LaRossians, or that their Lor led them.

As Christine hugged Becca close, her eyes drifted to the pink flower that lie wilting beside the crate.

"Kindly Mas," she addressed to the carry driver, "will yon help me down?"

~~~~~~~~~~

The sea of ponies parted before her, the ganist atop bowing heads as she treaded through with babe on hip. Though still dressed in mud-stained gani garb, her hair was free and dancing boldly in Sola's smile as she strode with a determined step.

They sat high upon ponies, one Lor of Zeria and one Lor of LaRosse, in heated discussion, this quickly cooling as they spotted her.

"Ah, Mine Lita," Lor LaRosse greeted with a bow of his head. "I am pleased to note yon lia is well."

"Naya thankings to yonself," the Lor of Zeria replied coldly.

"I have come to reclaim yon from these babe stelcherers."

There came an angry rumbling, and the LaRossian battlers
~~~~~~~~~~

moved in as the Leader of Lors put his hand upon the haft of his blade. Kynneth went one step further, pulling his from his boot, though his men reacted quickly, spurring their ponies forward to block him.

"Yon did waste yon travelings, Mine Lor," Christine spoke loudly to be heard above the ruckus. "I wish to return to Zeria."

Lor LaRosse gave a reverent bow of his head. "Christa, hear me."

"She has spoken," the Lor of Zeria snarled, keeping his hand firmly on his weapon. "And yon will address her as 'Mine Lita'."

"Did yon address her as such, then, as yon did force yonself inside of her?"

A murmur ran through the men surrounding them.

"Forgivings, Mine Lita," LaRosse addressed to her. "But yon does walk with one new limp. I did warn of such, did I nayat?"

The blade was pulled from its sheath so quickly, she did not see it till it was tipped at LaRosse's throat, the Lor of Zeria leveling it with a steady hand.

LaRosse was not near as hasty. He placed his hand upon his weapon with slow deliberation. "Does yon challenge this Lor to battle, then?"

"No, he does not!" Christine insisted.

"Do nayat fret, Mine Lita." LaRosse whipped out his blade, maneuvering it as only a master swordsman could, spinning it skillfully as a gunslinger might a revolver, the last revolution ending with a quick flick of his wrist which deftly directed the opposing blade away. "He will tuck his tippetly tail," he assured her, "as did his brathern. Only tippets do stelcher babes and force themselves upon litas." His tight grin disappeared as he dropped his eyes to her. "Come with me, Mine Christa. As Sola shines, I will nayat put yon at risking again."

"As Sola shines, I will rip yon blasted throat wide," Zeria threatened through clenched teeth.

Christine moved between the two ponies. "Yon will nayat! As Sola shines, yon will nayat, Jerrod!"

His eyes fell to her, then to the babe on her hip, and a rumbling growl escaped him as he re-sheathed his blade. He pointed a finger of warning at LaRosse. "One Lita Clavin has spoken. Same does wish to return to Zeria. Now yon and yon ganist will return to yon own hailing. If yon does ever come near mine again, there will be battlement. On this I do swear on Sola."

In a swirling flash, LaRosse re-sheathed his blade. "I look forward to such." His pony pranced as he eyed her, taking in her gani garb. "Yon is one skilled loper, Mine Lita. More so than I did know. But these bratherns do know yon skills well. And they know yon weakness." His eyes shifted to where Becca sat on her hip, listening attentively to his every word. "Return to Zeria, and there will be naya escaping. For the rest of yon sols, it will be yon keeper." He threw a look of disdain to the Lor before him, then over to his brathern. "One that does crawl with foul roggii," he added—then extended his hand to her.

The Lor of Zeria bristled. "She did—"

"Wait!" Christine cried, throwing up a halting hand.

The Leader of Lors looked to her incredulously.

She dropped her eyes from his so wounded. She didn't dare look toward Kynneth. She could picture his glare, his eyes shooting warnings of severe punishment. She could still feel the aftermath of his wrath, stinging imprints on bruised buttocks.

She looked instead to LaRosse. He was close, mere feet away, his blue eyes pleading, his hand beckoning. She had but to place her palm in his.

She saw the hand of the Leader of Lors move to the hilt of his blade. Lor LaRosse followed suit, curling his fingers about his own. All about, ponies fidgeted as their riders tensed. Seeming to sense discord, Becca leaned close with a pout, throwing tiny arms about her malla's neck and resting her head upon her shoulder.

The tears came of their own accord, dashing down Christine's cheeks in a sudden torrent. She closed her eyes, searching for the color of hope in the darkness—but all that appeared was a shiny, silver platter complete with shiny, silver, dome cover.

Pulling in a deep breath, she opened her eyes to the color of reality. "I have handed mine answer."

PART VI

CHAPTER 1

Christine pulled the covers over the sleepy-eyed child. "Give her kisses." Making kissing noises, Christine put the rag-doll to Becca's lips, and the child giggled and threw her arms around it, giving it an obliging smooch before pulling it to her chest in a tight hug. "Now malla." Christine leaned in, and Becca puckered dutifully, bequeathing a moist kiss with an exaggerated smack.

Lying down beside her, Christine propped on an elbow to run her fingers through the short curls, watching her eyes drift at the caress. Fallow sap had removed the dye. Her short locks were glowing a deep russet in the lamplight. Christine ran her fingertips down the line of her jaw, then over to a dewy, plump cheek. Leaning in, she placed a kiss upon it, then the nose, the forehead.

Settling her head into the pillow, Christine watched the doll rise and fall with every precious breath, watched the cherry-red lips smack in sleep, the dark lashes flutter. Her babe was safe, safe within the walls of Zeria.

Pulling the covers to her chest, Christine released a long weary sigh. She'd entered the gates of Zeria in the company of a thousand battlers—hooves clopping, drums beating, horns trumpeting. Within the cas, the litas had all greeted her with tears and hugs, Eubreena practically breaking ribs. Becca had been thrilled to see Bixten, bestowing him with unbridled hugs and kisses.

She brought a hand to her mouth as a yawn materialized. She would sleep well this lun in dry clothes and a soft bed, freshly bathed and fully fed. Rolling to her side, she took in the extravagant shalia displays, the opulently carved bedposts, the matching armoire and mirror. Her own private boarding.

Her keeper.

Running a hand along her brow, she rubbed at her forehead. She had wounded the Leader of Lors, he barely speaking three words on the remainder of the journey home—merely poking his head into the carry on occasion to inquire of her well-being.

Rolling to her belly, she patted at the side of the bed, then stroked the silky head that obediently moved within reach. "Did you miss me, Neema?" she asked, and the hound answered with a swing of her tail. "I missed you, too." Closing her eyes, Christine scratched behind the floppy ears, grinning as Neema groaned her express gratitude.

~~~~~~~~~~

"Mmm—get, Neema." Brushing the hound away, she rolled to her back and pulled the covers high, grinning at the sound of Hopper rustling through his bedding—till a thought slowly crept into her sleepy brain—the tippet was gone.

Slowly her eyes fluttered open.

With a gasp, she scrambled to a sitting position, pressing her back against the headboard. "Mine Lor! You—yon did startle me." Her heart thumped crazily. Instantly the air seemed thicker, the breaths difficult to pull in.

Seating himself on the edge of the bed, he eyed her where she cowered clutching the blanket to her chin. He was dressed in sleep pants and nothing else, save the chain around his neck, the gilded face of Sola hanging low on a chiseled chest. His hair was damp
~~~~~~~~~~

from bathing and combed back, his face cleanly shaven. He was impossibly handsome.

He dropped his eyes to the sleeping child, then to his own hand resting on the bed. "Does yon feel keepered here?" he asked, his eyes sliding up to hers.

She fidgeted beneath his gaze. "Well—the guardsganist—they are at mine side every grain."

"For purpose."

She nodded, then drew in a difficult breath as she brushed the hair from her eyes. "To keep danger out—or me in?"

His jaw flexed as a long breath filtered through his nose. "I will remove them during the sol, but they will return at lun."

"Thankings, Mine Lor."

"Jerrod," he corrected. Taking her hand, he rubbed it gingerly between his own. "LaRosse claims I did force mineself upon yon."

"Naya," she said with an embarrassed grin. "Was mineself did the forcing."

He returned her grin, then leaned closer to gently lift her chin. "I did nayat mind," he whispered as he leaned in.

"Wait!" She pressed her palms against his chest—and he pulled back, his eyes dark and wounded. He was recalling when last she had barked the word to him in front of LaRosse, in front of all his ganist—as was she.

"Apologies. It's just—I'm fretting about Dahla. Has there been any word?"

He shook his head and, raking fingers through his damp hair, rose from the bed, his veiled eyes moving to where Becca lie sleeping with her arms about the doll. "Sleep well, then," he said, before slipping away.

CHAPTER 2

Eubreena was crying, she was laughing so hard. Many of the litas were doing the like, wiping at eyes and clutching at bellies, the food at the table completely forgotten by all except Becca. The child was greatly enjoying the bread smothered with seedberry jam. Her face was smothered with it just as generously.

"One, two, three, four," Eubreena repeated, and an eruption of laughter ensued.

Christine nodded and took a sip of water.

"And all four blogarts did drop pants down?" Torna asked, shaking her head.

Christine grinned. "Aya, down over boots, down over blades. I could nayat have bound their ankles better with rope."

Eubreena lifted the knife from her plate. "Does this feel like mine tongue, blogart," she growled, sending the group to new heights of hysterics, some pounding on the table and stomping feet, some burying embarrassed faces in their hands. Vinova was positively braying.

"Oh, Mine honored, eyegrandly, kindly, wizened Lita," Tressa mimicked in a fear-stricken, mannish voice, "pleadings do nayat slice off mine ganispole!"

The litas howled and doubled over, gasping for breath.

"Yon does own more curves to boast, gani," Eubreena aped, the tears streaming down her face.

Christine pursed her lips indignantly. "Well, mine coat was overly thick," she defended.

Kylara, amply endowed even as pleasurers went, found this particularly amusing. Throwing her head back, she howled as she clutched at her heaving bosom.

"Lor Zeria!" Eubreena gasped, shooting to her feet, and the other litas followed suit, nearly knocking over chairs in their haste. Christine was slowest to react. Rising to her feet, she bowed her head.

He grinned from where he stood in the doorway, then moved aside, revealing Dahla where she stood hid behind.

"Dahla!" Christine cried, running to throw her arms about her, a hug which Dahla returned fiercely.

Becca scrambled from her chair with a squeal, and ran up to hug a leg, burying her jelly face in Dahla's gilt.

Dahla didn't seem to mind that her gilt was being soiled. She knelt to hug the child, then began to weep.

"She is well, Dahla," Christine assured. "She was nayat harmed."

"Thankings to Sola," Dahla sniffled, lifting the babe to her hip and kissing one jelly-stained cheek. "And to our Lor," she added, beaming up at the man by her side.

He acknowledged with a grin, then extended a hand to Christine, beckoning. There was a gleam in his eyes. "Might I have one word?"

Christine looked to where Becca sat perched upon Dahla's hip licking jelly from her fingers.

"Go," Eubreena urged, nudging her with an elbow. "Dahla will keep Becca."

~~~~~~~~~~

It was odd traveling the halls of Cas Zeria on the arm of its Lor. Her rebuff from the previous night seemed completely forgotten. He seemed of a fine mood as he interlaced his fingers with hers.

"Where are we going?"

There was a mysterious twinkle in his eyes as he looked down at her, as if a marvelous secret lie hidden there.

"Are we late, Mine Lor?" she laughed, running to keep up as he skipped down the stairs.

They came to a screeching halt on the landing, he leaning close
~~~~~~~~~~

with a reproachful frown. "Jerrod, Christa."

"Jerrod, then. Where are we going?"

He grinned and lifted her hand to his lips, placing a soft kiss on her knuckles. "I did speak with Dahla one long while. She is one fine litia. She need nayat go before one saker. I am certain she was nayat hired by Sherva Rostivane. And I am certain she did nayat know of Tavaka's loping. She is loyal to yon and yon lia."

Throwing her arms about his waist, she hugged him tight. "Thankings. I did know this."

"She is wisened for her aging," he said, reclaiming her hand to lead her down the remaining steps. "She does think Lor LaRosse the grandest blogart in of all Atriia." He chuckled softly. "She did insist on returning to Zeria gainst his wishings, and even knowing she might face loping charges here. She is more brazened than I did think."

"More than I did think," she admitted, feeling a sudden sense of dread as they turned down the hall leading to his boarding.

As if sensing her hesitation, his grip on her hand grew tighter. "Do nayat be angered with her."

"With Dahla?"

He stopped suddenly—not at his door—but her own, pushing it open and pointing in to the cage sitting upon the bureau.

"Hopper." Moving in, she leaned close to peer into the cage, tapping on the top. "Greetings, Hopper." The tippet poked his nose out from where he lie buried beneath fluffed straw, his whiskers bobbing. Realizing there was no food forthcoming, he pulled it back under. "Nice to see you too," she laughed, meeting the Lor's eyes in the mirror. "Why would I be angered with Dahla?" she asked of his reflection.

The Lor grinned, almost shyly. "She spoke of tears from Lazette to Banzine. I did force it from her," he added quickly. "Did twist her arm quite high."

"Oh," she breathed softly, feeling suddenly weak. Leaning heavily on the bureau, she looked down to where the tippet lie buried, wishing she could join him.

"Tears from yon heart, those were her words."

At the mention of tears, new ones formed, blurring her vision. “I—never meant to harm yon.”

“Christa.”

She couldn’t bring herself to turn around, even at his gentle coaxing. Facing his mere reflection was difficult enough. He seemed to tower where he stood in the doorway, his broad shoulders blocking the exit entirely. Her heart dropped as he stepped inside, pulling the door closed behind him—then floundered in her belly as he moved toward her, stopping just behind. Producing a medallion from his pocket, he brought it to his lips—then placed it over her head from behind.

He lifted her hair so Sola could rest proper about her neck, then slipped his hands about her waist, pulling her back against him. “Yon did drop this, mine Christa, at the foot of one tree deep in one woodland.”

She shuddered at the remembrance of the tree, of the woodslink wrapped so tight, snapping bones as fingertips caressed. The man wrapped around her was every bit as dangerous.

“It is back where it does belong,” he said, “as is yonself.” He leaned in to nuzzle her neck, bringing goose-bumps to life. The tingling traveled down her arms and torso, down thighs to shins and even toes.

While tingling traveled downward, his hands slid up to the buttons of her gilt. “Does yon remember mine words when first I placed one Honor of Sola round yon neck?”

“Aya,” she breathed as his fingers slowly worked their way down. “One heart brazened.”

She couldn’t pull her tear-filled eyes away from where Hopper hid beneath straw. She had caged him. But for his own good. He no longer had to fear giant roggii, or fry pans wielded by scullery litas—or flying boots. He was safest caged.

Lifting the gilt from her shoulders, the Lor let it glide to the floor, then slid his hands to her bare belly, his fingertips gently caressing. “One meant to pump life back to Zeria blood,” he breathed against her neck.

Sliding his hands into her undergarment, he slipped it neatly off.

CHAPTER 3

"There," Eubreena said as she finished off the last nail. "Now, do nayat touch one thing till one polish dries. Ten mounds, least."

Kylara held her hands out with fingers splayed as she rose to her feet. "Thankings, Eubreena. It is the perfect coloring of mine pleasuring gilt."

"Mine Lita," she addressed to Christine, bowing her head.

Christine reciprocated, then took her seat.

"Is yon locks dry, then?" Eubreena asked as she combed her fingers through Christine's hair.

"Aya, finhap," Christine replied as she shifted in the chair, trying to find a comfortable position for a tender body. "I miss my hair dryer."

Eubreena arched her brows in the mirror. "Hair dryer?"

"Aya. It blows air—to dry hair."

The arched brows furrowed. "As one flameblower?"

Christine pondered on this. "Aya, save *hot* air."

"How does the air get hot, then?"

"Well—there's a coil inside, a piece of metal that's heated."

Eubreena frowned as she picked up the hairbrush. "Yon can nayat put hot metals inside one flameblower. It will burn one hole, surent."

"Never mind," Christine said, waving the notion wearily away. "Forget I said anything."

"We do have Vinova," Eubreena offered with a grin. "Same does blow hot air plenty."

"Eubreena, shammer on yon," Christine chastised, closing her eyes as Eubreena began to brush. "Mmm, I am thinking braidings this sol."

"Naya. One simple bun is best." Eubreena leaned to her ear. "Much easier for large hands to undo," she whispered with a wry grin.

Christine felt the heat rush to her face. "Eubreena, we did only speak."

Eubreena's grin grew broader as she brushed. "One entire sol? Portent ganist speakings do nayat even last so long. And—Dahla claims Becca was brought to her boarding just before Sola wakened this morn. Did he wish to speak with yon some more, then?"

With an exasperated sigh, Christine turned her attention to the mirror, finding the group of litas being tutored at the long dining table, their fingers curled around plumed pens as they tried to form letters upon parchment. Dahla was painstakingly trying to pen the symbols, a feat near impossible with Becca holding the same pen, guiding it with giggles. Dressed immaculately as usual in tan pants and a crisp white shirt, Lessoner Talbot slowly strolled about the table, peering over shoulders.

"Do nayat paint mine nails. I wish to practice mine symbols."

"I must paint yon face, least, in case Lor Zeria does wish to—speak again this sol."

"Surely, he will nayat!"

Eubreena pursed her lips as she wound the hair into a bun and secured it with hairpins. "I am surent he will. Yon has three sols left of yon brooding allten. I am thinking he will wish to speak with yon each and every one."

"I am nayat his brooder." Christine watched as Eubreena placed a drop of oil upon her palette, mixing in a hint of pink with a tiny lip brush. "Besides, I've heard it spoken the Zeria bratherns can nayat fallar babes."

Eubreena stopped her mixing to peer anxiously over her shoulder. "Who does speak such untruths?" she hissed.

"Is it untruths, then? Nayat one babe between the two. Kynneth does call down pleasurers near every lun—two, three, four at once."

Eubreena dropped her chin to her chest and nodded as a deep sigh escaped. There were tears in her hazel eyes when she lifted them. "Even during their brooding alltens, gainst the rulings. I fear it is truths that he can nayat fallar babes." She wiped moisture from her eyes, then dipped the brush in the glossy pink paint.

"And our Lor? Most Lors have ten babes by his age."

"Hold still," Eubreena ordered as she leaned in to apply the gloss to her lips. "So much speaking did cause yon lips to swell," she teased, a grin tugging on the corners of her mouth. Though there was no hint of humor in her moist eyes. "Our Lor has had differed brooders over the segs, but—" She shrugged. "Mayhap Sola was waiting for the right belly," she said, giving Christine's a poke.

Christine gasped as he appeared in the doorway, the Lor of whom they spoke.

Leaning against the jamb, he smiled as the litas shot to their feet and bowed their heads. "How is yon lessonings this sol," he asked, and they all answered at once, tittering and tripping pathetically over rushed replies.

"They are quick lessoners, Mine Lor," Talbot offered, thrusting out his chest and brushing the silver bangs away from his spectacles.

"I did guess as much," the Lor confessed as his eyes slid to where Christine and Eubreena stood at the dressing table. "Christa," he beckoned, extending his hand.

"Mine Lor, I—"

"Go," Eubreena urged, giving her a nudge. "Our Lor does only wish to speak with yon."

And speak they did, at great length, a passionate discussion, one deep and heated. They spoke till she could speak no more, the only sounds left upon her lips mere breathless sighs that echoed through her brain. But he had much more to say, it seemed, years' worth of conversations stored. And she listened very closely, an attentive ear clinging to every golden word.

CHAPTER 4

As they exited the solasium into the gardens, Bixten gave a whistle. “So many differed colorings,” he sighed as he plucked a pink-petaled shalia from a shrub, bringing it to his nose. The Lor of Zeria broke off one matching and slid it behind Christine’s ear.

“I have nayat ever noted one garden so grand,” Bixten breathed.

“Nayor have I,” Christine confessed. It was grand, indeed, with trimmed hedges and shaped shrubs, all boasting brightly colored shalias. There were arbors crawling with vines, these dripping with shalias of different shades, shapes, and sizes. Trees were flowering—pink, white, yellow, red, and every possible hue of purple. The roses—or copes as they were known on Atriia—were enormous and of every imaginable shade. The Leader of Lors was especially fond of the tangerine copes, those tipped in dark orange. Pulling out his blade, he snipped a dozen stems to form a bouquet.

“We should have one garden like this at our cas,” Christine suggested, “on the grounds in front so that all can admire such when they enter. There’s plenty of space.”

He nodded, then interlaced his fingers with hers so they might stroll hand in hand. “Aya, there is that.”

“I would visit such every sol.”

“Aya,” Bixten chirped, interlacing his fingers with her free hand, “as would I. Note those trees, then,” he exclaimed. “Clouds!”

Christine looked to the tree exploding with shalias the color and consistency of cotton, indeed reminiscent of clouds. Closing her eyes, she breathed in of the light, clean scent they exuded, indeed what she imagined a cloud might smell like, fresh and pure. “It’s as if we walk with Sola,” she sighed.

“Aya, through clouds,” Bixten said, beaming ear to ear. His eyes widened as they exited the gardens into the cemetery. "So, this is it, then. One buriard." As they traveled the footpath, he eyed the stoic stones lined up like staunch soldiers. "I have nayat ever noted one," he admitted, "but I have heard of such. So many stones. Does one body rest neath every one, then?"

"Aya," the Lor replied. "Though some do rest in tempelles." He halted before one such tempelle, then knelt to place the cut copes within the urn at the base of the steps.

"So grand," Bixten marveled, throwing his head back to study the markings carved in marble above thick wooden doors. More marble spanned the front in the form of six pillars, and more in the form of two statues on either side of the doors—women dressed in flowing gilts, their hands and faces thrown to the heavens in a prayer to Sola.

"Can yon read the scribing?" Christine asked.

Bixten crinkled his nose. "Ta," he said, motioning to the first symbol, "and za, there."

The Lor nodded. "Good. It reads Tarriff Zeria. Mine fallar."

Bixten was intrigued. "What of yon malla? Is she there as well?"

He shook his head, pointing to a nearby stone. "There."

Bixten turned to study the stone across the distance. "Mine malla has naya stone. She ended fraigen dung."

"Bixten." Christine crooned, putting a hand on his shoulder. "Yon malla is with Sola. Look up."

Bixten threw his face to Sola, closing his eyes and smiling at the warmth.

"Does yon feel Sola's smile? Yon malla's smile does join with hers. She does smile down with pride on one gan growing more strong and wise with each new sol."

He nodded. "She would be proud of mine lessoning. Has yon heard, there are litias in mine grouping now?"

Zeria tousled his hair. "Does yon like being lessoned with litias, then?"

He nodded adamantly. "Aya. Flana is the brightest of us all. She does know all her symbols alreadied! And she does sit one pony better than any gani." He gasped suddenly and pointed. "Flutterfly," he cried, then dashed off after the flitting orange and purple beauty.

The Lor clasped her hand and turned to gaze upon the tempelle.

Christine gazed upon it as well. "How was he dropped, yon fallar?"

"Battlescores," he said, squeezing her hand. "His head near taken off."

"I thought Lors could nayat take turn in battlescores."

"Nayat any longer."

"And yon malla?"

He sighed deeply, a dark sound drawn from a dark place, one which compelled her to redirect her inquiry. "Why is she nayat in one tempelle with yon fallar?"

He shook his head. "Litas are nayat placed in tempelles."

"Why nayat?"

He looked to her with an amused grin. "Tempelles are for those of highest standing, ganist of honoring. I will rest in this one beside mine fallar," he said, moving his eyes back to the home of his future final resting place. "As will Kynneth."

"So, litas do nayat hold enough honoring, then, to be placed in tempelles?"

When he looked upon her again, it was with different eyes entirely. They ran the length of her, taking in her new riding gilt, one made special with ample skirting so as not to hinder her legs while straddling a pony. "Why must yon question every last thing, Christa?" He clasped her face between large palms to place a kiss upon her forehead. "It has been such from the beginning of segs," he said, placing a kiss upon one cheek, then the other. "I will place yon in mine tempelle, so to rest by mine side till the end of all sols. Does this please yon, then?"

She was given no time to answer, for his mouth was on hers, nibbling tenderly

Bixten cleared his throat, startling them both. "It did join one other and fly away," he announced with a sigh. "Of all Sola's creatures, I can nayat think of one more eyegrandly than flutterflies."

The Leader of Lors smiled down on the woman beside him. "I can think of one other."

Bixten grasped his meaning, then her hand. "But Christa *is* one flutterfly, Mine Lor," he insisted, beaming ear to ear. "Does yon nayat note her wings, the most eyegrandly wings of any flutterfly on Atriia? They do hold every coloring under Sola's smile."

"Aya, eyegrandly," he admitted, his grin dashing. "Most eyegrandly, indeed."

CHAPTER 5

She sighed as he traced her lips with the soft-petaled shalia. He traced it down her neck, then over to one breast, teasing terribly, before sliding it down to tickle her belly.

Bringing a hand to her eyes, she rubbed sleepily. "Does yon ever sleep?" she grumbled.

"How can I with the most eyegrandly flutterfly in all of Atriia in mine bunker?"

"Mmmm, mine wings are wearied," she mumbled. "I must sleep."

"Aya," he breathed as he crawled atop of her, running his fingers into her hair. "Sleep, mine flutterfly," he insisted, kissing one eyelid, then the other. "Do nayat let me waken yon."

"Mmmm." Running her hands up his back, she caressed his shoulders as he nuzzled her neck. "Yon was kind to Bixten."

"Mmhmm," he breathed, tickling her neck.

"He enjoys our outings."

He slid his lips to hers, caressing gently.

"I dropped his fallar," she whispered, the words slipping out without warning.

"Shhh." Reaching down, he slipped a hand behind her knee, drawing it up. "Do nayat fret, mine flutterfly. He is safe, now."

Gripping his shoulders, she dug in her fingers as he pushed inside.

~~~~~~~~~~

Every muscle in her body contracted at once, her hands gripping
~~~~~~~~~~

tightly to the fingers interlaced with hers, her thighs gripping tightly to the hips of the man pressed between them, her back arching, her neck arching further. Her body convulsed, forcing out a shuddering cry, and then again, rattling her addled brain.

Slowly, as her muscles relaxed, she settled back onto the mattress, as he did upon her. Running his fingers into her hair, he nibbled her lips.

"Jerrod," she spoke between ragged breaths. "You're killing me."

He pulled back to frown down at her, his thumbs gently caressing her temples. "Killing?"

She smiled weakly. "Dropping."

He nodded. "And God?"

She sighed, running the tip of her tongue out to wet her lips. "Sola."

"Fucking bastard?"

"What—I did nayat speak such!"

He grinned. "Naya, but I have heard yon speak such."

"Oh. Well…blasted blogart is close, I suppose."

He scoured her face as his thumbs caressed. "What lies beyond fraig lairs?"

Running her hands behind his neck, she fingered hair curled by dampness. "Yon has been speaking with Kynneth."

"Mine brathern thinks yon skewed."

"Kynneth—thinks *I'm* skewed? If that isn't the pot calling the kettle black."

He frowned, shaking his head slowly. "Speak Atriian, lita," he commanded, before swooping in to her lips.

CHAPTER 6

"Hold tight!"

Clinging to Christine's neck, Becca giggled as she rode the malla pony.

With fingers laced beneath the child's bottom to create a safe saddle, Christine galloped about the room. Halting at the window, she surveyed the real ponies beneath. The ganist atop were practicing their swordsmanship, the clanging of metal blades echoing throughout the courtyard. She searched for the pale pony belonging to Jerrod, but there were many pale ponies on this sol, and all wearing battle armor, as were their riders.

"Good morn," Dahla hailed as she sashayed in the open door.

"Greetings, Dahla." Christine galloped to the center of the room, then around and around a smiling Dahla. "Here we go," she sang, trotting out the door and down the hall with Dahla on her heels. "Greetings Tressa, greetings Ellira," she hailed as she passed the scullery litas pushing the firstsup cart.

"Greetings, Mine Lita," they chorused, both grinning broadly.

Becca squealed as Christine took the steps down, bouncing her like a rag doll.

"Where is one pony taking yon, Becca," Dahla laughed.

"We are taking the long way round this grand sol." Christine was reveling in her newfound freedom, traveling the halls without guards trailing behind. "Greetings, kind ganist," she hailed as she trotted past the guards at the courtyard doors. "Greetings Alaina," she said to the seamsewer pushing a cart overflowing with sheets and blankets. "Is yon having flustings?"

"Auggh, one blasted wheel is sticking."

"Mayhap it needs oiling. Dahla, here, take Becca to firstsup," Christine said, transferring the babe to the back of a new pony, one with longer legs and a silky blond mane. "I will be there shortly."

"Hold on, sweet babe," Dahla warned as she skipped back up the steps.

"Here," Christine spoke to Alaina, "you lift up on that end, and I will roll on mine."

~~~~~~~~~~

Vinova's jaw dropped at the sight of Christine. "What—oh—Mine Lita," she said with a bow of her head.

Christine motioned to the towel thrown over her shoulder. "Use kindness to lead, nayat cruelness, Vinova. I think yon will find yon litas far more receiving."

"Aya, Mine Lita," Vinova replied, nodding adamantly. "I do only use such to dry mine hands."

"Good. That is well, for if I hear differed, I will be forced to speak with Mas Oscarn."

"Naya, Mine Lita. Yon will nayat hear differed."

Christine nodded. "I do think I will speak with Oscarn on any account," she said, witnessing Vinova's face grow pale. She motioned to the litas at the wash bins. "Yon litas need handslips, those that resist water. And the lighting is hardly better than one keeper in here. And there should be one fire burning every sol of the seg," she said, motioning to the hearth at the end of the room. "To pull out dampness. And the walls need painting, a pleasant scene—trees and warm skies with Sola smiling down. And I do nayat think yon litas need sup on coarse every single sol. They labor hard and are deserving of better. From this sol forward, they will sup as grand as any pleasurer—goser, shike flays, fresh bread with jam, seedberries, sweetcakes."

Vinova's face was no longer pale. It was pink with flush, her mouth hanging open. The seamsewers at the wash tubs had stopped in their duties to stare, their own jaws gone suddenly slack.
~~~~~~~~~~

~~~~~~~~~~

Christine was grinning as she exited the room to the sound of profuse thankings. She could hear them still, echoing down the hall, even as she turned the corner and headed for the stairs.

Her grin slowly faded as she stopped in her tracks, one foot poised on the first step. Drawing in a deep breath, she closed her eyes, trying to ignore it—the voice whispering in her ear.

Slowly, her head swiveled, forcing her eyes to the hallway leading to the keeper. Suddenly her mouth was cotton dry, all the moisture having exited her pores to dampen crawling skin.

Her heartbeat quickened as she removed her foot from the stair and turned to face her fear.

The first step was the hardest. The rest fell into place of their own accord, one foot obediently following the other. The sound of rolling stones issued from the guards' room, then a gravelly voice swearing.

Her pace slowed as she passed their station. She was praying they would spot her, but overly occupied with tookets as they were, they never spied the loper who slipped past in plain sight. Slowly, the sound of tookets faded as she traveled deeper, the hall seeming to grow darker and danker with every hesitant step.

On legs grown weak, she stopped at the entrance to the keeper, peering down the cramped corridor lined with doors. She near screamed when she heard a scratching noise and saw a dark shape dart across the hall, then another. As her muscles tensed for flight, another sound caught her attention—moaning, low and constant. Behind her, the angry cursing of a guard echoed down the hall—lamenting over a tookets toss gone wrong while his opponent gave a howl of victory.

Fighting the urge to flee, she stepped across the threshold, and the dank air instantly became colder, producing a thin vapor with every labored breath. She hugged herself, rubbing at the painful bumps on her arms. The smell was unpleasant, twisting her stomach. The feeling was more unpleasant yet, as if a thousand eyes were
~~~~~~~~~~

upon her, watching her every move.

She knew where she was headed—fifth door on the left—her private prison for twenty sols and twenty luns. It had a new occupant this sol, one who moaned a lot. There was a faint light filtering through the food slot, flickering across the floor. The voice in her head was telling her she had faced enough of her fears for one sol. But her feet were listening to a different voice entirely.

Releasing a ragged breath, she stopped shy of the door to listen. The moaning was muffled but constant—a woman, and she did not seem to be moaning in distress.

Instantly, Christine was the Loper of Zeria yet again. Dropping to all fours, she went to her stomach, putting an eye to the slot.

The moaner was sitting on the cot. The candlelight showed her hair was a deep auburn, falling down to her waist, though her face could not be seen past the man who stood before her, his hands on her head holding her in place as he moved his hips in slow measured strokes.

"Ah, good litia," he purred in a low whisper. "That's mine good litia. Hold!" He stepped back suddenly, bringing the moaning to an abrupt halt—and bringing the litia into view.

She was bare-footed and dressed in a tattered gilt, but her hair was well kempt. It was gleaming in the lamplight. It wasn't her own. Even in the dim lighting, Christine recognized her own locks. She also recognized who wore them, the pleasurer Ryla. She did not have to see the man's face to know who he was.

"Does yon wish more, sweet Christa?" he asked.

Ryla nodded adamantly, her tongue darting out to wet her lips. "Aya, Mine Lor."

"How badly, then?"

"Badly, Mine Lor. Pleadings," she begged, reaching for his hips.

He obliged her, stepping between her parted legs and leaning into her parted lips.

She clutched at his hips, and the moaning resumed.

~~~~~~~~~~

The keeper guards never saw her as she barreled past. She was fighting back nausea as she took the steps two at a time. The doors leading to the courtyard were just opening as she was hurtling by.

She stopped at the commanding calling of her name, then slowly turned to face him. Lowering her eyes, she bowed her head. "Mine Lor." Fresh in from battle practice, he was dressed in armor, his helmet resting in the crook of his elbow. Reesal was by his side, holding his helmet as well, as were two other ganist.

"We will meet later," the Lor told his men, then took her arm, leading her back from whence she'd come. Stopping at the summit of the stairs, he motioned down. "Why was yon below?"

"I—was aiding Alaina, one seamsewer. Her cart did—one wheel did come loose."

He put a finger to her chin, lifting her face, his hazel eyes searching. "Why does yon fret?"

She wiped a tear from the corner of her eye. "I do nayat like that boarding. It is overly dark, overly damp. I feel badly for those litas."

She told him of the many changes she envisioned, and he grinned and nodded. "It is done. Now, do nayat fret," he said, brushing his fingertips along her cheek and into her hair. His eyes dropped to her lips, as did hers to his. Pushing to tip toes, she closed her eyes, savoring the sweetness of his gentle kiss.

"Well, now. Is this nayat sweet, then."

She pulled away, the kiss instantly soured by Kynneth's voice as he bounded up the steps. "Mine Lita," he greeted, grinning down at her with a glint in his eyes.

The Lor put a fist on one hip, his eyes narrowing. "What was yon doing below, Kynneth?"

"Speaking with keeper guards, brathern."

"Speakings, or tookets?"

"Mayhap both," Kynneth confessed with a grin.

"Yon will be at battle practice at midsol," he ordered gruffly.

"Aya, Mine Lor," Kynneth countered with an exaggerated bow.
~~~~~~~~~~

"As yon does wish."

"Aya, I do wish," he spoke to Kynneth's back as he sauntered away.

His demeanor softened as he turned back to her. "Has yon had firstsup?"

"Naya."

"I will meet yon at the lita's quarters in one turning. There is somebody I do wish for yon to meet."

~~~~~~~~~~

He was practically running down the entrance steps of the cas. Gripping tightly to his hand, Christine squinted against Sola's bright smile as she ran to keep up. "Are we late again?" she laughed, wondering if he could hear the juice sloshing in her belly.

Skipping down the last few steps, he picked her up and twirled her around. "Aya," he said, placing a peck upon her nose. "Let us meet quickly with this ganis. There is one other meeting we must attend—in mine boarding," he added with a sparkling wink.

The ganis approached with a courteous bow. "Mine Lor."

"This is Mas Dryor, Christa, gardencarer at one solasium," he introduced, and the ganis bowed in greeting. He was every inch as tall as his Lor, his shoulders just as wide. His hair was silver and pulled back in a tie. His teeth were very white, his skin deeply tanned—and deeply creased.

"Yon may call me Ervine," he said with a pleasant smile.

The Lor motioned to the vast grounds spread out before his cas, the length and width of two football fields, maybe three. "I do wish the most grand shalia garden in all of Atriia, one befitting the most eyegrandly flutterfly under Sola's smile."

Sola's smile was reflecting dazzlingly in his eyes as he looked to his flutterfly. "Tell Mas Dryor what yon does wish and where yon does wish it, and it is done," he promised. "I have alreadied ordered ten by two garbona trees," he said with a dazzling grin, "so that yon might walk with Sola every sol."
~~~~~~~~~~

CHAPTER 7

Her head felt light as she moved on top of him. Her palms pressed flat against his chest were all that were keeping her from listing over. He was watching beneath his lashes, his hands on her hips helping to guide her movements, his breaths deep and steady—unlike her own labored huffs. She faltered yet again, halting to rub at her forehead, wincing as a wave of vertigo swept through. Dropping her chin to her chest, she struggled to clear her senses.

He chuckled beneath her, his fingertips caressing her thighs. "Do nayat battle it, Christa," he purred, as one hand diverted to slip between her legs. And though his fingers did barely brush their mark, it was enough to send her collapsing upon him with a shuddering cry. Clutching him about the neck, she held tight, gritting her teeth as she spit and sputtered.

She cried out yet again as he rolled to lie heavy atop. "Allow me to lend aid," he said, nestling his mouth into her neck as he began a silky rhythm, one much smoother and controlled then her own had been.

Closing her eyes, she trailed her fingertips along his back, then up to his nape. "Mmm, Hannen," she sighed into his ear.

She realized her blunder instantly, even before he could push away to stare down with wounded eyes.

"Jerrod," she whispered, trying to counter the mistake much too late.

The pain faded just as quickly as it appeared, and a small smile formed. He let out a long, even breath as his fingers slid a curl from her dampened forehead. "He dropped her down," he confessed as he trailed the back of his fingers down her cheek. Slipping his hand behind her neck, he gently caressed. "Mine fallar. Dropped his brooder down for she did speak the callen of one other in his bunker."

A chill caressed her as amorously as the fingertips at her neck. He was speaking of his father taking the life of his mother—and in a voice entirely too calm.

He traced a thumb along her lips. "Spellering can skew one's brain."

"Jerrod, I—"

"Call me Hannen."

She bit her lip, trying desperately to fight back tears.

"I can be yon fraigen dropper if yon does wish." He restarted his rhythm—slow, silky strokes. "Is that yon wishing, Christa? Does yon wish it was yon brathern inside of yon?"

A whoof of air escaped her, his words striking her as solidly as a fist to the gut. Then she was screaming, kicking, striking with balled fists.

Pinning her hands above her head, he waited patiently for her struggles to cease. "Bastard," she wept, fisting the hands restrained by her ears.

"Fallier *is* yon brathern, then?" He watched her reaction with his talcar eyes, reading truths despite the slow shaking of her head. "Yon spoke such—in toskin fevering."

When she dropped her eyes, he released her hands to cradle her face.

"Do nayat harm him," she begged in a whisper thick with shame.

His lips dropped to hers, nibbling tenderly. "Naya," he breathed, "I will nayat."

Suddenly, she needed the mouth designed to devour to do that very thing. Clutching at his neck, she pulled him down, desperate to kiss the man who was not her brother. It seemed he was just as desperate as he began a forceful rhythm, each thrust forcing out a muted moan. Sliding his mouth to her neck, in burrowed in. "Speak mine callen, Christa," he demanded, his hot breath sending a shiver through her.

What little air she could pull into her lungs was exiting as undignified huffs. “Jerrod!” she forced out, sliding her hands down to grip his hips, needing desperately to pull him deep, the man who was not her brathern. She couldn’t stop the tears any more than she could stop the drawing in of labored breaths. They built till she was weeping openly, her body quaking, her chest hitching. Still, her fingers clutched.

He wrapped her tight as any woodslink, and the bed rocked beneath them. It was sturdy, with four wooden posts thick as tree trunks. Despite the Lor’s formidable attempts, it would not be collapsing into a broken heap. She was not so confident the same was true of herself.

CHAPTER 8

Curled on her side, Christine listened to the ganist in the courtyard below—the lusty cries of battle, the pounding of pony hooves, the clanging of swords. The Lor of Zeria would be amongst them. The night's rigorous affairs would not have tired him in the least. She, on the other hand, was beyond wearied, her body ravaged to what seemed like disrepair. She had been too wearied to pull herself from bed for firstsup—had trudged up to midsup with barely enough energy to spoon coarse to her mouth. As she lay on the bed peering at the child napping soundly beside her, the little food she'd managed to force down sat like a lead weight in her belly.

She felt a tear slip out as she gazed upon her lia, the pudgy cheeks, the pouty lips. As much as she hated it, she saw Sam in her.

Reaching out a weary limb, she ran fingers through the short, downy curls. "Aya, Sam. She is yours. She is. But mine heart is nayat. It is mine to give. It is mine. It is mine!" Burying her face in the pillow, she began to sob.

~~~~~~~~~~

The keeper hall was icy cold where she stood frozen in place. Shivering in darkness, she tried desperately to control erratic breaths as she stared at the floor, terrified by the candlelight flickering across it. There was moaning coming from beneath the door—a woman. She wanted nothing more than to turn and flee, but she was the brazened loper, and there was something she needed to see.

Dropping to the floor, she put an eye to the slot.
~~~~~~~~~~

The moaner sat on the rickety cot. The candlelight showed that her hair was a deep auburn, the luxurious curls cascading to her waist, though her face was not visible past the man who stood unclothed before her, his hands on her head holding her in place as his hips moved in and out with slow, measured strokes.

"Aya, good litia," he purred in a low whisper. "That's mine good litia. Wait, hold!" He stepped back, bringing the moaning to an abrupt halt, and bringing the woman into view.

She was bare-footed and her gilt was tattered and stained, and her eyes were closed as if sleeping while sitting. Even in the low light, Christine knew her own face. She didn't have to see the face of the ganis to know it was Kynneth.

"Does yon wish more, mine sweet Christa?"

The Christa on the cot lifted a small, pale hand to the back of her head. She winced as she nodded.

"That's mine good litia." Pushing her down on the cot, Kynneth lifted the gilt to her waist, then laid himself between her legs, pushing them wide. "How badly does yon wish it?"

With a groan, her head lolled toward the door. Her eyes were closed, her body limp, though she did stir briefly, swatting at him as he lapped her cheek like a hound. "Get, Necma," she mumbled groggily, then awoke with a gasp as he thrust, her fists beating at his back, her legs kicking.

"Shhh, be one good litia and I will leave yon pony."

Her body went mercifully limp in reply, though his was far from such, his muscles tightly bunched as he rocked the cot dangerously beneath them, the springs protesting in loud, creaking groans.

"Is such deep enough for yon, then," he huffed, his Pebbles ponytail bobbing. "Yon should have ripped it clear when yon had one chancing, Mine honored Lita."

In the blink of an eye, an eye with an arched eyebrow was on the opposite side of the slot, leering. "As if made of it…"

"Naya!"

She shot up in bed, clutching at her head and gasping for breath.

Dahla sat in the chair with Becca on her knee, both peering at her with wide eyes. "Lundevons, Mine Lita?"

Christine threw her hands over her face as she nodded. "How long has yon been sitting there?"

"Nayat long. A few mounds only. I did nayat think I should waken yon, so I did take Becca to play at the brooder's quarters. Buleea did finhap find her legs. She and Becca did run for turnings."

"What turning is it?" Christine asked, kneading at a forehead that throbbed.

"Lastsup turning."

"Lastsup! I did sleep four turnings?"

Dahla nodded. "Becca has been changed and readied."

Christine put a hand to her stomach. "I do nayat think I can sup."

"I will yon take her, then. Does yon wish lastsup sent down?"

"Naya."

Dahla frowned. "Our Lor has been overly eager with his—attentions. Mayhap he will let yon sleep this lun."

With a groan, Christine fell back to the bed, throwing an arm across her face. "I am thinking he might."

Dahla tousled Becca's short curls then kissed her head. "Yon bath has been readied. Mayhap such will make yon feel better."

~~~~~~~~~~

The water was much hotter than usual, the steam rising from the surface humidifying the room like a sauna. Resting against the side of the bath, Christine rested her chin upon folded arms to study the statue—the man pressed between the legs of the woman, his palms pressed flat against the floor on either side of her shoulders. She studied the strong line of his jaw, the chiseled features, the tight muscles along his arms and back. It could easily have been the Lor of Zeria, perfectly proportioned, perfectly handsome, perfect in every way.

She laid her cheek upon her arms, only to find just such a perfect
~~~~~~~~~~

man standing at the head of the bathing pool. "Mine Lor!"

He raked fingers through his hair, combing it back from his eyes. He was fresh in from battle practice, his clothes grimy, his hair slick with sweat. "Why is yon nayat at lastsup?" he asked, his bassy voice echoing about the room.

"I was nayat feeling well. But the bath has helped. I will join them now."

"Naya." His eyes fell to the statue at his end, the woman straddling the man lying on his back. Loosening the lacing at his chest, he slipped the shirt over his head and tossed it to the woman's back.

"I'll leave yon to yon bathing, Mine Lor."

"Naya," he said, undoing his belt. "We need to speak."

She dropped her eyes discreetly as he slid off his pants.

"I must hand apologies," he said as he descended the steps, the words bouncing off the water to echo about the room.

She shook her head with a sigh, cursing the tears that formed so easily. "It is I should hand such."

"Naya. It was nayat yon aiming to harm me. But it *was* mine."

She looked up to where he stood at the bottom of the steps, the water to his waist. "Yon does know now why I do nayat wish him harmed."

He trailed his fingers along the surface of the water to the pool's edge where he plucked a bar of soap from its dish. "Yon callens are differed. Yon does have differed fallars," he stated as he worked up a lather between large hands.

"Differed fallars and mallas."

He stopped his lathering to peer at her curiously. "How is he yon brathern, then?"

"We were raised as brathern and sasturn. I did always believe us to be such."

"Yon claimed he did nayat force hisself on yon."

"He did nayat. He—tricked me."

Depositing the soap back to its dish, he began to lather his hair, massaging at his scalp and briefly scrubbing at his face. Dunking under, he rinsed quickly before resurfacing to brush the water from his eyes. Retrieving the soap, he continued with his bath, running lathered hands along broad shoulders and down long arms. “He is nayat yon brathern by blood, and yon should nayat be shammered,” he said as he began to lather his chest.

She dropped her eyes, peering into the steaming water as she listened to him bathe. A tear fell, making a miniature splash, then another.

Depositing the bar of soap to its dish one last time, he dunked down to his chin, then began to tread water, headed toward her.

“Mine Lor,” she breathed in a voice that trembled.

He quickly closed length, trapping her against the side of the pool with hands on either side. “Now yon *does* aim to harm me, Christa.” Cupping her chin, he lifted her face. “Yon is to use mine first callen. And I do nayat wish to hear fearing on yon tongue when yon does speak it. And—I do nayat wish to note shammering in yon eyes. Fallier is yon past. I am yon present—and yon future.” He pulled her close, hugging her tight.

She held him just as tightly.

Wrapping her arms about his neck and her legs about his waist, she slid her mouth to his, the tender kiss turning instantly torrid.

CHAPTER 9

"Yon is pallored," Eubreena spoke as she brushed out her hair.

"Am I?"

"Yon did barely touch firstsup. I did think yon would eat as one pony after missing lastsup last lun."

"I am too wearied to sup."

Eubreena nodded her understanding. "Dahla speaks Becca did bunker with her the entire lun."

Christine ran a hand over her face with a sigh. "Eubreena, the ganis does nayat sleep."

"Mayhap yon should go back to yon boarding now. Sleep while he does practice battle skills. That way yon will be rested. Dahla can take Becca to one brooder's quarters to play."

Burying her face in her hands, Christine shook her head.

"Christa," Eubreena crooned, rubbing her back. "This is the last sol, and the sol holding the most portance." Leaning in, Eubreena hugged her from behind, wrapping her arms around her shoulders and smiling at her in the mirror. "Picture his sweet face. Picture him in yon arms, at yon breast—yon gan."

"Eubreena," Christine chided, shaking her head, "there will be naya gan. Yon does know this."

Eubreena grinned widely. "I have been praying to Sola, sol and lun, and Sola holds all power. Here," she said, pulling open a drawer, "this should raise yon spirits." She pulled a fireplace bellows from the drawer—carved wooden handles protruding from brown accordion leather. "Note," she said, turning it over to reveal a hole burned through the leather. "I did heat metal pegs and slip them in."

Christine brought the back of her hand to her lips to suppress the grin.

"I am hiding such from Mas Oscarn," Eubreena confessed. "Same will throw me in one keeper if he does find out."

"Of all Atriia," Christine laughed. "Give it to me, then. I will claim I laid it too close to one fire."

"And what of this one?" Eubreena asked, pulling another from the drawer. "And this?" she said, producing a third.

"Eubreena!"

"Sola did send me one sign," Eubreena said, tossing the damaged bellows back into the drawer so she could grasp Christine's hands. "I have noted him in mine dreamings—yon gan. Blazened-locked, Christa, like yon self, and the knowing eyes of our Lor."

"Eubreena," Christine sighed, closing her eyes as she dropped her chin to her chest. "I think I *will* take that nap."

~~~~~~~~~~

She awoke with a start. Voices had pulled her from a restless sleep. Slipping from the bed, she padded across the floor to put an ear to the door. Male voices could be heard from across the hall, then laughter.

"Six and ten turning, then," Reesal spoke.

"Aya," Lor Zeria replied. "Tell Hallis to roll out targets. We do all need arcing practice."

"Aya, Mine Lor."

Dropping down to her belly, Christine put her eye to the door crack, watching as the Lor disappeared into his room. A minute later, he reappeared bare-footed, headed toward the bathing room.

Sitting up, she rested her head back against the door and closed her eyes. She was wearied, a weariness that went deep.

She gave a yelp as a knocking sounded on the door. "Who's there!"
~~~~~~~~~~

"Midsup," Sheele spoke, his voice muffled through the door. "Sent down by scullery."

Rising wearily, she opened the door, nodding to Sheele as he handed in the covered tray.

"One carry-load of plantings has arrived on one front yard," he announced before shuffling away.

~~~~~~~~~~

"Mine Lor, the plantings have arrived!"

He smiled charmingly as he descended the entrance steps appearing tall and handsome and freshly bathed, his damp hair slicked back, his hazel eyes reflecting Sola's smile brilliantly.

"So I do note. Yon does work quickly, Mas Dryor."

Brushing his hands on his pants, the garden-master bowed to the Lor. "We did dig plantings all morn, Mine Lor. It will take a bit longer to dig the trees, but added shrubs and trailers will be arriving from Panize and Kinsear in the next few sols. Mas Sekars will also be arriving in a few sols."

Lor Zeria nodded. "One stone carver."

"Aya. The finest to be found."

"Well done. I was wisened to hire yon. Now if yon does nayat mind, I must stelcher one lita," he said, extending a hand to Christine.

"Naya, I need stay," she insisted. "I need show where each must go," she said, motioning to the many plants surrounding her feet.

"Yon can show him on the morrow."

"It can nayat wait till the morrow," she insisted. "The roots will dry. I do nayat wish all these fine plantings to drop, Mine Lor."

He frowned as he eyed the plants being unloaded. "One turning, then. The plants will nayat drop in one turning, surent."

Mas Dryor shook his head. "Naya, Mine Lor. They will be fine."

Stepping close, the Lor took her hands, bringing them to his lips. "Come, mine flutterfly," he beckoned, his eyes sparkling wickedly. "The grains are sifting through."
~~~~~~~~~~

“Naya,” she said, shaking her head adamantly. “That will nayat leave enough turnings to put them in the ground before Sola sleeps.” Leaning close, she ran her hands behind his neck, pulling him down to place a peck upon his cheek. “We will speak later this lun, Jerrod,” she whispered in his ear. “And at length,” she promised.

He did not look pleased as he pulled away. “I will send ten added ganist to help put them in the ground,” he insisted. “Ten by ten, if needed.”

“Jerrod,” she said, propping hands on hips to firmly stand her ground. “We will speak after lastsup. Now, then, Ervine,” she said, spinning on her heel. “Let us start with the copes.”

CHAPTER 10

Finished drying Becca's hair, Christine tossed the towel aside, then snatched up the tiny nightgown, slipping it over the babe's head. "Do I look pallored, Dahla?" she asked as she guided the child's arms through one at a time.

Dahla stopped toweling her own hair to glance over. "Naya, Mine Lita."

"Dahla, note closer. Surely I do look pallored?"

"Oh, aya, Mine Lita," Dahla agreed as prompted. "Yon does look overly pallored."

"Aya. I do nayat feel well, nayat at all."

"Yon does look quite ill. Dark circles do sit under yon eyes and yon cheeks seem flushed." Dahla put a hand to Christine's forehead. "I do think yon is fevering."

"Aya, I was bit here," Christine said, pointing to a red mark on her hand. "One green leafpitter. Mas Dryor speaks they hold poisonings."

"Aya," Dahla concurred. "Some leafpitters do."

Christine examined the mark further. "I do think I note swelling. Does yon note it?"

"Aya, I do."

"I think Becca and I will bunker early this lun. On yon way out, pleadings inform mine guards that I am ill. They should allow naya visitors. *Naya* visitors," she stressed. "Make it clear, Dahla."

~~~~~~~~~~

Lying in bed with the covers to her chin, Christine listened with
~~~~~~~~~~

acutely tuned ears. She thought she detected the drone of male voices on the other side of the door—then it was gone—trickery by ears overly tuned and nerves overly jumpy. Becca had gone out quickly, victim to a day spent at the brooder's quarters with Trayson, the torrential two-year-old, and one-year-old Buleea.

Christine trailed her fingers down the alabaster arm, them over to the bruise on her cheekbone. According to Dahla, Becca had fought valiantly when Trayson tried to stelcher her doll, this in spite of being half his size. She was tiny, but no dainty shalia. She was headstrong and stubborn to a fault. Like Sam.

Closing her eyes, she tried to force his name from her thoughts, a name that put an ache in her heart and a twist in her belly. She owed him nothing. Nothing!

~~~~~~~~~~

Becca seemed unfazed by her fallar's horrid scars. She was giggling where she sat upon his lap, her face flushed, her breaths shallow. Tentatively, the babe reached to his mouth, then squealed as he snapped at her fingers, striking quick and efficiently, ravaging the chubby fingers that had dared venture too close. Laughing and screaming at once, Becca yanked her hand away, fisting it in a tight ball to protect the vulnerable fingers. But she was no dainty shalia. Slowly, showing great courage, she made yet another daring attempt to touch the dangerous lips.

And they were dangerous—so very dangerous. "I can nayat stop mine heart from feeling as it does," they spoke where he knelt before her, clasping tightly to her hands. "I love you, Christa. More than life. Sola help me, I do!"

She squared her shoulders, trying not to show the turmoil raging within. "I love Jerrod," she stated pointedly.

She witnessed the shadow darken his features, and then he was probing, drilling with eyes intent on unearthing untruths in the words she'd spoken.

There came a prickling of panic. "I can't give you what you want! I can't. You're my..."
~~~~~~~~~~

Her voice faltered on the word, for even as she thought it, she knew it wasn't entirely true. The eyes peering at her did not belong to Sam. They were devouring her in a way Sam's never would. How many times had she lost herself within those very eyes?

"Aya, look closely, Christa," he rasped throatily. "Who do you see?"

She felt her resolve waiver. Suddenly her breaths were coming in quick succession. It was Fallier the fraigen dropper who knelt before her, his dark hair falling to below bare shoulders, a fierce fraigen inked permanently upon his chest. He was badly scarred, yes. He was magnificent, dark and wild and beautiful. The eyes, black and smoldering, belonged to one fraigen dropper. They riveted her in place with their shameless intensity.

He was leaning into her, and she to him, aware of the danger but unable to save herself. "Sweet Sola, help me," she breathed, her breaths mingling with his as their lips melded…

She was having difficulty drawing in breath when he pulled away to grin down upon her. Blinking away the grogginess, she tried to focus on the face so near. It was not immeasurably scarred with eyes dark and brooding. It was immaculately handsome with eyes light and laughing.

"Jerrod."

He placed a hand on her forehead, sliding it to her cheek, feeling for fever. "Should I summon one meshganis?" he asked with a grin.

"Naya," she sighed, clutching at his neck, pulling him down, desperate to devour the lips of the man who was not her brother.

~~~~~~~~~~

"Wha—" Coming suddenly awake, the Lor grabbed at Christine's arm as she tried to sneak from the bed. Dodging him landed her on the floor with a thud and sent her blanket to flying across the room.

Such an unceremonious collapse summoned forth a bassy chuckle from the Lor scrambling after her. "Does serve yon right for
~~~~~~~~~~

thinking to escape me."

"Yon was sleeping," she defended as she scrambled toward the door, locomoting on hands and knees. She struggled to her feet to pry on the handle.

"Naya," he growled, grabbing her about the waist and forcing her away. "Yon does wear nayat one stitch," he laughed as he dragged her away. "The guardsganist will have unpured thoughts." With a grunt, he tossed her back to the bed. "Stay," he ordered, pointing a finger of warning with one hand while the other combed the hair back from his face.

"I'm not your hound," she huffed—then rolled nimbly off the opposite side of the bed, making a second mad dash for the door.

He quickly blocked her escape route, stooping before the door with arms spread wide. His grin was just as wide. "Nayat mine hound," he conceded. "Yon is mine flutterfly, one that does try to flutter away." Plucking up the blanket from the floor, he spread it wide. "Mayhap I should catch it in mine netting."

"Jerrod! I do only mean to check on Becca."

He was chuckling as he moved closer, his blanket readied. "Becca is with Dahla. Now back to mine bunker, mine flutterfly."

He backed her toward the bed as he advanced, taunting her with the blanket while grinning ear to ear. Anticipating the throw perfectly, she dodged the blanket and dove across the bed, doing a lithe roll and landing on her feet at a run. She made it to the door, and even out a step, before she was apprehended yet again.

She was giggling madly as he dragged her back to the bed, the vision of the guards' startled expressions beyond priceless. Her giggling only intensified as she latched onto a bedpost, holding tight, forcing him to pry her away with an exaggerated grunt.

He was chuckling as he forced her to the bed, face down. Lying atop, he put all his weight against her back, pinning her hopelessly. "Bad flutterfly," he whispered into her ear. "Yon does force me to clip yon wings. Hold very still," he warned. "If yon does nayat struggle, it will nayat pain yon much."

With a growl, she tried to squirm from beneath him, but he merely wrapped her tighter, squeezing as any woodslink till her efforts were exhausted.

“Alright! I give,” she huffed.

“Yon will nayat escape me,” he vowed as he slid her to the edge of the bed, his palm spread across the bridge of her back thwarting any further attempts at flight. With one foot, he forced her two apart so that he might stand between. “Now,” he whispered, leaning close to her ear, “hold still.”

CHAPTER 11

"Hold still, Christa."

"Ow!" She gripped tightly to the chair arms as Eubreena tweezed the last few brows.

"Done, then," Eubreena said, tossing the tweezers to the table. "Now quit yon whining."

Christine leaned closer to the mirror to inspect Eubreena's handiwork. "What one lita must go through to be eyegrandly," she huffed. "Mas Oscarn does walk about with brows thick as bushes."

"Aiyee, but I would give mine right eye to take snippers to such," Eubreena admitted, and they both laughed. "Here." Picking up a jar, Eubreena pried off the lid. "Sola did burn yon nose."

Christine tilted her face so Eubreena could apply the salve with a gentle finger. "I did work the garden the entire sol, watering."

Eubreena grinned as she spread the salve over to her cheeks. "Nayat the entire sol," she corrected, making Christine fidget uncomfortably. "He must be spellered," she added, tapping Christine on the nose before grabbing a cloth to wipe her fingers clean. She lifted Christine's hand to admire the newest gift, a gold bracelet sporting a menagerie of dangling jewels. "Aya, he is," she chuckled.

Christine fingered the bracelet. "Did yon know his fallar?"

Eubreena shook her head as she popped the lid back on the jar of salve and leaned back against the table. "I have heard tale of him. Tarriff Zeria." She looked to where several litas sat talking on the settees, before leaning closer. "He did drop his brooder," she whispered, shaking her head sadly, "for she was spellered by one other, one battler, one of his closest ganist. *His* throat was ripped first so she might witness such." She shook her head. "It is spoken she did curse the Zerian name fore her own could be ripped, did swear it would end with their two gans. But such is mere—" She stood suddenly. "Mas Oscarn!"

He was huffing as he approached. "Ryla and Sheilla have been called down to Kynneth," he informed her, "and Tiatra and Kylara to one guard's quarters. And Mas Sheele does wish to speak with yon, Mine Lita," he said, turning to Christine with a humble bow of his head.

"Mas Oscarn, I was just having mine brows trimmed," Christine said with a grin. "Do they nayat look nicely shaped?"

Placing a pudgy finger to his chin, he tilted his head back and squinted, his bushy brows knitting as he pondered hers. "Aya, Mine Lita," he said with a nod.

"I do think yon own could do with one trimming. What says yon, Eubreena? Does yon have spare mounds to trim such?"

Eubreena yanked open a drawer to frantically fish out the snippers. "Aya," she said, a splash of flush surfacing suddenly upon her cheeks.

Oscarn eyed the snippers warily. "Well, uh, four pleasurers do need preparing, and this ganis was just about to sit down to one mug of spirits and one round of tookets."

"It will take but one mound," Christine said, standing to smooth out her gilt. "What does Sheele wish to speak with me on?"

"Mas Tulls did just arrive."

"Ah, one wall painter. I did nayat expect him till the morrow. Has he been shown to his boarding?"

"Aya. He is wearied from his travelings. If yon does wish, I will inform him yon will speak with him on the morrow."

"Naya, I will speak with him now. Now sit," she said, patting the chair. "I do insist."

~~~~~~~~~~

She sat in the darkness, grinning at the wall. Tulls had outlined the scene in charcoal as she'd described her vision—a scene from the solasium garden—Sola shining down upon several garbona
~~~~~~~~~~

trees—cloud trees, as Bixten liked to call them. To the left, an iron gazebo with flowering trailers housed a statue yet to be decided—perhaps a lita carrying a basket of fruits, perhaps a cherub child wrapped in bolts of silky cloth. Cope bushes would surround the gazebo and other flowering bushes would be scattered about. There would be birds and flutterflies and furry crouts peeking from shalia beds. It would be a magical scene, one taking away some of the drudgery of the abysmal life of seamsewers, those spending half their days bent over washboards.

She eyed the five washbasins beneath the proposed scene, her eyes drawn especially to the one which had near taken her life. Pulling her gaze away, she slid it around the room, surveying the changes already made. Fresh firewood had been stacked on both sides of the hearth, generous stacks at that, and six wall torches had been added to the original four. The one that still flamed flickered oddly as it was caressed by a gentle breeze, and Christine stood at the sound of movement outside the doors, what sounded like an angry mob parading down the stairs. The sound of angry voices accompanied them, one belonging to Kynneth.

Moving quickly, she pushed the doors closed, listening as they passed—then cracked them again as the procession halted at the end of the hall. A ganis was pleading not to be thrown in one keeper, his voice bouncing off the stone walls and echoing down the hall.

"I do only carry his message!" he swore.

"We are nayat fond of his message," Kynneth growled, "or his blasted messager. Yon was paid overly for yon services, and yon will nayat be handed one added slice, is such clear!"

"Aya!"

"Did yon think yon would ride into our cassing, to the doors of our very cas, and demand added rounds!"

"But—she did near slice off his kagege!"

Christine threw a hand to her chest, pressing it against a palpitating heart. "Hagis." The whispered name caught in her throat.

"We have heard the tales," Kynneth scoffed. "Four blogarts dropping pants to ankles! Yon kageges deserve ripping!"

"As Sola shines, we did nayat know it was she!" he swore. "The loper is skilled!"

"Yon *did* know it was she when yon took one club to her head, blogart!"

"She held one blade!"

"I will slice off both yon kageges and toss them to fraigens while yon does watch! Yon can send him this message, messager!"

"Enough," the Lor of Zeria spoke calmly, and the hand pressed to Christine's chest quickly flew up to clamp over her mouth. His voice was just as cold when next he spoke, the words frigid as the wintered winds. "One dropped messager can nayat deliver messages."

"But—Mine Lor," Hagis pleaded, "we did keep our word! We do spread to all will listen that was high-hillers did stelcher one babe! We have nayat betrayed yon trusting, and we will nayat, as Sola shines!"

"Aya, yon will nayat."

She heard Hagis groan, a sound filled with desperate despair, heard him struggle for his life—shouting, scuffling. Then all fell horribly still.

~~~~~~~~~~

There was a creature inside of her, deep in the pit of her belly, desperate to get out. She clutched at it, doubling over, but it would not be contained. It escaped slowly in the form of a moan, deep and guttural, building to a tortured howl.

It was howling still as she fled, drowning out the ganis who called her name, a ganis who was quickly gaining on her. Stumbling down the hall and up the stairs, she flew into the first open door—the conference room where the council gathered—then hurried around the table, clutching tightly to one of the many high-backed chairs lining it.
~~~~~~~~~~

An icy chill caressed her as he appeared in the doorway, the monster of a man seeming to tower, his shoulders barely missing the jambs as he stepped through. He was decked in boots to above his knees, the blade tucked neatly back inside. The shirt tucked in his pants was crisp and white, save for the fresh stippling of crimson staining his chest. His mouth was set in a firm frown, his eyes black and hard as two onyx stones. "Christa," he spoke softly as he approached the table, "mine loping flutterfly."

Pulling in a deep breath, she pulled her shoulders back, facing him squarely across the table.

Resting his fingertips lightly upon the tabletop, he studied her. "Christa," he whispered, cocking his head, "one stelcherer was dangerous."

"Aya," she spoke, the word sounding fragile as she felt, "for he did know the truth. Now I do as well."

Placing his palms on the table, he leaned closer, his eyes condescending.

Christine fought the urge to shrink back from him. Digging her nails into the supple leather of the chair, she held herself in place. "Yon did aid Kynneth in stelchering mine babe. Yon did likely lead the whole plan. You tricked me, Mine Lor. *You* are the grandest loper in all of Atriia, not me."

"Christa—"

"Yon did lope as the good brathern, when truths be—there is naya such thing. Yon is both foul devons, fouler than the stelcherer whose blood yon does wear." She swiped angrily at the tears. "Yon malla was right to curse the callen Zeria. You and your brathern will be the last of your blood. Aya," she said, grinning, even as the tears were falling. "Mine cycle's bleeding is started, so yon grand plan was for nothing."

She jumped as he thumped the table with angry balled fists, the thud resounding throughout the empty room like a cannon shot. "Yon did note how easy we did stelcher her!" he sneered, his composure breaking at last. "It could just as easy been high-hillers!"

"Does yon think this will make me search harder for yon lia?" she whispered.

Pressing palms upon the table's surface, he leaned toward her, a hint of fear in his hardened eyes. "Christa—"

"I will search to the ends of Atriia. To the ends of Atriia."

"Christa—"

"Fuck you! Fuck you and your fucking brathern too!"

She anticipated his move, and as he leapt over the table, she dove under, locomoting on hands and knees beneath it. She was weeping as she fled from the room and up two flights of stairs—then screaming as she burst into the lita's quarters.

Eubreena barely had time to turn from where she stood painting Kylara's face before Christine barreled into her full-force, sending them both crashing into the table, and sending Kylara toppling to the floor with the chair atop.

Vials of scentings went flying, as did jars of creams and face paint. The jewelwear box overturned, scattering jewelwear everywhere, as did the water pitcher, shattering on the floor beside Kylara, sending her to scrambling and screaming.

Christine picked up the first thing to reach her palm and hurled it at him as he rushed into the room—a line drive, the perfume bottle narrowly missing his head as he dodged it deftly.

Eubreena stepped between them, her large frame creating just enough diversion to allow Christine to put the supping table between herself and her pursuer, a table not near as sturdy as that in the conference room. "Will yon force yonself on me again!" she screamed. "LaRosse was right about such! He was right! I will return to him. As Sola shines, I will!"

He upended the table as if it was made of cardboard, tossing it aside, sending vases of shalias flying and bowls of fruit to tumbling—and Christine to stumbling and tripping over an overturned chair. He grabbed her about the waist as she tried to scramble away, hefting her from the floor as she kicked and screamed.

She heard the impact of the water bowl hit his head, felt him stumble forward several steps, then heard Eubreena cry out.

The large woman was in a choke hold, a guard restraining her from behind while she clawed at his arm.

Christine was helpless to help her friend. She could do nothing but scream her name as the Lor of the cas carried her kicking from the room.

~~~~~~~~~~

He was watching her from across the table, one entirely too small, a tookets table made only for two. She chose to keep her eyes averted from his, keeping them instead on the meshganis who stood behind him, stitching his wound. She watched as the last thread was snipped, then the salve applied, dabbed sparingly on the gash at the back of his head.

"Well, I do think most of yon brain was saved," the meshganis joked, trying to bring some levity to a room heavy with tension.

"One must own such to be saved," she mumbled.

The meshganis cleared his throat as he packed his supplies back into his bag. "One cold rag will help with swelling, Mine Lor. And naya battle practice for three sols, least."

"Aya, thankings, Meshganis Uldin," he said as he stood to usher him out.

Sitting on the edge of the chair, Christine kept her eyes safely averted as he pulled the door shut behind him. "May I go to mine own boarding, Mine Lor?"

"We must speak."

"I have nothing to say to you, and will have nothing to say to you ever again."

Crossing his arms across his chest, he leaned back against the door. "Take off yon underclothes."

Dropping her chin to her chest with a heavy sigh, Christine rubbed at her forehead. "I spoke untruths. I have nayat started mine bleeding. I did think it just to speak untruths that once, since yon has spoken untruths to me every time yon mouth has opened."

His only reply was to hold out his hand.

With a growl, she did as bid, slipping off her underwear where
~~~~~~~~~~

she sat and heaving them at him. She watched as he examined them, then tossed them aside. "Now may I go to mine boarding?"

"Naya. Yon may take off yon gilt and climb into mine bunker."

His words sent a bristling down her spine. She looked to where his boots sat discarded by the desk, then back to the Lor and the bloodied shirt he wore. "I would rather lie down with one dropped stelcherer."

He stripped the shirt over his head, tossing it to the floor. "If yon does nayat spend this lun in mine bunker, Eubreena will nayat spend this lun in hers."

She grinned, even as the tears welled. "Well, least you didn't send your little brathern to do yon dirty work. At last yon tippetly tail has untucked itself." She applauded his efforts, clapping clammy hands. "Good for you. But it is there all the same." Standing, she wiped her hands upon her gilt. "As one wisened ganis did speak, only tippets do stelcher babes and force themselves upon litas."

"I did what needed be done."

As he stalked toward her, she retreated from his angry advance, shuffling backward till halted by the obstacle of his unyielding desk. Pressing back against it, she craned her neck as he moved close.

"Yon would have dropped in the hands of that blogart," he insisted, "yon and yon babe both!"

Her hand brushed against his boot—and against the hilt of his blade. "I would leave with him again, one thousand times over, even if it meant mine dropping. I would leave with him this very grain if he stood before me, one ganis of honor, one who does nayat speak untruths every time his mouth does open."

He leaned closer yet, his eyes dark and flashing. "Lend ears, lita, for the words I speak this grain are truths, as Sola shines. You will leave this cas only if I lie dropped."

She curled her fingers around the haft.

He grinned tightly as he nodded. "Pull it free, then. Drop down this devon. Yon is naya stranger to slicing the throats of such. Slice deep, and yon is free to go with yon honored LaRosse."

The haft felt cold and wrong in her hand. She'd pulled it free once before—had driven it into the back of the man who was challenging her to repeat the deed. Desperation had prompted her to pull the blade free that day.

Releasing her grip, she dropped her eyes to his chest.

It was he who pulled it free to place it firmly in her hand. “Be certain, Christa,” he warned as he folded her fingers about it. “If yon does nayat drop me down, yon will spend this lun in mine bunker,” he swore, “and every lun does follow.”

“And if I *do*, I spend this lun in the bellies of fraigens!” she screamed, her composure crumpling. “If nayat for mine lia, the choice would be easy!”

There came an urgent rapping on the door, and Kynneth stuck his head through. He was shirtless, wearing nothing but sleep pants. “Is all well, Mine Lor?”

“I have handed over mine blade to Christa,” the Lor informed him. “If she drops me down, she is nayat to be punished for such. She is to be escorted to one Cassing LaRosse. I trust yon will carry out these orderings when yon becomes Lor, brathern.”

“Jerrod!” Kynneth barked, pushing the door wide to reveal a group of ganist huddled in the hallway, Reesal and several guards, all craning their necks to peer past Kynneth.

“She is nayat to be punished,” he reiterated as he spread his arms wide, giving her an open target. “Does yon hear mine words, Kynneth?”

“I hear them, brathern,” Kynneth spoke as he placed his fists staunchly upon his hips, his glare imparting a chilly warning to Christine.

“Does yon all hear yon Lor?” he asked of his men, though his eyes were firmly on her.

Fragments of noncommittal affirmations sounded, spurring Kynneth to step inside, halting just within the threshold.

She felt her grip tighten about the hilt, felt her breaths quicken, her knees weaken.

With a growl, she plunged the blade to the desk top where it imbedded with a hollow thunk, the blade wobbling a warble as the Leader of Lors grinned.

CHAPTER 12

A lilting voice drifted into her dream.

> "'Fret nayat mine fairest babe.
> Stave yon tears, mine fairest babe.
> All Atriia, she will surent save,
> she who hails from one fraigen cave.
> And all Atriia she will surent save.
> All Atriia she will surent saaaave.'"

She opened her eyes as Eubreena draped the cool cloth across her forehead. "Eubreena," she spoke groggily. "What is this?"

Eubreena grinned sweetly. "I thought mayhap yon was ill. Sola does sit high and yon is still in yon bunker."

"I am nayat ill," she assured, pulling the cloth away.

"Deck yonself, then, and come up," Eubreena suggested, grasping her hand and bringing it to her lips. "Midsup is being served. Yon did alreadied miss firstsup."

Christine pulled the large hand to her own lips, placing a tender kiss upon it. "Eubreena, I'm sorry," she said as the tears welled. "I should nayat have put yon between us. Apologies."

Eubreena took a deep breath. "Naya. I did react badly, but—Lor Zeria has been overly kind. He did come to speak to me his very self, before Sola wakened even. He did insist he was nayat angered, did swear I would nayat be punished." She broke at this, her voice temporarily lost as she wiped at an escaping tear. "He did praise this bligart for—for her brazenry, for protecting yon. As Sola shines, Christa, he did wrap his arms about me, did place his lips upon mine cheek." She began to weep, wiping the traitorous tears on her sleeve. "He should have handed me over to the bellies of fraigens. In the stead, he did hand thankings." With a ragged sigh, she regained control of her emotions, ending her tears as quickly as they'd begun. She placed her trembling fingers to the treasured spot on her cheek. "The very Leader of Lors did place lips upon mine cheek," she sighed, closing her eyes so to better relive such an event.

Christine closed her eyes as well. The very Leader of Lors had placed his lips upon her cheek as well, one turned to him in disdain. But they had not been discouraged. They had taken many liberties throughout the lun, and she hadn't the strength or the will to deny him. "So weak," she sighed.

"Aya," Eubreena agreed, her eyes popping open. "Deck yonself. Yon does need to sup. And our Lor did take early leave this morn, so yon will have many sols to gain back yon strength."

CHAPTER 13

She watched as three ganist slid the massive root ball into the freshly dug hole. “In,” Ervine shouted as he placed a plank of wood against the tree’s trunk to keep it from tipping. Snatching up shovels, his aides began to replace the dirt, shoveling it in around the roots.

Brushing the sweat from her brow, Christine dipped the pail into the water barrel, then hefted it out with a grunt to deposit it on the ground. All the new trees had been watered and most of the copes. Her hands were blistered, her face Solaburned, her muscles aching. After an entire cycle of laboring from dawn till dusk, the garden was quickly taking shape, the plants rooting, the leaves greening, the buds opening. She was certain that watching her creation come to life was the only thing keeping her heart from shriveling and dying.

As she dried her hands upon her apron, she felt her fragile heart lift a bit at the sight of the three babes running fast as their tiny legs could carry them—Becca, Buleea, and Trayson, all screaming as they attempted to escape the frightening beast pursuing them. With his arms thrown wide like a hulking monster, Bixten took awkward, lumbering steps, not seeming to gain on his fleeing prey. Neema was disturbed by his behavior. Barking impressively, she made numerous attempts to thwart him, lunging at his ankles and leaping at his flailing arms.

With a growl, Bixten switched direction, headed after the annoying hound, and she turned tail, tucking it between her legs as she dashed away, her back legs nearly tripping up her front in her panic to escape such a fearsome creature.

Crouching low, Christine scooped up the flushed-faced children as they ran into her arms, lifting all three at once and twirling them round as they screamed and giggled. “I’ve got yon, babes. Yon is safe."

"Saved by one brazened loper," Dahla heralded, coming up to tousle their hair. Their mothers, Corrita and Irva were close behind, both laughing as they rescued their babes from Christine's arms.

"It is coming along well," Irva said as she took in the surroundings.

"Aya," Corrita agreed. "It is quite grand what yon has done in one cycle. The copes are eyegrandly. So many differed colorings."

Dahla pointed proudly to the markers outlining the proposed paths. "The foot trails will wind throughout," she boasted, "so that all shalias and trees can be noted. And there will be seats of stone scattered about for one to sit upon, and stone carvings to gaze upon."

"What is that?" Irva asked, pointing to where two men were digging a large hole.

"Water pool," Christine informed. "For the gosers. One carving of one malla with babe in arms will stand in its center."

The two mallas with babes in arms beamed proudly. "I will walk in this garden every sol with mine babe," Irva declared.

"As will I," Corrita vowed.

"As will I," Dahla put in, grinning shyly as she rubbed her belly, one only beginning to show the slightest sign of swelling. "It is midsup turning, Mine Lita," she informed Christine as she reached for Becca. "We must get cleaned up."

Handing over the child, Christine put a hand to her own stomach. "Aya, mine nose tells me Becca is due for one changing."

Peeking down the diaper, Dahla crinkled her nose. "Aya, she is at that. I will change her while yon does finish here."

"Thankings. I need water a few more copes, then I will be in."

"Fine," Dahla said, rubbing Becca's back where the child rested on her hip with her head upon her shoulder and flush upon her cheeks. "Spiced swill is being served, and pickens covered in shike's cream. It can be smelled throughout one entire cas."

"Aya," Christine said, putting a hand under her nose, "I do smell such out here even."

"It is mine gilt," Dahla admitted. "I was in scullery speaking with Tressa. Mine mouth did water the whole while."

Christine swallowed hard, for her mouth was suddenly dry. "It is overly strong. It—" She threw a hand over her mouth to hold back the gag.

Dahla's eyes grew wide. "Mine Lita!" she gasped. "Is yon feeling ill?"

Clutching at her mid-section, Christine bent in half, placing a hand upon her knee to steady herself as she abruptly emptied her stomach to the ground.

~~~~~~~~~~

"I'm fine," she insisted.

"Put yon feet in this bucket, Christa, for just a few mounds," Eubreena insisted, pushing it toward her chair and forcing her feet into the water.

"Ah! It's cold!"

"And keep one rag on yon head," Eubreena chastised, pulling it from Christine's grasp to place it back across her forehead. "Keep fanning," she barked, and Dahla doubled her fanning speed, frantically waving a throw pillow.

"Naya, Dahla. I'm chilled!"

"Here." Eubreena placed a mug of water into her hands. "Drink it down, the entire thing."

"I did just drink one full mug! Yon will drown me!" Pulling the rag from her head, Christine flung it away.

Sheele ushered Kynneth in, his hair and clothes damp from battle practice.

"Mas Zeria," Eubreena greeted as she bowed, her cheeks instantly mottling with blush.

"I'm fine," Christine insisted as Kynneth placed his hand upon her forehead, then down to one cheek.

"She had to be carried in," Eubreena informed him.

"I was aided," she stressed, "nayat carried."

Standing back, Kynneth eyed her. "Need I call one meshganis?"
~~~~~~~~~~

Eubreena nodded adamantly. “Aya.”

“Naya! I did stay overly long in Sola’s smile, is all. I’m fine now. And I’m starving. I wish to go up for midsup.”

“Leave us,” Kynneth ordered of Sheele and the milling litas. “I need speak to Christa loner.”

He pulled up a foot stool as they filed out, sitting before her with legs set wide. It was an unsettling stance, one bringing to mind the crate in the horrid carry. He’d been keeping his distance since that lun, and that had been just fine. His proximity made her stomach queasy. His grin made her want to scratch his eyes out.

He studied her, his eyes roving over her face. “Yon is nayat fevering, yet yon cheeks stand blushed,” he pointed out, his eyes sparkling wickedly. “Is such from Sola’s smile, or from mine own?”

“Mine stomach *does* feel like emptying itself again, so mayhap it is yon.”

He grinned. “Or mayhap yon is with babe.” He tapped his fingers on his knees. “Yon cycle is late, is it nayat?”

Christine’s empty stomach made a slow, dangerous roll. “Does yon nayat have affairs to attend in one keeper with Ryla, Kynneth? Or should I call you Mine Lor?”

As his grin faded, her own formed. She thought he meant to leave when he stood—till he picked up the stool and flung it across the room, shattering the mirror in an instant. Shards of glass were sent flying around the room, and Neema was sent scrambling under the bed with a high-pitched yelping.

The guards burst into the room. Behind them, Eubreena and Dahla stood gaping in the doorway.

“Naya meshganis is needed,” Kynneth proclaimed as he made for the door, shouldering past the guards. “One blasted loper is live and well.”

~~~~~~~~~~

Dahla swept up a pan full of glass shards, depositing them into the waste basket with a clinking clatter. “Of all Atriia,” she
~~~~~~~~~~

muttered, “flector glass is everywhere. It is in yon bunker, even. I will have fresh bunkering brought up, but I do nayat think Becca should be allowed back in till the whole boarding is gone over. Or Neema. Both can bunker with me this lun. And yon as well, if yon does wish.”

Gripping the bars at the window, Christine heard her words, though it seemed they were drifting up through a dark watery tunnel.

“Hopper’s bunkering is full as well,” Dahla continued from the murky depths. “I hope he will nayat bite this lita if I try to take it out.” She brushed glass pieces from the bureau into the basket. “I know he is but a wee tippet, but I am spookered by him all the same.”

“I will do it.” Her own voice sounded muted, as if cotton had been stuffed in her ears.

“I am also spookered by Mas Zeria,” Dahla admitted in a lowered tone. “He is skewed. Yon should keep well distanced from him.”

Christine watched the man of whom they spoke arching arrows below. He was an impeccable marksman, hitting the target dead center near every shot. “He is but one tippet as well. As is his brathern.”

“Forgivings, Mine Lita, if I do speak out of line. But what thing did our Lor do to turn yon heart away? I did note it breaking when he was left behind at Lazette.”

Christine’s grip tightened on the window bars. “He’s one devon. One like no other. He did use trickery to fool mine heart. He did force hisself upon me again and again, and I didn’t even know I was being forced. Such does speak of skilled devonry.”

“I do nayat understand.”

Christine turned her eyes to the tall, slender litia with the strawberry birthmark. “He has dropped me down. Does yon understand this?”

Dahla shook her head, the welling eyes growing wide. “Naya.”

Christine looked back to the battlers in practice, some on foot shooting at targets, others on horseback arching arrows while at full gallop. “If anything happens to me, I wish mine lia returned to her fallar, one Hannen Fallier."

"Mine Lita!" Dahla cried, crossing the room to fall at her feet. Grabbing Christine's hand, she brought it to her lips to place a frantic kiss upon it. "Lor Zeria will nayat drop yon! He is spellered by yon! All do know such!"

Christine placed her hand upon the girl's hair, stroking tenderly. "I wish Bixten given over to Fallier as well. I know yon does nayat think much of Fallier, but trust me when I say he is one honored ganis. He will raise Bixten as his own. He did only drop Darris for he was sent by the tippetly bratherns to drop him down in his sleep."

Clinging to her hand, Dahla nodded as the tears began to fall.

"Tell him to travel as far from Zeria as possible, away from the devonous bratherns. Tell him to travel to LaRosse. He will be protected there. Yon would be wise to travel there as well, Dahla. Yon could help Hannen to raise Becca, and he will help to raise yon own babe."

"Mine Lita!" Shooting to her feet, Dahla wrung her hands. "If yon does fear Lor Zeria will drop yon down, let us travel to LaRosse."

"I can nayat. They will never let me go. I did seal mine fating when I walked back to mine keeper."

Dropping her chin to her chest, Dahla nibbled on a lower lip that trembled. "Naya, Mine Lita. Yon can," she insisted. "I am nayat one loper. I did tell LaRosse such, as Sola shines I did, but he did insist."

"Insist on what?"

Moving to the window, Dahla wrapped her hands around the cold bars as she looked out over the courtyard to where Kynneth stood draped in battle gear. "He will toss me to fraigens."

"Dahla."

Running a sleeve under her nose, Dahla turned to face her with a face gone pale. "I did draw one picturing on parchment so LaRosse would know which window was yon own."

"Window?"

Dahla put a hand to her belly. "White. If yon does wish to escape yon keeper, fly one flagging of white."

"And he will do what? Ride in with his grand battlean, dropping any did get in his way?"

Dahla shook her head, her birthmark dark crimson against her pallored skin. "Naya. He did ask if yon was ever permitted to leave the cassing walls, and I did—did speak of yon pony riding."

Christine nodded. "Still, many ganist would be dropped. I am always well escorted."

Dahla ran her hands over her pale face. "Kynneth will rip mine tongue free, as Sola shines. Then he will rip mine neck."

Christine put her arms around the girl, rubbing her back. "Yon will be far from Zeria if ever I fly white flagging, Dahla. I will see to that. But yon must nayat speak of this to anyone else, nayat ever."

CHAPTER 14

The fog was thick and suffocating and the taste in her mouth was bitter. She put a hand to the back of her head, wincing at the tenderness. "Naya, get, Neema," she moaned, pushing the hound from her lips.

"Yon should have ripped it free."

She kicked out, connecting with the crate, sending it to tumbling, then beat with balled fists at the man pressed between her legs. The carry was creaking as it rocked with his movements.

"Be one good litia and I will leave yon pony."

"Luckied Lita?"

He shushed her breathlessly.

"Mine babe!" she cried, gripping at his back.

"Shhh, she is safe."

"Mine Lor?"

"Yon can nayat run from fating."

She tried to blink away the fog. "Kynneth?"

"Shhh, close yon eyes."

"Kynneth!"

"Shhh…"

"Kynneth!" Springing up in bed, she threw the covers aside to claw at the strangling gilt. As she struggled to recapture her breath, she looked to Becca's unoccupied spot on the mattress, then to the bureau with the empty flector frame.

"Kynneth," she whispered.

~~~~~~~~~~
~~~~~~~~~~

The guards jumped as she flung open her door—then followed silently as she stalked down the dark and deserted hall.

The guards at Kynneth's door were equally as surprised. "Mine Lita," they chorused, bowing their heads in unison. Exchanging nervous glances, they stood aside as she pushed her way in.

"Mas Zeria," one called out, alerting Kynneth before she could slam the door behind her.

Kynneth was instantly awake and fumbling for the blade resting upon the bed-stand—then relaxed as recognition dawned.

Fluffing a pillow, he propped on an elbow, his eyes running her length where she stood just inside the door. "Has yon come to ask forgivings, loper? Or has yon become lonlied with mine brathern away?"

"You forced yonself on me—in one carry, while I lay injured."

His grin vanished in an instant. Pulling the covers back, he slid his legs from the bed to sit on its edge. "Naya."

"Yon did force me to drink leexer—chouster. I remember tasting it."

He shook his head. "Yon brain was skewed by one blow, surent."

"I did hope it was one foul stelcherer in the stead of yonself. I did pray for such."

His eyes drew to thin slits. "Did yon, now?"

"You're a roggi. A big, fat, disgusting roggi with a big, fat roggi tail tucked between yon legs."

He grinned devilishly. "That is nayat one tail, lita."

"Somesol, I will slice it off."

He slid the blade from the night-stand, running his finger along the flat of the blade. "It is freshly sharpened," he said, thrusting the handle toward her.

"Place that blade in mine hand, and I will use it—as Sola shines."

He stood to saunter toward her, not bothering to adjust the sleep pants riding dangerously low on his hips. Backing her against the door, he thrust the hilt into her hand. "Slice it off, if yon does dare, Mine Lita. But keep in mind, if yon does—yon will nayat ever know the pleasuring it can give." He stepped back, throwing his arms wide.

"I warned you!" she spat, taking a wide-arced swipe with the blade, one only meant as warning.

She gasped as he leaned in, forcing the tip to graze his chest. A slice appeared above his left nipple and the blood began to trickle, trailing down his belly toward his white sleep-bottoms.

A whoosh of air exited her lungs as she flung the blade aside. As it slid along the floor, he leaned his palms against the door, pinning her neatly. "Does yon feel bettered now yon has wounded mine heart?" he asked, the spirits strong on his breath.

"Naya blade is sharp enough to slice that stone," she sneered, facing his dark eyes with venom. "You forced me while I lay injured. Roggii will nayat attack prey while it is strong and abled. They wait till it is weak and defenseless."

His eyes fell to her lips, before drifting slowly back up. "Yon is nayat weak and fendless this lun. There is fire in yon eyes. And blood does pump through one heart strong as any battler's. I hear it," he whispered, leaning close to her ear. "Lay lips to mine, Christa, and I will forgive any falsed accusings did spill from them. Run hands behind mine neck and I will forget they did spill mine blood. Yon will lie with me in mine bunker this lun, in the stead of one keeper."

"Lead way to one keeper, then. I would rather lie down with one thousand foul roggii than the one standing before me."

He pulled away to frown down upon her. "Would yon, then?"

CHAPTER 15

A cry escaped her as she pulled her chin up from her chest. She strained her ears in the darkness, listening for movement, for the slithering of roggi tails, the scampering of tiny feet. But it was not tiny feet that she heard, but those of a big fat rat. When candlelight appeared under the door, she wrapped her arms about her knees, hugging them tight as the door was pushed open with an eerie creak.

Pushing it shut behind him, he held the lantern high to inspect her where she sat huddled on the cot in her lungilt. "How was yon lun? Did yon sleep well, then, yon and one thousand foul roggii?"

"Yon was tipping spirits last lun, Kynneth, so I forgive yon."

"How kindly."

"Aya." She hated that her voice shook. "I wish to return to mine boarding."

Setting the lantern on the floor, he approached the cot, putting his face in shadow. She didn't have to see it to know he was grinning like an idiot.

"How badly does yon wish it?" he asked, resting his hand upon his belt buckle.

Dropping her chin back to her chest, she shook her head. "Nayat so badly. I would have one thousand foul roggii sup on mine flesh first."

"As yon does wish."

She peeked, watching as he retrieved the lantern and prepared to leave. "What will yon brathern say when he returns to find me in one keeper?"

"Yon did spill the blood of his brathern. It did take ten stitchings to close mine wound."

"Blogart," she spat, dropping her head back down.

~~~~~~~~~~

"Bitch!" she spat, frantically brushing the fat roach from where it had crawled onto her shoulder. "Mother—"

She cocked her head, listening in the darkness, trying to discern the owners of the distant voices drifting under the door—most probably the guards playing tookets as they'd been doing for turnings. It was difficult to tell past a stomach that gurgled and grumbled. She had kept her spot on the cot, cowering beneath the covers as the roggii had feasted on her meal, squealing and clawing, this sending the bowl to clattering across the floor.

"Ten stitchings," she grumbled. "It will take more than that when I slice yon blasted throat, blogart. Just yon…"

Scrambling from the cot, she dropped to the floor, putting her eye to the food slot. "Who's there!"

"Christa!"

"Eubreena?" She could just make out the guards' boots as they trudged by, several sets, and a woman's gilt. Eubreena was weeping as they dragged her past.

"Eubreena!" she screeched, banging a fist against the door. "Kynneth! You bastard! Blasted bastard!"

~~~~~~~~~~

She swiped at the tears as she shivered in the darkness. "You're an idiot," she spoke to herself, her voice sounding hollow in the empty cell. "He'll have his way and there's nothing you can do about it." Rolling to her side on the flimsy cot, she pulled the blanket over her head, a barrier against the misery—and the roaches. Somewhere at the far end of the hall, Eubreena's muffled weeping had ceased, though this brought little solace. For the first time since he'd left, Christine wished for the Lor of the cas to return.

~~~~~~~~~~

She sat up suddenly at the latch releasing, wondering at how she could have fallen to sleeping. Shielding her eyes from the light, she attempted to focus on the figure behind it.

"Kynneth?"

"Did yon enjoy yon sup?" he asked, looking to the empty bowl overturned in the corner.

She sighed deeply. "One thousand foul roggii did enjoy it greatly."

"Yon does know the rulings," he said. "If yon does nayat place yon emptied bowl through one slotting, yon will nayat sup the next sol."

Christine rubbed at her forehead. "Pleadings, Kynneth, do nayat punish Eubreena for mine actions."

"She was spectless," he said, placing the lantern on the floor, then his hands on his hips. "She did come to mine boarding and demand I release yon. And Dahla is acting skewed as well. She did throw herself at mine feet, swearing on Sola she is nayat one loper. She speaks of white flaggings."

"White flaggings?"

"She claims such will free yon from one keeper."

"Oh—aya. I did tell her, in minc hailing, white flaggings mean surrender."

"Surrender?"

"It means I hand defeat. Yon has won this battle. I fly white flagging." Lifting the light-colored lungilt at her feet, she waved it at him in demonstration. "I was spectless and I hand apologies," she said, bowing her head.

He studied her where she sat, then ran his eyes about the cell, coming back full circle. "Yon is nayat to speak of such foul accusings again, is this clear?"

"I will nayat," she promised, standing up to wring her hands. "What of Eubreena?"

"What of her?"
~~~~~~~~~~

"She was only protecting me."

"Such is what mine brathern spoke when she put stitchings in his head. He is more forgiving than mineself."

Christine folded her hands in her lap. "If Eubreena stays in one keeper, then I stay as well."

He moved closer, his eyes narrowing. "Does yon wish this ganis to release her?"

She nodded, swallowing down the lump of dread, fearing the next question.

He stepped aside, pointing to the door. "It is done, then."

CHAPTER 16

"Big litia," Dahla crooned.

Grinning widely, Becca carefully maneuvered the eggs she had painstakingly procured with the tiny fork into her mouth.

"Aiyee, eggs and shike strips have nayat ever tasted so grand," Eubreena spoke through a mouthful.

Christine nodded, her own mouth too full to reply.

"What was is like, then, Torna asked of Eubreena. "Was yon nayat allowed to sup at all?"

Washing her food down with a gulp of juice, Eubreena wiped her mouth on a napkin. Though her eyes were still puffy, she was in good spirits, almost exultant at having survived such an ordeal. "Sup was sent, but I could nayat note such past the blackness, blackness deeper than any lun. Do I speak untruths, Christa?"

Christine shook her head as she took a healthy bite of shike strip.

"As Sola shines," Eubreena swore, "foul roggii did jump mine sup like starved wildhounds. Was one swarming! They did come from the walls, from under one door, from the very flooring. I feared they might sup on this lita if I did try to claim mine meal."

"Aiyee!" Torna squealed, throwing her hands to her lips. "One swarming?"

"Was ten least, mayhap twice such. Do I speak untruths?"

"Naya," Christine replied, pushing the remainder of strip into her mouth, then tousling Becca's hair.

Dahla wiped the babe's mouth before turning to Eubreena. "I could nayat believe Mas Zeria would throw yon in one keeper. Yon is his favored. I did think I was next when he came to mine boarding. I did throw mineself at his feet to hand beggings. I do nayat even remember what I spoke, I was fretting such."

"Kynneth was angered at me," Christine explained. "Poor Eubreena did only suffer for mine actions."

"As did I," Ryla imparted from where she sat at the far end of the table. "I did suffer in his bunker," she said with a tight grin. She was up early for one pleasurer, and accompanied by two others, Sheilla and Kylara, both of who paused in their supping at the startling confession.

"Ryla," Eubreena chastised. "Pleasurers do nayat speak of pleasuring affairs, lest they wish to lose their tongues."

Ryla paled as tears welled. "*She* does spill his blood, yet it is I do wear his handprintings on mine backside!"

Christine swallowed down her food in a gulp. "Ryla, I—"

Ryla stood suddenly, her chair grating along the floor. "Why does yon nayat just bunker him and be done with it!"

All at the table watched in silence as she fled from the room with Sheilla and Kylara following close behind.

Christine placed a hand upon her belly as firstsup began to churn. "Should I go speak with her?"

"Naya, I will do it," Eubreena offered, wiping her mouth on her napkin before pushing from the table. "I will have it known, I did nayat mind suffering for Christa's actions," she addressed to the table. "I would do such again with naya questioning."

Christine threw her hand over her heart as tears welled. "Eubreena, I do nayat deserve—"

"Mas Zeria did hisself release me from one keeper," Eubreena interrupted, her eyes blazing brightly. "He did pull me close, did wrap arms about me tight, did beg forgivings."

"Naya!" Torna gasped.

"Aya, and—he did lean in to place lips upon mine own."

There were gasps of shock, several litas throwing hands to their own lips.

"Swear it!" Torna insisted. "Swear it on Sola!"

"Well, to speak truths," Eubreena said, raising a finger high, "he did lay lips to mine cheek, but," she stressed, pointing to the spot, "it was overly close to mine lips. I am most certain I did feel his touch mine own, here on one corner."

"Sweet Sola!" Torna breathed. "I would spend one lun in one keeper for such!"

"Aya," Tressa agreed.

"Of all Atriia!" Christine cried. "I did just spend two luns in one keeper to avoid such! Is yon all so blinded by Kynneth's fair face, yon can nayat see the fat, foul roggi he is?"

All at the table gasped when a male cleared his throat close by.

Eubreena spun about. "Mas Sheele!" she stammered, throwing a hand to her chest. "I did nayat hear yon enter."

He bowed curtly to Christine. "Mine Lita," he spoke grimly. "One fat, foul roggi does wish to speak with yon."

~~~~~~~~~~

Kynneth dismissed Mas Sheele as he tightened the straps of his shoulder plates, tying the knot securely at his chest.

Christine gave a nod of her head. "Mas Zeria."

"Our Lor will be returning soon," he said, resting back on the dresser. "Yon will treat him with spects, Christa, as Sola shines, or yon will meet yon thousand foul roggii again."

"I will treat him with all the spects he does deserve."

He frowned. "He has spent the last cycle preparing this region for battlement—battlement brought upon us by yon actions. As I am surent yon has heard, yon honored LaRosse is banding the upper Lors gainst us."

Christine rubbed her clammy palms on the skirt of her gilt. She was completely aware of the troubles brewing between the regions. The litas could speak of nothing else. "Well, I guess I'm nothing but flustings. Mayhap yon can convince yon brathern to hand me over to LaRosse. Spare yon ganist and send me on mine way. Surent yon—"

"Yon and yon litar would be dropped within one allten," he sneered as he moved toward her.
~~~~~~~~~~

She held her place as he strolled around to stand behind her.

"And yon does carry his babe," he whispered, leaning close to her ear.

She willed herself to calmness, forcing herself not to whirl and knee him where it hurt most. "It is nayat yet certain I am with babe."

"I do nayat think I could convince our Lor to send yon away, even if it was mine wishing. And it is nayat."

"Of course not. Then who would yon have to torture for yon own entertaining?"

She felt his warm breath on her hair as he chuckled. Closing her eyes, she released the deep breath slowly. "Where is mine pale pony, Kynneth?"

He breathed deeply of her scent. "Safe," he said, placing his hands upon her shoulders.

Spinning, she shoved at him, an action which only managed to send her stumbling backward. "I want her back!"

"Does yon?" He moved to the dresser to retrieve his helmet, adjusting something within. "When one babe is birthed, yon will have her back."

Spinning about, she yanked open the door, startling the guards to attention. "What does one dropped lita need with one pony, you jackass!" she yelled as she hurried from the room.

CHAPTER 17

"Oh, Eubreena, I'm dropping."

Eubreena draped the cool rag over her forehead. "Naya," she said, taking her hand. "One babe is letting it be known that he is one to be reckoned with. Naya larger than one picken seed, yet alreadied landing yon on yon back."

Christine closed her eyes against the spinning room, placing her free hand upon her stomach. "I was nayat ill one sol with Becca."

"It is always the gans cause most flustings."

Christine opened her eyes to Eubreena's broad smile. "I fear he will cause untold flustings fore all is done."

Eubreena placed her free hand upon Christine's stomach, her eyes misting. "Our next Lor is in yon belly," she said. "Mine dreamings did prove truths. Sola is grand, is she nayat?"

Christine gently squeezed her hand. "Eubreena—there's something I must tell you." She moistened her dry lips with the tip of her tongue. "There's a good chancing this babe will drop me down."

Eubreena tried not to grin. "Naya, Christa. Yon does feel as if yon is dropping now, but in a few sols yon ills will be done with." She pointed to the newest vase of shalias reaching clear to the ceiling, a gifting from the Leader of Lors. "And in a few sols, our Lor will be returning. I can only wonder how many shalias will grace this cas once—"

"Eubreena, the babe will nayat fit past mine hips. Such are overly narrowed for birthing babes. Did yon nayat warn me of such over and again?"

Eubreena frowned as she nodded. "Aya, but—Becca."

"Just be prepared. I have alreadied spoken with Dahla. If I am dropped, I wish Becca and Bixten placed in Hannen Fallier's care. He is one good ganis, Eubreena. Yon must—"

"Christa, pleadings do nayat speak of such!" Eubreena wailed, her face turned ashen. "Mine heart will stop beating if yon is dropped birthing this babe!"

Reaching for Eubreena's other hand, Christine brought both to her lips, placing a soft kiss on one, then the other. "Yon heart is pure as Sola's smile. Yon has protected me at every turn, has risked yon own neck more than once. I could nayat ask for one better friend."

"Of all Atriia," Eubreena breathed, pulling her hands away to cover her face.

Sliding the rag from her forehead, Christine sat up in the bed. "I do nayat wish to make yon weep, but we must be readied. If I do nayat survive this birthing, I'm depending on yon to be strong, mine friend."

Keeping her face buried, Eubreena shook her head. "I am nayat yon friend. I am one bligart—one foul, devonous bligart. Mine heart is black, black as the blackest lun."

"Naya, Eubreena."

Eubreena dropped her hands into her lap like lead weights. "I spoke untruths," she confessed, swallowing hard and struggling to blink back tears. "Our Lor has nayat ever taken one brooder. Yon is the first."

"But—you…"

Eubreena wiped angrily at a tear. "He has been overly carefilled with the pleasurers, mindful of their cycles. He was—was waiting for yon." Her faced twisted as she fought back a sob. "Such were his very words. He has been waiting for yon all his sols."

Christine buried her face in her hands. "Naya, Eubreena," she groaned.

"Forgivings, mine Christa. He did come to me, did tell me yon was afeared of him, did ask for mine aid to open yon eyes, to open yon heart."

"To open mine legs!" she cried, dropping her hands from her face to pummel the mattress with balled fists. "Bastard! Fucking rat-bastard!" She clapped a hand over her mouth as a gag escaped—and Eubreena hurried to position a bucket under her chin.

"Here," Eubreena said when the cramping in Christine's belly finally ceased. "Lie back." Positioning the pillows, Eubreena helped her do so, then folded the rag neatly, placing it back into position. "Apologies, mine Christa." She sniffled as she smoothed the hair away from Christine's face with gentle fingers.

Christine closed her eyes as a numbness settled over her. "I am nayat angered at yon, Eubreena. He used trickery, as he did on me. He is devonously skilled at such." She placed her hands upon her belly, knowing in her heart that the next Lor of Zeria lie beneath them. "I did lie down with one devon, knowing it was wrong in mine heart. Now I must face mine fating."

CHAPTER 18

The deep beating of drums was at a much slower pace than that of her racing heart. Standing at the window, she and Dahla watched the procession enter the courtyard, a long line of prancing ponies five abreast. Sola's smile reflected brilliantly off the armor they wore and off the armor of the battlers commanding them. He was in the third row back, dead center, sitting tall upon his white pony, his face tilted up to her window.

She rubbed hands up and down her arms as a chill entered the room, then peered over her shoulder to where Becca napped upon the bed.

"Finhap she does rest," Dahla whispered.

Christine nodded. The babe was teething and irritable and had struggled against sleep.

"Yon is eyegrandly, Mine Lita."

Christine looked down to the finery she wore, a gilt of sea-foam green cut low at the chest. It was trimmed in olive velvet stippled with pearly beads. "I am thinking yon will be traveling soon, Dahla."

Dahla paled. "Is yon thinking to fly white flagging?"

"Yon malla is ill, is she nayat?"

"Aya."

"A visit is in order. And yon should take Bixten as company. He does enjoy traveling. And he will wish to take Neema." Gripping the bars, she looked down to the Lor on the white pony, he who was gazing up to her. "If all goes well, I will pick you up on mine way to LaRosse."

~~~~~~~~~~
~~~~~~~~~~

She went to him even before she was summoned, barging in as he was removing his armor. "Hand me over to LaRosse and end this battlement fore it does start."

He grinned as he shook his head. "Naya."

"Yon would note thousands of ganist dropped so to keep me in yon bunker?"

Unloosing his shoulder plates, he lifted them over his head and draped them over the back of his chair. "Even if I handed yon over, there would still be battlement," he said as he poured himself a mug of spirits. "LaRosse does boast loudly of protecting yon honoring, but it is mine standing he does wish."

"Aya, he did tell me this hisself. He believes yon standing will be handed to him if I am handed to him."

He gave her a sideways glance before lifting the mug. "I will hand him nayathing," he said, before downing its contents in a few hearty gulps. Seating himself at the desk, he pulled off his boots, casting them aside. "But I do wish yon in mine bunker. Yon is right about such. One cycle did seem as one seg." Refilling his mug, he leaned back to pour over her, spreading his legs to a wide stance.

"Mine Lor, his battlean could destroy this entire region. Hand me over and spare yon peoples."

"And what of mine babe? Will I hand him over as well?" He studied her as he swirled the liquid in the mug.

"I am nayat with babe."

"The entire cas does seem to think differed."

She fisted her hands, digging nails into palms. "Then there is naya longer reasoning for me to share yon bunker, is there!"

He emptied his second mug almost as quickly as the first before wiping his mouth on the back of his sleeve. "It is mine wishing. That is the only reasoning needed."

"I know of yon trickery on Eubreena, how yon did use mine closest friend gainst me." She applauded as he filled his mug a third time. "If yon has succeeded and I do carry yon babe, yon best prepare one spot in yon fallar's tempelle, for I will be joining him quite soon."

His eyes were cold when they lifted to hers. "Now who does use trickery? I have questioned every meshganis from here to Chaspia. Nayat one has ever heard of one babe being birthed through a lita's belly."

"Yon should speak with Meshganis Tieslen. And I gest yon does move him close when the time draws near. Same did save mine pony and her nippers. He may be able to save yon babe. He may be able to save mineself even, but I do nayat wish him punished if he can nayat."

Dark liquid splattered the desk as he slammed the mug down and rose to his feet. "Does yon think me one blogart?"

"Kynneth did note the scarrings on mine pony. That's why he sent her away. Ask him."

He stalked toward her, his lips set in a tight line. "Was I did send yon pony away. Yon precious gifting from yon precious brathern. Aya, Tieslen *did* slice her belly, but after her nipper was alreadied birthed. Yon skewed brathern did order him to do such, so to trick me to thinking yon does speak truths about yon own scarring!"

"I am speaking truths, as Sola shines!"

Striking swiftly, he snatched her wrist, pulling her close. "I am nayat one blogart. Do nayat mistake me for such. Fallier would stop at nayathing to get yon back in his bunker. But yon will nayat ever be back in such, for yon will be in mine, this lun and every lun after—if I need chain yon to mine bunkerposts."

Gritting her teeth, she yanked her wrist free from his grasp. "Gather yon chains then, Mine Lor. Chain mine wrists tight, else I will claw yon face to shreds. Chain mine ankles and pull them wide, for that is the only way mine legs will ever open to yon again."

"Is that right?" He hastily unfastened several buttons of his shirt and pulled it open to reveal the necklace hidden beneath, the fraigen scale nestled neatly in the cleft of his chest.

As her eyes slid to his, his face softened. "Christa, I do nayat wish to battle."

She placed palms against a queasy stomach. "You found him?"

"He found me. The blogart did wish to speak ganis to ganis. He did nayat take kindly to me telling him to leave his sasturn alone."

"You promised not to harm him."

"And I have nayat," he said, stripping the shirt over his head. She watched numbly as he lifted the necklace over his head as well, tossing it to the floor beside the discarded shirt.

"He did nayat hand such over willingly."

"Naya, he did nayat." Turning her about by the shoulders, he began to unfasten the buttons of her gilt, his fingers working their way quickly down.

"He was nayat harmed?"

"Naya," he replied as he slid the gilt from her shoulders so it could glide to the floor. Unfastening her binder, he slid it from her arms, then pulled her back against him, his hands eager to cup that newly freed. "We will speak of this on the morrow," he breathed, his breaths hot against her neck as he lavished it with kisses.

She took in a sharp breath as one hand slid downward into her undergarment, sliding it off. "He is safe?"

Pivoting her around, he guided her to the bed, gently pressing her down upon it. Though he did not lay himself down upon her as she expected. Instead, he dropped to his knees.

"As long as yon legs stay opened to me," he promised, pulling her to the edge of the bed to drape her legs over his shoulders, "yon precious brathern stays safe."

~~~~~~~~~~

His breaths were deep and steady in sleep, his chest rising and falling where it pressed against her back. Before she could attempt to slide from beneath his draped arm, he rolled in his sleep, landing on his back and freeing her to slip from the bed.

She found the necklace where he had discarded it on the floor. Lifting it delicately, she watched it dangle in the darkness, the hypnotic rhythm holding her spellbound for several mounds. An odd calmness settled over her as she watched it sway. The hand which took hold of the scale belonged to another. She watched from afar as a finger slid over the edge, testing its deadly worth. It seemed the legs she stood on belonged to another as well, as did the feet which
~~~~~~~~~~

took her to the side of the bed. She was gazing through the eyes of another as she looked upon him. He was magnificent as he slept, his face turned toward her, his lips slightly parted. It was a beautiful mouth, full and sensual, one designed for devastating devouring. His chest rose and fell with his every breath.

Her own breaths were just as deep and just as steady. The weapon clutched in her hand seemed tiny, weighing no more than a feather. It had taken a devon's life. She could not remember the name of such devon, nor his face. She remembered the blood. Black blood from a black heart. It had flowed into black waters. She had dived into those black waters to escape the very man who lie sleeping before her—the Lor of Zeria, the Leader of Lors, the most powerful ganis in all of Atriia. She had feared him more than black waters brimmed with fraigens, more than torturous tunnels. It had been wise to fear him.

It was another's body that leaned over him, and another's voice that gave a triumphant cry as the scale was dragged across his throat.

She was pulled to the bed beneath him in an instant, his blood raining down, a deluge of crimson. Spitting and sputtering, she fought against him, struggling against the strong restraining hands, against the drowning downpour. She blinked eyes blinded by blood. It was pouring from his throat and from his mouth as he tried to speak, his words drowned by the blood trying to drown her.

"Christa," he gurgled…

She blinked away the blood as he leaned in to her forehead—then her cheek, her lips, nibbling tenderly. "Yon is safe," he said as he settled between her legs, pushing them apart. "Was only lundevons."

She struggled to catch her breath and to stave her tears. "Pleadings, I must know what has befallen Fallier!"

He pushed away to stare down upon her. "Was yon dreaming of him, then?"

"Naya—one foul devon."

He smiled. "Overly foul by yon kicking and weeping."

"Foul as foul can be," she admitted, facing him squarely. "I did rip his throat wide, ear to ear. I was free at last—till I did waken to find him between mine legs, readied to force hisself upon me yet again."

His eyes dropped to her lips, and when they lifted again, they were veiled in dark shadow. Rolling from her, he sat on the edge of the bed to rake his fingers through his hair, then stood to move to the desk. Leaning heavily upon it, he hung his head between his shoulders. "Would yon rather it was Fallier between yon legs, then, yon own brathern?"

"I would rather open mine legs for one foul roggi than yonself, one foul fraigen even. The thought of mine brathern between mine legs does make me want to slice mine own throat wide, yet I would rather him to yonself, as Sola—"

She flinched as he swiped the spirit pitcher from the desk with a snarl, sending it somersaulting across the room—flinched again as he lunged at her, his hand snapping about her wrist like an iron manacle. His grip was bruising as he dragged her from the bed and out the door, past the startled guards and down the hall—the naked Lor leading the naked loper. They came upon Reesal in the arms of the pleasurer Kylara, both gawking as their Lor swept by. Down a flight of stairs and down the hall, they interrupted two guardsmen speaking to Kynneth at the entrance to the conference room, their conversation cutting short at the shocking sight.

"Are we battling?" Kynneth quipped with an infuriating grin as she was whisked past in unceremonious fashion.

Down the lower flight of stairs he dragged her, past the seamsewers room and to that of the keeper guards. Here, he snatched a lantern from the wall while the gaping guards stood stunned.

"Keys to Fallier!" he barked, and they scurried to locate them.

Christine tried vainly to cover herself. "Mine Lor—"

"He was warned to keep distanced," he growled as he dragged her down the dark hall. "But the thought of yon opened legs was too strong one luring. Here," he said, shoving the lantern in her hands and the key in the door. "Open yon legs for yon brathern, then," he suggested as he pushed open the door. "He would give his life to lie between such."

Shoving her in, he slammed the door shut, locking it securely behind her.

~~~~~~~~~~

With a trembling hand, she held the lantern high, casting the light to where he sat squinting upon the cot, shielding his eyes. “Sam?”

He shot to his feet at the sound of her voice. “Christa!”

“Sam! Wait—” She pressed against the wall as he flew toward her, unmindful of the shackle which bound his wrist. It halted his hasty advance, nearly ripping his arm from its socket.

“Shit—blast!” he growled, yanking on the chain till she feared his wrist might snap.

“Sam!” Shrinking back against the wall, she sucked in her breath as he stretched to the limit of the chain, groping out with his free hand, his fingertips coming within inches of grazing her.

“Christa!” he begged, straining against his restraint, the veins in his neck popping with the effort.

“Sam! Hannen!”

With a frustrated growl, he stepped back, his breathing erratic as his eyes ran down her length, seeming to suddenly notice she was unclothed.

“Just—calm down,” she said, placing the lantern on the floor, freeing her hands to cover herself. “I could use a blanket.”

His eyes raked over her, drinking in her nakedness.

“I’ll explain.” She motioned to the cot with her head. “Please, your blanket.”

He continued to stare, his free hand absentmindedly going to his manacled wrist.

“Your wrist is bleeding,” she said, hoping this might draw his eyes away. But they refused to leave her. They were dark and impossible to read in the dim light. “Sam, we might only have a minute or two. Can I have your blanket, please? We must talk.”

He hesitated, before pulling his eyes away to glance over his
~~~~~~~~~~

shoulder to the cot. Reluctantly, he retrieved the blanket, shuffling to the end of his chain to hand it to her.

"Sam, I—" She gasped as he struck, grasping her wrist and pulling her close. A struggle ensued, one she quickly lost.

Engulfing her in a tight embrace, he lifted her from the floor. "Christa," he breathed, burying his face into her neck.

"Sam!"

He silenced her with a kiss, his mouth hot and hungry, ravaging her lips as a man starved.

He pulled away suddenly, his eyes probing. "I smell him on you. I taste him."

She felt the shame flood through her, felt the tears well.

"It doesn't matter, Christa. Yon is safe, that's all that—"

"I'm pregnant, Sam."

The color drained from his face as he placed her back to the floor. "Naya."

Fishing the blanket from the floor, she wrapped it about her shoulders, clutching it tight about her neck. "What? No congratulations?"

The pale shock on his face instantly brought pangs of remorse. "Meshganis Tieslen, he did birth Luckied Lita's nippers by caesarean, did he nayat."

He nodded as his eyes filled with tears.

"Maybe he could do the same for me."

His eyes fell to the floor. "I don't know," he said, running a hand across his brow. "She did nearly drop. For several turnings, we did think she had. Her breathing was so shallow. She—"

They both looked to the door at the sound of shouting.

"Listen to me, Sam," she pressed, the words tumbling out. "If I can convince Lor Zeria to release you, you must go to LaRosse. Its Lor is planning to help me escape the Zeria devons, and probably very soon. I'll meet you there. Don't come back here again. They'll kill you. They will, Sam! You can't raise Becca if you're dead!"

"Christa—"

"She's going to need her father," she rattled out at the sound of the key rattling in the lock." Don't let her down. And there's a boy, Bixten. He's orphaned. I—"

It was Kynneth who came busting in, his blade drawn, his face in a snarl, pulling her away as the guards rushed in to beat at her brother with clubs.

Though she was imploring them to stop, her cries for mercy went unheeded as she was dragged from the cell.

~~~~~~~~~~

The Lor of the cas was seated at the desk when Kynneth ushered her into the room. He was wearing pants and a frown.

"He had foul hands on her, yon blogart!" Kynneth hissed.

"He did nayat harm me," she insisted where she stood wrapped in his blanket. "He would nayat ever do such."

The Lor ran his fingers through his hair. "Naya. Nayat yon honored fraigen dropper."

"He's promised to leave Zeria. I've made it clear he will be dropped if he returns."

"We made it clear he would be dropped if he came near this cassing," Kynneth sneered. "He did nayat heed our many warnings, and he will nayat heed hers. He must be dropped, Jerrod. Yon does know this as well as I."

"Naya! You did swear on Sola!"

A new pitcher of spirits had already been brought in. And the Lor had already lessened its volume considerably. He lifted his mug, finishing off its contents. "I need speak with Christa loner."

Kynneth bristled. "Jerrod, he will nayat rest till she is his. He is—"

"Kynneth!" his brother snapped, his mug hitting the desk with a resounding thump. "Leave us."

Kynneth was fuming as he strode from the room—and the Leader of Lors was frowning as he stood to face her.
~~~~~~~~~~

CHAPTER 19

Dahla rapped lightly before poking her head inside the door. "Oh, I was nayat certain yon would be wakened," she said, stepping in with Becca on her hip. "I did hear—I mean—our Lor did keep yon busied till late."

Turning from the window, Christine held out her arms, beckoning. "Becca, sweet babe," she crooned, taking the child from Dahla to shower her with kisses. The child was unusually subdued, grasping her about the neck and resting her head upon her shoulder.

"She did nayat get much sleeping as well," Dahla explained.

"Still teething, mine poor babe?" Returning her attention to the window, Christine stroked Becca's hair, reveling in the weight of her in her arms, in the silkiness of her hair against her cheek. She nuzzled the locks, placing kisses upon her head. Freezing suddenly, she leaned close to the bars. "There, mine babe. There is yon fallar."

Dahla stepped close to grasp the bars, her face turning ashen. "Fallier!" she gasped, throwing a hand to her mouth. "Here?"

He was being escorted to the carriage by what seemed like a hundred guards, his ankles and wrists heavily chained. "He's leaving," Christine informed her. "And he is nayat to be harmed. Jerrod promised me. He promised." Fighting back tears, she held tightly to Becca.

Dahla shuddered as he disappeared into the carriage with several guards crowding in behind. The rest mounted waiting ponies, riding alongside and behind as the carriage crept forward, trundling away.

"He promised," she whispered, clamping down on her bottom lip.

It came without warning, a blanket of gray fog rolling in. She quickly handed over Becca before leaning against the wall, in desperate need of its support as the legs beneath her grew suddenly limp. A sob erupted, buckling her knees, and she slid down the wall, collapsing to the floor in a heap. With legs tucked under, she buried her face in her hands, trying to smoother the hitching sobs that came one after the other, each racking her body in violent waves.

"Mine Lita!" Dahla railed, "should I fetch one meshganis?"

Christine shook her head adamantly, unable to speak past the savage sobs. Fisting her hands, she beat at the floor, each strike accompanied by a howl of pain.

Becca's muted cries pulled her from her miseries. Dahla was clutching the babe, and both had wide eyes and pale faces.

Christine wiped her face on her sleeve. "It's alright. I'm alright. Just—give me one mound," she said, hanging her head as she tried to catch her breath.

"Yon does need resting, Mine Lita. I will take Becca up to firstsup."

"Naya," Gathering her strength, Christine stood on wobbly legs to shuffle to the bureau. Pouring water from the pitcher into the bowl, she leaned over it to splash water onto her face. "I will change," she said, blotting her face with a hand towel, then peering at herself in the newly installed flector. "We will go to firstsup together." Stripping the lungilt over her head, she held it out for inspection. It was white and wet. "I did spill water on mine lungilt."

"Hang it over yon chair, Mine Lita," Dahla advised.

"Naya." Pulling in a deep breath, Christine released it as a slow exhale. "I will tie it to mine window bars. Sola's smile will pull out the dampness much more quickly."

CHAPTER 20

Christine took a seat on the stone bench, placing Becca on her lap, then placing the bright pink cope in the child's hand. "Sit, Dahla," she said, patting the seat beside her.

Gathering her skirt about her, Dahla sat with a sigh. "Such grand benches," she stated. "Overly sized. They could sit four easy."

Nodding, Christine looked out over the gardens, counting the newly placed benches, ten in all. Four ganist were busy installing the newest arrivals—trees dug from all over the region. The stone carver was busy as well, the sharp retort of his hammer ringing out as he chiseled away on the fountain carving—one malla with babe in arms quickly taking shape. Four more ganist were whittling away on the mountain of flagstones piled off to one side, the foot-trails winding through the gardens nearly half completed. She eyed the ganis in the straw hat who was laying these stones, piecing them together like a puzzle, he who had pulled her aside several days earlier. It had taken only four days for LaRosse to respond. The message had been only one word.

"Fivesol," Dahla whispered, looking about the garden. "Is yon surent, then?"

"Aya."

Dahla nodded, then looked to where Becca was pulling pink petals from the cope one by one. "I do hold great fearings, Mine Lita."

Putting her arm around Dahla, Christine pulled her close. "Do nayat fret, sweet Dahla."

With a sigh, Dahla rested her head upon Christine's shoulder. "What if yon is injured? What if Becca…"

"Shhh, Dahla, don't." She rested her cheek upon Dahla's head and rubbed her shoulder. “Is yon packed and readied to leave early on the morrow?”

“Aya.”

“Bixten is excited about traveling. Don’t let him feed Hopper overly.”

“Aya, Mine Lita.”

“And remember what I spoke. If something is to happen to me, yon must travel on to LaRosse without me. Find Fallier there. He will take care of yon.”

Dahla sniffled. “I do nayat wish Fallier to care for me.”

“Dahla, yon should nayat be afeared of him. He does look as if he should be feared—his sizing, his scarring—but his heart is kind. The kindest I have ever known.”

Dahla pulled away to wipe her eyes. “Yon is spellered by him.”

Christine kissed the head of the babe on her lap, then stroked the locks dancing so gaily in Sola’s warm smile. “More than he will ever know,” she whispered.

~~~~~~~~~~

The fingers caressing her belly slipped low to trace over the scar.

“Thankings, Mine Lor, for allowing Dahla to travel to her hailing. Her malla has nayat been well.”

“Mmhmm.” His fingers traveled back to her belly, trailing lightly back and forth.

“And Bixten was overly excited. It was kind to allow him to travel with her.”

“He’s one fine gani,” he whispered against her hair. “He will like the new painting Mas Tulls does work on. One flutterfly—the most eyegrandly of all Atriia.”

“Aya, he will like that. He spends turnings chasing them in the garden. I wish to hand thankings on such as well—mine garden. It is grander than I ever dreamed.”

“Grander than I dreamed. Yon has labored overly.”
~~~~~~~~~~

"Mas Dryor has done most of the laboring."

"Hmm. The ganis enjoys what he does."

"Aya. He has finhap agreed to take one sol for resting. The first since we began," she added, leaving out that she had insisted he do so. "Fivesol. I was thinking to go pony riding that sol."

He shifted behind her. "Naya."

"But…I was wishing to take Becca. She has nayat been pony riding in a long while, and she does greatly enjoy such."

He patted her stomach. "We must be careful."

She rolled to face him. "I will only walk mine pony, Jerrod. Pleadings."

Rolling to his back with a sigh, he laced his fingers behind his head. "I do have five Lors arriving over the next five sols. I will be busied with speakings. Yon does know this."

She placed a hand on his chest, gliding her fingertips along his still dampened skin. "Pleadings, Jerrod. I did promise her. I will be safe with yon ganist."

He closed his eyes at her gentle caress. "Mayhap within one courtyard."

"I did promise one pony ride, nayat to walk in circles," she said, slipping her hand lower to caress his belly.

He eyed her warily. "Yon does wish to ride that badly, then?"

She nodded with a pout. "I did promise Becca."

He drew in breath as her hand slipped lower yet, sliding beneath the covers. "Careful, Christa," he warned, "lest yon be riding much sooner than fivesol."

She leaned into his ear as she took hold of him, stroking gently. "Does yon wish me to ride this pony?"

A wry grin surfaced. "Mayhap."

Leaning down, she nibbled on his lips as her hand stroked a silky pony raring to be ridden. "I will ride hard this lun," she whispered against his lips, "but on fivesol, I promise, I will only walk mine pony."

He let out a ragged resigned sigh. "Fine then," he said, casting the covers aside.

CHAPTER 21

Eubreena paused in her braiding to study the flash-card, her brow furrowing. “Tot,” she said, her face breaking into a wide grin. “Christa, yon did nayat even try.” She gave an exasperated frown in the mirror. “What is wrong with yon this sol? Is yon feeling ill?”

“Naya, just wearied.”

“Mine poor Christa,” Eubreena crooned, leaning forward to kiss the top of her head. “I did think our Lor would nayat call on yon once yon did carry his babe.” She resumed her braiding, her experienced fingers nimbly weaving the separated strands in and out. “Yon is the grandest loper in all of Atriia, skilled at trickery. So trick the ganis. Tell him yon is ill.”

Christine sighed, looking to where Tressa sat, bouncing Becca on her knee. “That doesn’t work with him. He can hear untruths fore they are even spoken.”

Eubreena nodded. “Aya. He is skilled at such. As Sola shines, he is.” Pulling the braid to the back, she joined it with the one already dangling from the opposite temple to create a headband. “Mayhap he will be overly wearied this lun after so many ganist gatherings.”

“Eubreena, the ganis does nayat ever get wearied of such.”

Eubreena laughed as she took the seat beside. “We should all have such flustings.” She frowned as she took Christine’s hands. “Yon has dirt under yon nails again. Why do I even bother?”

“I did water copes all morn.”

“Auggh, where is it,” Eubreena growled, rifling through a drawer—then pulling out the nail cleaner. “Does yon wish me to paint them as well? Yon does have one guestive on the morrow.”

“Naya, I—I’m riding ponies in the morn. Yon can paint them after.”

Eubreena grimaced. "I do nayat think it wizened to ride ponies. What of yon babe? Yon must—" Her eyebrows shot up as Christine grasped her hand, pulling it to her lips.

"Yon is so kind to me, Eubreena!"

"Christa, is yon weeping?"

"I just—I want you to know how deeply I care for you."

"Sweet Christa." Eubreena patted her hand with an understanding nod. "Yon is missing Dahla and Bixten. Do nayat fret. They will return."

Christine felt her lips draw tight as she nodded. But the sobs could not be contained—even by the hand she clamped tightly over her mouth.

Eubreena looked about the room as the class of litas turned toward them. "All is well," she said, waving the stares away. "Christa is having brooding skews."

~~~~~~~~~~

He was not wearied in the least. It seemed being cooped up in meetings all day had only stored his energies. He was releasing them into her, watching closely all the while, sharp talcar eyes drilling deep as the headboard beat a steady rhythm upon the wall.

Fear consumed her, her racing heart more than mere exertion. Fearing he would see too much, she pulled him down to her lips—but he merely lapped them like a hound before pulling back to stare down upon her.

She closed her eyes against his probing as she fought to catch the breath escaping on thin feathery moans.

"Christa," he spoke, winded, but stalwart. "Do nayat hide from me, mine flutterfly. Open yon eyes."

"No," she gasped, the only response her laboring lungs could muster.

"Mine are opened," he whispered, running his hands into her hair. "Mine are wide opened," he said, before plummeting to her lips.
~~~~~~~~~~

CHAPTER 22

Becca clapped her hands and squealed as the sictins flitted about, the swarm taking a particular interest in the ponies and the insects they attracted. It was a brilliant day; Sola shining brightly in a pristine sky, a gentle breeze lightly lifting silky manes. With one arm wrapped about Becca's waist, Christine led her pony in the direction of the trees, the reins held tightly in a sweaty palm as her eyes scanned for movement in the distance. Despite the leisurely gait, she sat stiffly, grateful the ganist trailing behind could not see the sweat beading on her brow, nor that trickling down her back. She was grateful for Becca's squealing and giggling, else they might hear the racing of her terrified heart. And she was grateful fear didn't have a scent, lest she be reeking of it. As it was, the strongest scent was that of the green grass being trampled beneath pony hooves. Just beneath it, the faint scent of Becca's hair could be detected, a sweet flowery scent, as could the sun on her skin, a scent clean and pure.

As the trees drew nearer, she thought she detected movement, the sight compelling her to halt her pony. Wiping the sweat from her brow, she turned to face her escorts. "Kindly gentleganist, I'm afraid I need relieve mineself. I will go just in the trees there. If yon would be so kind as to wait for me here."

The lead guard nodded. "Fine then, Mine Lita."

There was an odd tilt to the man's grin. She studied it longer than intended, until her pony snorted, breaking the awkward silence. "Thankings," she handed as she turned her pony about.

The pony's nostrils flared as it approached the trees. Raising its head, it perked its ears forward. Christine looked over her shoulder at the men grouped together, all watching from afar, and all exhibiting the same forced grin.

It was her pony's skittish prance that turned Christine's head back around to find a man standing at the wood's edge mere feet away. She clutched Becca close as he moved forward wearing the same forced grin as those behind her.

"Mine Lor," she breathed as he took hold of the bridle.

His grin broadened. "Greetings, Christa. Is yon enjoying yon riding, then?"

Her eyes darted to the trees as more men materialized, Kynneth and Reesal among them.

"It is one fine sol for such," he said, reaching up for Becca. She went to him readily, reaching down, then giggling as he gave her a few playful shakes before tucking her into the crook of his arm. "Come," he said, extending his hand to Christine and motioning to the trees with his head. "There is something yon must note."

Her breaths had stopped, a throat constricted in fear refusing to let air in. Along with her breath, she held her place, peering longingly to the trees. It was wrong, all of it—the blue skies, the green trees, the flitting sictins, his forced smile. All blurred as her eyes welled. With no air to force the word out, she could only shake her head in response.

"I must insist," he said, the smile dropping from his face.

CHAPTER 23

"Christa, do nayat weep. Yon is safe now," Eubreena assured, rubbing briskly at her back.

"Naya!" Christine wailed, lifting her face from the pillow. "He did drop them all! All of them!"

"Grand," Eubreena hissed with a shudder. "Foul high-hillers!"

Christine let out a wretched wail. "Was nayat high-hillers! Was battlers! LaRossian battlers!"

"Such will lesson the blogarts for trying to stelcher yon. It is nayat safe to go beyond Zerian walls, Christa. Yon must nayat ever do such again. Swear it to me! Swear it on Sola!"

"He hanged them!" She buried her face back into the pillow as fresh tears erupted.

"Too quick one dropping, if yon does ask me. Our Lor showed mercy."

Rolling to her back, Christine sat up to fling the pillow across the room. "Fucking bastard! I hate him!"

"Lie back and take deep breathings," Eubreena insisted, pushing her down to drape the wet cloth across her forehead. "Yon does tremble as one tippet and yon face is blushed. Yon need rest before this lun's guestive."

"Fuck the guestive!" she snapped, yanking the rag from her forehead.

Eubreena motioned to the gilt draped over the chair. "Yon gilt was made special. Calara did spend one allten seaming it, and there are many Lors do wish to lay eyes upon yon wearing it this lun."

Christine clenched her jaw and her fists, beating them on the bed. "Blast the gilt! And blast the fucking Lors! I'm not fucking going!"

~~~~~~~~~~

"Lor Panize," she greeted with a tilt of her head.

He bent over her hand, running his thumb over the scar before gracing it with a kiss. "Mine Lita, yon does look eyegrandly this lun."

She nodded numbly. "Thankings, Mine Lor." Her eyes drifted over his shoulder to the newest self-portrait gifted to her by the Lor of the cas. The blazened-locked beauty draped in a gilt of sheer lavender stood amidst cope bushes, her exquisite wings spread wide. They were the most colorful flutterfly wings she had ever seen, owning every color under Sola's smile.

"I did hear of yon flustings this sol." Lor Panize frowned dutifully. "It is well yon was nayat harmed." He put a hand on the shoulder of the Lor standing stoic beside her. "Thankings to yon honored Lor. Well done. I do nayat think they will try such again, nayat any sol soon."

"Naya."

Lor Panize leaned in to his ear. "I hear many heads line the walls of yon fine cassing this lun, and that yon hand did remove each and every one." He gave his shoulder a hearty thump. "I am glad to be on yon side, ganis. I would nayat wish to be yon enemy."

"Nayor I," Lor Kinsear agreed, moving in to take her hand. "Mine Lita. Yon is even more spellerly than I did picture. Paintings do nayat do yon just."

They were the last words she heard—before falling in faint.

~~~~~~~~~~

A heart was beating, pounding loud in her ears, the rapid rhythm rushing blood through her veins like the Ralling River. Only the sictins could be heard above it as they whizzed by, roaring like fighter jets, their lavender wings shimmering in Sola's smile. It was dazzling where it filtered through the trees, throwing dappled light in her eyes as she spiraled slowly—so to take in all twenty heads impaled high upon poles in a surrounding circle. Sictins were swooping by them like miniature dive-bombers, the high whine of wings piercing in her ears. The sound issuing from her throat was just as piercing. Clutching at her head, she lifted her face to Sola as she shrilled, the ululating echoing through the forest.

Eubreena's sweet song tried to console her.

"'Fret nayat mine fairest babe.

Stave yon tears, mine fairest babe.

All Atriia, she will surent save,

she who hails from one fraigen cave.'"

They joined in on the singing, at first one voice, then a chorus, warped male vocals forced past ravaged necks. Christine covered her ears, clamping tightly with trembling hands. Yet the voices grew stronger.

"'Fret nayat babe, yon tears do stave.

Brazened battler will surent save.'"

"Naya!" She was spinning, and they were glaring with ghastly faces, garish lips moving to the simple song.

"'In Sola's smile her locks will blaze, she who hails from one fraigen cave.'"

"Stop!" Collapsing to the ground, she curled into a fetal position with hands tightly clamped over ears—yet their combined voices seemed to grow louder yet.

"'And all Atriia she will surent save.

All Atriia she will surent saaaaaave…'"

"Christa." Leaning over her, he shook her shoulder, forcing her awake. He smiled as his fingers brushed a lock from her dampened forehead. "How is mine flutterfly, then? Better?"

She struck his nose with a balled fist, the blow catching her off guard as much as it did him. Scrambling away, she narrowly dodged his clutches as she tumbled from the bed—then out the door.

~~~~~~~~~~~

The dark and deserted halls were alive with shifting shadows. They fumbled for her as she fled, frantic fingers snatching at hair, at her lungilt as she stumbled forward. She dared not look back. She didn't have to see the murdering bastard to know he was close. She was being hunted. Fresh kills had the beast lusting for his reward. He meant to devour her in the most primal of fashions, and her screams for mercy would go unheeded, for he was the almighty Lor of the cas.

Her frantic flight took her into the banquet room where she took refuge behind a long panel of drapery—in the corner where shadows were deepest. With a palpitating heart and bated breath, she put one eye to the seam, watching as the dark shadow appeared in the threshold, this followed closely by the foreboding figure, the Lor almighty. Despite his formidable size, he moved silently, a stealthy devon dogging the damned.

He came to a halt just within the entrance, and eyes like two shiny black stones swept the room. They fell upon the statue—that carved in the image of the most famed lita in all of Atriia. He approached it, a frown furrowing his brow as he pondered on the hardest of stone chiseled to resemble the softest of flesh. He stepped close to run a feathery fingertip along one cheek and then over to lips parted prettily.

The newest portrait captured his attention, that fashioned from his fantasies. "Flutterfly," he whispered, "yon can nayat go far with wings so clipped."

Fuck you!

Though the words were uttered only in her mind, he swiveled toward her, his attention drawn as if shouted aloud. She shivered at his approach, steps slow and measured—a predator stalking prey.

"Christa."

She closed her eyes at the cajoling whisper.

"I would nayat ever harm yon, Christa."

Her eyes snapped open as he snatched open the drapes.
~~~~~~~~~~~

"There is mine eyegrandly flutterfly."

Releasing a shuddering sigh, she brushed at a tear as she shook her head. "How eyegrandly is one flutterfly with naya wings? It's only a body."

"Yon is nayat only one body to me, Mine Christa."

"Yes I am," she spoke, hating that her voice quivered. "Yon has ripped off mine wings, has ripped out mine heart—shredded mine soul. That leaves only mine body."

He removed the blood trickling from his nose with his thumb. "Sol?"

She grinned. "Soul. One thing yon was born without. One thing yon will nayat ever own. It is what differs one ganis from one devon."

"If I am one devon for wishing to keep yon safe, then so be it." Lifting a hand, he ran the back of it down one tear-moistened cheek, and she shrank back at the touch, despising the hand which had beheaded twenty good men mere turnings earlier.

He frowned at her reaction. "Yon heart has been wounded—but it will mesh. And it will come back to me. It does know, deep down, I did only what needed be done."

"Their heads needed to be hacked off!"

He drew his shoulders back. "It is one lessoning to all. One does nayat come into mine hailing to stelcher what is mine."

"I am nayat yours! Mine heart will never belong to you, as Sola shines!"

His eyes ran the length of her. "Naya, such belongs to yon brathern, does it nayat?" He leaned close to her ear as if someone might hear. "The blogart did nayat heed yon warning, or mine own. He boards close, just off the skirts of mine cassing, waiting for *his* chancing to stelcher what is mine. One true devon would nayat think twice to place his head beside the others. Is such yon wishing, Christa?"

Dropping her eyes to his feet, she shook her head.

"Fine," he said, stepping back to extend his hand. "Back to mine bunker, flutterfly. I do so wish to claim the only part left to me."

CHAPTER 24

Becca's hair was dancing in Sola's smile, a shimmering shimmy.

"Naya, Becca," Christine warned when the child moved close to a cope bush covered in neon-orange shalias. "Ouchy. Sharp."

Undeterred, Becca whined and stomped in place, pouting and pointing to one of the bright beauties.

"Fine, then. Here," Christine said, carefully snapping off the flower head and handing it to her.

With a wide grin, Becca smashed it into her nose and inhaled, then proceeded to speak of how amazing it smelled, though the words were mere gibberish.

Christine grinned at the valiant attempt at communication. "Aya, eycgrandly," she agreed—then continued to trail along behind Becca as she meandered along the new trails.

As the child wandered, Christine's mind did as well—to thoughts she'd been trying to avoid—to Kyle, hating that she had hurt him, and praying that he could move on and be happy. To her mother and sister, both of whom she'd caused so much pain, hoping they could forgive her. To Sam, hoping that he was safe and that he had enough sense to stay away. To Dahla and Bixten, hating—yet hoping—that she might never see them again.

She brushed at a tear, just one of the many which had been plaguing her for days. Her magical garden, even, could not ease her pain. Not the birds testing the branches of the young trees, swaying precariously on limber limbs. Not the bumbles buzzing about the cope bushes, nor the sictins dipping and diving. Especially not the flutterflies flitting from one shalia to another. And certainly not the ganis in the straw hat, he placing the last few stones in the rambling footpaths.

Swiping at tears and swallowing down emptiness, Christine looked to the stone-carver who was busy rap-tap-tapping with hammer and chisel, then to Ervine and his two aides who were busy trying to wrestle a huge cloud tree to its hole. They had enlisted her two guardsmen to lend hand, and still they struggled.

When Becca climbed upon a bench to dismantle her shalia, Christine took the seat beside to watch numbly as petals fluttered to the ground. She felt an affinity to the cope, its delicate petals being peeled away one by one. Soon there would be nothing left but a stark stem. And in no time, that too would shrivel away and crumble to dust. She felt it inside—the withering. Every time he parted her lips, every time he parted her legs. And he did both with frequency since the savage slaughter. The fact that he had hacked off the heads of twenty decent men to keep her in his bunker had not seemed to ruin his appetite as it had hers.

"Mine Lita."

She jumped, throwing a hand over her heart. "Of all Atriia!"

"Apologies, Mine Lita," the stone-layer said, removing his hat to bow his head. "I—there are stones on mine carry yon must note. The, uh…coloring is much darker than the others."

Shielding her eyes against Sola's smile, Christine squinted up at the man. His face was sweaty and flushed, his jaw tense. "Darker?"

He shifted, shooting a nervous glance to Becca who was swinging her legs as she peeled away the last remaining petals. "One coloring is differed. I do nayat think I should use such."

"Fine, then," she said, standing to prop Becca upon her hip. Following silently, she focused on the back of the man who had delivered more than stones when last they'd spoken. He had unwittingly delivered the death of twenty LaRossian battlers.

"Yon does work loner, this sol," she pointed out.

"He is one devon," he replied without turning around.

Christine felt her heart skip into a bouncing trot. "Aya."

"Climb on mine carry, Mine Lita, and yon will nayat ever lay eyes upon him again."

She stopped in her tracks, her heart instantly galloping. “Is yon skewed!”

He turned to face her. “The blogart will nayat expect such so soon.”

“He will add yon head to those at Zeria’s gates!”

“So let him,” he growled, his eyes blazing. “I will be proud to lose mine head for the lita did drop PacMattin, same devon did drop mine lita, mine litar,” he said, his eyes dropping down to where Becca rested on her hip. “I was away when SalCossin did fall to his battlean—laying blasted stones.”

“I—I’m very sorry. But I still do nayat wish yon dropped on mine accounting.”

He glanced toward the guardsganist. They were struggling with the giant burlap-wrapped root-ball, inching it toward its destination. “I do nayat plan on dropping this sol,” he assured her. “This plan will nayat fail like the first, but we must move quickly,” he urged, pointing to the wagon.

She looked down upon the child perched upon her hip. Her hair was dancing gaily in Sola’s smile, a radiant rhumba. She held a stark stem in her hand.

“Becca, does you wish to play hide and find?”

A bright smile lit Becca’s face as she nodded. Tossing the stripped cope to the ground, she clapped her tiny hands.

~~~~~~~~~~

“Shhh, Becca, hide, hide.”

Becca pouted, then lay her head back in her mother’s lap.

Curled in the back of the carry, Christine tried to rein in her racing heart, tried to listen over it for the sounds of trouble. She could hear nothing above the clip-clop of pony hooves and the rattling of wagon chains.

They’d passed the first checkpoint without incident. The bridge guards had been lax, barely lifting the tarpaulin and not bothering to pull it beyond the barrier of stone-filled crates where the stowaways
~~~~~~~~~~

lie hidden.

Those at the cassing gates would be far more thorough. If they even made it that far, which seemed highly improbable with them trundling along at a snail's pace.

She was confused that he was in no hurry, confused further when they stopped much sooner than expected, and the covering was peeled away.

"Quickly," he said, extending his hand.

Sitting up, she hugged Becca close as she studied the small cottage nestled in a clump of trees. "What is this?"

"The last place yon Lor will search."

Lifting Becca, she carefully handed her over the side. "We're still in Zeria."

"Aya," he said as he took Becca. "Lor Zeria will search to the ends of Atriia." Extending his hand, he helped Christine down. "He will nayat think to search under his very nose."

"What of the hounds?" she asked as she grasped Becca's hand. "Surent they will find me here."

"I will take care of the hounds," he said, reaching into the back of the wagon and fishing out a package. He held it up with a wry grin. "Swill oil will draw them away. Now, quickly," he said, pointing to the small cottage. A man had opened the door and was patiently waiting for her. "Yon will hide here the next few sols," he informed as he re-fastened the tarpaulin then clambered back to the driver's seat with his package in tow. "Sola be with yon, Mine Lita."

~~~~~~~~~~

"Blast!"

The stately woman bowed her head regally. "Mine Lita."

Christine clutched tightly to Becca as she eyed the woman—her flawless skin, her hair darkened by socket root. "Sherva!"

"Yon is pallored, Mine Lita. Is yon nayat pleased to note me?"

Christine looked over her shoulder to the large ganis blocking the door, his face set in a smug grin that matched Sherva's. She
~~~~~~~~~~

recognized him instantly up close—the ganis from Woroff Woodland—the cruel face, the cold, deep-set eyes. He riveted her with these same, his grin growing wider.

"This is Tarrig," Sherva introduced. "Tarrig Trost. Yon may know the callen. Though he does also go by Boskiel."

Christine looked back to the tall man with his arms folded firmly across his chest. Though not near as dashing as his brathern had been, there were similar features, the dark hair and the tanned skin—and a similar dangling earing. His eyes were reminiscent of the devon PacMattin's. Though they were dark as PacMattin's had been light—they held the same eerie emptiness.

Sherva gave a smug nod. "Tarrig is also one loper, same as yonself. I call him one Loper of LaRosse." She tittered, tickled at her own cleverness. "He has been loping as one LaRossian battler. It was being whispered LaRosse did mean to reclaim yon. I did think I could use such to mine vantaging."

Christine felt the traitorous tears welling. "Was yon did hire those ganist to hunt me."

Sherva's grin disappeared as she pulled her shoulders back. "Was it yon thinking yon could come into mine cassing, into mine very hailing, throw me in onc keeper, then ride away into Sola's smile? Those are mine kin, bligart. Mine own blood." She lifted her chin to stare down her nose at Christine. "Tarrig here did also have blood in Rostivane—till yon did drop him down, yon and yon troller. I made certain Kaltica did meet his fating as was fit. Now yon will meet yon own."

Christine clutched Rebecca tight as the ganis glowered at her, one who had never asked nicely for anything in his life.

Sherva lifted the curtain, peeking out at the faint sound of hounds in the distance. "Searching has begun alreadied, then. Do nayat worry, Mine Lita. Mas Holten will lead the hounds away. The blogart does think hisself aiding LaRosse." She let the curtain fall back into place. "It was wisened, was it nayat, to strike while the Zerian Lor was busied gloating in the victory I did hand him?"

"Was yon did warn him of mine escaping?"

Sherva stuck a finger to her own chin and pursed her lips as if to ponder the question. "Mayhap."

"Sherva, was the same gloating Zerian Lor did force me to order yon dropping, as Sola shines! I did nayat wish to do such!"

"Then one Zerian Lor does show greater mercy then yonself. Yon would have me rot in one keeper the rest of mine sols."

"I knew yon brathern would nayat treat yon badly!"

"Did yon think he would drop me down—his own sasturn?" She shook her head. "Now I live exiled, mine hailing gone to me forever."

"Pleadings, Sherva. Mine babe."

The dark-haired Sherva held out her hands, beckoning for Becca, and a brief struggle ensued, with Tarrig stepping in to wrestle the child away.

"How is mine precious babe," Sherva cooed, propping Becca upon her hip to kiss an alabaster cheek. "How I did miss yon."

Becca remembered Sherva despite the dyed hair. She giggled, showing off all her new baby teeth as she pointed a pudgy finger at a dangling earring.

"I will pardon you! I own the standing to do such! Yon will be free to return to Rostivane!"

Sherva grasped Becca's grasping fingers and chomped on them, making the babe squeal and giggle. "Last we met, yon did break mine nose," she said, leaning in to place a peck on the top of Becca's head.

With her attention on the child, Christine did not see the blow coming, Tarrig's elbow snapping her nose and landing her on the floor in a broken heap.

CHAPTER 25

She came awake slowly, her eyes opening to a filmy haze. Her own bare feet came into focus first, then the hem of her gilt, saturated in blood. Her legs were not supporting her. It was the ropes which held her up, those wound round her wrists and stretched tight between two posts.

She swallowed down a mouthful of blood and weakly lifted her chin from her chest. The pain seemed distant, as did her thoughts. Darkness had fallen, enticing shadows into the room. It was a kitchen, dining, living, and bedroom, all in one. The low-burning sconce on the wall showed Sherva sitting in a rocker at the opposite side of the room, her eyes closed as she rocked a sleeping Becca. The Loper of LaRosse sat at the table preparing a snack. Through the haze, she watched as he carved several slices from a froma wedge and arranged them neatly on a crusty slice of bread. Much of the crust crumbled to the front of his shirt as he folded the slice in half and took an enormous bite, three quarters of the sandwich disappearing in an instant. It seemed he barely began to chew, when he shoved in the remainder. With cheeks crammed full, he retrieved his blade to prepare another, pulling the froma wedge close to carve.

"Ah, Tarrig, she has wakened."

With a growl, he gulped down the food, then plunged his blade into the froma wedge so to retrieve the whip draped over the back of his chair.

"Wait," Sherva ordered. "She will only fall to faint again. I wish for her to feel the pain, as I do every grain of every turning—banished from mine hailing, from all I have ever known."

Focusing on Becca's peaceful face, Christine tried to stay conscious. She knew the back of her gilt was gone, shredded by the savage bite of the whip. She knew her back was shredded as well. Her sanity was not much better. It was only Becca's sweet face which kept her from jumping over the enticing edge.

"I could nayat birth babes," Sherva confided as she stroked Becca's hair. "It was nayat mine fating. Such is why Sola brought yon and yon precious lia to mine cassing. I am surent of such. She does work in odd ways, does she nayat?" Leaning down, she kissed Becca's head. "If I must live the rest of mine life in hiding, least I will have mine litar to keep me company." She grinned blissfully. "I did know from the grain I set eyes upon her, she would be mine."

Christine tried to implore to Sherva, but the gag permitted only a pathetic moaning.

Sherva motioned to Tarrig. "Ten," she ordered, shifting Becca to procure a more comfortable position for the show forthcoming. Lastly, she repositioned the blanket over the babe's ears so it might muffle the sounds of the whip—and that of her malla's muffled cries.

~~~~~~~~~~

Eubreena was humming, the sweet lullaby drifting in through the haze. Christine hoisted her chin from her chest, her head listing left, then right. Fighting to hold it upright, she forced her eyes to open.

She could barely make Eubreena out through the haze in the room. She was rocking Becca as she hummed, her cheek resting upon the babe's silky hair.

"Ah, finhap yon is wakened," she whispered so as not to disturb the babe. "I have been waiting to present yon fating." It wasn't Eubreena's voice. And the hair was too dark, the face too thin in the flickering lamplight.

It struck her then. She was no longer stretched between two posts. She was bound to a chair, the ropes wound about her waist. Her hands were bound behind it, her ankles to the legs. She tried to focus on the man who stood in the middle of the room, and on the
~~~~~~~~~~

object at his feet. It was her fating—a crate covered with cloth.

A piercing shrilling sounded when the cover was whipped away, the roggii jumping about the cage in a mad frenzy. Instantly, the haze in her head cleared, and she joined in on the shrilling, a healthy portion of the high-pitched keening managing to seep through the gag.

~~~~~~~~~~

Panting cut through the darkness—tight, panicked huffs rushing in and out of her nose. She could hear the roggii scurrying about the small cubit, could see dark shadows streaking through the puddle of light spilling under the door. Incited by the smell of blood, they were becoming bolder by the minute, even braving tugs at the blood-soaked gilt at her ankles. Her muted screams and thrashing managed to send them away time and again, but lulls between bold advances were becoming briefer.

She jumped at the loud banging as a pounding shook the door. "Mine Lita," Sherva called, her thin voice squeezing through the cracks. "Does yon like yon keeper? I did nayat like mine own. I did think of yon every grain of every turning I did spend in such, did dream of this sol, when yon would suffer for crossing me." She pounded again, making the roggii scamper, several colliding with Christine's legs in their panicked frenzy. "I do so wish I could note with mine own eyes, but I also am spookered by roggii. Foul creatures, are they nayat? And these—these ones are overly hungered," she informed her. "They have nayat supped for five full sols."

Christine struggled against her binds, trying to twist out of ropes tightly secured.

"Brazened Loper of Zeria," the tiny voice taunted. "By the morrow, yon will be roggi dung. I did think yon roggi dung from the first I set eyes upon yon, so it is one just fating." She cackled, the mirth slipping through the cracks much easier than her voice. It echoed about the small cubit, sending the roggii to bouncing off the walls. "Yon honored troller did also end roggi dung," she continued.
~~~~~~~~~~

"I did have his head delivered to mine keeper. One fine gentleganist he was. He did keep me company, did keep the roggii busied. Was such nayat kindly of him?"

Christine strained against the ropes, blackness turning to red as she shrilled strangled obscenities. Her body lurched as she raged, the chair hopping in place as her muscles spasmed. It teetered precariously, then toppled backward. Fire engulfed her as she hit the floor—and her head.

~~~~~~~~~~~

Sola's smile shone warm upon her face. It owned a peaceful scent, one clean and pure. The cream cope she twirled between her fingers owned a scent more pronounced, like peaches and jasmine mixed. She held it to her nose, breathing deeply.

Birds were singing a warbled tune. Someone was humming in accompaniment.

"Mom?"

Her mother was perched upon the bench under the garbona tree, rocking a sleeping Becca. She was stunning as ever, her dark hair gleaming where it cascaded over her shoulders, her skin flawless. She lifted her face to smile warmly, then lifted a hand in greeting.

"Hi." Christine lifted her hand in return. "Do you like mine garden?"

Her mother grinned and nodded. "It is the most eyegrandly garden I have ever noted," she spoke in perfect Atriian. "And yon is the most eyegrandly flutterfly."

Christine peered over her own shoulder at the wings she boasted, the brilliant colors shimmering in Sola's smile. When she looked back, her mother's eyes were shimmering as well, and her voice shimmered when she spoke. "I love you, mine litar."

"I love you more." Christine expanded her wings fully, amazed at the ease with which they moved, then lifted them high till the velvety tips touched. "Take care of mine lia."

"She is *mine* lia, yon foul heap of roggi dung!"
~~~~~~~~~~~

She came awake screaming as tiny daggers ripped flesh from limbs. The roggii scattered at her thrashing, hissing and chattering at a meal disturbed. But they did not refrain for long. They had discovered sup beneath the bloodied gilt, and they hadn't fed in five full sols.

A muted scream sounded as teeth sank into her ankle. Her assailant scurried away as she struggled in the chair. A chattering ensued as another tried to move in on his territory, this escalating to squealing as they fought over the meal. While they squabbled, another braved its way near and nipped at her arm, a painful pinch, then more at her ankles, stabbing jolts of pain.

As she thrashed, it became instantly apparent that the chair had been damaged in the fall—and with the frame compromised, the ropes had loosened.

~~~~~~~~~~

She spotted Becca sleeping on the small bed, wrapped in blankets. The Loper of LaRosse was busy at the table again, but he wasn't supping. The froma wedge and bread loaf had been pushed aside to make room for Sherva. Her gilt was hiked up about her waist where she lie belly-down on the table, gripping its sides as Tarrig stood behind, pumping like a piston. "Aya," Sherva huffed as the table lurched back and forth, its legs on the verge of buckling. "Blast me! Blast me! Sweet Sola, blast me, yon blasted blogart!"

Christine's legs were weak, her determination strong as she crept silently toward them. One of the wooden floorboards groaned beneath her weight, but Tarrig's attentions lie elsewhere.

Sherva spotted her first. Her eyes grew wide as she screamed his name.

Wrenching the blade from the froma wedge, Christine plunged it into his back with two hands and a howl, embedding it to its hilt.

He sent her flying as he lurched to his feet, his arms flailing, attempting to grasp a weapon out of reach. While she was skidding along the floor on her back, he was stumbling sideways, then
~~~~~~~~~~

tumbling over a chair.

Sherva rolled off the table, landing on all fours like a cat, spitting and hissing as several roggii scurried by. By the time she scrambled to her feet, her mouth pulled back in a snarl, Christine was there to greet her.

Round and round they went, crashing about the room, a dance of death. Somewhere on a different plane, Sherva was screaming, Becca was crying, Tarrig was hacking. She could barely hear them over the snarling of the rabid beast that had forced itself inside her brain.

She took Sherva to the floor, then pounced atop, straddling her—strangling her, pressing bloody thumbs into a tender throat. She didn't feel the nails clawing at her wrists, nor the feet kicking at the floor. Worlds away, Sherva was gurgling, Becca was screaming, Tarrig was groaning. She could barely hear them over the guttural growling.

Long after Sherva's struggles had ceased, Christine continued to strangle her, till her body shook with the effort, till the sweat dripped from the tip of her nose. On a different plane, worlds away, Becca was wailing. Christine could barely hear her, for the beast in her brain was howling, an exultant ululating, the victory cry resounding throughout the vast wastelands.

CHAPTER 26

"Dahla!"

Christine's eyes fluttered open long enough to see Eubreena hugging Dahla tight, long enough to realize she was lying in her own bed, belly-down. There was no recollection of how she ended there—only vague memories of wandering along back roads, of clutching Becca to her chest—and of a wagon, a man and his son.

"I did nayat think I would note yon again," Eubreena whispered to Dahla. "I mean—there were whisperings yon may nayat return."

"I would nayat ever leave her," Dahla spoke numbly.

"She has been in and out of sleeping for sols. And naya leexer! Meshganist fear such may harm the babe."

"How badly is it, then?"

Christine felt the sheet lifted from her back.

"Oh, sweet Sola!" Dahla gasped. "This is mine doing! Sweet Sola!"

"Shhh, Dahla!" Eubreena warned in hushed tones. "It is being whispered yon did somehow aid LaRosse. If this be truths, yon must nayat speak of such. Lor Zeria will take yon head."

"Aya!" Dahla wailed. "As he did Sherva's! It does sit at Zerian gates with the others! And Lor Rostivane has been keepered, has yon heard? He could well lose *his* head!"

"Let him, then," Eubreena hissed. "Same as his sasturn, the bligart! The blasted bligart! She did lock Christa in one cubit with roggii! They did sup on her!" She blew her nose, honking loudly.

"Devon!" Dahla spat. "She has always been skewed. Thankings to Sola Becca was nayat harmed. And one babe. We need thank Sola for sparing him as well."

Eubreena sniffled. “Need we?”

“Eubreena, yon does nayat mean such.”

“What if he will nayat fit past her hips. If she drops birthing this babe, as Sola shines, I will do the like!”

“Hush now. We must trust in Sola.”

Eubreena released a desolate sigh. “Why does she hate our Lor so that she would risk all to be rid of him? There is nayathing he would nayat give her. His heart did near rip in two at the noting of her wounded. As Sola shines, I did note it in his eyes.”

“Aya. He is spellered,” Dahla admitted. “But her heart belongs to one other.”

“Fallier,” Eubreena hissed, a shudder in her voice.

Christine felt Dahla’s gentle caress upon her cheek. “I do nayat claim to understand such,” Dahla whispered. “But I did note her weep for him—as if her heart was being ripped from her very chest.”

“I hate him,” Eubreena swore, “he and LaRosse, both. Both blogarts did land her in the hands of devons. If one or the other does try to stelcher her again, I will drop him down mine very self.”

“And I will aid yon,” Dahla vowed.

PART VII

CHAPTER 1

He ran his fingertips over her back, caressing the latticework of scars as he caressed deep within—slow, agonizing strokes. Grasping fistfuls of bedding, she pressed it to her face to muffle the moans, and then the cries as he brought her effortlessly to the peak of devastation yet again. It consumed her in an instant, turning her knees weak, as well as the forearms supporting her weight—these trembling were they were propped upon the mattress to protect the prominent bulge of her belly.

As she struggled to regain composure, he calmly brought his hands around to caress the unborn babe. He gave a deep throated chuckle. "He is kicking me."

"Aya," she huffed, licking dry lips. "For his malla."

Chuckling, he pressed his palm against the spot of impact. "He owns one strong kick."

"He is angered. Yon does disturb his sleeping yet again."

He pressed his palm in deeper. "I am thinking to call yon Deele, mine gan. Kick if yon does like such callen. Ah," he breathed as the baby responded. "Deele it is, then. Am I disturbing yon sleeping, Deele?"

Lowering her forehead to the mattress, Christine closed her eyes, willing the baby to respond.

"Deele is silent," he whispered, sliding his hands to her back yet again, his fingertips gently tracing along the whipping welts. "As are the wintered winds."

His words opened her eyes in an instant, as well as her ears. He was right. The shutters no longer rattled as they had been doing for two cycles straight—the longest two cycles of her life.

"Oh, thankings to Sola," she sighed.

He chuckled as he slid his hands to her hips.

Clamping down on her lip, she grasped handfuls of bedding and locked her wobbly knees, bracing herself for yet another sleepless night.

CHAPTER 2

"One hound did chase one shike," the group recited in unison, reading from the parchments they held before them. It was a large group, too many to seat at the table, so chairs had been brought in, lined in rows like a lecture room. "One shike did kick one hound. One hound did turn to run. One shike did chase one hound."

"Well done," Lessoner Talbot said, removing his glasses to clean the lenses on the cloth in hand. "That is all for this sol's lessoning," he announced. "As yon all does know, in one allten, battlescores will be upon us, so one break is on order. I am certain Zerian battlers will make us proud this seg," he spoke with confidence, and the room responded with scattered applause.

"Five segs did pass so quickly," he mused. Gathering his papers together, he tapped them on the table to align them. "One large crowding is expected this seg, thousands even. Yon will have yon hands filled with preparing. But I trust yon will read if there are grains to spare. Our Lor has been kindly enough to open one bindboarding to all. I gest yon does take vantaging of such."

"Auggh, I hate battlescores," Eubreena grumbled under her breath as she shuffled her papers. "Our cas will be brimmed with guestings for alltens. There will be naya resting for anybody; pleasurers, scullery, seamsewers—me," she sighed.

Tressa stretched her arms out. "Torna was thinking battlescores might be overrid by battlement."

"There will be naya battlement," Eubreena assured her. "The upper Lors have tucked their tails."

Dahla nodded. "One blogart LaRosse is nayat nearly as skilled at uniting his Lors as he did think. They remain divided."

"Aya, while our region does band as one," Eubreena boasted. "Our Lor is truly one skilled leader."

"Thus his title," Tressa pointed out.

"I do naya think it was his skill so much as it was the wintered winds," Christine suggested. "Many long alltens to come to one's senses.

"Mayhap," Tressa agreed. "In any case, we all must contend with battlescores, like it or nayat."

Leaning back in the chair, Dahla rubbed her round belly. "I do think mine babe dreaming of battlescores. He does battle with mine insides."

Christine leaned back to rub her own belly, one of equally impressive proportion. "Mine does sleep soundly."

Dahla gave a tickled titter. "To make up for that lost last lun, surent," she teased.

Eubreena cleared her throat as she tapped the papers on her lap. "Dahla, yon has become quite skilled at painting yon face over these last cycles. Yon does paint it near every sol. Is there any special reasoning?"

Closing her eyes, Dahla leaned her head back, resting it on the chair. "Mayhap."

Christine exchanged glances with Eubreena. Dahla had been spending much of her spare time with Reesal since he'd escorted her back from Ramon, this despite the fact that he was twice her age.

Dahla massaged at her belly, trying to soothe the restless babe. "What if they are birthed on the same sol?"

"It may be close," Eubreena admitted. "Christa's belly has passed the sizing of yon own, even." There was concern in her voice—and in her eyes.

Dahla grinned. "What if they are both ganies, and both with blazened locks? How will we tell them apart?"

"One will have the heart of one Lor, the other one laborer."

They all turned to glare at Ryla where she sat rifling through papers behind them.

"What?" she piped, her eye popping wide.

"Laboring is honest work," Christine intoned. "Can yon speak the same of yon own duties?"

Ryla pulled her shoulders back. "Anybody can sweep and scull. Pleasurers own skills."

"How much skill does it take to lie on yon back?"

Ryla lifted her chin along with her brows. "Yon tell me, Mine Lita. Yon does spend more turnings on yon back then any pleasurer I know."

Several surrounding litas cried out as the slender Ryla was helped to her feet with the aid of Eubreena's large hands twisted in the neck of her gilt. "I will put yon on yon back, yon bligart!" Eubreena growled, leaning so close their noses nearly touched. "Hand apologies this grain!"

Dahla gave a frightened cry as she clutched at her belly. And so did the others cry out at the watery fluid puddling beneath her.

~~~~~~~~~~

Dahla's birthmark was a crude shade of crimson against her pale face. She seemed in the grips of melancholy as she looked down upon the bundled babe sleeping in her arms.

Sliding the chair close, Christine gazed upon him as well. "Yon did well, Dahla. He is most eyegrand."

Dahla nodded. "He does own one birthing mark."

"Aya, but it is small. And it can nayat be noted so low on his back."

Dahla's grin seemed sullen. "I wish mine malla could note him."

"She will, Dahla. She will."

"He owns blazened locks, like his fallar."

Christine felt a strange sensation in her chest, like a band tightening. "Aya." She gently brushed at the fluff of hair still damp from washing.

"And one heart of one laborer," Dahla added dully.

"Dahla, his fallar was one battler. He will be the same, doubtent. Though there is nayathing wrong with being one laborer."
~~~~~~~~~~

Dahla nodded. “Mayhap.” She pulled her eyes away from her babe to peer at Christine. There was a weariness within them, one more than mere physical fatigue. “What is it like to know yon gan will be one Lor one sol?” she asked. “That he will nayat ever labor one sol of his life, will nayat ever want for anything, fear anything or anyone?”

Christine felt the sensation in her chest grow more intense, the band tightening painfully, sending her heart to racing.

Taking Dahla’s hand, she leaned close. “Sweet Dahla—you tell me.”

CHAPTER 3

Slipping quietly into the bunker, he slid close to press against her back, his hand coming around to caress the swell of her belly. After a full day of greeting guests and overseeing battlescores protocol, she prayed he was too exhausted for anything else.

"Is Dahla off to Ramon, then?" he whispered against her ear.

"Aya. Thankings, Mine Lor."

"I do still think one allten overly young for traveling."

"Aya, but Dahla's malla does nayat have much longer."

His fingertips moved to the cropping of scars dimpling her right arm—the markings of roggii teeth imprinted permanently into her flesh—then upward to the sleeve of her lungilt, sliding it from her shoulder.

"I do nayat have much longer, either."

"Till yon birthing?" he breathed between tender kisses along her bared shoulder.

"Till mine dropping."

His affections halted instantly. "Christa, I have gathered the finest meshganist from every region."

"Meshganis Tieslen?"

He sighed heavily.

Rolling to her back, she placed her hands on the mountain of belly and met his eyes in the darkness. "If something is to go wrong, the meshganist must save our babe. Promise me, Jerrod. Do nayat let us both drop. And promise me, if I am to drop, mine lia will be returned to her fallar."

He flopped to his back with a disgusted snarl.

"Yon will have yon child. He should have his. And I wish it in scribing."

Throwing the blankets aside, he sat up on the edge of the bed to rake his fingers through his hair. With a frustrated growl, he stood and moved to the desk. "I will bring Tieslen in if such will put yon brain at ease," he grumbled as he poured spirits.

"Aya, it will. But if he can nayat spare me, yon must keep yon promise. Naya harm is to befall Fallier. And I wish him to raise Becca—and Bixten. Dahla has promised she will remain here to raise mine babe alongside her own."

"*Yon* will be here to raise him!" he growled.

"Mayhap, but if—"

"Fine!" he snapped, slamming the mug down. "It is done!"

CHAPTER 4

With hands folded across the ample swell of her belly, she peered out over fields crowded with commotion; colorful flags whipping, proud ponies prancing, clarion horns trumpeting, excited spectators rumbling. Thousands lined the sides of the fields for the much anticipated event, some seated on wagons, others on chairs and benches hauled in, most standing. An occasional chant broke out as flags were waved and mugs were raised, the proud boasting of loyal supporters, many of who had been celebrating the upcoming event for sols.

They had gathered to witness a coveted competition which only took place once every five segs. It consisted of only five categories; arrow arcing, blade battles on ponyback, blade battles on foot, blade and ax throwing, and jabbing—Atriia's version of jousting. Only five contestants per category per cassing were permitted to contend.

The competitors had been separated into groups of twenty-five, the finest from each cassing, each group sporting their colors in the forms of flags and clothing—vests and leggings specially made for the grand occasion. Those to be competing on this day were weighted down with resplendent armor—polished chest and shoulder plates reflecting Sola's smile, helmets sporting majestic plumes dyed to reflect the cassing colors, shields reflecting the cassing crests. The ponies were shielded in armor as well, metal molded to faces from forehead to muzzle, and across broad chests and rounded rumps, and down the crest of arched necks from forelock to withers. Colorful plumes bobbed on their heads to match those of their riders and more dangled the length of elaborately embossed saddles.

"It is one fine sol for battlescores," Kynneth spoke from where he sat beside her on the lavish platform built special for the occasion. It was covered in canvas bearing the colors of Zeria—black and crimson—and flying flags bearing the cassing crest—Sola with radiating rays.

"It's so grand to have yon back, Kynneth," Christine quipped. "Our Lor has been keeping yon busy. Doing his dirty work, doubtent. I can't begin to speak of how I've missed yon."

He chuckled as he looked out over the excited ceremonies. "And I yon, Mine Lita."

True to Kynneth's comment, it was a beautiful day. Sola was smiling brightly as hundreds of flags sailed on her gentle breath. Drawn by the insects drawn by the horses, sictins were plentiful, dipping and diving in every direction. Even a colorful flutterfly flitted by on occasion.

Christine located the white pony, the Lor of Zeria conferring with the other Lors as they officiated the opening of the much anticipated event.

"Yon is eyegrandly, Christa," Kynneth whispered, leaning close. "Brooding suits yon."

She turned her face away from him. "If I am to drop while birthing, I wish Luckied Lita returned to Fallier."

He gave a grunt. "I will note her dropped first."

With a sigh, she reached out to the hand that rested upon the arm of his plush chair, running her finger along the scar that matched her own. "If yon does care for me at all, Kynneth, yon will do such."

His eyes fell to the hand toying with his own, his jaw stiffening.

"Jerrod has promised to hand Becca and Bixten to him. He has put such to parchment," she added. "But, mayhap yon brathern does care for me more than yonself."

"Fine, then," he said, pulling his hand away to join the other in his lap. "Yon is truly skilled, loper."

She grinned. "Speaking of skills, why is yon nayat down on one field? I have noted yon skills at arcing."

"Such is nayat permitted," he said with a scowl. "I am next in line to one title of Lor of Zeria."

She let out a laugh. "Lor Kynneth Zeria. Does yon dream of such title?"

"I do nayat wish one blasted title," he grumbled, stretching out his long legs. "It is more flustings than nayat. And Leader of Lors is worsened yet. To constant lend ears to fellow Lors blowing over nayathing. Hand me one title does place me one standing above so I might keep them in order, and I might sider such."

"Ah, one king."

He gave her a sideways glance. "King?"

"In mine hailing, a king does stand above all the others. Even the Lors would bow before yon. King Kynneth," she mused. "It does have a nice ring."

The crowd commenced to cheering as the Lors dispersed, each leading their contenders to their assigned positions. Trumpets sounded as five from each group assembled in the center of the field where various targets awaited blade throwing.

"Let battlescores begin," the herald shouted.

The crowd erupted.

~~~~~~~~~~

Every Lor of the lower region was in attendance at the grand guestive, just one of the many to be held throughout the competition. It seemed every pleasurer was in attendance as well, parading about the room decked in the finest of gilts and sporting the finest of jewelwear. And each was flaunting ample portions of exposed bosoms above dainty, diminutive waists.

Her own waist seemed stretched to beyond physical possibility where it rested upon her thighs beneath the table. With the Lor of Zeria on one side and his brathern on the other, she hadn't much of an appetite, merely pushing the food around on her plate.

"Sola has blessed us with grand weather, least." Lor Lazette was
~~~~~~~~~~

saying. "Does yon recall last battlescores? Raining did fall near every sol."

The assembled Lors grumbled at the memory, nodding their heads in unison.

"And Sola does bless us with yon presence," he directed to Christine. "Mine ganist feel honored that yon is to present the medalings."

The surrounding Lors nodded affirmation.

"The honoring is mine," she said with a grin.

"It seems Alabas will be receiving two of such medalings. Well done," Kynneth said, raising his mug to its Lor, and the surrounding Lors raised theirs in unison, all offering words of congratulations. "Two of five medalings to one cassing," Kynneth mused. "All did expect Roddenson to medal in blade throwing, but where did yon find the railed ganis with such arcing skills? To hit his mark center three tries straight, and at full pony speed. Overly luckied, surent."

"Overly skilled," Lor Alabas corrected, his face flushed with pride and spirits mixed. "He is newly hired, but it is spoken he does rarely miss his mark."

"He does seem overly young to own such skills," Lor Zeria stated. "Is he as skilled with blade?"

"Auggh, naya," Lor Alabas assured him, waving off such a notion. "He does own one bad leg and does nayat do well on his feet. I do think one lita could handle one blade better. Naya offending tended, Mine Lita," he offered to Christine with an embarrassed grin, sending those at the table to chuckling.

"Does yon have any new hirings for jabbing?" Lor Zeria asked as he sawed off a large bite of shike flay and routed it to his mouth.

"Do nayat give his callen if yon does," Kynneth warned, "lest he come up missing fore the morn. Mine brathern does nayat take well to defeating."

Booming male laughter filled the room.

"I can attest to such," Reesal imparted. "As can any ganis ever to play tookets with him."

Kynneth found this particularly amusing, practically choking on his food. Hastily locating his mug, he washed it down with spirits.

"Lor Zeria," Sheele spoke over his shoulder, seeming to materialize from thin air. Leaning into his Lor's ear, he imparted whispered words as he placed a folded parchment in his hand.

Unfolding the letter carefully, the Lor skimmed over it—then refolded it, setting his jaw rigidly as he turned to Christine. His eyes dropped as he took her hand, lifting it to his lips. "Mine apologies, Christa," he spoke sadly. "I did fear one allten overly young for traveling."

~~~~~~~~~~

Even from miles away, the faint sound of trumpets could be heard drifting up from the valley where battlescores continued.

"Becca, come to malla."

Grasping Becca's hand, Christine watched with a heavy heart as the carry lumbered into the courtyard.

"Sweet Sola," Eubreena whispered, inching closer to Christine as she dabbed at her eyes with a cloth.

Tressa crowded in from the other side, her hands wringing a hanky as she sniveled. "I do nayat know what to speak to her."

"Just be there for her, Tressa," Christine offered. "Hold her, weep with her. That is all we can do."

"I did know it was overly soon," Eubreena sniveled. "I did tell her such."

"Hush now. She did lose her babe and her malla two sols apart. We need be strong for her."

Christine looked to where Reesal stood with two other ganist. His face was pale as he watched the carriage come to a halt.

Dahla's face was paler yet as she exited with numb, awkward steps.

When Becca broke away with a squeal, Dahla scooped her up, hugging tight, her pale face painted with nothing but pain. Christine approached her, putting her arms about the two of them, squeezing tight.
~~~~~~~~~~

"Sweet Dahla. Sweet, sweet Dahla," she whispered in her ear. "Be strong. Does yon feel the sizing of mine belly? Soon yon will be malla to the next Lor of Zeria."

Dahla hugged back fiercely as she began to weep.

CHAPTER 5

With fingers interlaced, Christine supported the weight of her enormous belly, trying to suppress the nausea which had been plaguing her since she'd wakened. Standing between the tall Zeria bratherns, she felt two feet tall and five feet wide. Tilting her face to Sola, she soaked in her soothing warmth.

Sola's smile was beaming for the medal ceremony, reflecting off the battle armor of the five victors who stood ready to receive their honors. The gentle breeze fluttering a thousand flags and ruffling countless colorful plumes was of a perfect temperature; not too cold that coats were needed, yet not so hot that the ganist were sweating beneath their armor. Countless fire pits were billowing white smoke—meat roasting in preparation for the feasting that was to follow. Combined aromas of shike, goser, and crout were adrift.

Sliding the tie from the scroll, the Leader of Lors unrolled the parchment and held it at arm's length. "Mas Lucas Roddenson of Alabas," he recited, his deep imperious voice hushing the murmurs of the crowd. "Yon does claim one honored title of most skilled blade thrower of one lower region—again," he added with a grin and a reverent bow of his head.

The crowd erupted, the rowdiest cheers coming from the fellow competitors who surrounded them. They chanted his name and beat on their chest plates as he stepped forward and removed his helmet. His face was flushed as he bent low to receive his metal.

Taking the tendered metal from Kynneth, Christine placed it over the head bowed before her. "As Sola shines," she proclaimed, and the crowd repeated the mantra, thousands of voices in unison echoing throughout the valley.

Roddenson was beaming as he kissed his metal and accepted his scroll. Thumping the Leader of Lors on the shoulder, he offered profuse thankings while grinning with giddy adoration.

Christine ran a hand along her brow, one feeling suddenly clammy. The celebratory clapping and cheering and whistling seemed distant.

Kynneth leaned close. "Is yon well, Christa?"

"Mas Surad Litagan, of Alabas," the adored Leader of Lors read from the new scroll in hand. "Yon does claim one honored title of most skilled arcer in one lower region. Well done, gani," Lor Zeria praised.

A ruckus resounded throughout the valley as he stepped forward. Pulling off his helmet, he bowed before her.

"As Sola shines," Christine spoke, placing the ribbon over his head.

There was a frightened look in the boy's brown eyes as he stood to face her, and Christine felt a similar expression come over her own face as she took in the locks cut short and dyed dark.

"They have him keepered, Mine Lita," the boy rushed out, raising his voice to be heard above the cheers. "Hannen—in Alabas, chained and laboring in the stone yards, whipped and beaten every sol! He will drop if yon—" He gasped as the tip of a blade flicked across his throat, the Lor of Zeria silencing him in an instant. Dropping to his knees, the boy clutched at his neck as his mouth tried to finish the sentence.

It was Kynneth who ended any further disclosures, his boot on a shoulder pushing the boy to the ground so he could push his blade through his heart.

A stunned hush fell over the crowd.

Christine clutched her cramping belly. A scream was lost somewhere inside, entrapped and desperate to escape. Hands helped her to the ground as her body convulsed—her legs kicking and arms flailing. She fought to direct the scream to her throat, but it was bent upon ravaging her insides first. Only upon having done so to its satisfaction, did it leave on a mere breathless whisper.

"Sura…"

CHAPTER 6

Christine squeezed Dahla's hand as the band across her belly tightened. Pulling breaths in and out in quick succession, she fixated on Neema who lay in the corner with her head resting on her paws, her brown eyes shifting nervously about the room.

Dahla jumped up as Lor Zeria entered the room in a rush. The three meshganist jumped up as well, all attempting to speak at once.

"Her laboring is going well," Meshganis Uldin spoke over the others.

"Is he coming?" Christine huffed.

The Lor lowered himself to the edge of the bed, reaching for her hand.

She yanked it away with a snarl. "Is he coming!"

He raked his hand through his hair. "I have sent for him. Alabas is one full sol's traveling, one way. It will be two sol's fore he arrives."

"Fine, then. I'll wait." She turned her face away from him and toward Eubreena who sat on the opposite side of the bed with a washcloth in her hands. "Have Becca readied," she ordered, "and Bixten. They will be leaving with Fallier when he arrives."

"Christa," the Lor spoke, "I did swear to hand them over only if—"

"Yon did swear many things!" she screamed. "Yon did swear on Sola yon would nayat harm him! On Sola!"

"I had naya choosing. The blogart would nayat stay away."

"Yon had naya aimings of handing over Becca!"

"Christa—"

"I want it in scribing! I wish to place mine marking before Saker

Odium! And where is Tieslen?"

"These are the most skilled meshganist in our lower region."

"One other promise broken, then," she wept.

Standing, he moved to the bureau to pour himself a mug of spirits. "I did nayat know it was his litar. I did nayat know it was one lita, even. What lita arcs arrows like that?"

Burying her face in her hands, Christine wept.

~~~~~~~~~~

Eubreena stirred beside her as she began to pant yet again. Rolling to her side, Christine tried frantically to steady her breaths while Eubreena massaged her cramping back as she'd been doing throughout the lun.

Meshganis Uldin stirred as well where he rested in the chair, reaching to the night-stand to turn the hourglass. "One turning," he mumbled. "Mounds should be dropping between laborings, and they are nayat."

Lor Zeria stood from where he sat at the bureau to rub hands wearily over his face. "Is there nayathing we can do?"

"Tieslen," she pleaded as the pain ebbed.

"She speaks Tieslen," Eubreena repeated.

The Lor raked the hair back from his face with an angry growl. "So he can rip her wide!"

"Naya," the meshganis stressed. "Of all Atriia! We can nayat be hasty. Some litas have longer laborings than others."

~~~~~~~~~~

"Shhh, Becca. Malla is sleeping," Dahla whispered.

Christine opened her eyes and smiled at Becca where she stood at the side of the bed, her chin resting upon the mattress. Her blue eyes were resonating concern for her sleeping malla.

Patting the bed, Christine prompted her to climb aboard with Dahla's assistance. The child was flaunting all her new baby teeth as she lie down beside her malla so their faces were mere inches apart.

"Sweet Becca," she spoke weakly, brushing her hair with trembling fingers. "I love you, mine babe."

"Malla."

Dahla's jaw dropped. "She spoke malla, Christa!"

Christine grinned. "Aya, malla."

"Malla," Becca repeated with a proud nod.

"Can yon speak fallar?" Christine asked, trailing a finger down one inviolate ivory cheek. "You have his eyes."

Becca giggled, then scrambled from the bed, of a mind to rummage through the toy trunk.

Christine took Dahla's hand as she seated herself on the bed's edge. "Dahla, yon must speak with Reesal. Jerrod may listen to him. He must bring in Tieslen. I have been laboring one full sol. We can nayat allow the babe to drop."

"Reesal has gone to escort Fallier from Alabas." She rubbed Christine's hand between her own. "Yon hand is cold."

Christine looked to where three meshganist sat eating firstsup at the tookets table brought in. "Dahla, I wish to note Bixten."

Dahla fought back tears as she nodded. "Aya, Mine Lita. I will have him brought in." She broke suddenly, burying her face in her hands. "Kynneth did drop mine only friend," she wept. "Pleadings do nayat leave me here loner."

Christine reclaimed her hand, pulling it to her lips. "Yon will nayat be loner, Dahla. Yon has Eubreena. And Tressa—and Reesal. He is spellered, Dahla. I do note it plain. Yon must—" She bristled as Kynneth appeared in the doorway. "What do you want! Has yon come to watch me drop, then! Mayhap yon will drive yon blade through mine heart as well! Mayhap Dahla's!"

"Pleadings, Mine Mas," Meshganis Uldin urged, moving to the door. "Yon should leave us."

"Yes, leave us! Go find someone else to drop, blogart!" she shrieked as he disappeared from sight. "Mayhap yon brathern can help you!"

"Dahla, Dahla," she groaned, groping for Dahla's hand as the band about her belly began to constrict and the muscles in her back to cramp.

~~~~~~~~~~

She leaned heavily on Eubreena and Dahla as they escorted her back from the lavatory. Lowering herself to the edge of the bed, she allowed Eubreena to lift her legs and swivel her onto the bed. Rushing to the other side, Dahla arranged the pillows, lifting her head gingerly to slide them under.

The Lor of Zeria seated himself beside her, waiting patiently for her to catch her breath, then held the cup steady as she sipped water.

"That will be the last trip," Eubreena informed her Lor. "She has naya strength left."

"The meshganist claim it is fine for her to move about."

A mixture of sob and laugh escaped Eubreena. "The meshganist do nayathing but prod her belly and scratch at heads. Apologies, Mine Lor, but—Christa is dropping fore our very eyes. Nearly two sols and her laborings are still one turning spaced! One babe is stuck! She did speak this would happen! Sweet Sola!"

"Eubreena," Christine whispered, wetting dry lips with her tongue and reaching weakly for her hand. "Sing to me, mine friend."

~~~~~~~~~~

Birds were trilling, the sweet warbling accompanied by the precious peeping of newly hatched chicks. The sun was shining, reflecting off their wings as they plummeted to the ground to pluck plump worms from the dewy grass before heading back to nests where necks stretched tall and beaks stretched wide. As she watched, a menagerie of shalias came to life, the buds burgeoning to blooms—high in trees, low in bushes, clustered on trellises. Gosers waddled about, honking out an occasional command to keep the goserlings marching behind in orderly fashion. Newly hatched sictins were trying out their wings, zipping and dipping in perilous nosedives. Flutterflies were emerging from cramped cocoons, spreading resplendent wings to dry in Sola's warm smile.

With fingers laced, she supported her round belly as she strolled along the path, reveling in the fruits of her labor.

"Labor."

Christine stopped, peering around for the owner of the voice.

"You're in labor."

She spun around, coming face to face with Sura. Her hair was long again and glimmering like spun gold.

"You're in labor, Christa." Taking her hand, Sura brought it to her lips. "Only mine fallar can save yon babe," she spoke sadly.

"Sweet Sura," Christine breathed, squeezing her hands. "One Lor of Zeria is afeared of him."

"Hannen will convince him. Does yon hear me, Christa? Christa…"

"Christa."

She felt her hand lifted, then the caress of soft lips.

She opened her eyes to slits. "Hannen," she breathed weakly.

"Aya. I'm here, Christa."

"Hannen." His face was thin and bruised, one eye swollen shut, the other brimmed with tears. "Mine babe," she breathed softly. "Tieslen."

His head swiveled angrily. "Where is Tieslen!"

Christine looked to the faces surrounding her, all etched with dread—Eubreena and Dahla, the three stooges who called themselves meshganist, the devon who called himself the Leader of Lors, his blogart brathern. Even Sheele was present, standing in the background among a throng of guards, a grim frown upon his gaunt face.

The Lor of Zeria rubbed at a stubbled chin. "He is close—just in case he is needed."

"What is yon waiting for!" Hannen snarled. "She is dropping!"

"She will drop for certain if he rips her wide!"

"I have noted him do the like on mine pony! He did pull two nippers through! They are strong seggins this sol!"

Meshganis Uldin cleared his throat nervously. "Mine Lor, she has been laboring near three sols. She will drop, as will one babe, if yon does wait any longer."

Christine squeezed Hannen's hand to draw his attention. "Hannen—Becca. Bixten."

The tears spilled over as he nodded his understanding, unable to speak past a mouth twisted in pain.

~~~~~~~~~~

She screamed as the vise tightened on her belly. Gripping tightly to the hands—Hannen on one side, Eubreena on the other—she panted, then screamed, vacillating between the two, then shrieked as the pain peaked.

As the pain ebbed, she lay trembling and gasping.

Leaning in with a wet rag, Eubreena dabbed at her face. Her face was pale, her eyes swollen. "Sweet Sola, aid her," she blubbered as she brushed away the locks plastered to Christine's forehead.

As if in answer, the resonating voice of thunder rumbled across the heavens.

"He's here!" Dahla cried from where she stood at the foot of the bed. Her eyes were swollen as well, her birthmark glowing.

She barely recognized him dressed in black. His lips were set in a tight thin line as he entered with his lita by his side, she toting a bulky bag in each hand. The crowd parted as he moved close to take her hand. "How long has she been laboring?" he asked, his eyes resonating concern.

"Three sols," Meshganis Uldin informed him. "One turning apart and getting naya closer."

Leaning close, Meshganis Tieslen captured her eyes, holding them as firmly as he was her hand. "Mine Lita," he spoke sadly, "yon does know what need be done."
~~~~~~~~~~

She searched for the breath—and the strength. "Aya."

"I have come readied," he whispered, his eyes hovering close. There were beads of rain in his hair and in his baubled beard dyed black with socket root. There was pain in his bloodshot eyes.

Christine searched out Katissa where she stood across the room. Her face was puffy, her eyes rimmed in red.

"Many thankings for arriving so quickly," the Lor spoke from his place beside the bureau. "I will hand many rounds for yon services."

Meshganis Tieslen straightened to face him. "Any rounds handed by yonself would be stained with blood," he spoke coldly. "I do nayat need such."

The Lor rubbed a hand wearily over his face. "Meshganis Tieslen, I can nayat hand apologies enough. I did nayat know it was yon litar."

"Mine babe has been dropped by yon hand. If yon does wish *yon* babe saved by mine, I gest yon do as I bid." Fetching his bag, Tieslen placed it upon the bed to rummage through it. "I will need cleaned rags, heated water, and an emptied boarding—save for one litia," he said motioning to Dahla. "I will need her aiding."

Meshganis Uldin stepped forward to voice his objections, but Tieslen quickly silenced him. "I spoke everybody!"

Pouring himself a swallow of spirits, the Lor downed it in an instant, before slamming the emptied mug beside the pitcher. "Everybody out," he commanded.

~~~~~~~~~~

She watched the shadows on the ceiling through her lashes. They were blurry, and Dahla's humming lullaby in her ear seemed distant. The fuzzy face of Meshganis Tieslen leaned close to lift a lid, peering beneath.

"Is she dropped?" Dahla whimpered.

She could not hear the muffled reply, only Dahla back at her ear, humming and crying at once.
~~~~~~~~~~

A drum roll was sounding for the big event. It was distant—a thousand miles away.

"Sweet Sola," Dahla prayed. "Sweet, sweet Sola!"

She could feel it, a strange sensation down low, a gentle tugging. She tried to shout, to warn him she was not fully under, but no words came out.

~~~~~~~~~~

The rumbling voice of thunder woke her. A babe was crying, a sweet bleating. Dahla came into her line of vision, leaning down, her face fuzzy. "Christa, mine sweet Christa. He is eyegrandly!" she wept. "Eyegrandly!"

She could feel the tug of the thread. He was stitching her belly.

"Out," he shouted. "I am nayat finished! Katissa, mine dearest," he spoke in a calmer voice, "yon can take leave as well. I will stay till she wakens."

"Sy," Katissa wept. "Pleadings!"

Thunder spoke again, the deep and commanding voice reverberating through her brain.

~~~~~~~~~~

He was weeping. She'd never heard him do so before—the Leader of Lors, his bassy sobs echoing about the room. She could feel the vague pressure of his head where it rested upon her chest, the vague pressure of the hands clutching at her arms.

A bassy rumble joined his sobs as thunder tumbled across the heavens.

~~~~~~~~~~

She came aware suddenly at the sound of shattering glass. She couldn't see past the blanket pulled over her face, but she could clearly hear Kynneth frantically shouting his brathern's name. And a
~~~~~~~~~~

woman was sobbing. Eubreena.

“Mas Zeria,” Tieslen spoke calmly, “yon must calm yonself. Yon brathern is but sleeping.”

“He is nayat sleeping!” Kynneth snarled.

“Here,” Tieslen said, “take one sip to settle yon brain.”

“Yon take one sip!” Kynneth screamed, his voice on the verge of hysteria. “Take one sip this grain or lose yon head!”

There came an eerie silence, followed by an eerie chuckling. “Fine then,” Tieslen spoke. “Take mine head, if yon must. But such will nayat bring yon brathern back. Yon is right. Same is nayat sleeping,” Tieslen spoke calmly. “Same was overly skewed at losing his brooder, so did beg me to poison his spirits. Take one small sip from his mug, and yon suffering will be ended as well.”

A growl sounded, one turning quickly to an angry bellow. A raging bull was stampeding through the room—flinging furniture, tossing chairs. Ganist were shouting, litas screaming. Above the chaos, she could make out Reesal’s voice imploring his Lor to waken.

Above it all, the thunder rolled.

CHAPTER 7

Mist swirled about her ankles as she strolled through the garden. She was walking amongst clouds. Sola's smile was a blinding, shimmering brilliance. Everything it touched shimmered, the skin on her arms, the locks of her hair—the velvet of her wings. It shimmered on his skin as well where he stood beneath the garbona tree, just one of a thousand stretching as far as the eye could see. It shimmered on the hair spilling over his shoulders, on the crisp white shirt he wore.

"Mine Lor," she greeted with a bow of her head.

"Mine flutterfly," he replied with a grin as he reached for her hands. Her eyes were drawn to the mouth that spilled such sweet words. She leaned up to him as he did down, his lips caressing with touching tenderness. "I did note him," he breathed against her lips. "Our gan."

She pulled away with a pang of guilt. "Naya. Was Dahla's gan yon did note, brought in by Meshganis Tieslen, hid in his bag. Same was nayat dropped in traveling." The gnawing guilt grew at the pain in his hazel eyes. "Apologies, Mine Lor. I did promise Dahla her gan would be Lor one sol. Our gan was carried out the same way. He will be raised with his sasturn by the ganis who owns mine heart."

He sighed heavily. "Samuel Clavin."

The pain came upon her suddenly, a throbbing deep in the recesses of her brain—and one other, low on her belly.

She awoke on a bed of stone. She was not alone. The body stretched out beside her was emanating heat like a stoked furnace.

"Sam?"

He lifted his head in an instant. “Sweet Sola,” he whispered as he scrambled to his feet to lean over her. Grasping her hand, he brought it to his lips. “I did think yon would nayat ever waken!”

She ran her eyes around the room.

“Tempelle,” he whispered, leaning close to caress her face. “It worked.”

“The babe,” she croaked past a dry throat.

“Safe with Lita Tieslen,” he assured, brushing the hair from her forehead, “as well as Becca—and the gani.”

“Bixten.”

“Aya. All in Huyetti. We will meet there, then head to LaRosse.” His eyes wavered. Pulling back, he squeezed her hand. “Meshganis Tieslen is dropped.”

“Naya!” The hand she moved to her stomach was heavy as a lead-filled pipe. Her head was heavy as well, listing to one side, this bringing into view the Leader of Lors where he lie on the stone slab beside her own. He was wearing a crisp white shirt.

Sam quickly moved to block her view. “Christa, I’ve brought a change of clothes, one hooded gilt. As soon as yon is able, we must be off. The entire cassing is in grieving—thousands lining the streets of Zeria, thousands more traveling from all over Atriia. There is a large crowding of mourners just outside one solasium, but there is a back way through the garden that Ervine has—”

“Is he dead, Sam?”

Sam stiffened, then nodded. “Poisoned by Tieslen.”

“But—that wasn’t the plan.”

Sam shook his head sadly.

“He could be sleeping.”

He squeezed her hand tenderly. “He is dropped, Christa.”

~~~~~~~~~~

She was confused by the pain twisting her heart. She despised the man laid out before her, had wished him dead more times than she could count. Still, she could not pull her eyes away from him.
~~~~~~~~~~

He was horribly handsome. Even in death, his mouth was sensual. She leaned in one final time to lips cold and firmly closed.

"Christa," Sam spoke softly behind her, "we must be off."

She slid her lips to his ear as tears slipped from her eyes. "I hope I was wrong, Mine Lor—and you do own one soul. May it walk with Sola."

CONCLUSION

Katissa seemed in a trance as she peered into the flames of the campfire. Seated on a crate, she wiped absentmindedly at a silent tear, just one of many which had fallen over the past allten.

Christine peered down at the sleeping babe bundled in her arms. She had shed a river of her own tears over the past sols. Whenever she looked at him, they would come without fail. He was breathtakingly handsome—as his father had been. "I am thinking to call him Deele."

Katissa nodded numbly. "One fine callen," she said as she pulled the blanket tighter about her shoulders. "Strong."

Shifting the babe in her arms, Christine beckoned to Bixten. "Bixten, can yon hand one babe to Lita Tieslen. Mine back is paining me."

Daxter stirred from where he was seated beside his malla. "Does yon need more leexer, Mine Lita?"

"Naya," she said as she transferred the babe carefully to Bixten's arms. "It is only mine back. Mine belly is meshing nicely."

Daxter nodded. "Mine fallar was one gifted meshganis."

"As will yon be," his malla prophesied as she accepted the bundle gratefully. Cradling the babe to her chest, she began to rock him gently. If she resented who his father was, it didn't show in the eyes peering down with adoration.

Bixten nodded adamantly. "He does alreadied know the differed leexers," he piped proudly. "Did yon know yaw leaves can mesh burns?"

Christine shifted upon the crate, pulling the blanket about her shoulders. "Naya."

"And slegg and chouster roots mixed can make babes sleep sound for turnings."

"Aya. That I did know," Christine admitted, glancing over at Katissa who was glancing back at her.

Becca giggled sweetly. Seated cross-legged on the ground with her doll in her lap, she peered into the cage occupying her crate, watching as Hopper devoured the froma, twirling it in his tiny paws as he nibbled the edges.

Seating himself beside her, Bixten reached over to pat Neema's head, spurring her tail to thump the packed dirt. "How many more sols traveling?" he asked with a sigh.

Sam stretched an arm out to poke a stick at the fire. "We are coming up on Chaspia, mine gani. Two added sols will land us in LaRosse."

"Will I be lessoned in LaRosse?"

Sam nodded. "I will lesson yon," he warned, giving him a sideways glance. "Reading, scribing—battling," he added, standing to point his stick menacingly at the boy, his legs set wide in a battling stance.

Bixten took the challenge instantly. "I must warn yon," he said, snatching up a stick of his own, "I am alreadied skilled at such."

"Bix!" Becca squealed as the two began to spar, the hollow clanking of sticks echoing through the still night. Unsure of how to react at such a disruptive display, Neema stood up to swing her tail, the movement traveling up her body till half of her was wagging.

Daxter chuckled as the skilled fraigen dropper maneuvered his opponent around to swat his behind with the stick. "Of all Atriia, Bixten! Do nayat let him treat yon as one blogart," he teased.

Bixten regrouped, then lunged with a growl, a move which only managed to spin him around yet again, exposing his backside for a second undignified swatting.

Daxter guffawed, doubling over where he sat, thus prompting Becca to giggle and clap her hands at such amusing entertainment.

Sam tisked his tongue as he tossed his weapon to the flames. "I do hope yon was better lessoned at pony riding."

Bixten's pout quickly turned at this, his eyes lighting. "As Sola shines, I am skilled at such," he swore, tossing his own stick to the fire. "Is it truths I will be lessoned in the training of seggins?"

Sam nodded as he took his seat with a groan. "If yon does wish. Hindler can always use aiding."

Bixten clapped his hands, beaming at the prospect. "Will he bring the ponies right off?"

"As soon as we are settled."

"I also wish to be lessoned in such," Daxter spoke up.

"Done, then."

"We will be lessoned together," Bixten chirped cheerily, trotting over to slap Daxter on the back as if they were the best of chums. "May I ride with Daxter on one supply wagon on the morrow?"

Hannen pondered this, then nodded. "Aya. Once Chaspia is safely behind us."

Becca was rubbing at an eye as she tottered over to her malla. In an unexpected move, she threw herself across Christine's lap, causing her to grimace as the pain at her belly reawakened.

"Becca," Hannen beckoned. "Come to fallar."

"Falla," she mimicked, running to him and throwing herself into his opened arms. She giggled as he showered her with kisses, then squealed as he tickled her belly.

Coming to her defense, Bixten quickly became the target. Locked in Sam's steely clutches, Bixten struggled to escape as he was viciously tickled.

Immediately, Daxter became protector, slipping up from behind to put Sam in a chokehold. Though Sam was thinner than she had ever seen him, he wrestled the boy effortlessly to the ground, pinning him on his belly while digging knuckles into his neck and back. "Does yon give?"

"Aya, yon blogart!" an indignant Daxter choked out. Upon his release, the boy staggered to his feet, brushing the dust from his pants—then made a surprise attack, jumping Sam from behind, putting the larger man into a new improved neck-lock, one which was quickly reversed, landing Daxter on his face yet again.

"Does yon forget who I am, gani?" Sam growled, digging knuckles into the boy's kidneys. "I am the most famed fraigen dropper in all of Atriia! One railed stick of a gani will nayat best me!"

Neema was beside herself, her golden coat shaking as she snarled and nipped at their ankles.

"Dax! Naya!" Becca barked, running to grab Bixten's hand."

Bixten found Daxter's predicament particularly amusing. "Of all Atriia, do nayat allow him to treat yon as one blogart. Kick him in one kagege!"

"Kaggeg!" Becca aped, making Christine gasp.

Laugher erupted—Sam and Daxter where they lie on the ground, Becca and Bixten where they stood hand in hand, Katissa where she sat cradling the babe. The matronly woman resumed her rocking as the babe stirred, then began to sing. It was a lullaby, one her malla had sung to her, and her malla to her, passed down generation after generation for as long as any Atriian could remember. The words had been slightly altered over the last few segs, but the tune was the same, as it would remain for generations to come.

"'Fret nayat mine fairest babe.
Stave yon tears, mine fairest babe.
All Atriia, she will surent save,
she who hails from one fraigen cave.
Fret nayat babe, yon tears do stave.
Brazened battler will surent save.
In Sola's smile her locks will blaze,
she who hails from one fraigen cave.
And all Atriia she will surent save.
All Atriia she will surent saaaave.'"

DICTIONARY

aiming - intention

allten - Atriian period of time consisting of ten days or sols

arc - *v.* to shoot an arrow from a bow

Atriia (a try a) - name of parallel world

Atriian calendar - An Atriian week consists of ten days (or sols) and is called an allten - onesol, twosol, threesol, foursol, fivesol, sixsol, sevensol, eightsol, ninesol, tensol. There are three alltens in one cycle. Twelve cycles make up one seg (one year).

aya - yes

babebunker - crib

battlean - army

battlement - war

battler - military personnel; soldier

battlescores - competition of varying battle skills between different cities

bind - book

bindboarding - library

blacktongue - name referring to one addicted to genopé

blasted - Atriian curse word

blazened - fiery

bligart - idiot (female)
blogart - idiot (male)
blow - nonsense
board - *v.* to room
boarding - *n.* room
brathern - brother
brazenry - bravery
brooder - lita used primarily for child bearing
broone - bear-like animal
bunker - *n.* bed; *v.* to bed or sleep with
bunkerboarding - bedroom
buriard - cemetery
callen - name
carry - wagon
cas - large castle, hub of the city and home to leader of the city
cassing - city
chouster root - root dried and ground into powder; medicine that brings down fever
cloth-carry - covered wagon
coarse - thick porridge
coneroots - carrots
cope - rose
cover-carry - carriage
crout - small burrowing creature, squirrel-like with long silky tail
cubit - closet
cycle - period of time similar to one month; consists of three alltens
deck - *v.*- dress
decking - clothes
devon - devil
devonous - devilish, evil
doubtent - without doubt
dricloths - diapers

drop - kill

eyegrand - handsome (male)

eyegrandly - handsome (female), beautiful

fallar - father

fallow sap - tree sap used to remove hair dye

fingerring - ring

finhap - finally

firstsup - breakfast

flameblower - fire bellows

flay - steak

fleecin - pheasant-like bird

flustings - trouble

footings - shoes

fraig - newly hatched fraigen found only in fraig lairs

fraigen - large reptile similar to crocodile with ridged back and razor sharp scales

frii - small, foxlike animals

froma - cheese

gan - son

gani - boy

ganis - man

ganist - men

genopé - crumbly black stone, when crushed and ingested - a powerful narcotic

gest - suggest

gentleganis - gentleman

gentleganist - gentlemen

gilt - robe worn by women

globeberries - giant grapes

goser - large fowl similar to geese

grand - wonderful, magnificent

grain - second (of time)

guardganis - guard

guardsganist - guardsmen

guestive - party, gathering of guests

hailing - home

high-hillers - mountain people

huganis - human

grain - second (of time)

jelt - gold

jelten - golden

jewelwear - jewelry

kagege - male private parts

lastsup - dinner

layerleaves - lettuce

leafpitter - caterpillar

leexer - medicine

lia - infant girl

lita - woman

litas - women

litia - young girl

litar - daughter

long - distance equal to approximately one mile

loper - spy, imposter

lotice - lice

lowerly - south

lowerly region - south region

lun - night

Luna - moon

lundevon - nightmare

malla - mother

mayhap - maybe

mesh - heal

meshganis - doctor

meshganist - doctors
midsup - lunch
mound - minute (of time)
naya - no
nayan - none
nayat - not
nayor - nor
neckring - necklace
nipper - young pony under one year of age
note - see, look, watch
pallored - pale
pickens - giant green beans
pleasurer - lita used solely for pleasuring
portence - importance
portent - important
railed - skinny
rezle - ranch; farm
rezler - rancher
ringling - black bird with rainbow colored markings around neck
ringroots - onions
rip - cut; slice
roggi - (row gē) large cat-size rat; also **roggii**-plural (plural pronounced with long i)
round - money; consists of twelve slices
saker - man who officiates trials; judge
saxter - medicinal salve
seedberries - large red fruit (cross between strawberries and tomatoes)
scribe; scribing - write; writing
scull *v.* - cook
sculler *n.* - one who cooks
scullery - that involved with cooking

scullie - cookie

seg - year

seggin - year old pony

serin - medicine for allergies

shalia - flower

shammered - ashamed

shike - large cow-like animal (cross between cow and buffalo)

sictin - bubble-eyed dragonfly

skirter - one who hails from the outskirts

skirts - outskirts

sleeper regions - west region

sleeperly - west

slice - money; one twelfth of a round

slige - topical medicine that kills lotice

slips - socks

socket - black root used to make black hair dye

sol - day

Sola - sun - worshipped as Goddess

solasium - church

solists - priests, high worshipers of Sola

spectful - respectful

spects - respect

spectless - disrespectful

spellered - put under a spell (in love)

spooker - scare

stelch - stolen goods

stelcher - *v.* to steal

stelcherer - thief

sup - *n.* food; *v.* eat

suva - red fleshy fruit (cross between plum and peach)

sweetstalk - sugarcane

swill - fish

swilling - fishing
talcar - large scavenger bird
tellings - details
tempelle - mausoleum
tention - intention
termin - sores
timer - elderly person
tippet - mouse
tippetly - cowardly
toskin - poisonous spider found in the woodlands
trailers - vines
tripe - woman of lower class with loose morals; whore
troll - *v.* police
troller - policeman
turning - hour (of time)
upperly - north
upper region - north region
veneing - intervening
wakerly - east
waker region - east region
wildhound - wolf-like creature
woodslink - serpentine creature inhabiting thickly wooded areas
worgle - legendary creature of the Woroff Woodland
wristring - bracelet
yon - you; your
zalt - Atriian dance originating in the upper regions

LIST OF CHARACTERS

Antiva - scullery lita at Rez Axermme
Bixten - son of blacktongue; adopted by Christine
Bocksard - Uncle to Mas Fallier
Buleea - one-year-old tot at brooder's quarters
Corrita - brooder - mother to Buleea
Dahla - Christine's aide/nanny; birthmark on face
Darris Keat - Zerian battler - father to Dahla's babe
Daxter Tieslen - son of Meshganis Tieslen
Dratsum - doctor from the Cassing Woroff
Ervine Dryor - master gardener in care of church (solasium) gardens
Eubreena - head woman in charge of litas quarters of Cas Zeria
Gaddion Fallier - deceased brother of Hannen Fallier
Gaile Liticea - bald-headed troller, second in command under Kaltica
Hannen Fallier - fraigen dropper
Harvin Trost - troller with scarred face
Hilfra - escort from Cas Woroff

Hindler - son of Bocksard; slow-witted yet master horse trainer
Irva - brooder - mother to Trayson
Jerrod Zeria - Lor of Cas Zeria
Katissa Tieslen - wife of Meshganis Tieslen
Kylara - frizzy red-headed pleasurer
Kynneth Zeria - brother to Lor Zeria
Larid Izaki - leader of blacktongue band
Myurna - dark haired pleasurer; PacMattin's loper
Neema - golden hound
Odium - saker of Zeria
Oscarn - man in charge of keeping the women in order at Cas Zeria
PacMattin - evil outcast trying to gain rule over the entire land
Penningcole - troller-supply wagon driver
Reesal - Lor Zeria's right-hand man
Rhyone - silver-templed traveler, father to Tagen
Rialla - escort from Cas Woroff
Roltin Kaltica - lead troller from Rostivane
Roth Izaki - blacktongue; brother of leader Larid
Sebatton Fallier - father of Hannen Fallier
Sherva Rostivane - sister of Lor Rostivane
Sura Tieslen - daughter of Meshganis Tieslen
Sy Tieslen - doctor from Huyetti
Talbot - teacher from Zeria
Tallia - woman in charge of food preparation at Rez Fallier
Tarriff Zeria - father to Jerrod and Kynneth
Tarrig Trost - brother of Troller Harvin Trost
Tasta - blacktongued woman; mother of Bixten
Tavaka Hassidy - Dahla's best friend from Rostivane
Torna - woman in charge of food preparation at Cas Zeria
Trayson - two-year-old at brooder's quarters
Tressa - woman who works in food preparation, duties are

coarse grinding and delivery of meals

Tulls - artist

Uldin - Zerian doctor

Valenti LaRosse - Lor of Cas LaRosse

ValCussin - saker of Toskeena

Vinova - woman in charge of laundry (seamsewing) at Cas Zeria

Fawn Bonning was born and raised in South Florida. She now resides in Tennessee with her husband, four sons, and six dogs.

Made in the USA
Lexington, KY
12 May 2014